RIDER'S RESOLVE

THE RIDER'S REVENGE TRILOGY

Rider's Revenge

Rider's Rescue

Rider's Resolve

 DEDICATION

This book is dedicated to a dear friend who is a large part of the reason I've made it as far as I have with my writing. Thank you for always believing in me and encouraging me to continue when I was scared and doubted myself. I wouldn't be where I am now without your support and encouragement.

A NOTE ON PRONUNCIATION

Members of the tribes have names that use an apostrophe after the initial consonant. For example, K'lrsa and G'van.

To pronounce these names, substitute an i or e for the apostrophe. For example, K'lrsa = Killrisa.

This is a full listing of the tribal names used in the book:

B'nin = Benin

D'lan = Dilan

F'lia = Filia

G'la = Gila

G'van = Givan

K'lrsa = Killrisa

K'var = Kivar

L'dia = Lidia

L'ral = Liral

M'lara = Milara

V'na = Vina

CHAPTER 1

The late day sun beat down upon K'lrsa as she gripped the small pendant hanging at her neck, feeling the curves of the metal as it circled back on itself in one continuous, unbroken loop. The "weapon" she'd brought back from the Hidden City, it allowed her to travel any distance or to send others any distance she wanted.

Unfortunately, the one time she'd used it on herself—to transport her and Vedhe back to the gathering grounds— she'd coughed blood for a week. Turns out it wasn't nearly as useful as she'd thought it was when she chose it.

But it was effective on her enemies. She'd used it to banish the Daliph's commanders back to Toreem and to scare his soldiers into leaving.

At least for a time. Until their fear of Aran, the current Daliph of Toreem, overcame their fear of her.

A breeze blew her black hair across her eyes, bringing with it the familiar scents of sage and dust, as she stared down at the small encampment of enemy soldiers at the edge of the barren lands. She tucked the stray hair into her braid and turned to look at the others. F'lia, her belly swollen with pregnancy, stood at K'lrsa's right hand. Luden—one of the defectors from the Daliph's army and a new member of the tribal council—stood at her left. Vedhe stood off to the side studying the soldiers with her onyx viewing tube—her "weapon" from the gods that let

her judge whether someone was good or evil—lost in her own world as usual.

She gripped the necklace, and its metal edges dug into her palm. She didn't like the thought of using it again. She was sick of people dying. Life was too precious. And with that many men, some were bound to die if she used it.

But…

Better those soldiers than one single member of the tribes.

She had the power to protect her people, so she would. But she couldn't act without the Council's approval. Too many were scared of what she could do with the necklace. One, a Rider formerly of the Tall Bluff Tribe, had even suggested taking the necklace from her so she wouldn't use it on any member of the tribe. Fortunately, they hadn't been able to agree who could be trusted with the necklace and she'd pointed out that the gods had given it to her and her alone.

Still. As much as it rankled, she deferred to the Council on the necklace's use. At least for now. While they all agreed.

K'lrsa looked between Luden and F'lia, both also members of the Council. If they agreed with her, they'd have three of six votes and she could act and end this threat now without lengthy debate back at camp. "So? Any reason I shouldn't send them back?"

Luden—taller than her by at least a hand-span, with a shaved head and flinty black eyes—shook his head. "No. Do it." He continued to stare at the camp, the muscle in his jaw twitching as he glared down at the camp.

"Do you know any of them?"

"Yes." He turned to face her. "But I'm a member of the tribes now."

He held K'lrsa's gaze for a long moment and she quailed at his intensity. Because it wasn't just about his loyalty to the tribes, it was about his loyalty to her. Or, more particularly, his attraction to her. He'd never pushed, never said anything direct about how he felt, but he'd made it clear he wanted her and that he thought she should want to be with him.

He talked often about stability and strength, urging "his men"—the former soldiers from the Toreem Daliphate who'd joined the tribes—to pair off and settle down, saying it would be best for all when they'd established who was with who. But that wasn't the way of the tribes. Two people could be together and never choose to marry. Especially if children weren't involved.

It was…an adjustment, to have so many men from the Daliphana be part of their tribe. They made up almost half of the members of the small tribe and, as K'lrsa had learned during her time in Toreem, the ways of the Daliphana were not the ways of the tribe.

She turned away from Luden. He was handsome. He had an intensity that women seemed drawn to—one that she might have been drawn to under other circumstances—but…

He wasn't Badru. He hadn't been chosen for her by the gods. And he didn't fill her every waking thought the way Badru did.

Which was foolish. Because Badru was dead. The minute he'd crossed into the Hidden City he'd sealed his fate. He couldn't return from there to the world of the living because he'd been brought back from the dead once using death walker magic.

But she could still go to him. And he'd be as real to her as anyone else. They could live together in the Hidden City for as long as they wanted.

All she had to do was leave behind F'lia, M'lara, and Vedhe. And every single member of the tribes. If she turned her back on everyone else she loved, on her home and her duty to protect her people, she could have the man she loved.

But what was the point? Not like they could ever have a real life.

He'd still be dead no matter how real he seemed. He'd continue on, never-aging, incapable of having a family, unable to leave the city, while she stayed by his side, growing older with each passing day, letting the life she could have had slip through her fingers until they eventually grew so far apart that she left or she killed herself to join him.

She loved Badru, but not that much.

K'lrsa looked to F'lia, one eyebrow raised in question. "Do you agree? Send them back?"

She nodded. "Yes." She absent-mindedly rubbed her swollen belly as she stared down at the camp.

How hard it must be for her to bring a life into the world during a time of such uncertainty and danger, especially when the love of her life, L'ral, was dead and the baby's father had left with the Black Horse Tribe. And with Luden pressuring her every day to choose from one of the newcomers so she was "properly settled" before the baby arrived.

Finally, she turned to Vedhe. With her pale skin and hair she was more of an outsider in the tribe than the men of the Daliphate who'd joined them. The red shiny patches of skin where the sun had burnt her on her journey across the desert made it worse. The members of the tribes shunned her—there was no place for the weak or infirm in the tribes—and the newcomers sneered at her because the scars had disfigured her face as well as her body.

But K'lrsa trusted her above all others. Only she knew what it had been like to journey to the Hidden City. And only she had an *Amalanee* horse like K'lrsa's. And…

She understood.

About losing your family and being alone in the world. About having to carry forward without the people you believed would always be there for you.

"Vedhe? What do you see?"

She didn't honestly care whether the soldiers were good men or not. They could've stayed home or turned back if they'd wanted, but they hadn't. They'd chosen to follow a man like Aran and invade her home and threaten her people. They deserved to face the consequences.

Before Vedhe could answer, F'lia added, softly, "We can't feed more mouths than we have now."

She was right.

The former Black Horse Tribe lands were mostly barren, the result of a failed attempt to use the farming techniques of the Daliphana. And their situation had been made worse by the lack of knowledge of the newcomers, who didn't understand the first thing about surviving off the land. They might've been the lowest soldiers in the Daliph's army, but even they'd had better access to food and supplies than the wealthiest of the tribes.

Sometimes she regretted letting them stay. It had seemed like the right thing to do at the time, welcoming those who wanted a better life and were willing to follow the ways of the tribes.

The tribes had always welcomed new members. It strengthened them to bring in new blood and ways of doing things.

But she'd underestimated the strain of taking on so many at once. It was different to bring one new member into a tribe. Someone who was in love, who willingly adopted the ways of the tribes, as much through necessity as anything.

But this…

With so many newcomers, everything was a fight. Every mention of "this is how we do this" was met with a counterargument for why it should be done differently now. Every meal without enough food or without meat, was met with sullen complaints and criticism. Every night spent sleeping in the cold was followed by comments about how nice it was to live in a home and sleep on a real bed.

The tribe was like a spotted snake trying to swallow an entire desert cat. Attempting the impossible and choking on the result. She rolled her shoulders, trying to dispel the tension that had settled there the last few weeks.

She glared down at the twenty enemy soldiers swaggering back and forth between their tents, well aware of the small party that watched from above. They occasionally pointed and laughed amongst themselves, hands stroking the swords at their hips.

Confident, arrogant, smug.

They reminded her of every moment she'd spent in the Toreem Daliphate, eyes cast to the ground, silent, afraid she might give offense, told over and over again to cover herself, to act properly, that women shouldn't ride horses or wear sensible clothing or…

One of the men thrust his hips at her and called something she couldn't hear as the others laughed. She didn't need to hear his words to get the gist of it.

She tightened her grip on the necklace and willed him back to Crossroads.

And just like that, he was gone. No sign of him remained.

The others stopped laughing, and K'lrsa smiled.

Served him right.

Too bad he'd probably survive the trip since she'd sent him alone.

The others wouldn't, though. Quicker than a thought, she willed them all back to Crossroads, leaving the camp empty.

The campfires continued to burn and the men's horses stood where they'd been tethered, chewing slowly on the small bitter grasses that grew nearby.

But the men were gone.

Just like that. Twenty men. Gone in the blink of an eye. Likely dead. The twisted remains of their bodies piled somewhere on the outskirts of Crossroads.

So easy.

Too easy.

Her hand spasmed around the pendant. A part of her longed to rip it off and throw it to the ground, to be done with all of this forever. To run back to Badru and spend what remained of her life with him and let the world do what it would without her. But she forced herself to be calm, to breathe deep and find the hunter's version of the Core.

She couldn't just run. She couldn't just walk away.

She was the only one standing between the tribes and a devastating attack from the Daliphana. If she left or refused to use the necklace, they would never stand against so many trained soldiers. She was their only hope.

Still the guilt settled into her bones. Twenty men dead. Just like that.

She pushed back against it. This wasn't her fault. It was Aran's. He'd ordered those men here. He was the one that wouldn't leave the tribes alone. And it was the men's fault. Because they'd followed his orders. Because they'd carried his evil to her people.

Without followers, Aran would be nothing.

But that didn't keep the bile from burning the back of her throat. She turned away from the empty camp and walked away from the others, hands clenched at her sides.

She was becoming exactly what she'd never wanted to be.

F'lia joined her. "You did what you had to."

K'lrsa nodded, too upset to speak.

Maybe now Aran would leave them alone, now that he knew she was willing to use the necklace against his men.

Maybe.

But he wouldn't. This was just the beginning. He'd keep pushing until they broke. Or she broke him.

CHAPTER 2

As Vedhe tucked the viewing tube away, K'lrsa longed to ask what she'd seen. Were the soldiers she'd sent back good men? Or cruel and twisted? Did they deserve to die?

Would it really matter, though?

Not really. It wouldn't change the horror of what *she'd* done to *them*.

M'lara ran up to them with all the energetic awkwardness of a young colt. At almost nine summers old she was already stunningly gorgeous, but in the unabashed way of a child. "You need to come back to camp. There's a situation," she cried, breathless.

K'lrsa pinched her nose. It never ended. "What kind of situation?"

M'lara darted a glance at Luden. "N'la knifed one of the newcomers."

"I told you not to call them newcomers. We're all part of one tribe now. Remember?"

"If you say so," M'lara grumbled, summing up with all the precociousness and honesty of the young exactly how the entire tribe felt.

"I do. Come on."

K'lrsa trudged back to camp, Luden by her side as always, longing for something or someone to punch. Leadership involved too many words. People always wanted to discuss things. You had to compromise and find

the best solution and work things out so everyone was happy.

She was sick of it. She just wanted to act. To have an enemy she could physically confront and defeat.

She was a trained warrior. She knew a hundred and five ways to kill someone. But it hadn't done her a lot of good lately. Because none of that helped change what people believed. Especially when they didn't want to change.

But something had to give. And soon. The tribe couldn't keep on like this.

The easiest solution would be to send the newcomers away—back to the Daliphana or across the desert, it didn't matter as long as they were gone.

But she couldn't do that. They'd sworn their oaths. They were as much a part of the tribes now as she was. And they were good men at heart—Vedhe had confirmed that. It wasn't their fault they'd been raised so horribly.

Not to mention, the newcomers occupied three of the six Council seats now. She couldn't send them away without violating the rules of the tribes. Of course, the rules of the tribes didn't matter to *them*.

They wanted to make new rules—ones that they said would work better for them. Compromise they called it.

But they didn't understand. If they wanted to survive, they needed to do things the way they'd always been done. The way that worked.

All anyone had to do was look at the Black Horse Tribe to see what happened when you tried something new in such an unforgiving environment. The Black Horse Tribe had destroyed their land by trying to adopt the ways of the Daliphana. And then been expelled for trading in slaves and leading outsiders across the desert, risking the protection of the gods.

If they'd just kept doing things the way they'd always been done, they would've never gone down that path.

Unfortunately, no one seemed to care what K'lrsa thought.

She was a member of the Council but in name only. Because she had the necklace and she refused to use it on their behalf if she didn't have at least some say in how it was used.

But no one actually listened to what she had to say. The newcomers were simply too used to taking orders from men to consider the opinions of a woman. And the existing members of the tribes were too used to a Council that consisted of elders to listen to someone so young. (Forget the fact that she'd almost single-handedly saved them from Aran's troops when they were all trapped in the gathering grounds.)

K'lrsa shook herself free of her black thoughts as they reached the "camp"—a scattered assortment of sleeping rolls and fires; they hadn't planned to stay long enough to set up actual tents.

Everyone was clustered in the center of the space, gathered around two people who were shouting back and forth at one another.

Luden pushed his way through, K'lrsa on his heels.

"Luden. There you are. Punish her. She knifed me." Murin, the biggest troublemaker of all amongst the newcomers, pointed at N'la, an attractive Rider from the Spring Winds Tribe who stood across from him, knife in hand, the end red with fresh blood.

"You deserved it, you gadja bastard." She turned towards K'lrsa. "He grabbed me and kissed me. Like I wanted his tongue down my throat." She spit on the ground, the deadliest insult in the tribes.

K'lrsa glanced at Luden.

He knew the rules.

It was simple. Any unmarried man or woman could be with any other unmarried man or woman. (Or with a married man or woman if their spouse gave permission.) But a man (or woman) who tried to force another against their will was castrated and sent into the desert to die.

The tribes were too small and lived too close together for that sort of thing to be accepted.

Unfortunately, life in the Daliphana was very, very different.

There, a woman wasn't even allowed to kiss a man unless she was married to him. The newcomers saw a woman like N'la—who seemed to pick a different man every single night—and they didn't understand. They thought that her giving herself to one man made her available to any man. They didn't grasp that in the tribes a woman could choose to give herself freely to one or more men and yet refuse another. In the Daliphana a woman like N'la would've been cast out of her family, and killed or sold as a slave for the shame she'd caused.

But this wasn't the Daliphana.

Luden and his men knew the rules.

They knew that touching a woman against her will wasn't allowed. And they knew the consequences, too.

Of course, N'la wasn't helping things by being so cavalier about it all. There was nothing *wrong* with what she'd been doing, but most members of the tribes cared a little bit more about how their actions impacted others. In her old tribe, the men had grown wise to her ways and simply ignored her until she had no one left to sleep with, which was one of the reasons she'd chosen to leave her old tribe for this one.

But the newcomers seemed incapable of ignoring her. Just a few days before, two of the men had gotten into a knife fight over her, and now this…

Didn't change the rules, though.

If Murin had tried to force her then he needed to be punished so all would understand the consequences of acting that way in the tribes. And so worse didn't happen later. If this continued, someone was going to end up dead.

Luden turned to N'la. "Is that all he did? Grab you?"

"Is that all? *All?* He thrust his tongue into my mouth."

Luden frowned. "But he just kissed you, right? He didn't…touch you elsewhere? He didn't…rape you."

N'la's glare was sharp enough to slice Luden into pieces. "Yes, that's *all* he did." She turned on K'lrsa. "Is that accepted now? For a man to grab a woman against her will and force his tongue down her throat?"

Luden turned to Murin. "What were you thinking? You know you can't just take a woman for your pleasure here."

K'lrsa clenched her fists at the word, *here*. Because, of

course, it was perfectly acceptable to do something like that in the Daliphana.

No man of the tribes would ever grab a woman against her will. Ever. But in the Daliphana a lone woman away from her family was fair game for any sort of abuse. It was her fault for straying from the protection of the men responsible for her.

"It wasn't a big deal." Murin's expression was petulant. "I just wanted a little of what everyone else had already had." He shrugged. "If she didn't want to give it, she could've just said no."

"I did. With this." N'la waved the bloody knife at him.

Murin flinched back. "Get her away from me. She's crazy."

N'la took a step closer, the knife clenched tight in her fist. "Crazy? You forced your tongue down my throat. You're lucky I didn't castrate you right then." She spat on the ground at his feet.

"How was I supposed to know you wouldn't be into it? You were with Luden just yesterday. And B'lar the day before. And Noler the day before that. It was just a matter of time until you got around to me."

N'la screamed in rage and lunged at him. "Never. You disgust me."

Luden grabbed N'la and twisted the knife out of her grip. "Enough." He held her close for an extra moment before signaling to two of the Riders standing nearby. "Take her."

As N'la protested, he pointed to two men from the Daliphate. "And you take him. Keep them apart until morning. We'll discuss this when everyone has had a chance to calm down a bit."

As Murin and N'la were dragged away, N'la kicking and screaming in rage about how this wasn't the way of the tribes, Luden turned to K'lrsa, speaking softly, "I know N'la's done nothing wrong according to your ways, but this has to stop. She's playing the men against each other. It was only a matter of time until something like this happened."

K'lrsa snorted. "It would help if the men in the tribe stopped sleeping with her. Was Murin telling the truth? Were you with her just last night?"

Luden's eyes burned with an intensity that made her uncomfortable. "She wasn't my first choice. But she offered and I knew it would mean nothing to her so I accepted. Isn't that allowed in the tribes? Or do I still not understand your ways?"

"Of course, it is. You're free to sleep with anyone who wants to sleep with you. I guess I just expected you to set a better example."

He stepped closer. "I would if you'd just say yes to me. It's for the good of the tribe for us to be together."

"Don't blame this on me." She turned away, shaking with anger.

She hated being made to feel like it was her fault because she'd refused him. It wasn't.

She had the right to stay alone if she wanted.

Luden *was* a good man. He was attractive, intelligent, someone she worked well with and who others respected. She *should* want him. But...

But it always came back to the same thing: He wasn't Badru.

And no matter how much she tried, she couldn't let go of that dream of what could've been if only Badru had lived.

She walked away, her hands clenched into fists, wishing she were somewhere, anywhere but where she was.

CHAPTER 3

K'lrsa leaned close as Fallion galloped across the plains, letting the wind whip at her hair, losing herself in the perfect harmony of rider and horse, moving as one. This was the one thing that was right in her life—Fallion, her beautiful golden horse that was so much more than a mere horse.

The moon was almost full—they could've flown if she'd wanted, soaring high above everything in that space that was and wasn't part of this world—but she needed the speed and immediacy of the ground churning beneath Fallion's hooves and the feel of the wind as it tried to tear her from his back.

She'd barely slept in the weeks since they'd left the gathering grounds.

The chaos of daily life in her new tribe was bad enough; the nights were worse. She hated sleeping alone, knowing Badru was never coming back to her, that she'd never feel the warm comfort of his arm wrapped around her waist and his strong body pressed against hers.

But she hated more being drawn to the land of the moon dream each and every night by meddling gods who'd taken everything and everyone she loved. So far she'd managed to avoid them by forcing herself to wake as soon as she found herself there, but eventually she'd have to face them.

She couldn't go on much longer with so little sleep.

They rode until the moon finally sank below the far horizon, ushering in the gray time before dawn. The Trickster's time—when only fools dared travel.

She longed to keep going, to keep moving, never stopping, never thinking, but if she did they'd be lost, led astray by the vile little brat and his cruel tricks. And as much as she didn't want to return to camp, she also didn't want to wander lost on those misty paths to nowhere. Or worse, find herself trapped and taunted, pinched and poked by the Trickster.

They found a good spot to rest that had a natural spring nestled at the base of a small hill. With water and protection from the wind, it was a better spot than many she'd known back when all she'd had to worry about was tracking the next baru herd and avoiding her mother's attempts to settle her down.

She'd give almost anything to go back to that time. To sit around the family fire and listen to her mother complain that Fallion smelled better than she did and watch her father try not to laugh as he winked at her behind her mother's back. To watch D'lan, so intense, so serious, work on shaping a new bow. To have M'lara crawl into her lap and beg for a story.

But her parents were dead, long since passed on to the Promised Plains where she could never see them again. And D'lan was off with the White Horse Tribe, his attention focused on his pregnant wife and building a life with her.

All she had was M'lara.

And Vedhe and F'lia, too. But…It wasn't the same.

She lit a small fire and stared into the dancing flames. What was she doing trying to lead a tribe that didn't even want to listen to her? If it weren't for the necklace, she'd be no one and nothing as far as they were concerned. It was too much, having to fight them every step of the way.

And this mess with Murin and N'la…

That man needed to go. Vedhe swore he wasn't evil, but he didn't have to be evil to cause harm.

At least he'd pulled his foolishness on a woman like N'la who hadn't hesitated to put him in his place. Another woman might have let it happen, unsure how to react to something so unexpected. F'lia certainly would have. At least when she was younger. Just look at the man she'd ended up with after L'ral died…

It was only luck that had saved her from a lifetime of misery and possession.

K'lrsa poked at the fire with a stick, sighing.

No.

Murin couldn't be allowed to stay in the tribe. The kind of belief that led a man to do what he had was a slow poison that would eventually spread and destroy them. He had to be removed now. As an example for all the others.

She rolled her shoulders, trying to release the tension she felt there. The Council wouldn't agree with her. Luden would say it was a minor matter. The other two newcomers on the Council would side with him. B'lar would, too, because he wanted to be liked by everyone all the time so never voted against the majority no matter what it was.

Which only left F'lia to stand with her, but F'lia would either keep quiet or argue to give Murin another chance because he was new.

Which meant the next time Murin pulled a woman aside and forced himself on her that woman wouldn't bother with the Council. And why should she? Especially seeing what had happened with N'la? She'd either castrate Murin herself right then—which is what K'lrsa would do if anyone ever tried that with her—or, worse, she'd let it happen and he'd keep doing it to her or to others. He'd just get smarter about choosing his targets.

Either way. It wouldn't be good for the tribe.

Fallion whinnied softly and whuffed at her hair. She scratched his nose, taking comfort in his steady presence. "At least I still have you, *micora*."

She turned her mind from the problems at camp to the men Aran had sent across the barren lands, but that was no better.

She hoped sending the men back to Aran would show

him he couldn't defeat them, but she worried this was just the beginning. Aran wasn't the type of man to accept defeat. And if he wasn't going to leave them alone…

Then someone needed to stop him.

Her. Because who else could do it? The tribes were hunters, not warriors. And no one else had a weapon that could challenge him.

But she didn't want to face Aran. She was done with the Toreem Daliphate. The time she'd spent there was enough for a lifetime.

Maybe she could convince the newcomers to go back and defeat him…

Turn his army somehow. He was just one man, if they all stood up to him, he'd be nothing. And that would solve all her problems…

But even as she thought it, she realized it wouldn't work.

It would take a thousand men like Luden to manage something like that. Unfortunately, the others weren't like him. They were outcasts and misfits who'd been too scared to return home in defeat.

Luden…

Luden was something else. A man who'd seen opportunity and taken it. The type of man used to winning, to getting his way.

She broke a small stick into pieces and threw them into the fire one by one.

She wished he wanted someone else. F'lia would probably take him. But no, he'd set his sights on her and wasn't willing to look elsewhere. He'd been patient so far—making it clear he was interested but not pushing it—but that wouldn't last forever.

And she didn't think he'd accept her explanation that maybe she just wanted to be alone. That it wasn't a matter of choosing the best option available to her, which he admittedly was. It was a matter of choosing what would make her most happy and that was…

She sighed and buried her face in her hands.

She wished they'd all just go away so she could live her pathetic little life alone in the middle of the plains hunting with Fallion and avoiding anyone and everyone and wishing that the man she loved wasn't already dead.

Of course, even Fallion was a problem. Now that she knew what he was—a gift from the gods that could fly and who knew what else—she really should send him back. She had no right to keep him when she wanted nothing to do with them.

But she couldn't bring herself to do it. She loved him.

And he'd also been a gift from her father—a symbol of his belief she could be a Rider. Plus, he'd been the only steady presence in her life through all that had happened. She'd almost lost him once through her own stupidity, she wasn't about to give him up now.

She just hoped he'd stay with her…

She glanced at his silhouette in the gray haze of early morning, wondering what would happen if the gods tried to take him away. Could they? How much control did they have over him?

She hoped not. She couldn't take another loss. Not now. Not after all that had happened.

Shivering, she wrapped herself in a blanket and curled up next to the fire, hoping for a few moments of sleep before she had to return to camp to deal with Murin and N'la and Luden and all the rest of it.

CHAPTER 4

B ut as soon as K'lrsa fell asleep, she found herself in the land of the moon dream. Everything was more vibrant there, more alive than in real life. The moon was so full and bright, it seemed close enough to touch. And the sky was full of stars, so many she could never hope to count them, even in an entire lifetime. Desert dunes stretched in all directions, so vast they made her feel smaller than the smallest grain of sand

She willed herself to awaken, like she had every other night, but it didn't work. She was trapped.

She started to walk, her feet slipping and sliding along the dunes, one direction the same as any other. There was no Hidden City in the distance, no mountain range, just wave after wave of dunes stretching forever in every direction.

A soft breeze caressed her skin, blowing softly against the thin strips of fabric entwined around her body—the garments of the Moon Dance. She tore at the gauzy fabric as tears ran down her cheeks, remembering all those nights she'd spent with Badru, dancing to the rhythm of the universe, their bodies moving as one.

The breeze shifted and strengthened until it whipped at her, throwing sand into her face and stinging her exposed skin as the moon disappeared, replaced by a sun so scorchingly hot it burned.

"Stop," a voice boomed behind her.

Father Sun. It had to be. She shivered and tried to keep going, but she couldn't. Her feet wouldn't move.

"Look at me," he commanded.

She turned, shielding her eyes against the glare of his presence. "I can't."

The light dimmed slightly—still glaring and brutally hot, but no longer blinding—and she lowered her hand.

Father Sun stood before her, a warrior about her father's age, his body crisscrossed with the scars of battle, his eyes smoldering like a banked fire.

She fought the fear that pushed her backward a step, focusing instead on her anger at what the gods had done to her. What they'd taken from her.

She spat at his feet, her hands clenched tight in a mixture of fear and fury.

He laughed. "Would you truly make me your enemy?"

"Yes. I hate you. I hate all of you."

"Why?" He tilted his head to the side, as if genuinely confused. "What have we done to you?"

She shook her head, unable to articulate something that had slowly built within her, day after day, week after week. "Those tests you put me through in the Hidden City. The dragon? And *my father*? Or, should I say, my fake father? What kind of cruelty was that?"

"You had to prove yourself worthy."

"And how did killing a dragon do that? Or walking away from my father? What did that prove?" K'lrsa turned away, shaking her head in disgust, but he stood before her once more.

She glared at him. "And you abandoned me in the Daliphate. You sent me there as a slave and then just…Let me stumble through on my own. You didn't even warn me what it would be like. Or who Badru was."

"It wasn't our place. Other gods rule there. And we didn't abandon you. When you fled, my wife opened the land of the moon dream for you, didn't she?"

"What about Herin? You *sent* her there and then did nothing to save her."

His eyes burned red. "Herin's fate is not yours to judge."

"You killed Badru," she cried, tears pouring down her cheeks.

"No. Badru made a choice. As you've made choices. Am I now to blame for all the foolish choices men make?"

K'lrsa crossed her arms. "You could've warned me what would happen if he entered the city."

"And then what? Watched you fail? Watched the tribes destroyed and the Hidden City given to Aran? Because one man's life mattered more to you than any other?"

"I would've found a way without him."

"Would you have? Do you honestly think you'd have made it through the challenges alone? Without Badru? And Herin? And Lodie? And Garzel? They all went there with you, knowing the price they were paying." He stepped closer, looming over K'lrsa, the heat from his skin beating against her like fists. "If Badru hadn't found you in that final challenge, would you have had the strength to leave your father behind? Would you have given your father up to save a tribe that was willing to believe the worst of you?"

K'lrsa bit her lip. She might have spent weeks or months there, thinking *just one more day* until it was too late. Only Badru's intervention had pulled her away in time.

Still.

"You should do more for us. What's the point in being a god if you can't protect your people?"

"Would you honestly want to live in a world where we made all of your choices for you? Where there was no challenge and you always won every time?"

She crossed her arms and shrugged slightly. "I don't know. Maybe. Would my parents and Badru still be alive in that world?" She glared at him.

He barked a short laugh. "Who can say? Everyone dies eventually."

"But not so young!"

"Some do. Some must."

"So now you're saying my parents and Badru *had* to die? For what?" She glared at him, willing him to try to explain that to her.

He waved his hand in dismissal. "That's not why I'm here. You made a vow. It's time you honored it instead of playing with this new tribe of yours."

K'lrsa tensed. "I already killed the man who killed my father. K'var."

"But that isn't all you swore to do. You also swore to destroy the Toreem Daliphate." His eyes burned like twin bonfires.

She shook her head, dismissing him. "Maybe I did, maybe I didn't. But I was naïve back then. I didn't know what I was saying. And are you *sure* that's what I promised? Maybe you heard me wrong."

He waved his hand and an image appeared of her standing over her father's body. She wiped the last of the tears from her cheeks and then sliced her palm with the knife she'd just used to kill him, letting her blood drip on to his body and the desert sands below it.

So young and confident.

So foolishly stupid.

The girl in the vision held her head high and shouted into the night, "I, K'lrsa dan V'na of the White Horse Tribe do swear in the name of the Great Father, Bringer of Light, Bringer of Life, Scourge, and Destroyer, and on my father's everlasting soul, that I will avenge him. I will kill the man responsible for his death and I will destroy the Toreem Daliphate. This I swear, by my own blood. I forsake all other vows. I forsake all other ties."

The image faded.

"See? You vowed to destroy the Toreem Daliphate. No confusion there."

K'lrsa shook her head. "I can't do it. It's impossible."

"But you made a vow."

She turned away from him. "I can't do it. The tribes need me. And so does M'lara."

"Too bad." He stepped closer, menacing in his intensity. "When you swore that vow, you forsook all other ties."

She flinched, but didn't back down and didn't step away. "I was young and stupid. I didn't know what I was doing then."

"Nonetheless. The vow was made."

"Find someone else." K'lrsa moved away from him. "I'm done with the Daliphana. I won't go back there. I can't." She snorted. "Plus, I'm a woman. I wouldn't even make it to Crossroads before someone killed or enslaved me."

"You made it there once before. And that was before you had the necklace or knew Fallion's true nature."

It was also before she'd known what she was up against. The bravery of the ignorant couldn't be underestimated.

She turned to him, studying the hard, unforgiving lines of his face. "What if I don't do it? Not like there's anything left for you to take from me."

Even as she said the words, her mind flashed to Fallion. And to M'lara. And F'lia. And Vedhe. And D'lan. She'd lost so much, but she still had too much left to lose.

She raised her chin. Just because that was true, didn't mean she had to let him see it. She suspected the gods had no actual power in the real world. They could bluster and threaten all they wanted while she was asleep, but they couldn't actually touch her or the ones she loved in the real world.

Father Sun's smile was cruel as he stared at her with eyes of fire. "Didn't you hear the words of your vow? You not only swore to me, you swore on your father's everlasting soul."

"You can't touch him. He's already moved on to the Promised Plains."

"No. He hasn't."

"But…He told me…He said he wouldn't be there in the Hidden City if I went back. He said he was going to leave with my mom and go to the Promised Plains."

Father Sun's smile broadened. "That may be what he wanted to do, but that's not what happened."

She shook her head, trying to deny his words. "What about my mother? Did she move on to the Promised Plains?"

"No. She stayed with your father. They're both trapped until you keep your word. For now at least." He crossed his arms, the muscles rippling as he shrugged slightly. "I can't promise she'll stay with him, season after season, year after year while they both slowly waste away into nothingness. How much does she love him? Enough to give away her chance at the next life?"

"Why are you doing this to him? He never did anything to you!"

"No. He didn't." He leaned closer, his eyes flaring. "He's a victim of his daughter's foolish and rash vow. And now you hold his fate in your hands. And your mother's too, it would seem." He stepped back, the cruel smile twisting his lips once more. "Choose wisely, K'lrsa dan V'na of the White Horse Tribe. Your parents' souls rest on your decision."

He held her gaze for a long moment, and then he was gone and she once more stood alone in the quiet peace of a moonlit desert night.

"I hate you!" K'lrsa screamed, but there was no one there to hear it.

CHAPTER 5

K'lrsa spent the next morning listening to N'la and Murin yell back and forth, both demanding the other be punished. She wanted to grab them both and smack them upside the head a few times, but she couldn't. She was a responsible leader now, after all.

Murin tried to call others forward to prove how freely N'la had shared herself around camp, but K'lrsa shut that down immediately. "It doesn't matter what she's done with anyone else, Murin. It matters what she did or didn't want to do with you. And I think we've well established at this point that the answer to that question is 'absolutely nothing.'" She turned to Luden. "Time to make a decision."

Luden frowned, but he didn't argue with her. Instead he stood to address the rest of the tribe who had watched the whole time with keen interest. As he paced back and forth, making eye contact and smiling at different people in the crowd, she hated him for how he always ingratiated himself with others like that. But the crowd loved it. They loved him. They hung on his every word.

He stopped in the middle of the cleared space, halfway between Murin and N'la. "I understand that what Murin did is a violation of tribal rules. And I know that the usual punishment for an act such as this would be to castrate him and send him into the desert to die. But surely that's too extreme a punishment for what was clearly a misunderstanding."

Most of the newcomers in the crowd nodded, speaking quietly with one another.

A woman who'd been part of the Desert Storm Tribe rolled her eyes while another woman glared at Murin, her hand resting on her knife.

"Misunderstanding?" N'la lunged at Luden, but the two Riders guarding her caught her by the arms and pulled her away from him.

Luden turned to face her, completely calm. "Yes. A misunderstanding. He misread you."

"Misread me? When? When I refused to talk to him? Or when I moved after he sat too close to me? Or…"

"Hush, N'la. It's the Council's turn to speak now."

N'la's face flashed red with rage and she fought to free herself.

K'lrsa held up a hand to stop her from speaking further. Let Luden say his piece. There'd be time to address his comments after.

N'la looked ready to kill, but she kept silent.

Luden nodded and turned back to the crowd. "As I was saying…This was a simple misunderstanding. We need to make allowances for these differences between our peoples as we all learn to live together."

"Allowances? Differences? Is that what you call this?" N'la demanded.

"Yes." He didn't even turn to look at her, his attention focused on the crowd. "If Murin had forced N'la to have sex against her will, then I agree that the traditional punishment of the tribes would be suitable."

A few of the newcomers in the crowd muttered to one another at that, clearly disagreeing, but no one argued with him. Didn't they understand that rape was as bad as murder? Perhaps worse? It killed a part of the victim but left them alive to relive their pain over and over again for the rest of their lives. At least murder was quick.

Luden continued, "But since Murin didn't rape her. Since he only tried to kiss her, the Council believes a lesser punishment is warranted here."

"The Council believes?" K'lrsa stepped forward, glaring

between him and the other Council members. "Funny. I don't recall voting on this. Or even discussing it."

He waved her away. "Not now, K'lrsa."

"Not now? Then when? Because last time I checked, I am a member of this Council and I have a right to an opinion. And my opinion," she continued as he opened his mouth to interrupt her, "is that Murin is a problem and will do this again. If not with N'la then with another woman. One less able to resist him. We can't have that in this tribe. And we can't let others think that what he did is acceptable in any way."

"So you'd kill him? For a *kiss*?"

"Yes, I'd kill him. But not for a kiss. For an attitude and belief system that are incompatible with the way we live."

He turned away, dismissing her. "Times are changing, you need to adapt."

"No. Not on this I won't. I will not allow the tribes to treat women the way you do in the Daliphana. It will not happen." She gripped the necklace at her throat, the metal curves digging into her flesh.

He moved closer, reminding her of Father Sun when he'd towered over her in the moon dream. "And who are *you* to decide this? Do you now speak for the entire Council? Or the entire tribe? Did you lie to us when you said we'd be equal members of this tribe? When you allowed us to elect leaders to serve alongside you?"

The air rumbled with the approval of his men as he glared down at her. She glared back, trembling in anger, hating this war of words that she knew she couldn't win.

She longed to just punch him, but she couldn't. If she did, they'd never listen to her again. "You're a *member* of the Council, Luden. One of six. You voiced your opinion. I voiced mine. Anyone else wants to voice theirs, they can. And *then* we vote."

"Fine." He turned to the others. "Anyone else have anything to say?"

The other members of the Council were silent.

"Good. All in favor of whipping Murin three times as punishment for what he did, raise your hands."

He and the other two newcomers on the Council raised their hands. Luden frowned at B'lar for a long moment, but then turned back to her. "So we have three votes for whipping Murin. And your alternative?"

"All in favor of expelling Murin from the tribe and sending him back to the Daliphana, raise your hand."

F'lia and B'lar raised their hands.

K'lrsa tried to hide how relieved she was to see that they'd both chosen to side with her rather than abstain.

Luden narrowed his eyes. "A tie. So now what? What do your *rules* say happens now?"

She looked around. "Normally, we'd debate until we reach a solution we can all agree to. But I'll tell you now, suggesting that we send him back to the Daliphana *was* my compromise. If I had it my way, he'd be treated like any other member of the tribes."

Luden snorted and turned his attention on B'lar. "You voted with the women. Do you honestly believe that banishment is a suitable punishment for an unwanted kiss?"

F'lia touched K'lrsa's arm and leaned close. "Maybe we should let it go this time. Is N'la really worth all of this?"

"We have rules, F'lia. We need to enforce them. No matter who is involved."

"And next time we can. But for now…" She leaned back. "Luden, I'd like to change my vote. I think whipping Murin three times should be sufficient. You're right. He is new to the tribes and our ways. And N'la can confuse some men. And it was just a kiss."

Fury coursed through her. K'lrsa gripped the necklace, fighting with every ounce of will she had not to send Murin, Luden, and F'lia all to the middle of the desert. Good bye and good riddance.

But she'd agreed to abide by what the Council decided. And if she truly believed that the rules that had governed the tribes for hundreds of years were what had kept them together and alive, then she had to support the decision, no matter her own personal feelings about it.

She glared at Murin. "Fine. But if he ever does it again, I swear, on all of our gods, that I'll send him back to the

Daliphana myself. In pieces."

She stormed off, pushing her way through the crowd, not caring what anyone thought of what she'd said. Because she would. And damn the consequences.

CHAPTER 6

That night, as she rode Fallion away from camp, she pointed him towards the place where the soldiers had camped. It was just this side of the barren lands—that vast swath of deadness that separated the Daliphana from the tribes—near the one spot where it was narrow enough for a horse to cross in a single day. (No one wanted to sleep in the barren lands if they could avoid it, although K'lrsa had twice now.)

It was a good spot for a camp, with a small stream running nearby and the shelter of a series of small hills, but K'lrsa would've never camped so close to such destruction if she could help it.

The tribe had already taken the soldier's horses and tents back to their own camp—resources in the tribes were too precious to waste—so she expected the area to be empty.

It wasn't.

She watched in silence as a small group of soldiers set up camp, their tents arranged in a ring around a huddled, miserable group of slaves, their ankles chained together by heavy iron links, their clothes so threadbare they barely covered each emaciated man's torso.

She shuddered as she counted fifteen soldiers and ten slaves. Seemed Aran wasn't done testing them.

And now they had another choice to make: Send all of them back like they had the last group of soldiers, or just send back the soldiers and rescue the slaves who hadn't chosen this fate and didn't deserve to die such a horrible death.

They couldn't keep the slaves. The men were clearly in no shape to contribute to the tribe. And resources were stretched thin enough as is. If they didn't move on soon, they'd have nothing left to eat.

And even if they could feed that many more…

Those men would tip the balance over to Luden. Chances were they'd side with him rather than some fool girl who had almost reached her seventeenth summer.

The tribe would never recover.

If she'd thought today was bad, what would happen when Luden no longer had to pretend to find a compromise?

Before she could think too closely about what she was doing, she grabbed the necklace and willed the men back to Crossroads.

All of them. Soldiers and slaves.

In the morning she'd convince Luden it was time to move on. If she was lucky no one would see the camp to know what she'd done.

She reined Fallion away and galloped into the night, wishing she could keep going until she'd left all of it behind, but she had to be back as soon as the sun rose.

She managed to avoid the gods in her dreams by waking as soon as she found herself in the land of the moon dream, but it meant she was cranky and stiff the next morning when she finally rode back to camp.

"There you are." Luden strode towards her, men and women stepping out of his way with quiet respect.

She hated him for that—for the arrogance of assuming others would make way for him and the fact that they all did.

"What's wrong?" She slid from Fallion's back, looking around for M'lara. And F'lia. Were they alright? Had something happened with the baby? Or N'la and Murin, *again?*

He loomed over her. "There was an encampment at the edge of the barren lands. Right where we saw the other one. We found it this morning. It was empty."

She struggled to keep the small twinge of guilt she felt from showing on her face. "And?"

"Are you really going to make me ask the question? Honestly, K'lrsa. Sometimes you act like a child."

She raised her chin and glared at him. "Fine. Yes, there was another encampment. Just like the first one. And I sent them back just like the *Council* ordered me to do last time."

"You're lying. This one wasn't just like the last one."

She narrowed her eyes. He'd trapped her. Deliberately. "Says who?"

She glanced around at the small group of people who'd crept closer to listen to their argument.

"Delin saw the camp last night. He said it included slaves."

"Yes. And? So? They were still invaders that we couldn't afford to feed."

He stepped closer. It took all of her strength not to shrink back from the anger in his eyes. "Didn't you wonder who they might be?" he hissed. "Delin recognized one of them. It was my brother."

"What?"

She shivered. If one of the slaves was Luden's brother then chances were all of the slaves had been related to the newcomers somehow. She licked her lips, glancing around at the others who were trying to hear their conversation. "Does anyone else know?"

He looked at her with such contempt, she felt herself shrinking before him. "No. And they won't. Delin brought the news straight to me and we rode out together to see them. But, of course, they were already gone."

She bit her lip. "I'm sorry, Luden. I didn't know."

"Would you have cared if you had known?"

She opened her mouth to say yes, but then closed it again. Sighing, she admitted, "I don't know. I would've

cared, but…I would've probably done the same thing. They were in bad shape. And we can't afford to feed anyone who can't contribute to the tribe right now."

Another difference between the tribes and the men of the Daliphana that they had yet to grasp. In the tribes, it was a fight to survive day to day, year to year. Which meant that if someone couldn't do their part—couldn't hunt or contribute to the tribe in some other meaningful way— they were expected to leave.

For the good of the tribe.

It was harsh, but it was what had kept them alive all these years. Putting the good of the tribe above the individual.

Those slaves would've required medicine and food, and would've slowed the tribe down as it traveled. And they couldn't have given anything back.

Any member of the tribes would've made the same decision she had. Even if they'd been the slave that was going to be sacrificed. But that wasn't the way of the Daliphana. They didn't understand what it was like to live in a world of constant privation.

She knew. She'd seen their baru herds penned behind fences, docile as can be, waiting for the slaughter. And their fields full of fruit trees and grain for as far as the eye could see.

They didn't understand. How could they?

Luden held out his hand. "Give me the necklace."

"What? No. It's mine." She gripped the necklace as she backed away from him.

"The Council voted last night. We can't trust you to act in the interests of the tribe anymore. Give it to me."

"The Council voted? What are you talking about? *I* am a member of the Council."

Luden continued to advance on her. "You weren't here when we met, so we voted without you."

"And what was the vote count?"

"Three for, two against."

"Then with my vote it's three-three."

He shook his head. "It's too late for that, K'lrsa. Give it to me."

She backed away another step, shaking her head. "I don't know why you even bother to ask the others to vote. Your men always vote with you."

He narrowed his eyes as he took a step closer. "That's because they understand what's best for this tribe."

She laughed. "Is that so? You can say this when you've never lived here. When you don't know what it's like. When you don't understand why we do what we do." She shook her head. "You're going to get us killed."

He took another step towards her.

She tightened her grip on the necklace. "One more step, Luden, and I'll send you to the middle of the camp."

He laughed softly, relaxing. "See? I told them you were dangerous. Would you really turn that weapon on one of your own? Just because we disagree?" He shook his head. "Admit it. You can't be trusted with a tool so powerful." He held his hand out once more and raised his voice. "For the good of the tribe, you need to surrender the necklace."

"No. The gods said I'm the only one that can use it. Ask Vedhe."

He tilted his head to the side. "What happens to it if you die?"

She stared at him a long, long moment, trying to figure out whether he was actually threatening her or just curious. "It goes back to the Hidden City."

He nodded once. "Fine. You can keep the necklace for now, but if you want to remain a member of this tribe you'll use it how we say to use it and when we say to use it. And only then."

He stalked away from her, back rigid. As always, everyone moved out of his path.

She glared at his back, fantasizing about how good it would feel to fling him into the very center of the barren lands. She imagined him wandering there forever, lost and starving and alone, until he died.

It was a good dream.

Unfortunately, she still needed him. Without Luden the newcomers would be impossible to control and their entire tribe would fall apart.

CHAPTER 7

S he found Vedhe sitting outside a tent—one from the Daliph's soldiers. Even though K'lrsa suspected Vedhe was even younger than she was, at times like this she seemed as old and wise as one of the wise ones. Silently, she offered K'lrsa a steaming cup of tea.

K'lrsa took it and sat down next to her. "So you've heard? They took me off the Council."

Vedhe shrugged one shoulder. "Just as well. You can't lead the Council and kill Aran at the same time."

"I don't want to kill Aran. If I never see him again, it'll be too soon."

Vedhe didn't say anything. She didn't have to. They had this argument most days. Vedhe thought Aran should die and she thought she and K'lrsa were the ones that would have to do it. She was just waiting for K'lrsa to come to the same conclusion so they could act.

"Luden tried to take my necklace, too."

"I'm not surprised. He wants to lead the tribe. That means he needs to control all sources of power. As long as you have the necklace, you're a threat."

"Did he ask for your viewing tube?"

Vedhe smiled slightly, her scars making it look more like a grimace. "No. But he doesn't see power in it. He thinks himself a good judge of others. He doesn't need this to see what he already knows."

K'lrsa sipped at her tea, savoring the slight taste of mint. "I don't understand. I thought Luden was a good man. Not the man for me, but still a good man. I thought they all were." She tried not to look directly at Vedhe as she said the words. It was Vedhe who'd vetted each one before they were allowed to join the tribes.

Why hadn't she seen the kind of man Luden was?

Vedhe shrugged. "I could give you a reason that each person in this tribe deserves to die. Even you. Like that man there? He took pleasure in whipping Murin. Does that make him a bad man?" She took a sip of tea before continuing. "I could also give you a reason each person here is good and should be saved. That same man? He adored his son. Would have done anything for him. That's why he joined the army. Because it was the only way to earn enough to feed his family.

"But his son was killed last year and his wife died of fever while he was away. So he left when he had the chance. But what he'd done in service to the Daliphate stayed with him. It corrupted him so that he enjoys an act like whipping Murin. But he'd never do something like that on his own. Only under orders. Only at the will of someone else. So how do I judge? What makes one person worth saving and another irredeemable?"

She turned to K'lrsa. "The viewing tube shows me the truth about someone, but I have to weigh what I see and judge it myself."

"What do you see when you look at Luden?"

She sighed. "He is a good man. He loves his family. Cares for those around him. Wants what's best for everyone. But he's arrogant. He believes he's right. Always. And he's rigid in his beliefs. He doesn't understand how different life here is. He doesn't want to change from what's worked for him in the past. So he won't. Unless he's forced to."

K'lrsa cradled the cup of tea in her hands, relishing the warmth against her skin as she stared into its watery depths. "I don't want to fight him, Vedhe. I don't want to fight any of them. But..."

Vedhe nodded. "I know."

After a long silence, K'lrsa told Vedhe about the camp from the night before and what she'd done and what Luden had told her when she returned.

She bit her lip, dreading the answer, but asked, "Would you have done the same? Would you have sent them back?"

Vedhe was silent for a long time while K'lrsa studied the angry red scars that patched her face and arms. K'lrsa thought of their time in the labyrinth and those two little kids chasing one another around the clearing as Vedhe sat with her family, laughing and happy.

She'd had a life once, and a family who loved her. Until the men of the Daliphana took that from her and made her a slave. A slave just like those men K'lrsa had sent to their deaths.

Vedhe set her cup down, but she didn't look at K'lrsa as she answered. "I don't know. I know the right answer— that they needed to go back because we can't feed more than we already have, especially since they were likely weak and diseased—but…"

She shrugged one shoulder. "I'm not sure I could've seen them that way. I would've seen a man with brown hair and thought of the man who crossed the desert with me but died the day after we found you. Or seen a man with a scar above his eye and thought of the man who lent me his strength when I was too weak to stand by myself that last day before we reached Crossroads…"

She looked at K'lrsa. "Knowing that, that they were men with stories like mine, I'm not sure I could've done it."

K'lrsa sagged under the weight of what she'd done. Even the soldiers she'd sent back. They'd each had a story, too. A life to go back to. A wife. A child. A mother. A father.

But she'd taken that from them in a moment. With barely a thought. And no effort.

Vedhe nudged her foot. "That doesn't mean you made the wrong choice."

K'lrsa nodded, biting her lip. "How do we stop this, Vedhe?"

Vedhe's lips twitched with the hint of a smile. "Kill Aran."

"I can't …"

"You'll have to someday. Or this will continue until he's destroyed us or we've destroyed ourselves."

CHAPTER 8

Things were actually quiet for the next few days. The tribe couldn't stay camped by the barren lands—they needed food and the land couldn't support them for any length of time—so they rode out onto the plains in search of a herd of baru.

It took them three full days to track the herd and bring down just two baru.

It would've gone better if the newcomers hadn't decided that they knew better yet again. They insisted that the herd could be ridden down from horseback, not understanding how fleet-footed the creatures were or how much better they could run on sand than any horse.

It was true that K'lrsa had once brought down a baru from horseback, but only because she was riding Fallion, and only because she'd spent the better part of a week trying. But the soldiers wouldn't listen to her. They assumed if she'd done it once, then they could do it, too.

They spent an entire day chasing the herd, shooting after them as the slender creatures bounded away to the safety of the desert.

One soldier was even foolish enough to chase the baru so far into the sands that his horse sank so deep it couldn't move. They'd had to stop and help the poor animal and his rider get free before they could regroup and try again.

Finally, finally, the newcomers bothered to listen and let

the Riders chase the herd towards a spot where five of their best archers waited to shoot as the herd stormed by.

Of those five, only two managed a kill shot. Luden and K'lrsa.

The newcomers surrounded Luden, patting him on the back, congratulating him on his kill. But none acknowledged K'lrsa or what she'd done. She exchanged knowing looks with a few of her fellow female Riders. The men might not see what was happening, but the women did.

And it wasn't good.

That night the tribe feasted on the baru and drank fermented mare's milk, singing and dancing until dawn. K'lrsa watched from the shadows, sandwiched between F'lia, who wasn't feeling well, and M'lara, who'd insisted on being part of the excitement but had fallen into an exhausted sleep shortly after the moon rose.

Vedhe, surprisingly, was right there in the midst of the dancing, showing everyone the dances of her home—which seemed to involve a lot of kicking and shouting—laughing the whole time.

K'lrsa wished she could put aside her past hurts and live in the moment like that, but she just couldn't.

No matter how hard she tried or how much she wanted to.

The next morning they turned back towards where the Daliph's soldiers had camped twice before, knowing, even though none of them said it, that Aran wasn't done testing them yet.

And, sure enough, there was another camp waiting for them.

But this time, instead of a huddled mass of slaves, they'd brought women and children. Twenty of them, the children ranging in age from babes held in their mother's arms to almost grown.

K'lrsa felt ill. She knew what she should do—send them back, there still wasn't enough food to feed them and showing Aran any sign of weakness would be a mistake.

But what she wanted to do instead was race down the hill and gather them close. Tel them they were safe now. That no one would hurt them ever again.

Her hands tightened on Fallion's reins. Even from this distance, the bruises on the women and older girls were clearly visible.

Vedhe watched the camp, her body shaking, her face twisted with hate.

K'lrsa tensed, ready to intervene if Vedhe moved towards the camp.

Luden rode his horse in front of K'lrsa, his eyes flinty with command. "Give me the necklace."

"No. You want a weapon from the gods, go to the Hidden City and get one for yourself."

"Maybe I will. But not today." He tried to ride his horse closer, but Fallion snapped at him.

He glared at Fallion before turning his attention back to her. "If you send them back, I'll kill you."

"You'll kill me?" she scoffed, surprised at how quickly he'd turned from wanting to sleep with her to wanting to kill her just because she wouldn't do what he said. "Tell me, Luden, if you're such a great leader, how much baru meat do we have left from our hunt?"

"None."

"And what else are we going to eat for the next week? Did we gather any greens? How much grain is left? Have any of *your* men killed a bird? Or a rabbit?"

"I don't know. Why does that matter right now?"

"It matters because if you want to save those people, you need to be able to feed them. And us. You want to be a leader, it's a good idea not to let your people starve."

"We'll figure something out. But we're not sending those children back."

"Don't you get it?" She leaned forward. "Aran is testing us. He's probing us for weakness. If we don't send those children back, he'll bury us under a flood of women and children until we starve. We can't support that many people. It doesn't matter if we want to, we physically can't do it."

"Then we starve. I'd rather do that than kill my own wife and child. Or watch you do it."

"What?"

Luden pointed towards the camp where the soldiers had gathered together to watch them, looking smug as they spoke back and forth softly.

He rattled off a series of names so fast she couldn't even catch them before turning back to her. "Those are our families down there."

"But not all of them." Delin rode his horse closer. "I see my son, but not my eldest daughter."

Luden nodded. "I know. Same here. My youngest daughter, my son, and my wife are down there, but he still has my eldest daughter."

As they watched, a small boy broke away from camp. Shouting for his father, he ran towards them, arms outstretched.

One of the soldiers slowly raised his bow, casually aiming it at the boy's back.

Without even thinking—or touching the necklace—K'lrsa willed the soldier into the midst of the barren lands, hoping he'd wander there forever until he died.

Luden flinched, but he didn't look at her.

Another soldier grabbed a bow and took aim.

K'lrsa banished him, too. And then all of the soldiers, leaving the women and children alone in the camp, staring around themselves in wide-eyed terror, unable to understand what had happened.

"Go," she shouted, reining Fallion away. "Comfort your families."

The men rode towards the camp, their families crying out in relief.

But Luden followed her and blocked Fallion's path with his horse. "You didn't touch the necklace this time."

She met him, glare for glare. "No. I didn't. Seems I don't need to anymore."

He lunged for her, but Fallion was too quick for him. He used his broad chest to block the other horse and bit at Luden's arm, missing by the merest breath.

A deliberate miss.

A warning.

Luden sat back. "Give me the necklace."

"No. I didn't use it against you, did I? And I didn't send your family away either."

"You wanted to."

"But I didn't."

This time.

The thought hung in the air between them as they stared each other down.

They both knew that if she stayed with the tribe long enough there was going to come a day when she'd choose to disobey the Council and follow her own conscience.

The way he looked at her, Luden wasn't going to let that happen.

Even if he had to kill her.

CHAPTER 9

All throughout camp that night fathers sat with their children, smiling, holding them tight, talking and whispering back and forth with soft loving smiles, as their wives sat by their sides.

K'lrsa watched from the shadow of her tent, remembering all the nights she'd sat at the campfire with her dad, talking to him about her day, asking him to show her how to make a snare or fletch an arrow. How he'd smiled patiently and leaned close, guiding her tiny hands in his, as he explained what to do.

She wanted to flee, to run away like she had almost every other night, but she couldn't. She was frozen, unable to escape the pain she felt at the sight of families reunited in a way hers could never be again.

Luden was nearby laughing his deep, throaty laugh as his son stood before him, arms stretched wide telling a story. His daughter slept in his arms, nestled against his chest, sucking on her thumb. His wife sat next to him, her hand resting on his knee, a soft smile on her face.

M'lara raced past the tent, giggling as some boy chased after her. They were playing a version of tag that involved kisses on the cheek instead of touches on the arm, giddy with the innocence of youth.

K'lrsa bit her lip. This was just a lull before the battle.

It was only a matter of time until Luden stopped asking

for the necklace and tried to take it from her instead. All it would take was one surprise blow to the head. She debated leaving, going to the Hidden City and Badru. Letting him have the tribe if that's what he wanted so badly.

But M'lara was so happy here. K'lrsa couldn't take her away from that, not after everything else she'd lost in the last year.

And what about F'lia? She wasn't handling the pregnancy well; she'd gone to bed already, her cheeks pale, complaining that she no longer had any energy. She couldn't leave her here. But she didn't dare use the necklace to move her either. Not knowing the damage it could cause. Which meant a frantic escape on horseback with at least some following in pursuit.

Luden might let her go, but he'd never let her leave with the necklace.

So she had to stay for now.

Which meant more conflict to come. Because Aran wasn't done. He still had the rest of their children, and he was going to use them to get whatever it was he wanted.

One way or another. Either overwhelm the tribes with too many mouths to feed until they collapsed under the strain, or use the children as hostages to extort the men to surrender or lead him to the Hidden City.

They'd do it, too. They wouldn't understand why it was so important to stand against him. All they'd see was that their children were in danger.

They wouldn't understand that letting Aran have access to the Hidden City would doom them all.

Because the one thing she knew for certain was that Aran could never be given that kind of power. She didn't know which weapon he'd choose—the sun orb that could burn anything, the walking stick that could drown the entire world, or something even worse, something she hadn't even been shown because it was so terrible. But she knew what he'd do with it once he had it.

He'd tear the world apart.

And then it wouldn't be twenty children that died, but every child. And man. And woman.

She couldn't let that happen. She wasn't sure how to stop it, but she had to. One way or the other, she had to be the one to stand against him.

CHAPTER 10

The next morning when K'lrsa crawled out of the shelter of her tent, it felt like everyone was watching her even though no one would actually look at her. Those whose children had been returned clutched them close as she walked past. Like she was going to send them away now.

What did they think she was? A heartless monster? How could she look into the eyes of a little boy barely able to walk and want to harm him in any way?

Those whose children hadn't been returned yet kept glancing in the direction of the barren lands, muttering softly to one another, and she noticed a small line of the newcomers stretched in that direction placed just close enough to one another to pass a signal if anyone else appeared there.

No chance she'd know before Luden did this time.

She found him and a few others standing together at the center of camp. They stopped talking when she reached them and the others walked away, glaring back at her as they left, leaving her alone with Luden.

She ignored them just like she'd ignored all the others, focusing her attention on Luden. "We need to move on. Gather some sour greens and desert flowers, maybe see if the White Horse Tribe has more millet they can share with us. Hunt more baru."

"No." He didn't even bother to look at her. "We'll stay here and wait for the next group to arrive."

She clenched her hands into fists, her nails digging grooves in her flesh. "We can't. Don't you get it? Life here isn't like life in the Daliphana. We stay alive by moving. Look around you. If we don't move now, what are we going to be eating three days from now? Or five days from now?"

He glared at her. "I'm not leaving."

"Fine. I'll go then. Someone has to."

"You can't." Luden stepped closer. "Unless you want to leave the necklace with me."

He held out his hand.

Like she'd ever do that.

"No." He took half a step closer and she backed away. Her hand went to the necklace. "Step any closer and I'll send you away."

"You can't threaten me like that," Luden said through gritted teeth. "I'm a member of this tribe."

"So am I."

"I didn't even touch you."

K'lrsa rolled her eyes. "I'm not going to fight about this. I felt threatened, I reacted." She crossed her arms across her chest. "So. I'm not allowed to leave camp now?"

"No."

She looked towards where Fallion stood next to Kriger. How exactly did he think he was going to make her stay if she didn't want to? Fallion would never let another touch him and she still had the necklace if it came to that.

Luden cleared his throat. "And to make sure you actually listen…" He waited until she looked back at him. "We have M'lara."

"You what?"

"She's safe."

"Where is she?" She stepped closer to him, fury pounding in her veins, wanting nothing more than to take the last weeks' worth of frustration out on him with her fists.

"Not here."

"You took a child! How dare you!" Her hand crept towards the necklace, needing to feel the smooth metal of its curves even as she fought the desire to destroy them all. To send each and every newcomer into the barren lands.

"It was the only way to assure your cooperation. I had to do what was best for my people."

"For *your* people? Is there even a Council anymore, Luden? Or do you just run everything now?"

He didn't answer.

She glared at him as the moments stretched between them, neither of them backing down.

Finally, he sighed and shook his head slightly, breaking eye contact. "This could've been so different, K'lrsa. But you had to fight me…"

He signaled to two newcomers who were hovering nearby. "Take her back to her tent." He met K'lrsa's fury with a cool calculation. "If you care about your sister, you'll stay there and won't give me any more trouble."

"Is that so?" She was so angry she was trembling, tears threatening to fall from her eyes because she wanted so desperately to hurt him but couldn't.

"Yes." He turned away, dismissing her.

She wanted to fight the men who moved to take each of her arms, but she didn't.

She couldn't.

She needed time. To find M'lara.

To think and plan and figure out how to leave and take those she loved with her.

But once she decided…

There wasn't a place in this world Luden would be safe.

CHAPTER 11

K'lrsa kept to her tent through the rest of the day, watching over F'lia who'd stayed in bed, her forehead hot with fever. Vedhe brought them food, but there was no news. She didn't know where they'd taken M'lara, only that it had happened at some time during the middle of the night, and that two of the newcomers were missing.

Two men—Luden's men, of course—stood outside her tent, keeping her inside and others from visiting her. Not that many tried, but a couple did, unsure what was happening or what they should do about it. K'lrsa paced the small confines of the tent, trying to figure out what she should do next.

She didn't think Luden would actually kill M'lara. Which meant her sister would be safe even if she left. But where would she go?

To find Aran and kill him? All by herself?

She'd tried that once.

And almost succeeded, admittedly. But, as much as she loved him, Badru wasn't Aran. Killing Badru would've been easy; Aran was far more crafty than that.

She also suspected he knew how to counter the necklace.

He wouldn't die easily. He certainly hadn't the last time someone killed him.

She could go to the Hidden City to be with Badru. And her parents, it seemed. But she couldn't. Not while Aran's

men were still threatening the border.

Which brought her back to killing Aran.

She needed allies.

Vedhe would go. But who else?

Her brother? No. He wouldn't care. Not enough to leave his family and tribe behind. Or if he did, he wouldn't see how she had a place in it. He'd go himself and order her to stay home.

Too bad Herin was dead…

She would've been the perfect choice to send after Aran. (Not that she'd done so well the first time she tried, but the clever old woman she was today was nothing compared to the naïve girl she'd been all those years ago.)

K'lrsa shook her head. She actually missed the grel-like woman and her acerbic comments. As unpleasant as Herin had been at times, she'd had a mind for politics and was ruthless in going after her goals.

If Badru were still alive…

He'd been a trained warrior. And he had been the Daliph. The soldiers might even turn on Aran if they had Badru to follow. And if being a death walker didn't disqualify Aran from being Daliph, it shouldn't disqualify Badru.

She sighed. Unfortunately, he too, was dead.

Everyone was.

Father Sun found her in the moon dream that night.

He stood before her, his body crisscrossed by the scars of a thousand fights, his eyes burning like twin suns, and waited in silence as they stood together in the midst of an empty plain, devoid of life, the sun so hot K'lrsa felt like she was melting.

Finally, she couldn't stand the silence any longer. "What? What do you want now?"

"Are you finally ready to kill Aran and fulfill your vow?"

She narrowed her eyes. "I didn't swear to kill Aran. I swore to destroy the Toreem Daliphate. Or don't you remember? You are, after all, the one who showed me that lovely little scene the last time we met."

He smiled fiercely, his teeth surprisingly straight and white. "What?"

"You know that's why you're my chosen one, don't you? The way you make everyone feel like they've just thrust their hand into a fire when they cross you?"

She snorted and looked away. Even her god didn't like her. "I wish you hadn't. I'd rather still be living my old life."

"That was never going to happen. Don't think that because I chose you I set you on this path."

She wanted to argue with him, to point out that if he'd chosen someone else she might still be…What? Huddled in fear in the midst of her tribe as someone else tried to save them? Or worse, hiding away somewhere, safe, as the soldiers of the Daliphana destroyed the tribes because no one dared oppose them. Watching from a distance, powerless, as the Black Horse Tribe led slaves across the desert and her people slowly lost their way, seduced by the luxuries offered by trade?

She frowned, wondering what she would've become without Fallion. And without her father's faith that she'd make a good Rider. Without the years of training and trial that had prepared her for…something.

She shook her head to clear away the thoughts. "So you chose me and the Lady Moon chose Badru and then you brought us together."

"Not exactly."

"Explain."

He raised one eyebrow at her tone, but a slight smile played across his lips. "I chose you. First. She chose him because he complemented you. If I hadn't chosen you, she would have chosen another. Or if she'd chosen first, I might not have chosen you."

"So it didn't matter that Badru was Daliph?"

"No. Actually, when he was chosen, he wasn't yet Daliph, and not likely to be."

K'lrsa wished Badru were there to hear that. He'd placed so much of his value in the fact that he was the

Daliph that he'd almost been destroyed by losing his throne. But here was a god saying it didn't matter, that it was something else about Badru that made him valuable.

Just like she'd tried to tell him.

She chewed on her lip, thinking. "And Vedhe? How does she fit into it? If you and the Lady choose champions that complement one another, then what does the Trickster choose?"

He laughed softly. "The unexpected. My wife and I are the balance, he's the chaos."

"Like that night when she led everyone to safety through the Trickster's lands…" She nodded to herself. It made sense. But…

"What happens when the balance isn't there? When one half of the whole dies?"

He studied her carefully. "I thought you weren't even sure he was the one for you?"

K'lrsa winced. "It's not easy to be told that someone was chosen for you by the gods. I mean, yes, I was drawn to him the moment we met and I trusted him when I really shouldn't have, and for no reason I could understand, and it turned out to be justified. But…" She sighed. "I like things I can see and feel and whatever it was between Badru and me, I couldn't grasp it."

"But you believe in it now? You see how being with him made both of you stronger players in the game?"

"Players? Game?" Her hands balled into fists. "Is that all this is to you? A game? This is my life. And Badru's life. And the life of every single one of those people sleeping in that camp right now. We matter."

"Yes. Yes. I know. Your precious lives. All fifty, sixty years of them."

White-hot fury burned in her chest. "How dare you be so…so dismissive?"

"How dare you be so short-sighted?" He stepped forward, glaring down at her, the heat from his body beating against her exposed skin. "You know this isn't all there is. It's just one step on your path. And a short one at that."

"Well, from where I'm standing, it's the only one that matters. Do you think I care that we die and go to the Hidden City or the Promised Plains? There's nothing there. It's just a place for holding onto something we've already lost."

"I'm not talking about the Hidden City or the Promised Plains. I'm talking about what comes after."

She crossed her arms. "And what exactly is that?"

"Does it matter? Isn't it enough to know this isn't the end?"

"No." She laughed harshly. "Because *this* is all I can see and feel. *This* is what matters for me. Here. Now. The rest is…Something I'll deal with when I get there."

He smiled. "A warrior through and through. You never answered my question. Are you ready to kill Aran?"

She turned away from him, gazing off into the distance as she chewed on her lip.

Aran had to die. Until he did, he'd keep coming after them. But did she really have to be the one to defeat him? Why didn't all those people who surrounded him, who knew what he was like and what he'd done, why didn't they act? Why didn't they say, "no"?

Even a man like Aran was powerless without soldiers willing to die on his orders. Not to mention all the others who implemented his will and grew his food and sold his goods to pay for his conquests. Maybe not powerless—he did know how to bring people back from the dead—but even there, someone had had to save him when he was killed.

All it would've taken to end this was for those who knew how to save him to stand aside and let him die. But they hadn't. And now it fell upon her to either act, unlike all those others who'd come before her, or to stand aside and watch him destroy the world she loved.

"Yes," she sighed. "I'm ready to kill him. But I don't know how. I can't do this alone."

"You almost succeeded before…"

"Yeah, well. Don't underestimate the power of ignorance. I know better now."

He grinned at her before turning away, arms crossed comfortably, as he thought for a long moment. Finally, he turned back to her. "What if I could bring him back?"

"Who?"

He smiling slightly. "Badru."

"What?"

Her stomach clenched. She didn't want to hope, but she couldn't control the soaring happiness that consumed her for a brief moment before she quashed it and shoved it away.

She studied Father Sun carefully. This was important. And dangerous. She needed to be careful. To be sure she understood what he was offering.

And what price he'd demand. Because nothing was free with the gods.

"Is that even possible?" she asked.

He nodded. "Yes. I think so."

"And he'd really be back? He'd be alive, like I am."

"Yes."

"But he's dead. He was dead the moment he crossed into the Hidden City."

He tilted his head to the side. "Yes…And no."

She wanted to shake him, but held back, waiting.

"Badru's dead if he leaves the city. Or if he continues on to the Promised Plains. Which is what usually happens in these situations. But as long as he remains in the Hidden City and takes care of his physical body as if he's still alive—eating and sleeping, for example—he still lives."

"All that knowledge you shoved into my head and it didn't include this?" She shouted, stepping towards him, fists clenched. She shook her head in disbelief. "This means we could've been together. Really been together. Lived in the Hidden City and grown old together and had children and…"

She stepped away from him. "All those memories of all those people who'd wasted away trying to keep their love going…And it was all a lie. Of course it was."

"No. It wasn't. All *those* stories were true. Those were stories of people who'd truly died in the real world and whose spirits had journeyed to the Hidden City. It's different when a death walker comes to the city."

"Why didn't you tell me before? Before I left him there? Before I committed to this tribe that doesn't even want me?"

"You needed to save the tribes. And to stay with them afterwards to protect them."

"You didn't trust me. You kept this from me so I'd make the decision you wanted."

He didn't answer, just waited for her to think it through.

Would she have really returned to the tribes and stayed with them all these weeks, especially after they'd started to turn on her, if she'd known Badru was back in the Hidden City waiting for her?

No. She would've probably saved the tribes—M'lara and D'lan and F'lia deserved that even if no one else did—but then she would've left, returned to Badru and her own little piece of happiness and left the tribes to fend for themselves.

"So why tell me this now? Don't the tribes still need me to protect them?"

He raised one eyebrow, a smile quirking the corners of his mouth. "Not the way you've been doing it lately. You've been banished to your tent. Luden has taken control of the tribe. And you let those women and children stay even though you know what will happen."

K'lrsa closed her eyes, fighting against the despair that threatened to overwhelm her. "I couldn't just kill them."

"Which is why you'll lose if you don't take the fight to Aran." His eyes flashed, glowing like a bonfire, as he stepped closer to her. "Because Aran will use any weapon, harm any person, to win. But *you*, given a choice of some of the most powerful weapons in the world chose that necklace. And *you*, knowing what it would mean, let those children stay. Your weakness will doom your people."

She glared at him, jaw clenched so tight her teeth hurt. "It's not weakness to care about others."

"It is in times of war. If you fight with compassion while your enemy fights with ruthless efficiency, you will lose every time."

"But…I don't want to be like him! I don't want to be the type of person who could kill a child."

"Which is why men like him win. Because there is always a point where you have to stand and fight with everything you have no matter the consequences. If you can't do that, you lose."

His words hit her like physical blows and she sank to the hot desert sands, pulling her knees tight against her chest and rocking back and forth.

He was right. Someone had to stand against Aran, no matter the personal cost. And no matter the monster they became because of it…

CHAPTER 12

Father Sun loomed over K'lrsa, the sun shining from behind him, outlining his dark form. "I need an answer. Are you ready to kill Aran?"

"Instead of destroying the Toreem Daliphate?"

"No. You still need to destroy the Daliphate to fulfill your vow."

She rested her chin on her knees. "Is that even possible? How do you destroy a whole society?"

But even as the words left her mouth she flashed to memories from the Hidden City—fainter now because she'd tried her best to ignore them—of civilization after civilization that had fallen over the millennia. Some under the weight of their own hubris, some victims to time and change, and some the target of determined enemies.

It was possible.

Not easy. But possible. Even the greatest could fall.

She chewed on her lip. "Can you bring Badru back?"

"I think so."

"What about Herin? And Lodie? And Garzel? They were the same, right? They entered the Hidden City in their physical bodies. And that dragon wasn't real?"

He turned and the sunlight flashed past him, blinding her for a moment. "Lodie never left the labyrinth."

"I could go back for her. Or Badru could. If we brought her out of the labyrinth she could come with us.

She did kill Aran once before."

He shook his head. "No. I'm sorry. It's been too long. Her physical body is gone. She didn't care for it."

"Oh." K'lrsa sat back. "But I can have Badru back?"

"Yes."

K'lrsa bit her lip, sensing a trap but not knowing what it was. She stared into the distance, thinking, trying to figure out what was nagging at the edge of her mind. "Balance…"

"What?"

She looked up at him. "Death walker magic requires balance. A life for a life. That's why Sayel had to die to bring Badru back."

He watched her, his face impassive.

"If you bring Badru out of the Hidden City, there has to be balance, right? You can't just let him leave. You'll have to kill someone to free him. He wouldn't want that. I don't either."

"Even if that one death could save the world?"

She shook her head. "I won't kill someone to bring him back. Not again."

"No. You just kill people to kill them."

She flinched. "I killed those men to save the tribes."

"You could've sent them back one-by-one and let Aran kill them instead."

K'lrsa bit her lip. It was true. No one had forced her to kill those men. She'd chosen to do so. Because a part of her had wanted to punish them for coming to her home and threatening her people. For following a man like that.

She shook her head. "This is different. I don't want Badru back if you have to kill someone to make it happen."

"I won't kill anyone. I just need to use the last life spark of someone who's already dying to open the door."

"Who?"

He didn't answer.

She stood, glaring at him. "Answer me. Whose death are you going to use to bring him back?"

He met her gaze, his eyes burning steadily. "It doesn't matter. They're already dying."

"Who. Is. It?"

He shook his head. "We don't have time for this. Will you kill Aran if I bring Badru back to you?"

"This person, they're already going to die no matter what I say?"

He nodded.

K'lrsa hesitated a moment longer. But she needed to defeat Aran. And she wanted Badru back. More than anything. And Father Sun said whoever it was was already dying. She wasn't killing them, just giving their death meaning.

"Fine. Yes. I'll do it."

"So be it." The sun flared so bright she had to shield her eyes.

When she lowered her hand, Father Sun was gone, leaving her alone in the midst of desolation. She shivered, suddenly scared.

CHAPTER 13

She awoke to screaming.

It was the darkest time of night and F'lia's screams tore through the air, throbbing with agony.

K'lrsa scrambled free of her sleeping roll and made her way across the tent to F'lia's side. Her best friend—sweet and kind and bright as a summer's day—writhed on the ground, her face sheened with sweat, the cords in her neck sticking out from her skin as she screamed once more.

"Help," K'lrsa shouted, surprised no one was there yet.

Luden entered the tent, a small bag tucked under his arm.

"Go away. I don't want you here."

F'lia's hand clutched K'lrsa's as she screamed once more, her face contorted in agony.

"I'm the best healer we have."

K'lrsa didn't care. She didn't want him there. She didn't trust him.

F'lia screamed again, the sound wrenched from her body as if someone had reached down her throat and grasped her insides and yanked them out.

Luden pushed K'lrsa aside, resting his hand against F'lia's forehead and then pulling back the horsehair blanket covering her. F'lia's body arched off the ground as she keened through gritted teeth, the muscles of her belly contracting.

Luden dug through the bag until he found a small packet of herbs. "Here. Take these. Steep them in boiling water until the liquid turns dark brown and bring it to me."

"What do you know about women in childbirth?" K'lrsa demanded.

"Nothing. Now go."

As K'lrsa continued to hesitate, Vedhe pushed her way into the tent, a pile of blankets in her arms. "I can help. I have the knowledge I learned in the Hidden City."

"You learned healing there?" K'lrsa searched her own memories but found nothing. "I didn't."

Vedhe smiled, her scars twisting into a horrible sort of grimace. "I lasted longer, remember?"

F'lia screamed once more, and Luden turned on them. "Get hot water. Brew the tea. My grandmother was a healer. She used to use that when women were having a difficult labor. Your friend is dying while you stand there doubting me."

K'lrsa showed Vedhe the packet. She nodded. "He's right. It will help. Go." Vedhe pushed K'lrsa out of the tent.

K'lrsa stumbled out of the tent, glaring at the small crowd that had gathered outside. "Well, don't just stand there. Someone get a fire going. We need hot water. Lots of it. And a drinking cup."

As F'lia's screams spiraled into the night, K'lrsa paced outside waiting for the water to boil, wondering why she was bothering. Father Sun had said she was dying. That he was going to take her life spark to free Badru.

Why hadn't he told her it was F'lia she was trading for Badru?

It wasn't fair. Hadn't she lost enough already?

K'lrsa spent the rest of the night trying to figure out what was happening inside the tent from the sound of F'lia's screams. As the moon slowly slid towards the horizon, they became weaker and weaker, until, finally, in the gray time between when the moon set and the sun appeared—the Trickster's time—the screams stopped altogether.

Before K'lrsa could push her way into the tent and demand to be at her friend's side, Vedhe emerged.

"The baby?" K'lrsa froze, staring at the small, small cloth-wrapped bundle cradled in her arms.

Vedhe nodded, tears pooling in her eyes and running down her scarred cheeks. "He was too young to survive. He couldn't breathe." She shook her head as she clutched him close.

"There was nothing you could do for him?"

Vedhe frowned. "You don't need the memories of the Hidden City to know that a child born this early can't survive."

"I know. I'm sorry. I just…" She reached out a hand and touched the cloth. It was soft, and there was a small design stitched in the corner—F'lia's work. The yarn and fabric had to have cost a fortune, but F'lia would've wanted the best for him. "Can I see him?"

"No. He wasn't…right." Vedhe stared into the distance as if hearing someone call her name. "I have to go."

Without another glance or word to K'lrsa, she walked out of camp, the baby still cradled in her arms, disappearing into the gray of pre-dawn. K'lrsa wanted to run after her and insist on seeing the baby, but Vedhe had already disappeared into the Trickster's land. Instead, K'lrsa ducked into the tent, holding her breath, scared that F'lia too had died or was dying.

But Luden knelt at her side, wearied, but triumphant.

F'lia slept, her chest rising and falling softly.

"Will she make it?" K'lrsa knelt by his side, stroking F'lia's sweaty hair back from her forehead.

"Yes, I think so. She'll be weak for a few days. She lost a lot of blood. But I think she'll recover given time and rest."

K'lrsa started to cry—great, big wracking sobs that she couldn't hold back.

It wasn't for the baby—she'd grieve him later. It was because her friend had survived. She was overcome with relief that the price she'd paid for Badru's return hadn't been F'lia's life.

It was wrong to be so happy in a moment like this. F'lia had loved the babe with all of her being no matter what type of man the father had been, and she'd be devastated when she finally awoke.

But, nonetheless, K'lrsa was relieved. She couldn't lose anyone else. She didn't have any more to give.

Luden stood. "You should get some rest. We all should."

K'lrsa glanced at F'lia one last time then stood and followed Luden from the tent. He was right. She needed her rest.

Badru was coming back. And together they would kill Aran and destroy the Toreem Daliphate.

CHAPTER 14

T he early morning sun blinded K'lrsa as she stepped outside the tent.

Knowing that F'lia was alive, she finally let herself succumb to the terror and exhaustion of the night before, standing just outside the tent, her entire body trembling. When she could finally move again, she stumbled in the direction of the tent Vedhe and M'lara had shared. As much as she wanted to be close to F'lia right now, she couldn't sleep in the same tent as her—it stank with the bitterness of blood and the reek of sweat.

"K'lrsa. Wait." Luden ran after her and she turned slowly, too exhausted to even focus on his face as he approached.

Had something happened to F'lia? So soon?

He walked right up to her and, before she could react, snatched her necklace. The chain broke with an audible snap as he jerked his hand back.

She lunged for him, but two men she hadn't even noticed held her back as Luden calmly walked away, whistling softly to himself.

"Luden! That isn't yours. It's mine. Give it back."

One of the men tightened his grip on her arm until she winced in pain. "He's the leader. He should have it."

"It was given to me by the gods." She tried to wrench herself free, but she was just too tired.

"Then maybe they'll take it back for you," the man sneered.

They shoved her inside the tent, and she collapsed to her knees, too exhausted to fight. Or to even really care.

It was all falling apart.

How was she supposed to save her people when she couldn't even protect her sister and best friend? And how was she supposed to defeat a man like Aran when she couldn't manage to stand against one mortal man whose only strength was his ability to lead others?

She curled up on Vedhe's sleeping roll, and willed herself to sleep, praying the gods would leave her alone for just this one night.

In the morning she'd figure out what to do next.

For now she just wanted to hide.

CHAPTER 15

By the time K'lrsa awoke it was well past midday. Vedhe sat just outside the tent, flanked by two of Luden's men, quietly sewing a piece of the saddle she'd finally agreed to use for Kriger. She nodded towards the fire where a small pot hung, full of water, a small amount of sour greens, and what looked to be the carcass of a rabbit. "Help yourself."

K'lrsa spooned up a bowl full of the soup, grateful for something fresh to eat rather than a ration bar taken from Daliph's soldiers. "Thank you. How's F'lia?"

"Not well. As soon as she woke she started crying uncontrollably and screaming for the baby and for you. Luden forced her to drink a sleeping draught, but I'm not sure how much good it's doing other than to keep her quiet."

K'lrsa glanced at the two guards. "When did these two arrive?"

"They were waiting when I returned." She nodded to her right. "He's mine." And to her left. "He's yours." She pointed with her chin towards the horse pickets. "Pretty sure they tried to hobble Fallion and Kriger, too."

K'lrsa leapt to her feet, almost spilling what was left of the bowl of soup, looking for Fallion's familiar golden coat. She couldn't see him.

Or Kriger.

"Where are they? If he harmed Fallion…"

Vedhe patted the ground at her side and waited for K'lrsa to sit back down before she answered. "I'm almost certain they fled. Don't worry. They can take care of themselves. And it's better they're free. They'll be there when we need them."

"Do you really think they'll be alright?" K'lrsa took a bite of her soup, not even tasting it.

Vedhe laughed softly. "Oh, they'll be just fine. It's the men who tried to take them who might need some time to recover. Murin's arm is in a sling and Noler's hand is bandaged. He cussed me out when I saw him. Said Kriger bit him. I said, 'good'. Served him right for touching my horse."

K'lrsa laughed. She hoped Fallion was the one who'd put Murin's arm in a sling.

She finished her soup, licking the bowl to make sure she got every last drop, and then watched Vedhe's slow, delicate stitching for a while before finally adding, "Luden took the necklace."

"I heard. And saw. He's wearing it now, of course. Strutting around camp making sure everyone sees." Vedhe jabbed her needle through the thin strips of baru hide and cursed as the needle stuck into her finger on the other side. She sucked on the small wound for a moment, before resuming her stitching.

K'lrsa studied the camp, itching to do something. But what?

The camp had transformed overnight.

Before they'd been a small tribe of warriors—Riders and former soldiers, with M'lara and F'lia the only ones that weren't—nimble and ready to move on a moment's notice, usually not even bothering to put up tents, or, if they had, putting them up anywhere they wanted, scattered near one another like a handful of pebbles tossed on the ground. The Riders and soldiers had melded together, sharing tents and meals.

But now there was a small circular enclosure off to the side of the camp ringed with the tents of the newcomers. Children ran amongst the tents and into and out of the enclosed space, but the women from the Daliphana were hidden away behind the barrier.

Two soldiers stood guard at the entrance. She wasn't sure whether it was to keep the women in or to keep the rest of the tribe out.

The Riders' tents were still scattered where they'd been before, but large gaps marked the spots where the newcomers' tents had been. Even as she watched, though, the Riders were tearing down their tents and moving them closer together. To a spot opposite the newcomers.

Where one tribe had existed, two were forming.

Did Luden notice?

Did he care?

CHAPTER 16

V edhe and K'lrsa sat outside their tent the entire day, watching the tribe break apart, slowly and silently, the distrust between the two groups growing with every passing moment.

Because of where their tent had been placed, she and Vedhe found themselves in the no-man's land between the two camps. By the end of the day it was just their tent and the one where F'lia still slept. All the other tents were clustered together on either the newcomers' side or the Riders' side.

Luden had checked on F'lia a few more times throughout the day but he hadn't bothered to acknowledge them as he stormed past. K'lrsa smiled to see him so frustrated, but she worried about what was going to happen next.

They'd managed to make the soup last through lunch, but as the sun set K'lrsa's stomach was grumbling and the soup was gone. She had a few ration bars still, but she didn't want to eat them.

Vedhe was studying the two camps with her viewing tube. She hadn't said what it showed her, but she'd had it out most of the day.

"Be careful with that. Wouldn't want it falling into the wrong hands."

Vedhe nodded and tucked it away in her vest.

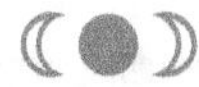

K'lrsa stood. "I'm going to see if N'la has some food to spare."

Given her friendliness with so many in the camp, N'la was also an excellent source of information. And a highly accomplished Rider. If K'lrsa wasn't allowed to leave camp to get more food, maybe N'la could. It was either that or they were going to need to move camp soon.

As she walked towards N'la's tent she nodded to the Riders she passed, trying to convey confidence instead of defeat. Even though she was no longer on the Council and Luden had taken the necklace, she still felt responsible for these people.

She'd been the one to suggest forming a new tribe, and the one who'd told the newcomers they could stay. (Although someday she was going to need to have a talk with Vedhe about what made a man a good man because it seemed she'd made a few mistakes where that was concerned.)

Before she could reach N'la, Luden intercepted her. "Where are you going? Are you behind this?" He nodded towards the Rider encampment.

"No. You are. Or did you think they wouldn't notice when you walled your women away and put them under guard. What did you think they'd do? Steal them? Kill them?"

"Don't be ridiculous. The women were uncomfortable being around so many strange men. They wanted something familiar. That's all that was."

She pressed her lips together, not wanting to argue with him, but she couldn't stop herself from making one more comment. "Well that's not what it looked like. And you're members of the tribes now. You need to act like it. We don't separate our women like that."

"Funny. I don't remember that being part of the vow I swore."

She exhaled through her nose, wanting so much to hit him even though it wouldn't help. "Don't you see how this divides the tribe?"

"We have a right to our beliefs."

A young girl, about M'lara's age, darted from the enclosure, chasing two young boys, all three laughing.

"Your beliefs? I've been to the Daliphana. I've seen what you believe. That girl." She pointed to the girl who had just caught one of the boys and was now running away from him. "What will become of her? If she wants to be a Rider, will you let her? Or will she spend the rest of her life behind those walls? Because that's the way it always was in the Daliphana."

His lips twisted into a sneer before he could stop himself.

K'lrsa shook her head. "I don't understand you, Luden. Before the women and children arrived you were at least willing to listen. And you treated us with respect. But now…What changed?"

"That was before I knew you were willing to kill my family to protect yourselves."

"It wasn't…" She pinched her nose. "I wasn't thinking of them as your family. You have to understand. In the tribes we're always struggling to survive. There's never enough food or shelter. It…We all know this…We all…"

She shook her head. It was too hard to explain how everyone grew up knowing they might need to sacrifice themselves for the tribe, and how every decision the Council made was for the good of the whole, not the individual.

She changed the subject instead. "Look. I know you won't listen to me, but you can't stay here. There's not enough food in this area to feed this many people. Go to the other tribes. Ask for help. They'll do what they can."

Although she was afraid it might not be enough.

It was the very beginning of spring. Most would be surviving on the last of their winter stores, and they'd all already taken in extra mouths to feed at the gathering grounds.

"We'll find a way." He didn't even bother looking at her.

"How?"

He touched the necklace. Her necklace. "I have a few ideas. With this we can cover much more ground than on horseback."

"Luden. Be careful. The one time I traveled using that necklace it almost killed me and Vedhe."

"I've heard the story. It made you too scared to try again. Because of that you failed to see the possibilities."

K'lrsa shook her head and turned away.

Let him kill himself. What did she care?

"Where are you going?"

"To see if N'la has some food she can spare. Unless, of course, Vedhe and I are allowed to leave the camp to hunt for ourselves?"

"No. And go back to your tent. I'll have one of my men bring you something to eat."

She turned on him, glaring. "Are you telling me I can't even talk to anyone else in the tribe?"

"Not right now. No. Now, go. Before I make you." He touched the necklace, staring her down with his flinty black gaze.

Rolling her eyes in disgust, K'lrsa stalked back to her tent. It was a good thing Badru was on his way or she would've probably done something very, very foolish.

CHAPTER 17

Luden's men did bring them food. And the next day she learned what he'd meant by using the necklace in new ways. Luden and four men left the camp in the early morning and returned towards dusk with the mangled remains of five baru.

None of the men looked particularly well; one was coughing up blood.

"See?" Luden grinned at her, basking in the glory of his triumph. "We'll have plenty to eat now that I have the necklace."

"What did you do?" She stared at the twisted carcasses in horror as grel gathered at the edge of camp with their beady red eyes and greasy gray feathers, calling out to one another at the sight of the bloody feast.

"We found a herd of baru off in the distance and I used the necklace to bring five of them to us. Barely took any time at all."

She paced closer to the pile of bones, hide, and meat, studying the remains. "Did you even think about *which* baru you were killing?"

"What are you talking about?"

"See that? You killed a nursing mother. Now her calf will probably die, too. And there? You chose at least two young bucks. When we hunt we always aim for the old who are past their prime."

"And it shows. I haven't had a decent meal since I've been here. Either the meat is so stringy I can barely eat it or completely tasteless because it boiled all day."

She bit her lip, wanting to slap him. "It keeps the herd healthy and alive so we can hunt them another day. You keep killing the young mothers and bucks and there won't be a herd left for you to hunt."

"Then we'll find another."

"And when that one's gone?" She glared at him, wondering if he really was this stupid.

"If you don't want any of it, don't eat it. I need to clean up before dinner." He stalked away as his men started butchering the meat.

K'lrsa watched him go.

She needed to take the necklace back. Luden didn't understand how delicate the balance was between the tribes and the land. A few more hunts like this one and the damage might take years to fix.

She sighed. Just what she needed right now.

Aran was a threat, certainly. An immediate threat to the very existence of the world.

But men like Luden—who only saw their own needs and interests and ignored the impact of their actions on the wider world—were just as likely to destroy everything given enough time.

Which meant she needed to deal with him, too.

And first.

CHAPTER 18

The next day there was a new camp of the Daliph's soldiers on the edge of the barren lands. Luden didn't even bother to call a meeting of the Council—what little remained of it with F'lia drugged and K'lrsa under guard. He simply used the necklace to send the soldiers away and brought the new women and children back to the camp.

As the five women and fifteen young children made their way to the newcomers' enclosure, J'ver stepped forward to confront Luden.

He was the oldest of the Riders in the tribe, but still only twenty-five summers old. His father was on the Council of the Spring Winds tribe. He'd left it to find his own way, but so far he hadn't done much more than lounge in the background and follow the orders he liked and ignore those he didn't.

He glanced back at the other Riders, wiping his sweaty hands on his pants.

"What do you want, J'ver?" Luden asked, barely looking at him.

"We need to talk."

"Well, then, talk." Luden crossed his arms and stared J'ver down.

For a moment, K'lrsa thought he'd run back to the safety of the other Riders, but he surprised her by lifting his chin and meeting Luden's condescending sneer. "The

Council didn't meet before you banished those soldiers and took in the women and children."

"And?"

"And that's the way we do thing in the tribes. The Council meets and decides, and anyone who wants a say can have one."

Luden shrugged, every line of his body conveying confidence and command. "I decided we don't need a Council anymore."

"But…That's the way we do things."

The Riders who were close enough to hear what Luden had said were muttering back and forth, their expressions dark, but Luden didn't care.

"Not anymore. Not now that I have this." He touched the necklace at his throat.

"But…You don't understand." J'ver glanced towards K'lrsa. "She was right you know. About hunting the healthiest of the herd and hunting too many at once. You need to listen to us. And…We can't keep taking on all these new mouths to feed. You have to send them away."

Luden loomed over J'ver, snarling. "If you don't like the way I'm running this tribe then leave."

J'ver stood up straighter, his eyes flashing with anger. "No. That's not how we do things here. Maybe *you* should just go back to the Daliphate where you belong."

K'lrsa flinched as J'ver spat, not at Luden's feet, but on his face.

Before she or anyone else could react, Luden grabbed the necklace, screaming in incoherent rage, and J'ver disappeared.

For one heartbeat, the space before Luden was empty. Every one stood, frozen, staring at him, trying to understand what had just happened.

And then the space wasn't empty anymore.

Before Luden was a pile of twisted flesh and bones, all white and red and dripping. But enough was left of J'ver for everyone to know what had happened.

Luden glared at the Riders. "I am the leader of this tribe now. If any of you dare to oppose me, you'll meet the same fate J'ver did. Now, everyone back to your tents." He gripped the necklace in his fist, slowly shifting his gaze across the crowd until people crept away, fleeing to the false safety of their tents.

K'lrsa stayed where she was.

J'ver was dead because she'd let Luden take the necklace from her.

It was her fault.

And her wrong to fix.

CHAPTER 19

L uden walked towards her, slowly, calmly, his expression one of contempt. He stopped five steps away. "You saw what I did to J'ver. Do you really want to defy me right now?"

She swallowed heavily, licking her lips, wanting to run back to her tent like everyone else had, but she couldn't. "It's because of what you did to him that I *have* to defy you."

He laughed softly. "And how do you think you're going to do that? Without your magic horse or necklace? You're just a girl. How old are you anyway?"

She lifted her chin, fighting not to quail away from him. "Almost seventeen summers."

"Seventeen? You're a child. Go to bed."

"No." She braced herself even though there was nothing she could do if he chose to use the necklace on her. "I can't let you do this. I know you think you did the right thing—fighting back against someone who challenged you—but… You didn't. Can't you see that?"

He reached for the necklace. "How dare you…"

K'lrsa focused on the necklace and willed it towards herself, thinking about how she was the one the gods had given it to, not Luden, calling to it to obey her, not him.

The necklace trembled slightly, vibrating on its chain, but it didn't fly through the air to her hand like she'd hoped it would. And then Luden's fingers closed around it, holding it in place, taking control of it.

She shivered. Any moment she might be turned into nothing more than a pile of meat and sinew, but she refused to quit. Not until he actually killed her.

She tackled him to the ground, surprising both of them with the speed and impact of her attack as she wrapped her arms around his legs and drove him to the ground with the weight of her body.

Luden let go of the necklace as he landed. The next moment he'd kicked free of her grip and grabbed her, pinning her to the ground, his fingers wrapping around her neck as he tried to choke her. She broke the hold, smacking his arms to the side and reached for the necklace, but he grabbed her wrist and twisted it painfully to the side.

She used her other hand to hit him in the side, causing him to release his grip just long enough for her to twist free and lunge for the necklace again.

She could hear the Riders and newcomers gathering around them, but no one stepped forward to intervene.

They struggled back and forth, evenly matched as they struck and counterstruck, grappling back and forth, neither one gaining enough advantage to grasp the necklace and use it.

Finally, Luden grabbed both of her wrists in his hands, his grip too strong to break and pinned her to the ground with his body. She fought to free herself as he slowly pressed her wrists towards one another, clearly meaning to hold them pinned with one hand as he used the other to grab the necklace.

K'lrsa turned her attention to the necklace. She only had a few more breaths before he'd succeed. She focused, drawing on its power the same way she had when she'd banished those soldiers without touching it.

She met Luden's flinty black eyes as she willed him into the heart of the barren lands with every ounce of strength she had.

She was rewarded with the sight of his eyes widening in fear for just one instant before he disappeared and the necklace dropped to her chest.

CHAPTER 20

K'lrsa lay on her back, eyes closed, relishing her victory for one, long, sweet moment. And then she had to scramble to her feet as the Riders and newcomers moved closer, ready to fight one another.

"Stay back. All of you." She glared them down, the necklace clutched tight in her fist. "Whether you want to believe it or not, we're all one tribe and it's about time we started acting like it."

She waited to make sure she had their attention and then nodded once. "Good. Now everyone gather round. We need to talk."

A few of the newcomers looked like they might argue but she brandished the necklace at them and they sullenly came closer.

She nodded towards the enclosure. "I want the women here, too."

Murin crossed his arms and planted himself between her and the women. She smiled at him, willing him to defy her so she'd have an excuse to be rid of him once and for all. He stared back at her for a long moment, but then nodded to one of the younger newcomers to get the women, and moved off to the side, hands held up to show he wasn't a threat.

K'lrsa watched him while she waited for the women to join them.

Only when everyone in camp was there—except F'lia—did she continue. "Alright. I'm going to say my piece. You can all do with it what you will. I say this as a former Council member and as the one who rightfully owns this necklace. And as a member of this tribe." She made eye contact with as many people as she could as she spoke. "It's pretty clear to me that we've failed as a tribe and we cannot continue the way we've been going."

"We should just send them back where they came from," a Rider in the back of the crowd shouted.

"No. We can't. These men are as much members of the tribes now as you are. They swore the same vow to the gods as the rest of us. And we offered them a home here. I won't take that back." She met the eyes of each Rider, stopping on the most stubborn ones for an extra moment or two. "And neither will any of you."

N'la stepped forward, hand on her knife. "How are you going to enforce that? Turn us into a pile of blood and guts like Luden did?"

"No. You'll do it because those are our rules. Members of the tribes don't attack one another. And anyone who does attack a member of the tribes is expelled. *That's how we survive.* By following the rules that have kept us alive for hundreds of years."

They clearly didn't agree, but she continued, wanting to get to the heart of what she had to say while they were still listening. "Look. We've failed as a tribe. Maybe given enough time we would have worked through our differences and found a way to honor our existing ways while also accepting the experience of these newcomers, but we don't have that time anymore. And now that these women and children are here, I don't think it will ever happen. Already we've split into two camps. And look how willing we were to fight one another. Which leaves only one choice."

"What's that?" N'la asked.

"Riders return to your original tribes. Newcomers stay here and form your own tribe. Or go with the Riders and join an existing tribe. But if you do, you'll be fully subject to the rules of the tribes and the governance of the Council that already exists for that tribe." Her gaze lingered on Murin as she said that last bit. "Any Riders who'd prefer to stay here as members of this new tribe, can."

Murin sneered at her. "What if we don't want them here, meddling in how we do things?"

K'lrsa sighed. After today she was never, ever going to let herself be put in a position to lead others ever again. "If you refuse to at least allow members of the other tribes to join you or to allow your members who want to join the other tribes to do so…" She made a point of meeting the gaze of the boldest women amongst the newcomers. "Then at the next tribal gathering the tribes will have to decide whether to allow you to continue to be members. Because that's not our way. All are allowed to freely move between tribes if they so choose."

"What's to guarantee you won't do that to us no matter what we do?"

"I can't guarantee that, Murin. I don't speak for the tribes. What I can tell you is that locking your women away behind barriers like you've done is likely not going to go over well with the other tribes. Especially if those women don't want to be locked away. You are welcome to make a new start here, but I'd suggest you find a way to put aside some of the beliefs and practices you brought with you from the Daliphana."

Murin turned away, ignoring her, but some of the new women moved closer to one another, talking softly amongst themselves.

"I'll also add what I've been trying to tell Luden for days now. You cannot stay here and expect to feed this many. You will starve."

"We could if we had the necklace," one of the new women said.

K'lrsa winced. "The way Luden used the necklace to hunt would've destroyed us all in time. You need to find a way to live in balance with this land. You can come join the other tribes and learn that way or you can find a way on your own. But I can't allow that type of short-sighted slaughter to continue."

K'lrsa wished there were a way to make them understand what she was telling them, but all she saw from the newcomers was sullen resentment. When their children started to die of starvation she had no doubt they'd blame her for it, but what she was doing was right.

Not just for these people, but for all of the tribes.

"What are *you* going to do?" N'la asked, interrupting her black thoughts.

"Find the man who sent these women and children here and kill him. For good this time." She glanced to the newcomers. "Once he's gone you can return home if you want to."

A few nodded, but others shook their head.

K'lrsa shrugged. "Anyway. That's what I have to say. Do as you will. But I, and the necklace, aren't going to be here either way." She met Vedhe's eyes. "It's time we ended this threat for good."

CHAPTER 21

F 'lia thrashed around in her sleep, tears running down her cheeks as she whispered L'ral's name over and over again. K'lrsa knelt by her side and gently squeezed her hand, wishing she could take all of her friend's pain away.

It hurt to hear her calling for L'ral—the man who'd led K'lrsa's father to his death—but it wasn't a surprise. Even though F'lia hadn't spoken of him since she'd come back from the Black Horse Tribe—L'ral's betrayal had hung between them like a rotten fruit, ready to burst at the slightest touch—it was clear she still loved him.

She was too kind-hearted to believe he could've betrayed K'lrsa's father without a good reason. And to K'lrsa there was no reason good enough for what he'd done even though he'd begged her forgiveness and sworn he hadn't meant for her father to die. (Something she hadn't told F'lia, because then she would have had to tell her that he was waiting for her in the Hidden City.)

K'lrsa winced as F'lia cried out for L'ral once more. She should've told her about him before this, but she hadn't wanted to doom her friend to living a half-life with a man who was already dead. And what about the baby? He would've been raised alone in a city surrounded by dead people.

But now…

There was nothing to lose. The baby was gone and F'lia was so devastated she might never recover. She'd already tried to give herself to the sands once before when L'ral and K'lrsa disappeared. This time, there'd be no one to stop her…

L'ral's love might be the only thing that could save her. Which meant that if K'lrsa wanted F'lia to survive, she needed to take her to the Hidden City. Now.

Before she went after Aran.

It was a risk.

What if F'lia chose to join L'ral in death?

But it was the best chance she had. The only chance. And if F'lia did make that choice? At least she'd be making it to be with the one she loved. She wouldn't be alone.

Vedhe ducked into the tent. "How is she?"

"Devastated." K'lrsa wiped at the fresh tears on F'lia's cheeks before turning to Vedhe. "I'm going to take her to the Hidden City. To L'ral."

Vedhe pursed her lips. "What about Aran? I thought you were finally ready to kill him."

"I am. But I need to make sure F'lia is safe first."

"You aren't just going to hide there until it's over?"

"No." She stood so she'd feel less like a child being scolded by her mother. "I…I didn't tell you this yet." She lowered her voice as she glanced back at F'lia. "Father Sun said he'd bring back Badru if I agreed to kill Aran. He's also holding my father's soul hostage against my vow to destroy the Toreem Daliphate. Which means my father is still in the Hidden City, too. I'd like to talk to him—and my mother—and maybe Herin if she's still there, before we go after Aran."

Vedhe frowned. "I thought Badru was dead. How is Father Sun bringing him back to you?"

She bit her lip, staring down at F'lia, finally letting the guilt of the bargain she'd made settle onto her shoulders. "Not really. According to Father Sun, because he's a death walker, he'll only actually die when he leaves the city. But Father Sun was able to free him without it killing him."

"How?"

She swallowed. "He traded a life for a life."

"Whose?"

"He said the baby was going to die anyway. That he was just taking a life spark that was already going to be lost and giving it a purpose."

"And you believed him? That the child was already going to die."

K'lrsa flinched. "Yes."

Vedhe pulled the viewing tube from its pocket and studied her. "Hm. Well, if nothing else, you believe what you just said."

"What does that mean?" K'lrsa stomach clenched.

"It means the gods have lied to you before to get what they want. Why should they tell you the truth now?"

K'lrsa stumbled backward a step. Could what Vedhe was implying be true? Had Father Sun taken the life of the child in order to bring back Badru?

No. It couldn't be. F'lia had been feeling ill for days before he made his offer.

He'd been telling her the truth. He had to be.

But then, why had he needed her permission to act? Why not just do it?

Because he wanted her to agree to kill Aran?

Or because he'd lied and the child wasn't going to die, not without her agreement.

K'lrsa clutched at her stomach, feeling ill. "He didn't even tell me who was going to die when he made his offer. If I'd known…If I'd thought…I never would've…"

Vedhe touched her arm. "That's what matters. That you would have never willingly sacrificed the life of F'lia's child for Badru."

"Is it?"

Vedhe shrugged. "It has to be."

As K'lrsa stared at Vedhe in horror, F'lia stirred, slowly opening her eyes. "K'lrsa? The baby. Where is he? Is he okay?"

K'lrsa knelt by her friend's side, tears pouring down her cheeks. "I'm sorry, Fi. He didn't make it."

F'lia wailed and started tearing at her hair and clawing at her cheeks. K'lrsa grabbed her wrists, struggling to keep her from hurting herself, but she was inconsolable.

Vedhe poured a thick gray liquid into a cup and knelt down next to them. "Here. Drink this." She forced the liquid down F'lia's throat, not letting her duck away until it was all gone.

F'lia continued to struggle against K'lrsa's hold until the medicine finally took effect and she drifted back to sleep.

K'lrsa stared at her friend, running a finger along one of the shallow cuts in her cheek from where she'd raked her face when she heard the babe was dead.

What had she done?

It was no excuse that she hadn't known who was going to die. She should've known. She should've…

Vedhe wiped the cup clean and stood. "That should hold her for a while. If we're going to the Hidden City, we should leave as soon as possible."

"You're coming with me?"

"Of course. Come on. We have lots to plan before we go."

K'lrsa followed Vedhe out of the tent, letting the logistics of finding the horses, packing up their tents, keeping F'lia drugged until they could reach the Hidden City, finding Badru, finding M'lara, and defeating Aran distract her.

But her mind kept circling back to whether Father Sun had lied to her. Had she given him permission to kill an innocent child—her best friend's child—just so she could have Badru back?

She hoped not.

She loved him. But he wasn't worth that.

CHAPTER 22

Fallion and Kriger returned on their own while Vedhe and K'lrsa were discussing what they could or couldn't take with them. They'd already ruled out using the necklace to return to the Hidden City. It had damaged them too much the first time and they were even farther away this time. Plus, that let them pack a tent and the small amount of provisions they still had.

Most of the Riders were already packed up and ready to leave. The newcomers had moved, too. They'd set their tents up right at the entrance to the barren lands, which was good, but they'd kept the walled enclosure for the women and children.

Ah well. She'd done what she could and now she had to focus on bigger issues. As they turned their attention to finding out where M'lara had been taken, a woman approached them, looking cautiously to each side, her hands clenched in determination.

She had the same dark skin as Sayel and for a moment K'lrsa couldn't breathe past the ache of loss that squeezed her heart. He'd been a good man. She owed it to him and all the others like him to end this. To give them a better world to live in than this one.

The woman reached her just as a man appeared in the distance, coming from the new camp, his expression dark with anger. K'lrsa recognized him as one of the more

89

troublesome newcomers, but she didn't remember his name. The woman saw him, too, and bowed her head, turning back towards him.

"Wait. Can I help you?" K'lrsa moved to stand between her and the man.

The woman forced herself to meet K'lrsa's eyes, her entire body shaking with fear.

K'lrsa hid the flash of anger that burned through her veins as she remembered all those days she'd spent in the Toreem Daliphate being told she had no right to raise her head or make eye contact with strangers just because she was a woman.

How hard must it be for a woman like this to approach her, to set aside an entire lifetime of rules and conditioning and reach out to a woman who dressed and acted so differently.

K'lrsa pulled the woman into the shadow of a nearby tent. "What is it?"

The woman swallowed. She had to be only twenty, maybe twenty-two, summers old. "You said we could go with the Riders if we want? Join the other tribes?"

"Yes. Of course. If you want to leave with the Riders and go to one of the other tribes you can."

The woman glanced in the direction of the man who Vedhe had moved to intercept. "My husband…He doesn't want to leave."

"Then go without him."

The woman stared at her wide-eyed. "But he's my husband. I have to obey him."

K'lrsa bit back the five or six things she wanted to stay about that. She had to remember that this woman's experience was completely different from her own.

She took a deep breath and tried to find the right words to explain to the woman how things worked in the tribes.

"Here, a wife doesn't obey her husband no more than a husband obeys his wife. They're equals. Yes, they should think about each other's needs and wants. You can't just act without realizing that your actions impact on your spouse. But you can still make your own choices, no matter what.

If he wants to stay here and you want to leave, that's fine."

"But he's my husband. My place is by his side." The woman bit her lip, fighting back tears.

"Then stay. But only if that's what you want to do."

The woman stared at the ground, her brow furrowed in concentration. "I don't want to stay. But he won't let me leave. I asked him to set me aside and he refused."

K'lrsa puffed out her cheeks as she desperately searched for someone else to handle this problem, but no one was nearby.

She tried again. "In the tribes you're allowed to leave your husband. Even if he doesn't want you to. You can make that choice."

"But he'll beat me if I leave him."

"No he won't. And I'd like to see him try." She gripped the necklace, glaring at the man where he stood with Vedhe, his face a storm of anger.

"But…"

K'lrsa rubbed the back of her neck. It was getting late and the Riders would be leaving soon and she still hadn't found M'lara. She didn't have time to discuss the difference in marriage practices between the Daliphana and the tribes.

"Look. It's simple. Go with the Riders or don't. That's *your* choice. And if anyone tries to stop you, I'll stop them. Now. What do you want? To go? Or to stay?"

The woman shook her head and wrung her hands. "I…I don't know."

K'lrsa grabbed her by the arm and dragged her over to where N'la was directing a group of Riders to saddle up their horses. "N'la, I need you to deal with this woman."

"Who is she? What do you want me to do with her?"

"I don't know. She thinks she might want to go with the Riders rather than stay here. But she's worried her husband will beat her if she tries."

N'la glared in the general direction of the newcomers. "Not if I have anything to say about it."

The woman cringed away from N'la's evident anger, and K'lrsa was certain if she let her go she'd slink back to that enclosure and never emerge again.

K'lrsa sighed. "I don't have time for this, but I suspect there may be more women than just this one who'd like to leave if given the chance. Can you…deal with it?"

"Me? Why me?"

"Because you at least know most of the men."

"Not in a way that will help with this!"

K'lrsa held her hands up in defeat. "Then find someone who does. I need to figure out where they've taken M'lara before you leave. And I really, really don't want to be in the middle of this."

N'la snorted. "Like I do? Fine. Leave her here. I'll figure something out."

K'lrsa let go of the woman and she started to back away from both of them, but N'la threw an arm around her shoulder and leaned close, talking to her quietly. Slowly, the woman relaxed and started to nod.

K'lrsa walked away, feeling a small twinge of guilt for basically forcing the woman to go through with her desire to join the Riders, but she shoved it aside. Better than staying with a man who'd beat her for wanting to leave. And hopefully she'd see that eventually.

If not…

Well. She could always go back to him.

K'lrsa didn't have time to think about it anymore. She needed to find M'lara. Where was she?

CHAPTER 23

Fortunately, M'lara was an easy problem to solve.

K'lrsa stormed into the center of the newcomer camp and threatened to send every man, woman, and child back to Aran in bloody pieces if someone didn't tell her where her sister was.

Now.

Two men immediately pointed her north, deeper into Black Horse Tribe lands. They said M'lara wasn't far, just a few hills away.

K'lrsa thanked them and raced off on Fallion to retrieve her. If the men were lying…

As she left what remained of the new camp, N'la and two other Riders were headed for the newcomers' camp, the frightened woman who'd approached K'lrsa trailing behind them. She hoped they found a way to work through things without anyone getting hurt, but she didn't care enough to stay and make sure of it.

Luckily for the two men who'd given her directions, M'lara and her guards were right where they'd said they'd be.

As soon as Fallion crested the small hill above their camp, M'lara ran past her guards, crying, arms held wide. K'lrsa slid to the ground and pulled her into a hug.

"Are you okay?" she asked, looking M'lara over for any signs of damage.

"Yes, I'm fine."

"They didn't hurt you?"

"No. They just wouldn't let me leave. I told them you'd find me and that you wouldn't be happy when you did."

K'lrsa hugged her sister again. "You're right. I'm not. But we have bigger things to deal with than these two."

She stopped just long enough to tell the men that Luden was dead and the Riders were leaving, and then she and M'lara rode Fallion back to the camp.

Things had become more heated since she'd left—she could hear shouting from the direction of the newcomers' camp—but they seemed to be under control.

She resisted the temptation to intervene—they needed to work this out themselves; she wasn't going to be there in the coming days to help, so there was no point her threatening people into doing things her way.

While she was gone, Vedhe had taken down both of the tents and packed them away. She was sitting next to F'lia, waiting.

K'lrsa helped M'lara down from Fallion's back and knelt in front of her, biting her lip, unsure how to tell her sister she was leaving her again.

"No." M'lara backed away from her, shaking her head side-to-side.

"I haven't even said anything yet."

"But you're going to. You're going to leave me. Just like everyone else has. You promised! You promised." Tears streaked down her cheeks as she took another step backward.

"M'lara, wait. Please. Let me explain." She moved closer and grabbed M'lara's shoulders, staring into her sad eyes, trying to find a way to explain why she had to leave. And why M'lara couldn't come with her.

But at the sight of M'lara's tears, she realized she couldn't break her sister's heart like that.

K'lrsa bit her lip, thinking.

She had planned on leaving M'lara with one of the Riders from the White Horse Tribe and asking them to take her back to D'lan. But maybe…

If what Father Sun had said was really true and her parents were still in the Hidden City…

Maybe she could give M'lara what she desperately wished she had—more time with their parents.

K'lrsa swallowed, suddenly nervous for no reason she could explain. "I'm not going to leave you. Not yet. I have an idea. But it'll require you to be very, very brave. And...I don't want you to get your hopes up...but..."

"What?" M'lara thrust her lower lip out and crossed her arms, clearly not trusting a word K'lrsa was saying.

K'lrsa nodded towards where Vedhe and F'lia were sitting, waiting for her. "Vedhe and I are taking F'lia somewhere she'll be safe. She lost the baby and she's very sad right now, and I don't want her to be alone."

M'lara wiped at her cheeks. "She lost the baby?"

"Mmhm. So we're going to take her somewhere she can recover. Somewhere special. I was going to have you stay with D'lan while we did that, but I think maybe you should come with us." She bit her lip again, anticipating M'lara's reaction. "Problem is, you'll have to stay there with her. You can't come with us when we leave."

M'lara glared at her. "You *are* going to abandon me."

"Well...No...Not really." K'lrsa didn't want to mention their parents. If Father Sun had lied, it would be like losing them all over again. But...She had to. Or else M'lara would be a nightmare the whole way there. "This is a very special city we're going to, M'lara. Sometimes, not always, the dead go there after they die."

"The dead?" M'lara wrinkled her nose, confused.

K'lrsa nodded. "Mmhm. Like Mom and Dad."

M'lara's eyes widened and she wiped her snotty nose on her arm. "Mom and Dad are there? I can see them again?"

K'lrsa held up a hand to calm her, wondering if she'd made a mistake mentioning it. "I don't know. They *were* there, but they were supposed to leave. But maybe they didn't and are still there."

"I can see Mom and Dad again?" M'lara looked so happy, so hopeful, that it broke K'lrsa's heart.

"For a little bit. But you have to remember, if they are there, they're still dead. The people you see there..."

She couldn't tell her it wasn't them, because it was them.

It just…wasn't the same.

"I can see Mom and Dad again!" She grinned ear to ear, jumping up and down in excitement.

"Maybe…"

K'lrsa grimaced. It was too late to tell M'lara not to get her hopes up. She closed her eyes for a moment, wishing she hadn't said anything at all. "We'll see when we get there, okay? But if we're going to leave, we should do it now."

K'lrsa glanced towards the newcomers' camp. They were still shouting back and forth. But it wasn't her problem anymore.

M'lara scrambled into Fallion's saddle and looked down at K'lrsa, eager to be off. K'lrsa laughed. "Let me get our things, okay?"

"Okay." M'lara was so excited, she was practically bouncing in the saddle. Good thing Fallion was such a mellow horse.

As K'lrsa checked the small bag Vedhe had packed for her, she shoved down the swirl of emotions that filled her at the thought of returning to the Hidden City. Part of her worried that Father Sun had lied to manipulate her and they'd return only to find her father and mother were gone, long since started on their journey through the Promised Plains.

But she was equally scared to find that they really were trapped there, possibly forever, against their will, because of the foolish vow she'd made.

She didn't know which would be worse. The disappointment in her sister's eyes if they were gone, or in her parents' eyes if they weren't.

Either way. She wasn't exactly eager to leave.

"K'lrsa, come on! Let's go!"

"Alright. I'm coming." She swung into the saddle and looked around one last time at the crumbled remains of the tribe she'd tried to found, hoping the newcomers could hold Aran's troops back long enough for her and Vedhe to defeat him.

If they couldn't…It might be too late for all of them.

CHAPTER 24

As soon as the moon rose, they flew the horses, soaring over the plains and then the desert, Fallion shining as if a thousand suns lurked just under his coat, his powerful wings beating through the air, Kriger, silvery and equally gorgeous, flying silently next to them.

Once again, K'lrsa found herself in that world that wasn't her world. The horses' powerful wings beat the air and large swathes of ground passed beneath them with each stroke, but it was oddly quiet and peaceful as they flew. There was no breeze to stir her hair, no birds flying near them. Just the moon and the stars, so close she felt she could touch them if only she dared.

M'lara pointed out everything she saw below—a herd of baru, a desert cat, a tribal camp far in the distance—until exhaustion finally overtook her and she leaned back against K'lrsa's chest, snoring softly.

Vedhe, sitting on Kriger's back, was serene, even with F'lia asleep in front of her, almost bigger than she was.

These between places seemed made for Vedhe in a way the real world wasn't. She'd done better at interacting with the newcomers than K'lrsa had, but there was always a part of her that was somewhere else. Like she had one foot in this world and one foot in the gods' world.

It was hard to realize—seeing her like this, so confident and strong—how young she was. Especially with all she seemed to know after their experience in the labyrinth. Both had earned the knowledge of that place, but Vedhe had lasted longer so absorbed more of it. And she'd made an effort to actually use the knowledge so she could keep what she'd gained through such pain.

Unlike K'lrsa who had wanted to forget it as soon as she'd learned it, and had shut it away behind a wall where she didn't have to think about it.

Hopefully someday it would be gone and she could go back to who she'd been before she learned about the wider world and all its complications and gray spaces. She didn't like thinking about the ten different explanations for everything. Or understanding why something she didn't like was the way it was because of *history*.

Vedhe smiled at K'lrsa. The angry red scars on her face had turned silver under the moonlight and were almost beautiful. K'lrsa smiled back, remembering the first time Vedhe had flown Kriger, looping through the sky on his back like a child.

She relaxed, letting herself enjoy the simple pleasure of flying, trying to remember the last time she'd truly felt at peace. Or happy. It seemed like forever.

She wished she could just stay in this world that wasn't a world. Take Fallion somewhere new, somewhere free of Aran and the tribes and the Daliphana. She'd find Badru and they'd escape together.

Let someone else carry this burden.

But as soon as it appeared, she shoved the thought aside.

It was too tempting to think that way, to think that if she just stayed away from the troubles of the world that eventually someone else would step up to solve them.

She knew better. She'd seen how people in the tribes had worried about what was happening. How they'd talked about the changes they were seeing. But had anyone other than her father dared to step forward, to speak up, to try to stop it?

No.

They'd worried, but they'd kept right on with their lives, hoping the threat just went away.

Most people didn't want to fight or struggle, not unless they had no other choice. They'd rather talk themselves to death while the tribes slowly rotted from the edges inward.

They didn't understand that some things, once broken, could never be put back together again. That you could go so far down the wrong path, there was no coming back.

So, no. She couldn't just fly away and leave it to someone else. Because no one else would care enough to pick up her burden.

If she wanted Aran defeated, she'd have to do it herself.

No matter what it cost her.

CHAPTER 25

As the moon set on the far horizon, the horses landed outside a small cave in the desert, the opening just tall enough for the horses to shelter in during the heat of the day.

K'lrsa had never realized before the Lady Moon pointed it out that the caves were provided by the gods.

It made sense. They always seemed to be there when someone needed one. And to have food to eat for both humans and horses and wood for a small fire. They weren't as grand as K'lrsa would've made them if she'd had the power of a god, but they were enough.

And that seemed to be what the gods were willing to provide. Enough. Never more.

She carried a sleeping M'lara towards the cave, stumbling under her sister's weight and the exhaustion of flying all night. A sound up ahead startled her and she saw Midnight standing at the entrance to the cave, his coat more sleek and black than she remembered, the white teardrop in the center of his forehead marking him as an *Amalanee* horse.

That meant…

Gently, she lowered her sister to the ground and hurried forward, trying not to run, her heart soaring with anticipation even as she told herself he might not be there.

K'lrsa couldn't stop the smile that broke across her face or the tears that filled her eyes at the thought of seeing

Badru again. All these weeks she'd told herself that what she'd felt for him had been no more than a crush—a physical attraction to a handsome boy by a girl who'd just lost her father and needed someone, anyone, to fill that gaping hole in her heart.

But as she quickened her steps and brushed past Midnight with a quick pat to the neck, she knew she'd been lying to herself. What she felt for Badru was so much more than that, so much deeper. It was like Father Sun had said—Badru balanced her. He completed her in some way she couldn't put into words. And she didn't want to name it. To try to define what it was that existed between them.

What mattered was what she felt. And with Badru she felt whole, complete.

Happy.

He was just waking up, rubbing at his face blearily as he sat up in his bedroll.

"Badru!" She fell to her knees and hugged him.

He fell back a bit under the sudden assault, but then he hugged her back, the fierceness of his embrace driving the air from her lungs.

She could barely breathe, but she didn't care.

He was back. Alive. Real.

"K'lrsa." He buried his face against her neck and she could feel his tears as he held her.

"Badru." She clung to him, never wanting to let go.

She hadn't wanted to believe, hadn't thought it could be possible...

That Father Sun...

She tensed and pushed away from Badru, remembering the price that had been paid to bring him back.

"Did...Did Father Sun tell you?" She glanced towards the entrance where Vedhe was helping a bleary-eyed F'lia lie down.

He nodded once, whispering so softly she could barely hear him, "He said the babe was already going to die."

"And you believed him?" She searched his face, desperate for him to say yes.

He grimaced, watching as Vedhe settled F'lia in the

corner and forced her to drink more of the sleeping draught. "Yes."

"Really? Truly?"

Badru stared at her with his impossibly blue eyes, and she longed to hug him again, to pretend she'd never asked the question. But she held back. This was too important.

"I had to. If I didn't…If I thought…" He clenched his jaw. "I didn't want anyone to die for me, ever. Especially not a child."

K'lrsa flashed to that moment after Herin had brought Badru back to life and he'd said something similar about Sayel. She remembered how Herin had lectured him, reminding him that people had died for him every day whether he'd acknowledged it or not. Slaves in the fields. Soldiers at battle.

It was true for all of them. Whether they knew it or not, somewhere someone was dying so they could have the life they did.

They were, all of them, beneficiaries of the sacrifices of others.

She sighed and settled down next to him. No point in sharing that thought. He'd either argue or be as depressed by it as she was.

Instead, she squeezed his hand. "Did he tell you? We're going to kill Aran."

"Good."

"And destroy the Toreem Daliphate."

He frowned. "Why? Why do you need to do that? Aran's the one that's evil."

She raised one eyebrow, remembering the way she'd been treated in the Daliphana and how evil it had felt to her while she was there, but kept silent. She didn't want to have that argument either. Not when she'd just found him again.

Instead, she told him the truth. "Because I swore I would when my father died. And Father Sun is holding me to my vow. If I don't do it, my father will be trapped in the Hidden City forever, never allowed to continue on to the Promise Plains."

She glanced towards where Vedhe had just settled M'lara down, speaking softly. "Is he still there? In the Hidden City? My father? And my mother? Is she there, too?"

Badru nodded.

K'lrsa nodded. That was good. For M'lara's sake at least. She wasn't looking forward to what they'd have to say to her, but she was glad she'd get to ask them for their thoughts before she challenged Aran.

She leaned against the wall, her shoulder touching Badru's. "So he told the truth about that, at least."

Badru took her hand in his and kissed it, a slight smile playing upon his lips. "I never thought I'd see you again. All those weeks I spent waiting for you to return, hoping…But with each day…" He shook his head.

She twined her fingers through his. "I didn't know…When I left…That you were still alive. I thought you were already dead. I thought if I went back you'd be there, but it wouldn't be you. You'd never age or be able to leave, and I'd be stuck there with you as I grew old and bitter and…"

"I know. I'm sorry." He moved away from her to stoke the fire and put a small pot of water on to boil.

"So why didn't you tell me?"

He knelt by the fire, keeping his distance from her. "You needed to save your people."

"Did you doubt me, too, then? Father Sun thinks I wouldn't have left if I'd known."

He placed a small pinch of herbs into three cups before answering her. "No. I didn't doubt that you'd save them." He held her eyes with his impossibly blue ones. "I knew you'd sacrifice anything you had to to save your people. I just…"

He looked away. "I didn't want to watch you make that choice. Better for you to think me dead and not worth choosing than to know that I lived and still chose to leave me."

"Badru!"

He smiled sadly and moved back to her side, taking her hand in his and kissing it. "It sounds worse than it is. I figured you'd come back to me in time, after you'd done what you needed to for your people. And then, surprise! You'd find out I was alive and that it was even better than you'd thought."

Vedhe dropped the horses' saddles on the ground and moved to join them. She poured the now-boiling water into the three cups.

"Welcome back." She handed Badru the first cup and K'lrsa the second.

"Thanks."

K'lrsa cradled the cup in her hands, savoring the aroma of mint and the steady warmth against her palms.

Vedhe looked back and forth between them as she blew on the tea to cool it. "You know he can't come with us, right?"

"What are you talking about?"

K'lrsa tensed. She'd just found him again.

"To the Hidden City. He'll have to stay here. Father Sun created a gate to free him, but if he enters the city again he'll be as trapped as he was before."

K'lrsa looked to Badru. "Is that true?"

He was just as devastated as she was.

Vedhe laughed softly as she took a sip of her tea. "It's only for a few days. You'll be back together soon enough. And maybe he can put the time to good use."

"How?" K'lrsa asked.

"By talking some sense into his former soldiers."

"Oh…That's a good idea…"

Badru frowned, clearly confused. "What? What are you talking about?"

As Vedhe set about making something for breakfast, K'lrsa told Badru all that had happened to them since they'd left the Hidden City. He listened and asked questions, intrigued and surprised by what they'd done and how things had progressed.

By the time she reached the point where the first camp had appeared outside the barren lands, Vedhe had made a breakfast of porridge with dried fruit and nuts in it. Trust the gods to provide the most tasteless meal possible, but at least it was filling and would give them the energy they needed to continue their journey.

K'lrsa finished the rest of the story while she ate, choking the porridge down without looking at it, Vedhe adding colorful commentary that made K'lrsa glare but Badru laugh.

When she was done with both the story and the meal, she asked him, "So? What do you think? Can you talk sense into them?"

He sat back, sighing. "I don't know. None of them will recognize me. And even if they do, then they'll know I was brought back with death walker magic and probably try to kill me."

"Aran was brought back with death walker magic and no one tried to kill him."

"That's because no one can be sure that's what happened."

"Same with you. Now. If you'd come back the day after that mess in the audience chamber they would've all known that you'd been healed with death walker magic. But now? Who can say? Maybe you were seriously injured and just had a really long recovery time."

Badru tapped two fingers against his lips, thinking. "Good point."

K'lrsa watched him with narrowed eyes, wondering what was going on in that mind of his.

He better not be thinking he could be Daliph again. Because there was no way she was going to live in the Toreem Daliphate for the rest of her life.

No. Way.

Plus, she was going to destroy it.

Vedhe scrubbed her bowl clean with a handful of sand and put it away. "One problem."

"What's that?" K'lrsa handed her the other two bowls.

"Does Badru really know any better than the newcomers how to survive here?"

Badru opened his mouth to object, but then closed it again. Vedhe was right. What did he know about living in the tribes? His parents might've been born there, but it wasn't like that conferred some magic knowledge on him.

"We'll just have to tell him what to do, then." K'lrsa grinned at him.

Vedhe nodded. "And it's really just to give him something to do for a few days while we visit the Hidden City so he doesn't feel useless."

"Hey! I'm right here, you know."

Vedhe met his outrage with a completely bland expression. "Sorry. But it's true."

Badru shook his head—in amusement, not anger. He'd changed—for the better—from the deposed ruler she'd fled Toreem with. He'd come to understand his failings, but he was also more comfortable in his strengths.

She liked this new Badru.

K'lrsa yawned, unable to stop herself. She'd gone so many nights without sleep and been so tense for so long…

It was all catching up to her.

"Maybe we can have that conversation over dinner? Unless you have the energy to explain it all to him right now?"

Vedhe shook her head. "Not really. I'm as tired as you are after the last few days." She nodded towards F'lia, reminding K'lrsa that she'd also stayed up all night the night the baby died.

"Well, then. Let's get some sleep and talk about this later." As Vedhe made her way to where M'lara and F'lia were already sleeping, K'lrsa turned to Badru. "You were just waking up when we got here, so I'm sure…"

He shook his head. "You think I'm going to pass up the chance to have you in my arms again?" He lay down on the bedroll and patted the hollow space in front of him. K'lrsa cuddled against him, grateful for his steady presence once more.

She'd missed him so much…

She fell into a deep, dreamless sleep, finally getting a small part of the rest that had eluded her for weeks.

CHAPTER 26

That night they parted ways with Badru and continued towards the Hidden City. It wasn't easy to leave him behind again, but at least this time K'lrsa knew she'd see him again. Soon.

As they flew through the silent night, he was all she could think about.

What would their lives would be like after this was all over?

Would he agree to live with her in the tribes? She certainly wasn't going to live with him in the Daliphana, no matter how much she loved him. Maybe they could travel together. Go North to where Vedhe's people were from. Or to the ocean she'd heard about but never seen…

Then again, she wasn't sure she wanted to see so much water in one place. To think that people traveled it in vessels made of wood!

No, perhaps not that. She was brave not foolish.

M'lara shifted in her sleep and K'lrsa checked to make sure she was still secure. She was.

K'lrsa's thoughts turned to Aran.

He had the benefit of death walker magic, but was that all? If it was, he'd be relatively easy to kill. She could just use the necklace on him. But she suspected he knew how to counter it. Badru said he'd studied all the histories and knew all the hidden lore.

Which meant she needed some other way to kill him. A simple arrow would do it as long as she could get close enough and keep his death walkers from resurrecting him in time. Or a knife to the heart for that matter.

The question was how to get close enough.

She ran her thumb along the curved lines of the necklace, wishing she'd chosen the staff of power or the sun orb when she'd had the chance.

How much easier it would be to defeat Aran—and destroy the Toreem Daliphate—if she had that power instead of the necklace. She wouldn't even have to be close to kill him, she could just burn him and everyone around him to the ground…

She sighed.

She'd made her choice, and she couldn't take it back now. She was stuck with what she had and would just have to make the best of it.

There *had* to be a way to kill him. He was mortal after all.

They stopped in a cave the next morning as the moon was setting and ate a quick meal and rested for a bit, but then continued onward, riding the horses across the shifting sands.

Halfway through the day, when the sweat that had poured down her neck in the morning was dried and salty against her skin and her tongue was swollen from lack of water, K'lrsa realized what a foolish choice it had been to try to travel during the day. Even the horses, normally so strong, were flagging, stumbling as they struggled against the shifting sands beneath their feet.

K'lrsa touched the moon stone at her neck, silently begging it to find them shelter. It pulsed softly, glowing a gentle blue color as she felt a tug towards their left.

"This way," she croaked as she turned Fallion towards the hope of water and shade.

It was just over the next rise. A cramped space, but enough of one for all of them to squeeze inside. And blessedly cool with a small bubbling spring in the back corner.

K'lrsa was careful to pace herself and the others as they quenched their thirst.

She sent a silent thank-you to the gods when Vedhe handed her a jar of salve to smear across her reddened skin. "I'm sorry. I shouldn't have pushed onward this morning. It's just…" She glanced to where F'lia lay, mumbling to herself. Within just the few days since the death of the babe she seemed to have faded away, shrinking in on herself.

Just like K'lrsa's mother had after her father died. But her mother seemed to have burned down to her core and found her strength there. F'lia was just melting away to nothing.

In another day or two she'd be gone.

She drank the sleeping draughts, but refused to eat or speak or do much of anything for herself. And when she was awake she just huddled in on herself, rocking back and forth in quiet agony. The twin losses of L'ral and the babe were too much for her delicate spirit.

K'lrsa longed to talk to her. To explain that there was so much left for her in this world and remind her of all the simple things she'd found joy in before—a gorgeous sunset, a flower growing all by itself out of cracked earth, the soft luxury of a piece of silk—but it wouldn't work.

Even if F'lia heard the words, they wouldn't bring her back from that dark place.

Their only hope was L'ral. Assuming he didn't convince F'lia to join him in the Promised Plains and leave this life of suffering behind.

She'd kill him if he did that.

But what if he did?

Was it K'lrsa's place to tell her friend to go on living when the man she'd loved her entire life was on the other side, waiting for her?

No.

But she'd still try. She was selfish enough to want her best friend by her side as she grew old. They were like night and day, F'lia the crafter who could find beauty in anything, K'lrsa the Rider who could master any physical feat. They balanced one another.

And she didn't want to lose that. She didn't want to lose anyone else she loved. Ever again.

Yes, she had Badru, but…That was different. A lifelong friendship like the one she had with F'lia was a deeper bond than she could ever form with Badru or anyone else. They'd grown up together, side by side, two trees twining their branches, supporting one another as they reached ever higher.

K'lrsa chewed on her lip as she watched F'lia sleeping. She hoped she'd made the right decision, because it was too late to go back now.

CHAPTER 27

T hey waited until the moon rose and started on their journey again, reaching the Hidden City by the time the moon was directly above them—half-full, half-shadow.

It was just as K'lrsa remembered. The wall was tall, stretching in a gentle curve in each direction, the buildings that showed above it hard-edged. It was a city built for a siege not beauty.

From the outside, the main thoroughfare of the only entrance appeared deserted, its surface of fitted stone tiles perfectly clean.

That was an illusion, of course.

Once they crossed the threshold into the city the streets would be full of thousands of people of all colors, talking and laughing in a thousand different languages, oblivious to the strangers who walked through their midst. There'd be no scents—no city stench of unwashed bodies and food—no vendors, nothing but the people.

The recently dead. Gathered together for as long as they chose to stay until they finally passed through to the Promised Plains, and from there to…

Who knew?

Somewhere else.

Some place beyond.

K'lrsa stared at the writing engraved above the entrance. She could read it now, thanks to the knowledge she'd gained from the labyrinth. That skill she'd chosen to retain, practicing in private until she could scrawl an approximation of each shape.

"Only the living may pass through this gate," it read.

Somewhere, on the other side of the city, but not in this world, was another gate where only the dead could pass through. The Hidden City was a waypoint, a small oasis where the living and dead stood side-by-side for just a little while.

A flaw in the world. The product of a god's misguided sympathy.

The god and the two lovers who had led her to create this place were long gone, but the city remained, a dangerous oasis that had destroyed hundreds of lives with the promise of a false eternity.

It was also home to the most deadly of weapons, those granted by the gods that men had proven unable to control.

K'lrsa took a deep breath and turned to Vedhe. "Ready?"

Vedhe shrugged as if to say, *why not?* They'd been through the city once before after all. What was there to fear?

Nothing for Vedhe, maybe. But in the center of that city, at the heart of the labyrinth, was K'lrsa's father. And her mother. Both prevented from moving on to the Promised Plains because of the foolish vow she'd made while in the throes of grief.

She licked her lips, nervous. She wasn't ready.

But waiting wouldn't change things.

It was time.

"Okay. Let's go, then." She urged Fallion forward.

CHAPTER 28

J ust as before, as soon as they passed through the gate it was midday, and the hundreds of people crowded in the street seemed to melt away from them, caught up in their eternal conversations, oblivious to the living, breathing people who rode through their midst. This time, knowing where they were going and without Lodie looking for her husband in every face, they made quick time reaching the heart of the city.

They crossed from the main thoroughfare onto a deserted road that gently curved away into the distance on each side, following a wall that contained the heart of the city. They sat their horses, alone, the dead left behind on the long avenue, and stared across the street at the entrance to the labyrinth.

Fallion shook his head and shifted his back legs, gently urging K'lrsa to dismount. She didn't want to, but when Vedhe slid from Kriger's back and pulled F'lia down with her, and Kriger turned and left like he had the time before, she gave in.

She helped M'lara to the ground before kissing Fallion on the cheek. "Don't abandon me, *micora*."

Fallion whuffed her hair before strolling away down the center of the road.

She envied him his confidence.

K'lrsa studied the entrance to the labyrinth, wondering

if they'd have to do it all over again—fight the dragon, solve the puzzle, overcome the temptation to stay with their loved ones—but then Vedhe pointed to a small door off to the side. "Was that here before?"

"I don't think so."

M'lara slipped her slender hand into K'lrsa's, her eyes wide with awe as they approached it. She'd been silent the whole ride through the city. Unlike K'lrsa she'd never been in a city before. Any city. And she certainly had never been around so many people crowded together—people who were so dark and so light, dressed in thousands of outfits unlike anything seen in the tribes.

K'lrsa winced. She should've explained it or at least offered comfort, but…

She had wanted to. Once started, M'lara would have had question after question after question and either K'lrsa wouldn't have been able to answer or she'd have found herself delving into those memories she'd never wanted.

She squeezed M'lara's hand, offering what silent comfort she could, but kept her attention focused on the door.

F'lia was awake enough to walk on her own, but she swayed with each step and Vedhe had to hold her firmly by the elbow lest she wander away.

K'lrsa stopped just shy of the door and waited for Vedhe to join her. "Do you want to go first or should I?"

"You go. If there's something to fight, M'lara can step out of the way easier than F'lia can."

"Step out of the way?" M'lara stood a little straighter. "I'm going to be a Rider someday. Riders don't step out of the way of a fight."

"They should." K'lrsa squeezed her hand to take the sting out of the words as she placed her other hand on the door handle. She paused, turning to M'lara. "If I say run, run. No bravery, understood?"

"Yes." M'lara rolled her eyes in sullen agreement.

K'lrsa smiled slightly as she turned her attention back to the door and cautiously opened it to reveal a hallway, entirely white with closed doors spaced along either side at irregular intervals—just like the second hallway in the center of the labyrinth.

K'lrsa relaxed a little.

Definitely a better start than the dragon's attack that had greeted them when they entered the labyrinth. But she didn't let go of M'lara's hand as she slowly stepped through, peering around, looking for danger as they made room for Vedhe and F'lia to join them.

"Now what?" She looked to Vedhe who'd retained more of the knowledge of this place.

Vedhe nodded down the hallway. "Only one direction to go."

K'lrsa released M'lara's hand and wiped her sweaty palms on her riding leathers. She didn't know why she felt so nervous. She'd been here before. Chewing on her lip, she led the way forward.

She was tempted to try some of the doors, to see where they led, but she didn't. What if they revealed more hallways? What would she do then? Better to continue forward on the one path they'd been given.

If they were lucky, this hallway led to the room at the center of the labyrinth.

They walked for what seemed like forever, the hallway never changing, just one long stretch of white walls and floors and ceilings alleviated with doors every once in a while. At one point, K'lrsa paused, ready to turn back, but there was nowhere to go back to. The hallway ended in a blank wall a short distance behind them.

Vedhe noticed and shrugged. It was what it was.

But K'lrsa had to force herself to stay calm, to breathe slowly, in and out, in and out. The walls—at least the one behind them—really were closing in on them. She felt light-headed and had to brace herself against the wall nearest her.

"Here." M'lara offered her a waterskin and K'lrsa drank the last of it. How long had they been walking?

Vedhe squeezed her arm and stepped past her, leading the way onward. K'lrsa followed along with the others. What other choice did they have?

Eventually, with F'lia so exhausted she needed both Vedhe and K'lrsa to keep her standing and even M'lara's boundless energy flagging, they reached the center of the labyrinth—the same circular room she remembered from before with one door on each side and another hallway opposite them.

The Lady Moon stood in the center of the space, waiting, her eyes shining silver from the midst of a beautiful, ever-changing face.

First she appeared to be a young maiden in the first blooms of womanhood and then slowly, too slowly to notice, her face changed until she was a woman as old as K'lrsa's mother, the lines of age touching the corners of her eyes like butterfly wings, but still more beautiful than any mortal woman. And then, oh so slowly, she transformed into the ancient crone, the wrinkles so deep they doubled back on one another. But still, somehow, impossibly, beautiful.

And through it all that gaze—that silvery intensity—never shifted or faded.

"Welcome back." Her voice danced like the trickle of cool water over rocks.

K'lrsa glanced around. "Where's my father."

The Lady laughed. "Ah, child. You never change, do you?" She waved towards the opposite hallway. "He's waiting for you in the room where you last saw him. Go. Refresh yourselves. See your loved ones. But then we must talk."

She nodded toward Vedhe. "I must talk with you as well."

Vedhe released her hold on F'lia and stepped aside. "Then I'll talk with you now. I'm not that tired."

"But…" K'lrsa's heart clenched with fear, turning to look at Vedhe. Her friend. Her support through these past few weeks.

"Your family is in there."

"I know. But…"

Vedhe met K'lrsa's gaze with a pained stare. "Your family. Not mine. I'd rather stay here if you don't mind."

K'lrsa winced. She hadn't realized how painful it would be for Vedhe to see K'lrsa reunited with her parents—again—when all of Vedhe's family was dead and could never be brought back.

And L'ral and F'lia would be reunited as well. And M'lara and…

K'lrsa nodded. "Okay. I'm sorry. I…We'll see you in a bit?"

Vedhe nodded.

K'lrsa led F'lia and M'lara towards the other hallway. M'lara clutched at her, sucking her thumb like she hadn't since she was little, her gaze darting around the room, her eyes wide with fear.

F'lia walked like one in a dream, unseeing and uncaring. Just in case he'd already left, K'lrsa hadn't told her about L'ral yet. She hoped seeing him would jolt her friend out of her stupor. If it didn't…

There was nothing else she could do except hope that enough time would pass to bring her back to herself.

As they crossed into the hallway, K'lrsa glanced back towards the Lady Moon and Vedhe, wondering what it was they needed to discuss.

The last time they'd been there Vedhe had almost chosen the sun orb instead of her viewing tube. And she'd said she might use it not just on the Daliphana but the tribes as well…

She'd already made her choice. It shouldn't be an issue now.

But K'lrsa didn't trust the Lady. Or, to an extent, Vedhe. Not when it came to revenge…

CHAPTER 29

K'lrsa pushed those thoughts aside as she led the others down the hallway to a large room full of tall trees and leafy green plants with a large grassy area in the center. Somewhere nearby she could hear the sound of the small stream that ran through the place.

And there, in the center, standing near a fire surrounded by camp stools, were her parents.

M'lara broke free, and ran forward.

"Mom!" She flung herself at her mother, wrapping her arms around her waist with a sob.

K'lrsa's mother laughed and stumbled backward, "Oh, M'lara. It's so good to see you."

She hugged M'lara tight for a moment until M'lara wiggled free and rushed to hug her dad, too.

"Dad!" She clung to him as he ruffled her hair and smiled down at her.

K'lrsa watched them, her throat too tight to speak, tears burning the backs of her eyes. F'lia drew away, wandering into the trees. K'lrsa let her go—there was nothing in the room that could harm her and L'ral wasn't there.

After a long moment, M'lara drew back. "I thought you were dead."

K'lrsa's father smiled gently. "We are, little one. This is just a special place that lets us see one another again before your mother and I move on."

"But…"

He ruffled her hair and stepped past her to face K'lrsa. She flinched, expecting him to be angry, but he wasn't. He was unusually calm. "You saved them?"

She nodded. "For now."

"Good."

"Dad…I'm…I'm sorry."

He shook his head slightly. "For what?"

"For trapping you here. Didn't the Lady tell you? The reason you can't pass through to the Promised Plains is because I made a vow to destroy the Toreem Daliphate. And, I…I did it on your soul."

"Oh, that." He shrugged slightly and turned back towards where M'lara and her mother were sitting together laughing and talking excitedly.

K'lrsa frowned. Why wasn't he more upset? Why didn't he care? She watched her mother, laughing and talking with M'lara, and that too seemed strange. It wasn't that her mother hadn't been loving and affectionate, she had.

But…

It wasn't like either of them to accept their fate so easily. She'd expected them to be angry, to demand that she help free them, to have plans and ideas for how to destroy the Daliphate so they could go free. But instead they were just…

This.

K'lrsa watched in unease as her father wandered back to join M'lara and her mother, sitting on a stool next to them and laughing easily at something M'lara said. They weren't faking it. There was no sign of tension or fear or anger. They were genuinely happy and relaxed.

They appeared younger and healthier, too.

The last time she'd seen her dad alive he'd been weighed down by worry, the fine lines around his eyes and mouth deepening by the day, more gray than black in his hair. Now he looked like a man in his early thirties, vigorous with health.

Her mother's transformation was even more dramatic. She'd burned down to her essence after K'lrsa's dad died, shedding the soft flesh of a mother until all that was left was a deep, burning anger.

She'd fleshed out again and she, too, looked younger than she was.

K'lrsa joined them. "You've changed."

Her mother smiled, a smile of such happiness and beauty that it hurt, because she'd never once looked that way when she was alive. At least, not that K'lrsa had ever seen.

"Of course we have. When you're dead you can look any way you want. Within reason. You still have to look like yourself, but you can choose to look like the best version of yourself."

"Oh."

F'lia joined them, her gaze still unfocused, and sat down by herself a short distance away.

"What happened to her?" Her mother nodded towards F'lia, a small frown marking her brow before disappearing.

"She was pregnant, but lost the baby. Since it happened she won't eat or speak or do anything except cry. Vedhe's been keeping her asleep as much as possible, but she can't go on like this. So I thought…" She glanced around. "Is L'ral still here? He said he'd wait for her."

Her mother nodded. "Yes. Your father can get him. Can't you, dear?"

Her father looked up from whatever conversation he'd been having with M'lara, smiling, and nodded. "I'll do it right now." He bounded away down the hall opposite the direction they'd come from.

Her mother started humming softly to herself, tapping out a rhythm on her knee as they waited.

K'lrsa watched her, the feeling of unease in her stomach growing with every breath. This wasn't her mother. Her mother would've demanded to know all that had happened since K'lrsa left. She'd be angry that she was stuck here and unable to continue on to the Promised Plains. Or she would've at least taken her young daughter into her arms and talked to her, but instead she had her eyes closed, ignoring all of them as she hummed to herself.

"Mom? What's wrong with you?" K'lrsa blurted. She leaned closer, eyes narrowed, remembering the last time she'd been here. "Are you really my mother? Or is this another of the gods' tricks?"

Her mother laughed. "Oh, K'lrsa. So serious all the time. Yes, I'm your mother."

"Then why are you so…So happy. Why aren't you upset with me? I thought you wanted to go on to the Promised Plains."

"Oh, that. Yes, we do." The little frown appeared and disappeared once more.

She stared off into space for a long moment. "But we've been enjoying ourselves here. It's good. To have time together away from the worries of the world. And it's beautiful here, don't you think?" She smiled, a vacant smile unlike any K'lrsa had ever seen from her before.

K'lrsa stared at her in horror.

But she didn't ask anything else. There was no point. This creature that was supposed to be her mother wasn't capable of more than the most superficial of responses.

She'd save her questions for the Lady.

Who'd better have a good explanation. Because K'lrsa wasn't leaving until her parents—her real, flawed, possibly unhappy, parents—were restored to her.

CHAPTER 30

Her father returned with L'ral a few moments later. He at least looked the same as she remembered. And he seemed genuinely concerned when he saw F'lia. He immediately knelt in front of her, taking her hands in his.

"L'ral?" She blinked as if waking. "L'ral! But…you're dead? How can this be? Am I dead, too?" She smiled with such hope that it broke K'lrsa's heart.

"No, my love. This is a special place where we can spend time together, you and I, but you're still very much alive." He smiled at her, his face full of love.

K'lrsa clenched her jaw against the anger that flooded her veins. How was it fair that the man who'd betrayed her father and led him to his death, could also be the man who loved her best friend with all of his heart?

She wanted to rip him away from F'lia's side and tell him to never come back. To just die already and leave her and hers alone.

But watching as F'lia touched his cheek and smiled—a smile so bright it was like the sun appearing from behind a bank of clouds on a hot summer's day—K'lrsa held back.

This wasn't about her. It was about F'lia and what would bring her back to herself. It was about her friend's happiness, not her own.

That didn't mean she had to watch them together, though.

She turned away, deliberately standing so she couldn't see them. Which meant watching her parents and M'lara, all three sitting together, laughing and talking as if the world wasn't falling apart.

She knelt down next to her father. "Is Lodie still in the labyrinth?"

He nodded, smiling happily.

She narrowed her eyes. Something was definitely off with him and her mother. "What about Herin and Garzel? Are they still here? Or did they continue on to the Promised Plains already?"

"They're still here. I think. We don't see them much. Do you want me to get them for you?"

"Yes, please." She forced a smile.

Maybe they could tell her what was wrong here. And, of anyone alive, they probably knew the most about Aran.

Her father left to get them, her mother smiling after him like a love-struck girl. Her parents had always loved one another and never hesitated to show it, but this...This was something else.

She paced the room as she waited, weaving her way between the trees, trying to avoid the sight of F'lia and L'ral cuddled close together, talking happily, and her mother and M'lara, laughing as they played a game of stones.

M'lara sounded happier than she had in weeks, but...

It wasn't right. Something was very, very wrong here.

She clenched her fists as she passed the hallway that led back to the center of the labyrinth and Lodie.

If these weren't her actual parents...

If the gods were playing some sort of trick on her, trying to manipulate her into doing their will...

She shook her head. Poor M'lara...To think she had her parents back for a little bit of time and then find out it wasn't really them. It had been hard enough for K'lrsa to experience that, but a little girl like M'lara? Could the gods truly be that cruel?

If they were...

She'd kill them.

She didn't know how, she didn't even know if it was possible, but if they hurt her sister, she'd do it. Somehow, someway, she'd make them pay for this.

Just as she'd made up her mind to confront the Lady and demand answers, her father returned with Herin.

"You missed him," she said, her voice like two rocks rubbed together. "He's already left to find you."

K'lrsa laughed in relief, glad someone in this place looked and sounded like they should. Herin was the same grel-like, acerbic, unpleasant woman she'd always been right down to the maimed fingers and wrinkles.

"Herin! It's so good to see you." She nodded towards Herin's hands. "I thought…Now that you're dead and you can change things that you'd…"

"Make myself all pretty and young? Maybe fix these?" She wiggled her fingers, the top joint of each one missing where Aran had removed it.

K'lrsa nodded, swallowing. She'd forgotten how scary Herin could be.

"Pzah. This is who I am." She crossed the room to stand before K'lrsa. "I *earned* every single one of these and I'm not going to give them up just because I'm dead."

K'lrsa smiled, some of the tension she'd felt since seeing her parents breaking free. "It's good to see you, Herin."

Herin snorted.

K'lrsa stepped closer, glancing towards where her father had rejoined her mother and M'lara. "Herin, are those my real parents?"

"Of course. Who else would they be?"

"Well, it's just…They're different. I thought maybe, like what happened in the labyrinth, they were some sort of illusion. I mean, you met my mother when she was alive. You know how strong-willed she was. And my father might have been more restrained, but he certainly wasn't like this."

"Oh, I know. You should've seen them when they found out they couldn't continue on to the Promised Plains. I was certain your father was going to tear this place to the ground."

"So what happened?"

"Father Sun came. Your father tried to strike him and he…did something. They've been like this ever since." She grimaced. "They don't get upset about anything."

Herin grinned wickedly. "On the days when I'm particularly bored I remind them that they're stuck here and that Father Sun did something to them. They get upset for a moment or two, but then they go right back to…that." She spat on the ground.

"Where's Garzel?"

"In our rooms."

"Is he like you? Did he decide not to…?" She waved her fingers.

Herin glared her down with that grel-like gaze of hers, but K'lrsa waited her out.

"He can speak when he wants to." She pointed towards L'ral and F'lia with her chin. "What's she doing here?"

"She lost the baby and I thought that seeing L'ral might bring her back to herself. It seems to be working…" She managed to keep the bitterness out of her voice, but just barely. She leaned closer. "Father Sun said he could use the death of the babe to release Badru from here. Do you know…He said the babe was already going to die, but…?"

Herin laughed, the sound like broken glass being ground to dust. "Don't ask me about the gods, child. I don't know them any better than you do." She glanced towards M'lara. "Why'd you bring your sister?"

"So she'd be safe while Vedhe, Badru, and I go kill Aran."

Herin smiled. "So you're actually going to do it, finally?"

"I hope so."

Herin snorted. "You better do more than hope, girl. Aran won't be easy to kill. And you certainly can't kill him with that little trinket." Herin shook her head in disgust. She'd been the least amused of everyone when K'lrsa came back from choosing her "weapon."

K'lrsa touched the smooth metal of the necklace. "You think he has a defense against it?"

"Yes. Aran knew more than anyone about the objects of power stored here. If there's a counter to that necklace that exists in the real world, he either already had it or has it now. You go after him with a weapon he knows about, you'll die."

K'lrsa's father stood, clapping his hands. "We should eat. Celebrate the arrival of my daughters. And of F'lia, who was as much a daughter to me as my own daughters." He beamed at F'lia and she answered his smile with a shy one of her own.

Herin stepped away. "That's my cue to leave."

"But wait. I need to talk to you."

She waved K'lrsa back. "After you've eaten and rested. There is no way I can eat a meal with that man's constant inanity." She glared at K'lrsa's father a moment longer before scuttling away.

K'lrsa's father watched her go, a smile on his face, not the least bit concerned or insulted.

Sighing, K'lrsa went to join the others.

She *was* starving and did need some rest, but she didn't know if she could survive an entire meal with her parents acting this way either. Not to mention, watching F'lia and L'ral be so cozy.

And where was Vedhe? She still hadn't returned.

And what were they going to do if Aran really could counter the only weapons they had?

CHAPTER 31

S omehow, K'lrsa survived the meal without hurting anyone or anything. It helped that the meal had all of her favorites, even the ones from the Daliphana that she occasionally dreamed of. Meats floating in rich, creamy sauces with just the hint of spices. (None of the really spicy ones appeared, thankfully.) Dates drizzled in honey and stuffed in tangy cheese. Small discs of bread that melted on her tongue…

She delighted in watching M'lara try them for the first time, in sharing with her all the wonders she'd seen on her travels through the Daliphana. Fresh oranges and apples. Honey-coated pastries filled with nuts and cinnamon…

Toreem hadn't been all bad. If she could've kept all the luxuries and lost all the people, she would've gladly stayed there forever. Unfortunately, the two came together, entwined like a chokevine wrapped around a sapling.

After dinner she took a bath—the sheer luxury of soaking in an entire tub full of fresh water still amazed her—and then found her way to a tent for a long night's sleep. It was the best night of sleep she'd had in months. No gods stalking her through the moon dream. No tribe to worry about. Just simple, blissful, uninterrupted sleep.

But the next morning as she lay there not wanting to actually wake up, all the worries and problems came back to her. Her parents, Aran, the tribes, M'lara, F'lia…

Sighing, she dragged herself out of her tent and followed the smells of breakfast to where the others were already up.

Vedhe intercepted her with a bowl of porridge before she could reach them. K'lrsa grimaced until she noticed the small sausages piled on top, still sizzling, their greasy scent wafting towards her nose, and saw the small bundle of cheeses and fresh fruit in Vedhe's other hand.

"We need to talk." Vedhe led the way to a small space away from the others.

"What is it? What did you find out from the Lady?"

Vedhe shook her head. "Not about that."

"But what did she tell you?"

"It doesn't matter. Not right now."

K'lrsa bit into one of the sausages, relishing the way the skin burst under her teeth and the delicious combination of spices and meat. "Then what is it?"

"Lodie."

"She's still in the labyrinth." K'lrsa popped a slice of orange into her mouth, sighing in contentment at the sweet burst of flavor. She'd hated the Daliphana, but she did miss their food…

Vedhe nodded. "We need to bring her out."

"But she didn't want to leave. Shouldn't she be allowed to stay there if she wants to?"

"She's been there for weeks with nothing but her imaginings of what her husband and child were like. She can't…" Vedhe frowned. "I don't have all the knowledge I should, I just have fragments, and the Lady won't tell me the rest. But…" She shook her head. "Staying there, in the labyrinth this long…It jeopardizes everything. It's not a safe space. Not like the rest of the Hidden City. If she doesn't move on soon, she'll never be able to."

"But what's there to move on to? The Promised Plains? By herself?"

Vedhe frowned and looked into the distance as if searching for something just out of reach. "It's what's beyond that that matters. She can truly be reunited with them there. But not here."

K'lrsa forced herself to take a bite of the porridge. It turned out to be surprisingly tasty. Someone had drizzled honey on it and included small berries that burst with flavor. "What happens if she stays in the labyrinth?"

"She'll disappear."

"And? So?"

"We can't let that happen." Vedhe furrowed her brow. "I can't explain it, but I know we have to help her." She grabbed K'lrsa's arm. "Lodie helped rescue me from the slavers. She didn't have to—she was comfortable where she was—but she did it. For me."

"I don't know…"

Vedhe stepped closer, her blue eyes pleading. "Please. I can't do this without you."

"Why not? How are we going to save her anyway? We can't go back through the labyrinth, can we? And even if we did, we wouldn't see her because she wasn't traveling it with us."

"We can enter the labyrinth."

K'lrsa clenched her jaw, remembering how awful it had been the first time. She didn't want to go back. Even to save her friend. "I'm not killing another dragon."

"You won't have to. We'll enter it from this side. The challenge isn't the same, which is why I need you."

"What do you mean?"

Vedhe bit her lip, but forced herself to meet K'lrsa's gaze. "We'll have to face our worst memories or deepest fears. And then we'll be able to find Lodie."

"No." K'lrsa took a step backward. "I don't…I can't…"

She'd spent months reliving the day her father died, seeing his body staked to the sands, his eyes gone, his belly sliced open…She couldn't do that again. She couldn't live that moment a second time.

Vedhe stared her down. "How bad are your worst memories? Truly?"

"I…"

Vedhe stepped close enough that K'lrsa could smell the remains of breakfast on her breath. "My entire family was slaughtered. Even the little ones. I was burned by the desert sun until my skin cracked and broke and bled. And then…in that tent…after you joined us…" She held K'lrsa's eyes, the fact that she'd been in that tent because of K'lrsa hanging between them. "What G'van did to me…"

K'lrsa looked away. She'd helped Vedhe escape. Wasn't that enough?

But no. It wasn't. It would never be enough. Because Vedhe carried those memories with her every single day.

And K'lrsa still owed Lodie for not telling Harley, the leader of the slave caravan, that her injuries were self-inflicted. "Okay. Fine."

"Good. Let's go."

"Now?" K'lrsa looked around, trying to find some reason to wait, but there wasn't one.

"Yes." Vedhe stalked down the hallway, not even bothering to look back.

Reluctantly, K'lrsa followed.

She was going to regret this, but she had to do it, or she wouldn't be able to live with herself.

CHAPTER 32

They made their way back to the center of the labyrinth. The Lady was waiting for them. K'lrsa glared at her, wondering if she knew about what had been done to K'lrsa's parents, but didn't say anything. That conversation could happen later.

"You're sure you want to do this?" she asked in her melodic voice.

"Yes." Vedhe stepped up to the door leading to the labyrinth. "Open it for us. Please."

The Lady looked to K'lrsa. "And you?"

K'lrsa shrugged and moved to Vedhe's side. "I guess."

The Lady looked as if she wanted to say something, but instead she waved her hand and the door to the labyrinth disappeared, replaced with a gaping, black hole.

Involuntarily, K'lrsa reached for Vedhe's hand. Last time she'd stepped into the labyrinth she'd almost been burned to death by a dragon. And when she'd stepped out of that door she'd been brought to her knees in agony.

She did not want to go back there.

Vedhe squeezed her hand gently and pulled her forward until they stood side by side directly in front of the black, empty space. "Ready?"

No.

K'lrsa shivered, reminding herself this had to be done.

She nodded, chewing on her lip to hold back the fear.

"Then let's go." Vedhe sounded so confident, so sure of herself, but the way her hand shook as she stepped forward showed that she, too, was scared.

K'lrsa followed her into the darkness.

She held her breath, tensed, waiting for pain or fire to strike her down.

All she felt was cold. Bitter, bitter cold, worse than anything she'd ever experienced before. There were trees—monstrosities as big as three men across that stretched high into the leaden sky. Their branches were heavy with a white substance that also covered the ground and the building ahead of them.

K'lrsa stared, her mouth hanging open. "Is this…?"

"My home. Yes. They came for us in winter. They knew we'd all be there and wouldn't be able to survive if we fled." Vedhe's voice was flat, like she had shoved every bit of emotion away somewhere else.

Her hand trembled, as she stared at the building ahead of them. It was a low, sturdy building with a sloped roof and small, narrow windows. A large wooden door dominated the front of the place, and smoke escaped from two spots on the roof, one at each end.

K'lrsa tried to move forward, but she was frozen in place. "What do we do now?"

Vedhe took a shuddering breath and raised her chin. "We endure."

"Endure what?"

"Our memories. Our fears." She clenched her jaw, her gaze fixed on the building in front of them.

"How many of these do we have to go through before we reach Lodie?"

"I don't know." Her voice was soft and low, full of fear and determination.

K'lrsa stared at Vedhe in horror. What had she agreed to?

She glanced behind them. The doorway was still there. It wasn't too late to leave. Lodie wanted to be here, why not just let her stay? Why put themselves through whatever was coming?

Just as she was about to suggest that they go back, the

crunch of boots through snow brought her attention back to the house. Men appeared from the trees, covered in layer after layer of animal skins to the point that they were barely recognizable as men.

Vedhe hissed as a man stepped forward, and her fingernails dug into K'lrsa's hand like claws. "That's Ivan."

"You knew him?"

She nodded, tears already in her eyes. "Yes. He was my father's friend. They'd traded together for years. Broken bread together just the week before. He knew all of us by name. We knew him. We trusted him."

K'lrsa shivered as Ivan signaled for his men to spread out alongside the house so they wouldn't be visible from the door. After they were in place, he called out a greeting and knocked. A man answered, smiling and laughing, holding his arms out to hug his friend, the warmth of the fires that burned inside shining bright on his pale hair.

"Papa," Vedhe whimpered.

Ivan ran him through with a sword and shoved his body to the side as he stepped across the threshold. His men rushed after him, swords drawn.

From where they stood, K'lrsa and Vedhe couldn't see what was happening, but the sounds of screaming that filled the air told their own story. Women and children, crying and begging for mercy. Men shouting about betrayal and being damned by the gods.

A young girl, her clothes covered with the bright red of freshly-spilled blood dashed outside, dragging an even younger girl with her. "Go. Run." She shoved the younger girl towards the woods and turned to fight.

"Is that you?" K'lrsa asked, scared to break the silence, but desperate to know.

"Yes."

Vedhe-in-the-vision looked so young, so vulnerable, standing there in a simple dress, two long daggers clutched in her hands as the first of the men came for her. He laughed as he reached for her, but she ducked under his grasping hand and buried her dagger in his belly, slicing hard to the side. He stumbled backward, clutching at his

guts as she stepped back into the doorway, ready for her next opponent.

As the men came for her, she slashed and parried and ducked and screamed in wordless rage. She should've been defeated immediately. They were men—twice her size— and they had swords, but she fought with the unbridled fury of a berserker with nothing to lose.

Two fell, then three, then four as she cried and screamed and fought.

Vedhe's grip tightened on K'lrsa's hand until it felt like her bones were grinding together. "My family were all dead. The only one left was Anya. I knew I was going to die, too, but I was going to take as many as I could with me before I went. Give her as much of a chance as I could."

Vedhe-in-the-vision fought on, slashing and screaming, the ground at her feet slick with blood, until the men withdrew, eyeing her warily. She screamed at them to attack her, to end this. But they hung back.

And then K'lrsa saw why. A man snuck around the edge of the building, moving silently from shadow to shadow.

Vedhe growled low in her throat, struggling to move forward and rescue her younger self. But they were trapped, powerless to act as the man crept up behind Vedhe-in-the-vision and struck her. She collapsed across the threshold as the men inside cheered.

"What should we do with her?" one of the men asked.

"Save her for the slavers. They'll pay a pretty penny for a pure one like her." He nodded towards the woods. "And find the one who fled. We can sell her, too."

K'lrsa glared at the man, memorizing every line of his face. If she was ever given the chance, she'd kill him— without remorse or hesitation.

From the way Vedhe trembled at her side, only if Vedhe didn't get there first.

《●》

As the scene finally dissolved into mist, K'lrsa allowed herself to breathe again. "Did Anya get away?"

Vedhe shook her head. "No. They found her." She clenched her jaw and turned away from K'lrsa, her hands balled into fists.

"Was she…Was she sold with you?" There hadn't been a young girl with the caravan when K'lrsa found it. Which might mean that Anya had died on the journey.

"No. She was sold to someone else."

"Who—"

Vedhe shook her head, cutting off the question, as a swirling mist formed around them, finally resolving itself into a desert scene.

K'lrsa glared around them. "What's the point? Why do the gods always have to torture us like this?" she asked as the sun beat down on them, chasing away the chill of Vedhe's homeland.

"It tests your will. Do you want it enough? See?" She nodded towards the door which still stood behind them. "We can leave anytime we want. We just won't find what we seek if we do."

Vedhe glanced around as the scene continued to resolve itself. "This is yours, not mine."

K'lrsa's stomach clenched as she recognized where they were—the cavern where she'd found her father.

But earlier in the day.

She tried to move forward, but she was stuck, forced to watch, unable to act. She screamed her rage, hating the gods, wishing she could leave before the vision started, but knowing she'd stay and watch.

One, to save Lodie. Two, to repay Vedhe. And three, because she wanted to know what had happened to her father before she'd arrived. To see if L'ral had told her the truth.

No matter how much it hurt.

She held her breath as her father and L'ral rode over the crest of a nearby dune, her father alert, scanning the horizon, not knowing that the man he needed to fear most rode by his side. L'ral was fidgety, his horse jerking sideways as he handled it too roughly, glancing around for the men he knew were waiting for them.

K'var stepped out of the shadows of the cavern, his bow drawn.

K'lrsa shouted, trying to warn her father, but he didn't hear her.

Even though it was pointless, she screamed and struggled and beat her fists against the air as K'var pointed the bow at her father and released.

L'ral saw it before her father did—because of course he'd known K'var would be there.

He moved his horse into the path of the arrow, shoving her father's horse to the side. The arrow buried itself in his horse's side and it cried in pain. L'ral pushed at her father, urging him to run, as he turned his horse towards K'var and the men who'd flooded out of the cave behind him.

K'lrsa fought back tears. She hadn't known he'd done that. She'd known he'd betrayed her father by bringing him here, and that he'd changed his mind at the last moment, but she hadn't realized that he'd put himself between her father and his attackers. That he'd sacrificed the horse he'd raised from birth to try to save the man he'd betrayed.

She swallowed heavily.

She still hated him. He'd still brought her father to his death.

But…Not quite as much.

What happened next was swift and brutal. L'ral was struck by three separate arrows, one after the other thunking into his flesh. K'lrsa's father tried to flee but they shot his horse out from under him and dragged him from its back before he could recover.

The horse staggered away, bleeding and wounded, disappearing over a nearby dune.

K'var's men forced her father to his knees at K'var's feet and K'var spat in his face, yelling at him for daring to stand against the future and believing he, one man, could oppose a tribe as powerful as the Black Horse Tribe.

Her father met K'var's gaze, defiant and strong. "You can kill me, K'var, but it won't stop what I've begun."

"We'll see about that."

As K'var's men carried her father over the dune to the

place where he'd been staked out to die, Vedhe and K'lrsa seemed to follow them although they were still rooted to the same spot.

Her father fought the men, struggling and kicking and screaming. He never quit, never stopped, even as they held him down and drove long metal spikes through his hands and feet, and he screamed in agony.

Only when they took his eyes did he stop fighting.

K'lrsa wept seeing the moment her father realized he wasn't going to survive. He sunk into himself then, finding the Core, disappearing somewhere they couldn't reach.

They kicked him, they taunted him, they stabbed at him, but he remained untouched, relaxed and calm.

Finally, K'var had had enough. "Die old man," he spat as he sliced open her father's belly and pulled the two flaps of skin wide, exposing the glistening organs inside to the hot desert heat.

He and his men stood aside, keeping the grel at bay as they waited for the fire ants to appear and crawl all over her father's flesh. But even as they swarmed his body and bit and tore at his body, her father remained calm. His chest rose, slow and steady, showing he was still alive, but the tortures they'd inflicted on his body didn't touch him.

K'var and his men left, abandoning her father to die alone on the hot desert sands.

Time passed.

Her father twitched if the grel came too close, but otherwise he lay there, silently suffering his fate, waiting to die, detached from the pain.

Until K'lrsa arrived.

Until she brought him back to his broken body with her tears and her cries and the water she tried to pour into his mouth.

K'lrsa of now stood above them and watched, sobbing, as her younger self pulled the stakes from his body and fought with him over her desire for revenge.

She forced herself to watch as her younger self pulled her dagger and plunged it through that gaping wound and into his heart, fulfilling his last request—to die at last.

Only then did she turn away, sobbing. Vedhe held her close as she wept.

As they both wept, remembering how powerlessness they'd been in the face of evil.

It wasn't right.

What had been done to her father.

What had been done to Vedhe's entire family.

It wasn't right that men like that could exist.

"They should die," Vedhe whispered.

"K'var is dead."

"All of them. They should *all* die."

K'lrsa nodded.

She was right. They should *all* die. No matter what it took.

CHAPTER 33

The horrors continued as Vedhe and K'lrsa stood there, powerless to act.

Some of what they witnessed were real experiences like what G'van had done to Vedhe each night in that tent.

(When that one appeared, Vedhe stood still, unblinking, her hands clenched into fists, tears pouring down her cheeks. K'lrsa tried to convince her to look away, but she refused, determined to endure whatever the gods threw at them. All K'lrsa could do was stand by her side and witness. If G'van hadn't been dead already, K'lrsa would've tracked him to the ends of the earth just so she could drive a knife through his heart. Repeatedly.)

Other scenes were born out of their deepest, darkest nightmares.

Beasts stalked through the shadows, howling for blood, their bodies twisted and grotesque as they tore their prey to pieces.

But somehow it was the horrors of what men, and a few women, were capable of that struck the deepest. K'lrsa stood there, shaking, full of hatred, wanting the world to burn and take every single person with it.

Better that than allow even one man like K'var or Aran to spread his poison.

Vedhe didn't speak after those first few visions, but she too trembled with emotion, her jaw clenched, her eyes hard as rocks.

Finally, as the day wore on and she became almost numb to the horrors in front of her, K'lrsa turned towards the black doorway they'd come through. "I can't watch another one."

Vedhe turned a cold, angry gaze her way. "You've been through so much already, why quit now? Why would you throw that all away? What's the point?"

"What if it never ends, Vedhe? What if we just stand here until we can't take it anymore? It's too much. I can't do this."

Vedhe turned away. "Then go. I will endure alone until the end."

K'lrsa stared at the doorway and then back at her friend as the sky darkened and a howl filled the air.

It was so tempting. To quit. To say she'd had enough. To walk away and let Vedhe carry the burden alone.

She'd succeed. She didn't need K'lrsa to stand by her side anymore.

But…

But Vedhe was her friend. And the horrors they'd seen already…To let her friend face those alone…

She couldn't do it.

"How many more do you think there are?" she asked, resigned.

Vedhe shrugged, her arms wrapped tight against her chest as a scene materialized before them of a nondescript room, Anya crying in the corner as some large man loomed above her.

"It isn't real." K'lrsa pulled on Vedhe, trying to get her to look away. "It's just your fears manifesting themselves. Vedhe, are you sure we just stand here and endure this? Isn't there something we can do to break free of it?"

Vedhe twitched as the man reached for Anya.

"Vedhe! Listen to me. You're feeding this. It stopped showing us things that actually happened a long time ago. This and all the other horrors it's showing have to be coming from us. We have to fight back."

"How?" Vedhe's voice was full of anguish as the little girl screamed and cried for help but no one came.

"The Core. You have the memories, yes? Find the Core."

It was the hardest thing K'lrsa had ever done to find the Core while Anya cried out, helpless and scared and unable to fight back against the man who was hurting her.

It could be M'lara in that room…

Even as she thought it, it *was* M'lara in that room, screaming in pain and fear.

K'lrsa told herself this wasn't real. It wasn't M'lara. This wasn't happening. It was just her fear feeding the images.

She needed to master her thoughts so there was nothing for the gods to use against her. She needed to find the Core—that place outside of time and emotion where she could see and act without being distracted by the world around her.

She struggled to reach it.

Her entire being wanted to fight back against the horrors she was seeing, but to reach the Core she had to let that go. Let the anger pass. Let the visions flow by her like they were happening to someone else somewhere else.

She needed to be like the summer sky—pure, blue, and calm.

Slowly, oh so slowly, she set aside her emotions.

Her anger.

Her fear.

Her sorrow.

Until, finally, at last, she found herself floating in the Core.

Only when she was sure that she'd finally found her way there, did she turn to Vedhe who was still struggling to master herself, her scarred face contorted in rage, her cheeks wet with tears.

K'lrsa took her hands and held her gaze, anchoring Vedhe to the moment, to the truth that all was illusion.

Slowly, Vedhe calmed her breathing. The tears stopped. Her chest rose more and more slowly as she took control of herself and of the world around them.

And then, just like that, the visions were gone.

They stood alone in the midst of trees, birds singing in the distance, a small stream running somewhere nearby.

Before them was a red-tiled path.

Lodie's path.

They collapsed to the ground, neither one speaking as they simply absorbed the peace of the place, letting the birdsong and babbling sound of water sooth away the horrors they'd just experienced.

A part of K'lrsa wanted to stay there forever. To never again face the horrors of life.

But she had to continue. Somewhere out there Aran was working to destroy not only his own people but hers as well. He had to die.

They all did. Every last person like him.

"Ready?" K'lrsa asked.

Their eyes met. Vedhe's anger mirrored her own. She nodded.

CHAPTER 34

They walked along the red-tiled path as it wound its way through the midst of the trees until they finally reached a small clearing. The same one where they'd left Lodie weeks before. There was a small pond and a tent surrounded by verdant, green grass that was soft under their feet.

That first time she'd come to the clearing, K'lrsa had been struck by the strangeness of a woman as old and withered as Lodie snuggled close to an attractive young man, their fingers intertwined like the lovers they'd once been.

Now, she was struck by the fact that Lodie was no longer the Lodie she knew.

Gone was the wrinkled old woman with the scarred ear of a slave and the red-stained teeth of a bitter root addict. Now a young woman was there with the man—a match for him in age and beauty.

The child from before slept contentedly in the young woman's arms.

A perfect family.

K'lrsa could see Lodie in the shape of the woman's face and her surprising height, but this woman's eyes were soft with love and contentment as she smiled at the man by her side.

She'd been transformed.

If it hadn't been for what they'd gone through to reach her, K'lrsa might have turned back then.

Vedhe, as if sensing her thoughts, grabbed her wrist and whispered, "She can't stay here. She has to move on. Before it's too late."

Reluctantly, K'lrsa stepped into the clearing. Lodie frowned when she saw them, but didn't speak as they moved closer and sat down across from her, cross-legged. Somewhere nearby a bird sang, trilling its little heart out with happiness.

Lodie stroked her daughter's silky soft hair, not looking at them. "I'm happy here."

K'lrsa bit her lip, remembering how happy she'd been in this place. How much she'd wanted to stay even after she'd known the truth. "This isn't real, Lodie. You know that."

Lodie shrugged, leaning her head on the shoulder of the man at her side.

"You let yourself die, Lodie. You weren't really dead."

"I know that. I drank the poison, didn't I?" She glared at K'lrsa, the sorrow in her eyes at odds with her young, sweet face.

"You deliberately killed yourself?"

Lodie snorted. "Of course I did. It was the only way I could return to the woman I was when I left them behind."

"How? Did they give you poison? Did the gods do this to you?"

"Pzah. No. I brought it with me."

"You knew? The whole time we were making our way through the labyrinth you knew what the challenges were and that you were going to stay here?" K'lrsa wanted to slap her.

"Of course."

"Why didn't you warn us?" K'lrsa wailed.

"And take that small moment of peace from you? You needed that."

"Didn't it even occur to you how much it would hurt after? When I found out that it wasn't my father I'd spent time with but some imaginary version of him?"

Lodie narrowed her eyes and leaned forward. "I'm sure it hurt when you finally learned the truth. But I bet in your darkest moments, when you don't know what to do next or you doubt yourself, you remember what that man told you. You remember how much he loved you and had faith in you. It doesn't matter that he wasn't real; the emotions you experienced were."

"But my real father was waiting for me in the center of the labyrinth. If I hadn't been caught up here, I could've spent more time with him."

Lodie didn't back down. "Did your real father give you more comfort than the memory of him you spent time with here?"

K'lrsa bit her lip and looked away. No. Of course he hadn't.

How could the real man ever compare to her perfect imaginary version of him?

Vedhe cut them off. "We need to go."

"Then go."

"You need to come with us."

Lodie shook her head. "No. I'm happy here."

The little girl in her lap stretched and wiggled free, running to the edge of the nearby pool where she buried her chubby little feet in the mud as she tried to catch the water bugs buzzing just above the surface of the water.

"This isn't real. And it isn't safe. You'll fade away if you stay here. You need to continue your journey."

"I don't want to." Lodie crossed her arms, her gaze focused on the little girl who was now splashing happily at the water.

"But you must."

Lodie raised one eyebrow, but didn't respond.

K'lrsa tried. "Lodie. Are you even listening to us? It won't stay like this forever. They'll fade away. You'll fade away. And then that will be it."

"I know. That's why I want to stay."

"But…" K'lrsa looked to Vedhe for help. "Your husband and your daughter are somewhere out there. They've passed on and are waiting for you, somewhere ahead."

The little girl ran back to Lodie and once more snuggled against her. Lodie smiled as she smoothed her daughter's hair. "You know one of the best things about this place? I never have to clean up after her." She held out the little girl's foot. It was completely clean. No sign of the mud she'd been wallowing in a moment before.

Vedhe frowned at her. "The battle isn't over, Lodie."

Lodie glared back at her. "It is for me."

"Would you really do that to them?" She gestured at Lodie's husband and child. "And to Herin and Garzel and all the others you've known? Would you really leave them to fight the next battle without you at their side?"

Lodie sighed and rested her chin on her daughter's head. "I spent twenty-five years trying to kill Aran. I sacrificed everything—my tribe, my husband, my child—to defeat him. And I failed. Haven't I been through enough?"

"No." Vedhe picked at the grass, shredding each blade with her fingernails before tossing it aside. "I can't explain it, Lodie. I don't know what comes next. I just know you need to continue onward. That we all do when our time comes. None of us can stay here and hide from what must be done. We get a moment to pause, to recover, but then we have to move forward." She glanced back and forth between Lodie and K'lrsa. "This world is just the beginning."

K'lrsa winced. "Don't say that. I want this to be over when I die. And you're telling me, what? That we all keep fighting in the next life or world or wherever we go?"

Vedhe shifted uncomfortably. "I can't see it fully, but, yes. I think so."

Lodie met K'lrsa's gaze, raising her eyebrows. "And that's why I want to stay here. I've had enough."

Vedhe stood, pacing back and forth angrily. "They need you, Lodie. They're somewhere ahead of you on the path and if you stay here they travel alone. Scared. Uncertain. Unloved."

"Don't you manipulate me, child." Lodie stood, looming over both of them, her face a mask of anger.

"I'm not manipulating you. I'm telling you the truth." Vedhe took a half-step back and knelt before Lodie, her head bowed. "You saved me. I owe you. Please. Let me save you now."

Lodie spat to the side. "Save me? From the only place I've ever been truly happy? Pzah."

Vedhe stayed where she was, head bowed.

Lodie stared down at Vedhe's bowed head for a long moment and then at her husband and daughter who were watching her closely. "I'll make my way out eventually."

"No. You're already fading. Can't you feel it?"

Lodie paced to the edge of the clearing and back. "I'm not ready, yet."

K'lrsa stood and risked touching her, resting a hand on her shoulder. "Lodie? Are you fading away already? Can you feel it?"

Lodie shrugged the touch away. "Maybe."

"Then you have to leave. Now. Before it's too late."

"I'm tired. I don't want to keep going."

"So am I. But if we don't keep fighting, then they win."

"Who are they?" Lodie asked. "What is this place I'm supposed to move on to?"

"I don't know. But if Vedhe says it's there, I believe her."

Lodie glanced at the still kneeling Vedhe and rolled her eyes. "I should've never let you convince me to leave that camp."

"Don't pretend you didn't want to save her. Or that you didn't do everything in your power for every single one of those slaves." She gestured around the clearing. "Is this really enough for you? Sitting in the grass, watching your child play? When you know somewhere others are suffering? Others that you can help?"

Lodie pressed her lips tight together.

K'lrsa stepped closer. "I'm not saying you didn't deserve the time you had here. But you need to move on now. To do something that matters."

Lodie grimaced, but still she stayed where she was.

"Please, Lodie. We need you to help us defeat Aran. Tell us all you know. And then move on to the next place. Find your husband and daughter. The real ones."

Lodie turned towards her. "Do you think I'll know him

in the next world?"

Vedhe stood, stretching her neck to the left and right. "Yes. Good always knows good."

"Pzah. Where'd you learn that crap?" Lodie asked, but there was a spark in her eye that hadn't been there before.

Vedhe raised one scarred eyebrow, the movement twisting the scars on her face.

Lodie stared her down for a long, long moment, but Vedhe didn't budge.

Finally, K'lrsa stepped between them. "It's time to choose, Lodie. Even now Aran is moving against the tribes."

"Fine. Give me a moment." She embraced her husband and they stood close together, hands tracing the outlines of beloved faces as they whispered softly back and forth before, with one last, fierce hug, they stepped apart.

Next, Lodie turned towards her daughter. The girl was back by the pond's edge, playing in the mud. Lodie knelt by her side, stroking her soft curls, talking and laughing with her for one last time before she kissed her softly and stood.

The girl ran to her father and he took her hand. Together they turned and walked away, disappearing before they reached the trees.

Lodie wiped the tears from her eyes with the back of her hand. "Alright. Let's go."

An arched opening appeared, wide enough for all three of them to walk through together. The space within the arc was inky and black, giving no hint of what lay on the other side.

K'lrsa flinched, remembering the last time she'd left this place.

But she had to continue. She'd come too far to stop now.
She had to end this.

Steeling herself, K'lrsa took Lodie's outstretched hand in hers and waited until Vedhe took Lodie's other hand. Together, they stepped through the arch.

CHAPTER 35

Nothing happened. They simply found themselves back in the center of the labyrinth with the Lady Moon waiting for them. As Vedhe led Lodie away down the hall, K'lrsa turned to the Lady, glaring at her. "We need to talk."

The Lady raised one exquisite eyebrow in question. "Would you care for some refreshments first?" She waved a graceful hand at a small table where a silver pitcher suddenly appeared, its sides beaded with water.

"No. I want you to fix my parents."

The Lady frowned slightly. "Are you sure you want that? They were very unhappy when they found themselves trapped here. We were worried they'd do themselves harm."

K'lrsa snorted. "My parents would never harm themselves."

The Lady didn't say anything—her expression said it all, reminding K'lrsa that her mother had essentially killed herself by challenging the Black Horse Tribe with only two others at her side.

"I need my parents back to themselves if you want me to defeat Aran. I need their help and counsel."

"What can they do for you that you can't do for yourself?"

K'lrsa shook her head. "Did you never have parents?"

After a moment, she sighed. "What am I thinking? Of course you didn't. You were born from the dust of the universe or whatever. Well, for us mere mortals, our parents are a vital source of support and advice and I'd like theirs before I have to leave this place."

"I don't know that it's possible."

K'lrsa stepped forward, her hand on her knife. "Are you telling me you've permanently harmed them? That they'll be like this forever?"

The Lady's eyes flashed silver and K'lrsa found herself frozen from the neck down. She stepped closer until their noses were almost touching. "Would you dare to attack me, child? Don't think that just because I appear in a form you can understand that I am anything like you or that there is anything you can actually do to harm me."

K'lrsa was flung backward, slamming into the wall with a heavy smack. She stumbled back to her feet, leaning against the wall, stunned, her body aching from head to heel.

And then the fury started to burn through her veins.

After all she'd been through…For the Lady to so casually attack her…

She was done. Done with the gods and their manipulations. Done with their petty little tests and hollow threats.

She didn't move towards the Lady or reach for her knife again, although she wanted to. Instead she pulled herself up straight and met the Lady's silver gaze. "I may not be able to harm you, but I can oppose you. I can stay here forever and refuse to kill Aran or destroy the Toreem Daliphate."

The Lady's face flickered briefly, revealing something dark and fathomless lurking underneath. "Do that and the world will end."

"So be it."

"You don't mean that."

"Those horrors you forced Vedhe and I to witness?" She shook her head. "The things that we've been through, that others have been through. Maybe it's time for it all to end."

"You must do this." The Lady's eyes blazed silver.

"No."

The air in the small space swirled as if they were caught in a spring storm, whipping K'lrsa's hair about her face. K'lrsa stood firm in the midst of the storm and smiled. The gods wanted her to believe that they were all powerful, but she knew the truth. They weren't. They depended on mortals like her to act for them.

She moved towards the exit.

"Where are you going?" The Lady's voice shook with thunder.

"I'm tired. I think I'll rest for a bit. And when I'm done, I hope you'll have a different answer for me about my parents. Because I promise you, if you don't, I won't be helping you defeat Aran."

She was almost at the doorway when the Lady hissed. "What about Badru? We freed him to help you. Would you leave him out there alone?"

K'lrsa paused on the threshold—she'd forgotten about Badru, but she couldn't let the Lady see her worry. "He was a Daliph, he can take care of himself." She turned back. "Just remember, you aren't his gods. If he wins, alone, without my help, who knows what will happen to you."

The wind whirling through the room whipped higher and the silver pitcher flew through the air, slamming into the wall next to K'lrsa's head.

With one last feral grin, K'lrsa fled the Lady's wrath.

CHAPTER 36

K'lrsa found the others gathered together around a small fire in the tree-filled room, Herin and Garzel huddled off to the side, K'lrsa's parents chatting happily with Vedhe, Lodie, and M'lara, F'lia curled up asleep at L'ral's feet.

K'lrsa headed for L'ral, wondering what she could say, what she wanted to say, but knowing she had to say something about what she'd seen.

She still hated him for leading her father to his death, but she knew now the truth of what L'ral and her father had both tried to tell her—that L'ral had changed his mind in the end. More than that, that he'd sacrificed himself to try to save her father.

L'ral tensed as she came closer, his hand moving to touch F'lia's hair, as if protecting her.

K'lrsa stood far enough away so he'd know she didn't mean him harm but close enough so she wouldn't have to shout. She swallowed, searching for the words to say. She wasn't going to apologize. He didn't deserve that. But he deserved something.

Licking her lips, she finally managed, "Take care of her, please. I *know* I can *trust* you to look after her while I'm gone."

She held his surprised gaze for a long moment until he nodded slightly.

Satisfied, she turned away.

It probably wasn't as much as he deserved, but it was the best she could do. She'd carried her hatred of him for too long to just let it go.

She glanced at her parents, but there was no point talking to them until the Lady fixed them. They were babbling like a small stream and with about as much direction.

M'lara pulled free of them and ran up to her. "Guess what?"

"What?"

"Garzel is teaching me how to speak with my hands. See?" She made a small gesture next to her hip. "This means 'be careful'." She made another gesture that involved brushing her ear. "And this means 'listen, do you hear that?' Isn't that neat?"

K'lrsa looked towards Herin, Lodie, and Garzel who were now watching them. "Is that how you've been communicating all this time? With your hands? You mean those grunts of his don't actually mean anything?"

Herin shrugged. "Eh. Sometimes they do, sometimes they don't." She bared her teeth in what for her passed as a grin. "You think you've figured out my secrets, child. You don't even know the half of them."

K'lrsa shook her head. Even after all the time they'd spent together and fleeing the Daliphate and coming here, Herin still kept her secrets. "You know, Herin, it might be about time for you to give up the last of your secrets. What if one of those little things you're holding so close to the chest is the difference between defeating Aran and losing to him?"

Herin snorted. "Pzah. Obviously I'm not the one to give advice on defeating that man." She wiggled her stunted fingers in front of K'lrsa's face. "See how many times I tried and failed. At least Lodie managed to kill him. Too bad she couldn't make it stick."

"But that's exactly my point. If Lodie had known that he was a death walker, she might've killed him in some other way. But because you didn't tell her, he died in such a way they were able to bring him back."

Lodie came to join them and Herin flicked a glance at her. "Prettied yourself up I see."

Lodie's form shifted until she once more looked like the old woman she'd been when K'lrsa met her. But then her hands closed into fists and she glared at Herin as she reverted back to the young woman she'd become in the labyrinth. "And why shouldn't I? Isn't that one of the perks of being dead? Getting to look like I want to and not what time has forced me to become? What's wrong with choosing to claim back the years I lost to Aran and revenge? You might try it yourself."

Herin cackled, her laughter like two rocks rubbing together. Tilting her head to the side, she too transformed. Gone was the old, wrinkled hag that K'lrsa had always known. In her place sat a woman almost as beautiful as the Lady Moon herself, her hair long and luxurious, cascading around a face with high cheekbones and stunning green eyes, her form svelte and lean, skin a deep, rich ochre.

"Is that how you used to look?" K'lrsa couldn't help but stare.

Lodie laughed. "Hardly."

And then she too transformed to look stunningly beautiful, her skin shining with health and vitality, eyes sparkling with mirth.

K'lrsa looked back and forth between them. They were still themselves, still recognizably Lodie and Herin, but somehow the best, most perfect versions of themselves. "So I take it neither one of you actually looked like this in real life?"

Lodie shook her head. "No. You've lived in the tribes, you know that wouldn't be possible. Too much time spent outdoors, never enough food. But if we're going to be our younger selves, why not be the best versions we can be, right?" Lodie turned to Garzel. "What about you, old man? Ready to shed the years you lost to Aran?"

Garzel shook his head and flashed a short series of hand signals at her before leaving the room.

Lodie shrugged and settled down next to Herin. K'lrsa glanced towards where Garzel had disappeared, but then back to Herin and Lodie once more. There was something transfixing about such beauty. She didn't understand it, but she could feel it tugging at her attention, demanding her focus, obliterating her focus.

"What did Garzel just say?" She forced the question out, trying to focus her attention elsewhere.

"He said he earned those years and he wasn't about to give them up like they'd never happened." Sighing, Herin shifted back to her older self, maimed fingers and all.

Lodie crossed her arms, keeping her younger appearance.

Herin snorted. "Not like it matters. As soon as we pass beyond we'll shed these bodies anyway."

K'lrsa moved closer. "Where is beyond? Do you know? Where do we go after the Promised Plains?"

Herin shrugged one shoulder. Lodie didn't even acknowledge the question.

Frustrated, K'lrsa turned towards Vedhe and her parents. "So, Vedhe, what do we do now? Just wait for the Lady to decide whether she's going to heal my parents or not?"

Vedhe stood and motioned for K'lrsa to join her away from the others. K'lrsa glanced back at Herin and Lodie, but neither one seemed to care, and her parents were a lost cause. The roof could fall in and they'd keep on talking as if nothing had happened.

She joined Vedhe. "What?"

"I think it's time I tell you what the Lady and I discussed earlier."

"You talked about more than just rescuing Lodie?" K'lrsa stiffened, suddenly wary.

"Yes. I asked if we could choose more powerful objects than the ones we already have. Ones that can actually defeat Aran." She met K'lrsa's eyes. "Like the sun orb."

K'lrsa shuddered, imagining the damage that would be done if the orb fell into the wrong hands. Look what Luden had managed with just the necklace. Imagine what he could have done with the power of the sun…

But at the same time, a small part of her thrilled at the possibility of having access to that kind of power.

How easy it would be to defeat Aran and destroy the Toreem Daliphate if she could just burn them to the ground. Destroying not just Aran, but all of those men who'd chosen to support him in his evil rather than stand against him. All the slavers and abusers like she'd seen in the labyrinth. All those who caused harm, spreading the poison of their hate throughout the world…

It would just take a moment. One thought. And they'd be gone. Purged from the face of the earth in god's fire.

She stepped back, shaking her head to clear it.

"What is it?" Vedhe asked.

"I'm not sure that's a good idea."

"Why not?"

K'lrsa bit her lip. "Because I'm not sure I can trust myself to stop with just Aran. Not after the visions I saw in the labyrinth. I'm not that strong, Vedhe."

Vedhe's smile was fierce and predatory. "And why should you stop with just Aran when there's so much evil in the world and we'd finally have the power to stop it?"

CHAPTER 37

K'lrsa dragged Vedhe farther away from the others, into a deep shaded nook. "Who else would you attack, Vedhe? The slavers? The other Daliphs?"

"Them. And more. All who are evil or support evil." Her eyes blazed with fervor.

A chill rolled down K'lrsa spine. "All who support evil?"

Vedhe smiled slightly, like she was confused by K'lrsa's question. "Yes. We'll start with all of the people in the Daliphana."

"Not just the Toreem Daliphate. All of them?"

"Of course. Why is the Toreem Daliphate deserving of destruction but the others aren't?"

K'lrsa didn't have an answer to that. "What about the women and children?"

"The women raise their sons and daughters to be that, don't they? Let their daughters be locked away? Live their comfortable lives on the backs of slaves? Raise their sons to treat others as contemptible?"

"But..."

"What? You think they can't fight back? Resist? Refuse to be part of it?"

"They'd die if they did. You haven't been there, Vedhe. You didn't experience what I did. Every single day they beat you down, make you doubt yourself, tell you over and over again that you're less than, that you're nothing. You don't understand how that can wear at you. And I was grown when I went there. What do you think it's like to be raised in that?"

Vedhe shrugged the argument away.

K'lrsa stepped closer, grabbing at her arm. "They may not be chained like the slaves, but the women of the Daliphana are as much victims as the slaves."

Vedhe snorted. "Except the slaves want to be freed. The women will just rebuild what they know and understand. You saw that for yourself with the women Aran sent across the barren lands."

"You can't know that! And some of the men don't like the way it is either."

Vedhe shook free of her grip. "Have you so easily forgotten how quickly Luden turned on you? How he kicked you and F'lia off the Council and took control?"

"That wasn't...He was trying to protect the women and children. It wasn't about..."

"About being used to having his way and not wanting to be thwarted by a *woman* who was stepping outside her place?"

K'lrsa shook her head, trying to clear it. "We can't just kill everyone who thinks differently than we do."

"We can if their beliefs cause harm." Vedhe's voice was flat and cold, determined.

K'lrsa wasn't willing to give up just yet. "Define harm."

Vedhe shrugged away the question.

"Vedhe? Define what you mean by harm."

Vedhe met her eyes. "If they make the world a worse place by being here, then they should die."

"But what does that mean? Where do you draw that line?"

Vedhe shook her head, looking away, arms crossed. "I can't explain it. But I know where it lies."

K'lrsa half-laughed. "But...Where does it stop?"

"When all who need to be, are dead."

"That would be...Thousands? Maybe more?"

"And?"

K'lrsa covered her mouth to contain her growing horror. "I saw the same nightmares you did in the labyrinth, but…What about those people you kill's children? Or their spouses? Or their parents? Or their…anyone? Their neighbors. Their friends. Think how much harm you'd do. How much harm you'd cause."

The look Vedhe gave her froze her soul. "Would you want a man like Ivan as your father? Would you want him to come home, his hands bloody from the murder of innocent women and children, to play stones with you? Would you want to be married to a man like that? To lay with him at night knowing what he'd done that day? Or to give birth to a man like that? To know you'd been responsible for creating someone like him? That you had brought him into the world to do that kind of harm?"

Vedhe shook her head, dismissing K'lrsa's argument. "We'd be doing those people a favor by killing the evil ones."

"It's not that simple. I saw Harley with Mistress Hawthorne. No matter what he'd done to you or me, he was a good man to her. He treated her well."

Vedhe's expression went flat. "Well. As long as he was a good man at home, who cares how many slaves he left to die in the desert? Or how many he whipped so badly they were permanently scarred."

"That's not what I was saying!"

K'lrsa paced back and forth, trying to work through the conflict between what her gut was telling her and what her mind was telling her. "Look. A part of me wants to wipe every single person like that from the world. But another part of me is screaming that that's not the way to solve this. That the more people we kill, the worse it's going to get. The more deaths, the more pain, the longer the hatred lasts."

"So we should leave Aran to do whatever he's going to do?" Vedhe raised an eyebrow in scorn.

"No. I'm not saying that. He's proven over and over what kind of man he is. But beyond him…I mean look at Badru. He was raised in the Toreem Daliphate, but he's a good man. If we kill them all, we kill good men like him."

"What makes you so sure Badru's a good man?"

K'lrsa's heart skipped a beat as she turned to look at Vedhe. "What are you saying?"

Vedhe refused to answer.

"Vedhe? Did you look at him with the looking glass? Did you see something I should know?"

Vedhe shook her head slightly, dismissing the question. "No more than I see with every person I look at. We are, none of us, pure or clean. We have all inflicted pain on others. We have all put ourselves first when we could have helped another. It's just the way we are."

"So where does it stop then? If none of us are any better than the others? If we're all flawed?"

Vedhe didn't answer, but the expression in her eyes said it all. For Vedhe there was no stopping. If she took up that type of power, she'd break the world.

K'lrsa's stomach dropped.

Vedhe would be no better than Aran…

She might even be worse.

K'lrsa buried her face in her hands. What was she going to do now?

CHAPTER 38

F ather Sun strode into the room.

The only part of him that burned were his eyes, but K'lrsa backed away from the sheer intensity of his presence as he stomped over to her.

She quailed before him, wanting to run and hide.

But she couldn't.

Not if she wanted her parents to be restored to themselves.

It took all of her will to stand tall and meet his gaze, but she managed it even though tiny tremors coursed through her entire body. The man was a god. One thought and he could probably erase her from existence.

He didn't, though. Because he needed her. And as long as she was willing to say no, she had the power to demand his assistance.

Didn't make him any less intimidating as he loomed over her, though. "You make demands when you're the one who can't keep your promises?" he roared.

"I do." She raised her chin, forcing herself to meet his eyes. "What's the point in keeping my vow if my parents are already gone?"

His eyes flashed fire and it was all K'lrsa could do not to step back. "They're not gone. They're right there."

"*That* is not my father. It looks like him, but what made my father who he is has been destroyed or removed. Same with my mother. Whatever you did to them, reverse it."

Father Sun laughed. It was an ugly sound, full of contempt, and K'lrsa had to fight herself not to cower at his feet and apologize for ever daring to challenge him.

"You're just a child, how dare you speak to me that way?"

She bit her lip. "Because you need me."

"Do I?" He turned his attention to where Vedhe stood, watching them. "Would you kill Aran for me, scarred one? And destroy the Toreem Daliphate? Burn it to the ground with my fire?"

She didn't hesitate. "Yes. Give me the power of the sun and I'll happily kill them all for you."

"You can't let her do that." K'lrsa stopped herself just short of grabbing Father Sun's arm. "She won't stop with the Toreem Daliphate. She'll kill everyone in all of the Daliphana."

"Even better." Father Sun's grin was fierce and merciless. He turned towards Vedhe, dismissing K'lrsa entirely.

K'lrsa moved so he was facing her again. "She won't stop there, you know. She'll go after the tribes next."

"Is that true?" He studied Vedhe. "Would you turn on us? After all we've given you? Kriger, a home, a chance at revenge…"

Vedhe sniffed. "I wouldn't turn on you. Or the Trickster. Or the Lady. But the tribes didn't want me. They still don't. They think I'm weak. Flawed. They think I should die because of these." She touched the scars on her face. "Why should I let them live when they don't want me to?"

Father Sun crossed his arms and rocked back on his heels. "Because they belong to me and I've promised them my protection."

Vedhe didn't answer, but it was clear that wasn't a good enough reason to stop her.

K'lrsa stepped closer to him. "What about the people of the Daliphana? Hasn't some other god promised them protection? If you give us the sun orb, won't that free their gods to act directly against you or us?"

A shadow passed across Father Sun's face. It was just a flicker, but it made K'lrsa's blood run cold.

He glared at her. "Don't concern yourself with the ways of the gods."

"Don't concern myself? Isn't that how Herin ended up tortured by Aran all this time? Because you crossed the line and she paid the price?"

His eyes burned like twin bonfires. "It was worth the risk."

"Worth the risk? She lost her entire life because of you. So did Garzel. So did Lodie." She searched his face for some trace of remorse. "Don't you even understand what you've done to them? Don't you even care?"

He backhanded her.

K'lrsa crashed to the ground, cradling her cheek where the flesh burned like she'd been branded.

She whimpered as Father Sun towered over her, growing taller and taller as she watched, his entire form limned in flame, his eyes black and empty.

Lodie hurried to K'lrsa's side, a metal pitcher full of water in her hand and a pile of cloths tucked under her arm. "Get back, you overbloated fool. What do you think you're going to do? Kill your chosen one?"

Father Sun glared down at her as she held a dampened cloth to K'lrsa's burned cheek. Lodie ignored him.

K'lrsa stared up at him, trembling in fear. "Lodie…"

"Shh. I'm fine. What's he going to do? Kill me?" She glared over her shoulder at Father Sun. "I stood up to Harley after he'd near beaten a slave to death, I can stand up to this one." She closed her eyes and held her hand palm up. A small ceramic pot appeared in her hand. Opening the pot, she smeared a soothing balm against K'lrsa's cheek, but frowned as she touched the tender skin.

She stood and confronted Father Sun. "Heal her."

"No." His voice rumbled, shaking the trees.

"Why not?"

K'lrsa tugged at Lodie's leg, but Lodie ignored her, her attention focused on Father Sun.

"She needs a reminder of who she's dealing with. *I* am her god."

Lodie snorted. "You can't force someone to worship you, you know. And…This? Is it any wonder some of us have chosen to turn our backs on you?"

His jaw clenched, and K'lrsa was sure he was going to burn Lodie to the ground right where she stood. Instead, he slowly shrank back to his normal size. The flames racing up and down his limbs disappeared.

Lodie still didn't budge. "Are you going to heal her?"

"Later. After she's had time to consider her choices."

He looked down at K'lrsa. "I don't need you to kill Aran or destroy the Toreem Daliphate." He looked pointedly at Vedhe who stood nearby. "But you'd be the best choice to do so."

He stalked away towards where K'lrsa's parents sat, talking as if nothing had happened. K'lrsa held her breath as he approached them, unsure what he was going to do. He walked up to her mother and pressed his hand to her forehead, muttering to himself. He did the same to her father.

When he was done, he stepped back, arms crossed and waited. K'lrsa held her breath, waiting.

Her parents shook themselves as if awakening from a dream, and her mother reached for the knife at her belt, standing to confront him.

Father Sun flicked a finger and the knife went flying. "I see where you daughter gets it from. But I've had enough of people defying me for one day. Sit down, shut up, and be grateful."

Against her will, K'lrsa's mother sat. Her father wrapped his wife in his arms as he glared at Father Sun, but he'd already turned away, headed back to K'lrsa.

He glared down at her. "I'll be back tomorrow for your decision. Make sure it's the right one."

He disappeared.

K'lrsa bowed her head for a moment, letting the fear she'd held back pass through her body in trembling waves.

What had she been thinking, to challenge a god like that? She was lucky he hadn't destroyed her.

Or her parents.

She scrambled to her feet and ran to them. "Are you okay? Are you really back to yourselves?"

They smiled and nodded as she threw herself to the ground and hugged them.

She ignored the pain in her cheek as she clutched them close, her eyes closed, all the fear and worry of the last few days overtaking her as she wept in their arms.

CHAPTER 39

K'lrsa wiped the tears from her eyes, looking back and forth between her parents. "Are you okay? Really?"

"I think so." Her father shook his head slightly. "I remember everything that happened after you left, but it's fuzzy. Like it wasn't really me experiencing any of it." He smiled a rueful smile. "Not that all that much happened. This isn't the most exciting place to spend a lot of time."

K'lrsa's mother rubbed at her forehead. "I remember wanting to be angry so many times, but then it would just disappear…" She looked towards Herin and Garzel. "Sorry. We weren't the most enjoyable to be around, were we?"

"That's an understatement." Herin came closer, Garzel trailing along behind her, and sat down next to them.

K'lrsa looked around. "Where's M'lara?"

Herin pointed her chin towards the trees where M'lara was hiding, peeking out from behind a tree twice as wide as she was.

"M'lara." K'lrsa frowned. "Come here. Mom and Dad are finally back to themselves. Don't you want to see them?"

M'lara crept closer, glancing around, her eyes wide with fear. "Is the scary man gone?"

"The scary…oh, Father Sun. That's right. You'd never seen him before. Yes, for now. But he'd never hurt you. He's our god."

K'lrsa's mother snorted. "Are you sure of that?"

K'lrsa opened and closed her mouth. Was she? What did a god care about the life of one little girl? Probably nothing. She gestured for M'lara to come closer and grabbed her hand when she was finally close enough to do so.

M'lara put the thumb of her other hand in her mouth as she stared at her parents, leaning her weight against K'lrsa.

Her father reached towards them. "M'lara, sweetie. Don't be afraid."

M'lara stayed where she was, studying him.

"M'lara!" He frowned at her. "I'm your father. Come here and give me a hug."

Reluctantly, M'lara let go of K'lrsa's hand and moved forward to let her father give her a hug, but she was stiff and awkward in his embrace.

Her mother huffed in annoyance. "Take your thumb out of your mouth. You're too old for that."

K'lrsa flinched, worried that the angry tone would drive M'lara back into hiding, but it seemed that was exactly what M'lara had needed. She removed her thumb from her mouth and flung herself at her parents with a small cry. She clung to them, crying, "I missed you so much. You were so different. I didn't know what had happened to you."

K'lrsa watched, tears in her eyes. She kept forgetting how hard this must be for M'lara—losing her parents, traveling to this strange city, finding her parents so changed...

She winced. She hadn't been a very good sister lately.

"Tell me you won't leave again. Ever." M'lara pulled away, looking back and forth between her parents.

"Honey..." K'lrsa's mother shook her head slightly. "We can't stay here. We need to go on. To the next life."

K'lrsa met her father's eyes and winced. Did her mother know they couldn't leave yet? Did her father?

Her father leaned forward. "What was the vow you made, K'lrsa?"

"He didn't tell you?" She looked around, wishing for some sort of escape, but there wasn't one.

"No. He just said I couldn't leave until you fulfilled the vow you'd made."

K'lrsa took a deep breath, wondering how her father was going to react when she told him. He watched her, stoic and strong, no trace of disappointment or judgement.

Yet.

"I…" She couldn't look at him. "I swore that I'd kill the man responsible for your death…"

"Which you did."

She nodded. "Yes. But I also…" She glanced at his face and away again, unable to meet his eyes. "I also said I'd destroy the Toreem Daliphate."

"You what?"

K'lrsa bit her lip as she finally met his eyes.

He stared at her, mouth half-open in surprise. "Why would you swear something as impossible as that?"

"I don't know. I was angry. You were dead. And I thought they'd done it. I wanted them to die for what they'd done to you."

He didn't say anything, but the way he sat back, withdrawing somewhere inside, hurt more than if he'd screamed at her.

Her mother rocked M'lara—who'd crawled into her lap—softly side to side. "So how are your father and I a part of this?"

K'lrsa gulped. "Ummm…When I made my vow…I…Um…" She took a deep breath and said in a rush, "I swore on Dad's soul."

"You did what?" Her mother's question struck the air between them like a slap.

"I didn't…It's just something you say. I didn't…know. I didn't realize that Father Sun would actually believe me or hold me to it."

Her mother sighed, clearly disappointed.

K'lrsa chewed on her lip. "Can you blame me? I never really believed the gods were real before then. I mean, yes, I had the moon stone and it guided me to shelter or warned me about storms…But that's not the same as a physical, living god standing before you and demanding that you fulfill your vow or he'll keep your father's soul for eternity."

Her father shook his head. "What's done is done. You made the vow, now we have to figure out how to meet it."

He was clearly disappointed, but he pushed it away as he leaned forward. "So you have to destroy the Toreem Daliphate in order to free me. To free us."

K'lrsa glanced at her mother. "Mom can continue onward at any time if she wants."

Her mother reached out, lacing her fingers with her husband's. "No. We will not be parted again. If your father is trapped here, then so am I."

K'lrsa bowed her head, trying not to cry.

Both of her parents trapped and the only way to save them was to do something she didn't want to do.

"K'lrsa?" Her father touched her knee, gently.

She met his eyes.

"Do you have to destroy the Toreem Daliphate to save us?"

She nodded, not trusting herself to speak.

Vedhe, who'd been standing off to the side, brooding, came forward. "I don't think he cares who destroys it as long as it's destroyed. I'll do it."

K'lrsa clenched her jaw, refusing to look at Vedhe.

Her father nodded. "Alright, then. Vedhe can do it."

"You don't understand, Dad. Have you ever been to the Toreem Daliphate? Do you know how many people there are?"

"How many?"

She looked to Herin who thought a moment before answering, "At least a hundred thousand."

"A hundred thousand?" Her father shook his head. "I can't even picture it. How many is that?"

"Too many." K'lrsa sighed.

She glanced at Vedhe. "We don't have to kill them all, though, to destroy the Toreem Daliphate. I didn't promise to murder every man, woman, and child. I just said I'd destroy it."

Vedhe shrugged away the comment. She'd already made it clear what she intended to do.

K'lrsa turned to Herin. "What would you do? Would you take the sun orb? Kill them all? Destroy just the palace? What?"

"I'd kill Aran. Horribly."

K'lrsa slashed the air with her hand. "That's a given. But what about destroying the Daliphate? Killing Aran isn't enough to do that."

She turned towards Lodie who'd quietly come to join them. "What would you do?"

Lodie spread her hands wide, palms up. "I prefer to heal rather than kill. I'd kill Aran, but no one else."

"But if I do that, I won't have fulfilled my promise. My parents will be trapped here forever."

"So be it," her father said, his voice strong and firm.

"But you could never leave this place."

He shook his head, dismissing her concern. "I'd rather that than know thousands of innocents died to save me."

K'lrsa glanced at Vedhe, but she had moved away, no longer concerned with the conversation. "Vedhe thinks none of them are innocent. That they are all a part of the system, so are all responsible for what it does."

"Do *you* believe that?" Her father leaned forward, holding her eyes with his kind, brown one.

"I don't…I don't think so. But it's so hard to know. It seems like such a reasonable argument when she makes it."

"What about Badru?"

She frowned. "What about him?"

"Do you think he deserves to die for his role in that system?"

She hesitated for a brief moment. "No. He's a good man."

"Then think about it. How can *he* not be guilty but every young child is? He was the leader of Toreem, K'lrsa. If the leader isn't guilty, then how can anyone else be?"

"But if I'm going to destroy it, *some* people have to die."

"You don't have to destroy it."

K'lrsa bit her lip. "But then you'll be trapped here forever."

"I'd rather that than see you betray everything I raised you to be."

K'lrsa stared at him.

What was she going to do?

CHAPTER 40

While the others ate their meal and talked and laughed around the fire, K'lrsa paced the edges of the room. She couldn't let Vedhe have the sun orb—she'd burn the world to the ground with the hate that coiled in her soul.

But there was also a small kernel of truth to what Vedhe had said.

Yes, Aran was the leader, the one pushing to attack the tribes and find the Hidden City. But he wasn't acting alone. He stood at the center of a network of supporters and enablers who made the evil he did possible. Without them, he'd be nothing. Or maybe not nothing—he had access to knowledge and magical power not granted to most—but at least far less of a threat.

How many of those men (and women) who surrounded Aran and made his evil possible deserved to be destroyed, too?

Did any of them deserve a second chance?

Perhaps.

Maybe without the influence of a man like Aran they would be good, decent human beings. Maybe they were scared or felt powerless to say no to their hereditary leader, the man they'd always been raised to believe was the absolute authority in their world.

But...

She bit her lip.

What happened if she was wrong? If she spared too many and they stepped into Aran's shoes? What then?

Spare too many and this would never end. The sickness at the heart of the Daliphana would continue to spread.

Kill too many and she became as bad as or worse than Aran.

Her father's words echoed in her head. I'd rather be trapped here forever than see you betray everything I raised you to be.

She crossed her arms and leaned against a tree, watching her parents sitting side-by-side, laughing and talking, real and vivid and wholly themselves once more. They deserved the chance to move on, to go to that place beyond the Promised Plains that waited for them, whatever it was.

But to do that she had to not only eliminate Aran and those closest to him but also destroy an entire society.

It wasn't fair. What did Father Sun get out of that kind of destruction? Why was he holding her to the impetuous vow she'd made in the throes of grief?

Didn't he see that if she did that there would be consequences? The other Daliphana wouldn't just stand aside and let her destroy the Toreem Daliphate without retaliating. Which would put the tribes in danger.

So her choice was to save her parents, who had loved her and deserved better than this nowhere place, or to save the tribes, hundreds of individuals, some of whom had done nothing to her, but some who'd turned their backs and believed the worst of her.

She studied Vedhe sitting silent by the fire, at ease, relaxed. She didn't care about the tribes. She might even use the orb on them herself before the Daliphana could act.

It was tempting. To let her choose the sun orb and destroy the Daliphana and then move against her when she turned towards the tribes. Allow her to be a convenient person to blame—the crazy slave, tortured beyond the ability to reason, who'd turned her rage against those she blamed for the death of her family...

K'lrsa could let her act while she stood to the side with the moon power, ready to step in and stop her. To be the hero. No one could turn against her then, could they?

But would those other gods—Aran's gods of darkness and death—really stand aside and let Vedhe choose the sun orb without balancing the scales in some way? Without giving Aran weapons just as powerful?

And if K'lrsa hesitated to choose a weapon a second time, would she be dooming her people, by failing to be strong enough to protect them?

She shivered, turning away from the others. As much as she wanted to refuse to choose a weapon, to keep her hands and her conscience clear, to avoid the hard choice of who should die and who should live, she couldn't.

If she was allowed into that room once more, she'd choose the deadliest, most powerful weapon she could find.

It was her only hope. To be stronger than everyone else.

She just prayed she'd have the strength to use it when the time came.

And to set it aside after.

CHAPTER 41

When Father Sun returned the next morning, K'lrsa met him at the entrance before anyone else could see him. She drew him to the side, under the shelter of a small group of trees. "I'll do it. I'll kill Aran and destroy the Toreem Daliphate. But on one condition."

Father Sun studied her, his crossed arms covered in scars, eyes burning like embers. "What condition?"

"That you don't let Vedhe exchange her viewing tube for a different weapon."

He roared with laughter, rocking backward on his heels. "It wasn't enough that I gave you your parents back? Now you have to thwart your competition, too."

"Bringing my parents back was just human decency. Then again, I guess that's something you wouldn't know much about."

He stepped closer, the heat of his body beating against her skin. "You forget yourself, child."

She suppressed the tremors of fear that threatened to undo her and met his eyes, holding her chin up in defiance. "You need me. All I ask is that you treat me fairly."

He smirked and stepped back. "Fine. K'lrsa dan V'na of the White Horse Tribe, do you swear that you will kill Aran Palero and destroy the Toreem Daliphate if I give you the weapon to do so?"

K'lrsa started to object that he hadn't mentioned her

condition about Vedhe, but he held up his hand. "If so, I swear that I will not allow Vedhe Kanaatanva to exchange the viewing tube she now has for a different weapon." He traced a symbol in the air and it burned between them for a moment before disappearing once more. "You have my word. Do I have yours?"

"Yes."

"Then say it." He spoke through clenched teeth, his burning eyes fixed on her face.

K'lrsa fought to hold his gaze. "I, K'lrsa dan V'na of the White Horse Tribe swear to you, Father Sun, Scourge and Destroyer, Bringer of Fire, that I will kill Aran Palero and destroy the Toreem Daliphate if you give me the weapon to do so."

His grin was fierce and brief. "Good. Now give me your hand."

K'lrsa didn't want to, but she'd come too far to stop now. She held out her hand.

When he took her hand in his, it started to burn like he'd plunged it into a fire pit. She struggled not to scream for what felt like forever but probably only lasted the space of a heartbeat, until he dropped her hand and stepped back.

Etched into her palm was the same symbol he'd sketched in the air.

"What did you do to me?" she yelled.

"It's a binding. As long as your path takes you in the direction of completing your vow, you won't even notice it. But should you veer away from that path, the binding will start to burn and it will keep burning until you continue."

She stared in horror at the lines burned into her skin. "How..." She licked her lips. "How does it work? How strict is it?"

"What do you mean?"

"If I have one last meal with my family am I going to be in excruciating pain the whole time? What if I stop to hunt for food? Or to sleep?"

He smiled slightly. "No. You'll only feel it if you turn your back on your vow."

She chewed on her lip, suddenly scared.

She intended to keep the vow, so it shouldn't matter, but seeing those marks burned into her skin upset her in a way she couldn't explain. "And what happens when I'm done? When the Toreem Daliphate has been destroyed and Aran is dead for once and for all? Does it just disappear?"

"No. You'll have to return here for me to remove it."

"What if I don't want to?"

He quirked one eyebrow. "If you don't return, what will happen to F'lia and M'lara? Do you think they'll just find their own way across the desert and back to the tribes?"

K'lrsa blinked at him.

How had she forgotten about F'lia and M'lara? She'd been so concerned with saving her parents and choosing the right weapon it hadn't even crossed her mind what would happen to them after she left.

She'd never thought beyond the fact that they'd be safe here. But of course they'd need her help.

Hers and Vedhe's. Vedhe who…

She winced. She hadn't meant to betray Vedhe, but she'd had to do it—for everyone, including Vedhe. She couldn't let her friend give in to that kind of destruction. She just hoped Vedhe understood.

Father Sun turned towards the hallway. "Are you ready to choose your new weapon?"

"You promised you'd heal the burn on my face."

"Oh yes, of course." He touched her cheek and the pain and tightness that had bothered her all night disappeared. "Now are you ready?"

"Yes." K'lrsa moved to stand next to him, taking a deep breath to calm herself. She was shaking, just the littlest bit, but she'd made her choice and it was time to fulfill it.

"Very well."

He turned towards where the others sat around the fire, watching them. "Vedhe. Come. It's time to select your new weapon."

"What?" K'lrsa stared at him. "What are you talking about? You just swore…"

The fierce smile he turned on her was one she was sure his victims had seen on the battlefield right before he gutted them. "I promised you I wouldn't let her exchange the viewing tube for another weapon. And I won't. She's free to keep it for as long as she wants."

K'lrsa's heart dropped. "You mean…But…"

He turned away, dismissing her as Vedhe joined them and he led the way down the hall.

K'lrsa followed in a daze. What was she going to do now?

CHAPTER 42

K'lrsa drifted behind Father Sun and Vedhe as they walked towards the center of the labyrinth. The first time they'd stepped into that room she'd been able to convince Vedhe to choose the viewing tube rather than the sun orb. But this time…

Vedhe was going to choose the sun orb.

There was no question about it.

After being reminded of the horrors that men and women could commit, she wouldn't hesitate. K'lrsa's only hope was that the sun orb wouldn't appear as a choice for her this time. The room never displayed all of the weapons available, only those that the chooser desired and was capable of wielding.

Although, that was a bit of a gray area. The mirror they'd seen the first time—the one that showed someone at their most beautiful—had almost ensnared them both. It was all K'lrsa had been able to do to wrest her gaze away from it. And Vedhe would've been trapped there forever, staring at herself, if K'lrsa hadn't saved her from it.

She shivered. Every single object in that room was twisted somehow. It took away as much as it gave, never quite meeting its owner's needs. Even the necklace had caused more harm than it helped.

Which meant they needed to be careful with what they chose. But Vedhe would take the sun orb, no question.

And…

K'lrsa already knew which object she wanted, too.

The staff.

It had called to her like it was made for her. She'd turned away from it, scared by the destruction she could cause, but now it was what she wanted.

But if she chose the staff…

There'd be no one to stop Vedhe. She'd burn the world to the ground. K'lrsa could choose the moon power instead. It was the only object that could counter the sun orb.

But…

She didn't want it.

She wanted a weapon.

The Lady met them at the door, calm and regal, with an air of authority K'lrsa had to fight to resist. "Once more, my children, you will enter this room and make a choice. This is not as it normally is. Usually, you enter this room once, full of the knowledge of the labyrinth. Most choose not to take any object away with them, seeing how it could turn against them and those they love. Some few, like you the last time you were here, choose an object out of desperation, knowing they have no choice but to risk allowing the object into the world once more."

K'lrsa wiped her sweaty palms on her pants as she glanced at Vedhe, wondering if she felt as nervous as K'lrsa did, but she was completely at ease, her hands folded peacefully in front of her.

K'lrsa shivered as the Lady continued, "Last time, I allowed you to enter the room together." Her eyes flashed silver as she looked at K'lrsa. "I believe that was a mistake. It's what led us to this moment."

K'lrsa lifted her chin and met the Lady's eyes. She didn't regret her prior choice.

The Lady gestured towards Vedhe. "You, Vedhe Kanaatanva, will go first. Choose wisely. This is the only chance you will be given to make up for your prior error."

Vedhe held out the viewing tube, but the Lady shook her head. "No. You may keep it."

"But that will upset the balance."

"Yes." The Lady looked at K'lrsa once more. "But we have no choice in the matter. Father Sun swore that he wouldn't make you exchange this for a new object of power, so you may keep it. Go. Choose wisely."

K'lrsa moved to block Vedhe's path. "Wait. What happens if she keeps them both?"

The Lady sighed. "As Vedhe said, it upsets the balance. She will have two objects of power. Normally, any one person should only ever have one. When they acquire more than one—it occasionally happens through deceit or conquest or death—the balance is upset."

"And? What happens then?"

The Lady breathed in through her nose, eyes flashing in annoyance. "The pendulum swings. For a little while, the world is out of balance." She shrugged slightly. "But eventually, it returns to the center. It always returns to the center after enough time has passed."

"How? How does it do that?"

The Lady's face flickered for a moment, showing that darker something that lurked beneath the beautiful surface. "It depends. On what caused the imbalance, how powerful the objects are, how the person uses them…"

The Lady pushed K'lrsa aside. "Enough. It is what it is. Aran must be defeated. We'll deal with the consequences after."

"Does he have objects like these? Is that why we can choose more than one? Or by choosing, will we enable him to become more powerful?"

The Lady pressed her lips together, refusing to answer.

K'lrsa turned to Father Sun. "Tell me. I need to know so I can make the right choice."

"The right choice?" He laughed, his voice a deep rumble. "You'd need thousands of years of knowledge to even understand the battle you're a part of, and then you'd see that there is no right or wrong choice. There's just the next move, the next skirmish. You are an imperfect piece on a never-ending game board. Choose as you will. You won't break the world. Not permanently at least."

"But we could break it." She glanced at Vedhe who was looking off into space, seemingly not even listening to the conversation. "For how long?"

"A hundred generations, maybe? Probably no more than that."

"A hundred generations!"

"At its worst. Likely less. The world is resilient." He leaned against the wall as if the prospect of the world being broken for a hundred generations meant nothing to him.

It probably didn't.

"It's time." The Lady opened the door. "Go, Vedhe. Choose wisely."

Vedhe stepped through, not even glancing at K'lrsa.

CHAPTER 43

K'lrsa paced the hallway, left, right, left, right, over and over again until she thought she'd wear a groove in the floor. The Lady had entered the room with Vedhe so it was just K'lrsa and Father Sun alone in the hallway, but she ignored him. He'd betrayed her. He'd made a promise he knew he wasn't going to keep and then broken it as soon as he could.

True, he'd technically kept the promise he'd made, but he'd known what she wanted. Which meant he'd broken the spirit of their agreement if not the actual words.

She stopped and turned towards him.

He was watching her, his eyes banked coals, belying his casual pose as he leaned against the sleek white wall opposite the doorway. "Why are you letting her choose a new object of power? If you know it will upset the balance, why do it?"

He smiled, pushing off of the wall and coming to stand before her. "You really care? You really want to know?"

"Yes."

He leaned closer. "I don't trust you."

"What?"

"I don't trust you to keep your promise. Even with the binding burned into your flesh, I don't think you'll do it."

She tried to hold his gaze, but she couldn't. "I said I would. And I know what happens if I don't. My parents will be stranded here forever and I'll be in perpetual agony." She flexed her hand. She couldn't feel the binding, but it was there. "Will they fray away into nothing like Lodie would have if she'd stayed in the labyrinth? Or will they just be stuck here forever?"

"They'll disappear eventually. But it will take hundreds of years, maybe more."

"I don't want that to happen." She glanced at him and away again, unable to hold his gaze. "So I'll do what it takes to save them."

He harrumphed, but didn't argue with her further.

She flexed her hand, wondering if she could really do it. If she could really destroy an entire people just to save the two people she loved most in the world. From…What? Spending an eternity together in a place where they had everything they could want?

She pushed that thought away.

They didn't want to stay here. No matter how pleasant it was. And there was somewhere beyond that they needed to go to.

She studied Father Sun as he once more leaned against the wall. "What does it mean to you to destroy the Toreem Daliphate? Is it enough to remove Aran from power? Or do I have to raze it to the ground?"

"For me?" He chuckled. "You're the one that made the vow, not me, so you're the one that has to be satisfied you've done it."

"Me?"

He nodded.

"Fine." She shrugged and turned away from him. "Then I've met it. We're done. Free my parents."

Nothing happened.

And then, slowly, her hand started to burn until it felt like someone was pressing a branding iron against her flesh, digging it deeper and deeper as the fire consumed her.

She collapsed to her knees, screaming, as Father Sun watched, his face impassive, not even moving from where he leaned against the wall.

Tears ran down her face as she clutched her hand to her chest, whimpering.

Father Sun pursed his lips. "It seems you don't believe that."

"Of course, I don't."

"Well, then…"

She glared at him through the tears still streaming down her face as the fire in her hand slowly retreated. "You did that," she accused.

"No. The binding did. As soon as you decided to turn away from your vow, the binding struck."

"I didn't decide to turn away from my vow. It was just words. I was just speaking." She slowly stood, cradling her hand close to her chest.

With a twitch of his chin Father Sun directed her to where a pitcher of water had appeared on a small table. She plunged her hand into the water, almost crying out in relief as the water cooled the last of the heat.

When she was finally sure it wouldn't keep burning, she withdrew her hand. It looked the same as it had before—as if she'd long ago burned her hand and it had healed over— but it ached with the memory of pain. "It didn't do any damage."

"No. It won't. But it doesn't really need to, does it?"

She flexed her hand, wincing. She never wanted to feel something like that again.

She glanced towards the doorway. "You don't have to give Vedhe another object of power. I'll do what I said I'd do."

"Too late." He pushed off the wall just as Vedhe came out of the room, the orb of fire cradled in her hands, her eyes glowing with an inner fervor that sent a chill down K'lrsa's spine.

CHAPTER 44

"Your turn." The Lady said, following Vedhe out of the room with a satisfied smile.

K'lrsa hesitated. "Was it like before, Vedhe? Were the choices the same?"

Vedhe barely managed to tear her attention from the orb. "No. I had more choices than before, but some were also missing. The staff wasn't there. Neither was the moon power that could neutralize the orb." She held the orb before her face and it cast a brilliant light on her scars, etching each ridge and shiny patch of redness in bright light, making them more gruesome than before. "But this was all I wanted. It seems fitting to bring fire to the people who did this to me." She touched her scarred cheek with her fingers.

K'lrsa tried to hide the horror she felt at Vedhe's smile, but when their eyes met she knew she'd failed.

Vedhe clutched the orb to her chest. "Don't forget who your enemy is. I've done nothing but help you."

"I won't."

K'lrsa shivered as she turned towards the doorway. She risked a glance towards where the Lady and Father Sun were standing, talking quietly. How much of this—the constant conflict and struggle—was actually the gods' fault? Without objects like the one cradled in Vedhe's hand, would men really turn on one another the way they had?

 185 

Without a god to fight for, would they care so much to take what wasn't theirs to take?

The Lady came back to the doorway.

"Choose wisely," Vedhe called as K'lrsa joined her.

K'lrsa nodded, not trusting herself to speak.

As the Lady opened the door, Vedhe added, "Oh, and don't worry about the imbalance. I left the viewing tube behind. I don't need it now."

K'lrsa turned back in surprise. "Really? I thought it helped?"

Vedhe's upper lip twitched in a snarl, making her look like some sort of feral beast. "I don't need to know that the man I'm about to kill loves his wife and child. Or that he gives food to the homeless every week."

"But…Wouldn't it be good to know that he's not such a bad person?"

"No."

"I don't…"

"I don't care anymore. They're all bad in some way."

"All men?"

"All people."

"All?" K'lrsa remembered Vedhe's earlier comments about Badru, her stomach sinking.

"All." Vedhe met K'lrsa's eyes and K'lrsa shivered at her unflinching certainty. For Vedhe the world had become black and white. All shades of gray were gone. People were evil or would become evil, so must die.

K'lrsa turned back towards the doorway. She'd promised to defeat Aran. She had to do it. And to destroy the Toreem Daliphate.

But…

But Vedhe was as much of a threat as anyone. Which meant she needed to choose something that would allow her to not only defeat Aran and destroy the Toreem Daliphate but protect Badru and everyone else she loved, too.

Assuming that was even possible…

CHAPTER 45

K'lrsa stepped into the room. It was small, like before, with shelves lining the walls, but this time the shelves were empty.

A single table dominated the center of the room.

On it were only two objects: the bowl full of moon power and the staff—both of the objects she'd considered choosing before. One would neutralize the sun orb and maybe other objects, and perhaps do other things she didn't know yet, the other could call water from anywhere in the world.

She turned to the Lady. "Where are the other objects? Vedhe said she had more choices this time around. Why don't I?"

"The room responds to the individual who has come to choose. It shows those objects the individual is likely to want and can actually control."

"I can control other objects." K'lrsa's heart raced. Had there been so many more last time because Vedhe was more powerful than her? What did that mean for her chances of defeating both Aran and Vedhe?

The Lady's laugh was as bright as sunlight on a spring morning. "That staff is the most powerful object ever made. You weren't given other choices because the only two you want are the two that lie before you. So now the question is…Which will you choose? To neutralize? Or to destroy?"

K'lrsa stared at the objects on the table for a long moment. Her hand itched to touch the staff just like it had the first time. She was drawn to it as if it had been made for her. But she stayed where she was.

If she touched it, she'd choose it. She wouldn't be able to set it aside once she took it up.

She turned away from the table, focusing her attention on the Lady. "Can the staff defeat the sun orb?"

The Lady tilted her head to the side, studying K'lrsa. "Why would you need to do that? Vedhe is your friend and ally."

Maybe.

"What if someone takes it from her? Luden took the necklace from me."

"Vedhe won't lose the orb. She's stronger than that." The Lady's eyes flared silver and K'lrsa flinched at the rebuke in her words.

She glanced at the staff, longing to pick it up.

What if she wasn't strong enough to keep it? What if Aran or someone else took it from her? What kind of destruction would she be bringing into the world if she chose it?

But what if she didn't choose the staff and the sun orb wasn't enough to stand against Aran? He might defeat Vedhe…

K'lrsa shook her head. "I don't get it. Why let us come in here and choose weapons that could destroy the world? Don't you even care about what could go wrong?"

A wind whipped around the room. The Lady seemed to grow, filling the small space as she loomed over K'lrsa. "What do you know of any of this, mortal?"

"Only what you tell me." K'lrsa shouted in frustration. "If there's something else I should know, then reveal it so I can make the right choice!"

"Ha. The right choice." The Lady slowly shrank back to her normal size and the wind disappeared. "For whom? You? Or us?"

"What does that mean?"

The Lady walked around the room, running her hand along the empty shelves. As she did, ghosts of objects appeared and disappeared, so many they seemed to stretch forever into the distance.

The Lady finally stopped at the table and stared down at the two objects lying there. "It means that what is best for an individual man or woman isn't always what is best for that individual's god."

"So killing Aran? Is that for you or for the tribes?"

The Lady pressed her lips together, refusing to answer.

"And what about Toreem? Why do you want so badly for me to destroy it? What does it matter?"

Once again, the Lady kept silent, running a hand along the table, studying the two objects before her, ignoring K'lrsa's glare. "It's time to choose, K'lrsa dan V'na of the White Horse Tribe. Which will it be? The moon power or the staff?"

"Why won't you answer my questions?" K'lrsa demanded, stepping closer.

"Who are you to demand answers from a god?" The Lady's eyes flashed like lightning as she stalked around the table.

K'lrsa shrank back from her at first, but then stood her ground, hands fisted at her sides for courage. "I'm the person you're asking to kill a man. And destroy an entire civilization. I deserve to know why you want me to do it."

The Lady's lips twitched into a slight smile. "Because you promised you would."

K'lrsa glared at the Lady. "Sometimes I really hate you, you know."

The Lady's laughter was like a sudden rainstorm on a hot day—there and gone in a moment. "It's time to choose. Which will it be?"

K'lrsa stared at the two objects on the table, torn.

CHAPTER 46

K'lrsa sighed as she looked back and forth between the two objects on the table. They looked so simple. But even from where she stood she could feel the power emanating from them.

The staff called to her, tugging at her soul as if it had been made for her. Whispering how powerful she'd be if she controlled one of the basic elements of the world, especially in a land where water was precious and capricious.

But the moon power could neutralize the sun orb…

And maybe other objects, too.

Which choice would save the world she knew?

Which would destroy it?

If she chose the moon power but then Vedhe wasn't strong enough to stand against Aran on her own, the world was doomed. K'lrsa had no doubt he'd come to the Hidden City, break into this room, and take every object he could.

What would he care about balance?

He was ruthless and cruel and wanted power more than anything.

But if she chose the staff…

She might defeat Aran and then fall to Vedhe. Water couldn't stand against the power of the sun. And then the world would be just as broken as if Aran had won.

There was no right choice. She needed them both.

"It's time to choose, child." The Lady stepped closer and K'lrsa moved away, not trusting her.

Carefully, she removed the necklace from around her neck and placed it in the center of the table, between the two objects, delaying her final decision for just a moment longer.

"You don't need to return it."

"Why not?"

The Lady's lips twitched into a grimace. "Because that necklace is like a single grain of sand in the entirety of the desert compared to either one of those objects. It won't make a difference."

"So then why let me take either one?" K'lrsa glared at the Lady across the length of the table.

Standing this close it was all she could do not to grab the staff.

"It's what's needed."

"But what about the balance?" K'lrsa wished she'd paid more attention to the knowledge she'd received from the labyrinth before it faded away. Now she just had a vague memory that the balance was crucial to survival, but she didn't understand how it worked or what happened when it was disturbed.

"Sometimes the world gets out of balance. It happens." The Lady's voice was as cold as the snow K'lrsa had seen in the labyrinth.

K'lrsa paced away from the table, searching for that lost knowledge, but it was gone. Faded away. She wished she could ask Vedhe a few questions, but if she left the room that would be it. She couldn't come back.

She stopped and turned to the Lady once more. "Are we the ones taking the world out of balance? Or will choosing these weapons help return it to balance?"

The Lady crossed her arms. "It's time to choose."

K'lrsa eyed the objects on the table. "Is it possible to take the world so far out of balance that it can't right itself?"

The Lady tilted her head, considering. "Yes…But no object that exists is powerful enough to do it."

"What about a combination of objects?"

The Lady studied her carefully, her silver eyes like drowning pools. "Which objects?"

"These three."

"All three of them?"

K'lrsa shivered slightly, but nodded. "Yes."

The Lady smiled, a beautiful smile full of life and joy, like the early days of spring.

K'lrsa wasn't fooled. She'd seen what lurked beneath that surface, she knew the darker creature behind the mask.

She held her breath, waiting for the Lady's answer.

The Lady thought about it for a moment. "No. These three together aren't powerful enough to permanently disrupt the balance."

"So if I took all three of these objects on the table with me, I wouldn't upset the balance?

Even as she asked the question a small part of her mind was screaming at her that she couldn't trust the Lady, that taking even one of the objects could destroy the world she knew. Look at what Luden had managed with just the necklace. What damage could all three objects do? Especially when combined with the sun orb? But she pushed that voice away, ignoring its warning.

She had to take the moon power and the staff. It was the only way to destroy Aran *and* protect her people from Vedhe. And it was only for a little while. Just long enough to defeat Aran. She'd be careful. She wouldn't even use them if she didn't have to.

Surely a week, maybe two, wouldn't be enough to change the course of her world?

The Lady ran her hand along each of the objects, her gaze far away.

"Lady? Can I do it? Can I take all three without breaking the world?"

The Lady smiled at her. She was in the guise of the young woman now, her cheeks pink with the first blush of womanhood, her hair long and lustrous as it flowed down her back. "Yes. You can take all three. It won't break the world."

"Good." K'lrsa grabbed the bowl full of moon power and it turned into a small stoppered jar that easily fit into the pouch at her waist. She considered leaving the necklace behind, but she might need it. Quickly, before she could change her mind, she put it on.

Last, she grabbed the staff.

She'd been right. It fit her hand perfectly. And the power it contained—such immense power, more than she could've imagined—coursed through her body like a song, lifting her up, leaving her almost dizzy with possibility.

Anything was possible. She could remake the world. Bring rain, raise mountains, call the oceans.

Anything.

Before that voice of warning screaming in the back of her mind got any louder, she turned and stepped through the doorway, the Lady following behind her.

She'd made her choice. What was done was done.

Vedhe was waiting for her. "What did you choose?"

"Isn't it obvious?" K'lrsa planted the staff on the floor, resisting the temptation to use it to call water right then and there. It sung to her, begging to be used.

Vedhe eyed her warily. "But you kept the necklace?"

"The Lady told me it wouldn't make a difference."

Vedhe glared at the Lady. "Why did you lie to her?"

The Lady smiled, a soft, benevolent smile tinged with malice. "I didn't lie."

"You told her it wouldn't make a difference."

"No. I answered the question she asked me. Which was whether keeping it would break the world. It won't."

"Let her put it back. Now, before it's too late." Vedhe grabbed K'lrsa's arm and dragged her towards the room, but the door was closed and no amount of pushing or banging would open it.

"It's too late for that. She made her choices. The pendulum is in motion." The Lady smiled with the fierceness of a desert cat about to pounce.

"What? What did I do?" K'lrsa looked to Vedhe. "Vedhe?"

Vedhe turned away, but not before K'lrsa saw the very real fear etched on her face.

CHAPTER 47

Before K'lrsa could ask Vedhe again what she'd done, the Lady stepped between them. "It's nothing. Time to say your goodbyes."

"No. Wait." K'lrsa pushed past the Lady, earning herself a look so dark she flinched. "Vedhe? What did I do?"

Vedhe turned on her, fear and anger warring on her face. "Don't you remember anything about what we learned when we came through the labyrinth?"

K'lrsa half-shrugged. "Some of it."

"What parts? The parts about fighting? I've seen you practicing new attacks each day. Or about finding food or water?"

"And why not?" K'lrsa crossed her arms defensively across her chest. "Those were the parts I could actually use. Do you really think I need to know what happened in a bunch of long-dead civilizations that have nothing to do with me? Far better to learn how to survive in *this* land than how other people died in theirs."

Vedhe shook her head in disgust. "We were given knowledge unlike anything anyone has ever received before. Even the wise ones of your tribe who used to come here didn't receive the amount of knowledge we did. But you just threw it away."

"Because it didn't matter. It was a bunch of worthless

information clogging up my head every time I tried to think."

"Which is why you just did the stupidest thing imaginable."

"What? Keeping the necklace when I took the staff?" K'lrsa snorted. "The Lady told me that the power of the necklace compared to the power of the staff, or your sun orb for that matter..." She jammed a finger at Vedhe's chest. "Was nothing. That it wasn't going to upset the balance if I kept it."

Vedhe turned on the Lady. "Did you really tell her that?"

The Lady raised her chin, silver eyes flashing. "No."

"Yes, you did."

"No. I told you that the power of the necklace compared to the power of the other two objects was like a grain of sand compared to the entirety of the desert."

"You told me I could take the objects and it wouldn't upset the balance."

Vedhe laughed before she could stop herself.

The Lady glared her down before answering. "No. I told you that the three objects in that room could not break the world. Taking any object from that room upsets the balance."

K'lrsa couldn't breathe. Taking any one object from the room upset the balance? Then what did taking three objects do?

"So we upset the balance. For a little bit. Until Aran is defeated. And then we bring them back here. And it's fine. It goes back to how it was."

Vedhe shook her head. "No. It doesn't work that way."

"What? Why not?"

"Because as soon as you took those objects out of the room, it freed Aran's gods to act to restore the balance." Vedhe pressed her lips together, the scars on her face standing out in stark relief. "It was already going to be bad with you having the staff and my having the orb, but now that you have the necklace, too..."

"But you said they'll act to restore balance, right? So we'll be matched? Maybe this was just balancing out his death walker magic?"

"No." Vedhe glanced at the Lady for confirmation. "I think the sun and moon stones balance the death walker magic. And when we took the viewing tube and the necklace that allowed Aran more power to balance it. But now…" She shuddered. "He'll have enough power to balance the orb, the necklace, and the staff. Perhaps combined into one object. One that could break the world. And how do we stand against that when each of us can only use one object at a time?"

K'lrsa touched the pouch at her waist where the moon power was hidden. As scared as Vedhe was, what would she think if she knew K'lrsa had also taken it?

She turned on the Lady. "Why didn't you tell me? Why did you let me choose more than one object?"

The Lady shrugged one shoulder. "I was bored. You try living through four hundred years of peace."

"You were bored? So what now? You just sit back and enjoy the show as we all die?"

The darkness that lurked underneath the Lady's beauty surfaced for a moment in her silvery eyes as she smiled.

K'lrsa turned away from her in disgust.

"Vedhe? What can we do? Can we neutralize one of the objects? Can you burn the necklace with the sun orb maybe?"

Vedhe shook her head. "No. It's too late now. As soon as you left the room the balance shifted. All we can do now is confront Aran before it's too late."

K'lrsa buried her face in her hands. This couldn't be happening. Why hadn't anyone warned her? Why had the Lady let her do it?

And what would a man like Aran do with that kind of power? How many were going to die because of her mistake?

CHAPTER 48

As K'lrsa and Vedhe walked back to where they'd left the others, K'lrsa couldn't help but fiddle with the pouch at her waist where the vial with the moon power was stored. She hadn't told Vedhe about it because if she had to use it against her she didn't want her to know. But if just keeping the necklace had shifted the balance that much…

What had taking the moon power done?

K'lrsa swallowed heavily. She didn't want to know, but was scared she was going to find out at the worst possible moment.

"You can give the necklace to Badru," Vedhe said, walking along beside her, trailing her fingers along the walls.

"The Lady said we can't let anyone use the objects."

"Luden already used your necklace. And F'lia used my viewing tube. Clearly you won't be struck down by lightning if you do it."

"No…But I wonder if what happened with F'lia and the baby might have been caused by it?"

Vedhe shrugged. "Doubt it. And even if it did, it didn't kill her. Better to deal with the consequences later than let Aran win."

K'lrsa nodded. Vedhe was right. But if Badru was going to use any of the objects he needed to use the moon power, not the necklace. Of course, if she was going to

keep what she'd done secret from Vedhe, then she'd need to give both to Badru to keep her from being suspicious.

And then trust that he'd use them the right way and wouldn't stop Vedhe *before* she destroyed the Toreem Daliphate.

Her stomach clenched at the thought of giving up an object that powerful. Even to the man she loved.

She'd missed him and wanted him in her life. And she knew he loved her and that she loved him. But…

Trusting him with that kind of power…

Trusting *anyone* with that kind of power. She wasn't sure she could do it.

She shook her head. What a fool she was. She'd trust him with her life and her happiness, but she wasn't willing to give him the moon power.

She sighed.

She didn't want to do it, but she had to. Didn't she?

There wasn't another option.

If Aran had enough power to defeat all the objects combined, then Badru had to be a part of their plans. Which meant telling Vedhe about what she'd done.

She glanced sideways at her friend, licking her lips nervously. How do you tell someone who has come to be a friend that you didn't trust them not to burn the world down so you probably did something that would break the world anyway?

"What?" Vedhe nudged her arm. "Are you okay? You're looking at me funny."

"Yeah. Yeah, I'm fine. Just…worried, is all. I wonder what kind of weapon they'll give Aran to balance out ours. Do you think it'll be one weapon? Wouldn't it make more sense for it to be multiple weapons?"

Vedhe shrugged one shoulder. "It would if there were multiple people on their side who were standing against us. But from everything I've heard about Aran, he doesn't share his power. He'll want all of it for himself. Which means one weapon powerful enough to stand against all of ours."

They walked along for a moment in silence before K'lrsa asked, "Why do you think the gods allowed this? If we hadn't taken those weapons out, then none of this would be happening." She barely stopped herself from mentioning how the Lady had almost encouraged her to take all three objects.

Even though she didn't mention it to Vedhe, it did niggle at her mind. There was something she was missing.

"Who knows why the gods do anything? Why did my gods let Ivan kill my family and sell me into slavery? Why did one of your gods give me Kriger? They aren't human, you know. As much as they look like us."

K'lrsa grabbed her arm and pulled her to a stop, looking back to make sure the gods weren't nearby. "What are they? Do you know?"

Vedhe shook her head. "No. I've sifted through all the knowledge I received, but it isn't there. Neither is anything about the nature of the place we go after this one. It's like there are these paths I can follow, but when I get to a certain point they just end abruptly. Like walking off a cliff. Everything past that point is missing."

K'lrsa wanted to ask more, but Vedhe continued walking and they reached the room with the others in it before she could think of anything more to say.

Herin met them at the doorway. She took one look at the staff in K'lrsa's hand and gave a sharp nod. "About time you started thinking like someone who wants to actually win."

K'lrsa winced. "Glad I could please you, Herin." She met her father's eyes. "But I'd like a little time alone with my parents if you don't mind."

Herin harrumphed but turned her attention to Vedhe without further comment.

As the others gathered around to see the sun orb, K'lrsa pulled her mom and dad to the side. "I need your advice. Come with me."

She led them to a far corner, behind a stand of trees, hoping it was far enough away that no one else would be able to hear them.

If anyone could tell her how to fix things, it would be her parents...

She hoped.

CHAPTER 49

"What is it?" Her father peered into her face, his brow wrinkled in concern.

K'lrsa bit her lip and glanced back towards the others. "I made a mistake."

"What did you do?" Her mother stepped closer, arms crossed. "I don't want to be trapped here for eternity."

"V'na." Her father's voice was stern as he pulled his wife back. "I already told K'lrsa that I'd rather stay here forever than see her act against everything I taught her."

"Everything you taught her? What do we owe the people of the Daliphana, B'nin? What have they ever done but try to exploit us?"

"V'na. They're people, too. Don't they deserve to live their lives in peace?"

Her mother snorted.

"You won't be trapped here. I promise."

"Do you? Is that a promise you can keep?" Her mother stepped closer, staring her down, and K'lrsa had to avert her gaze.

For a brief moment she almost wished Father Sun hadn't cured her parents. At least, not her mother.

"I'd do anything to save you. And…" She glanced towards where Vedhe and the others had been a moment before. They must've moved to the fire. "If I can't bring myself to do it, I'm sure Vedhe will. I don't think the gods care as long as it happens."

Her mother nodded once, satisfied.

Her father studied her, the questions he wanted to ask written on his face, but he kept silent.

K'lrsa twisted her hands together, feeling like she was M'lara's age and trying to work up the courage to explain how she'd let a prized horse lame itself. "There's something else, though. Something happened in there."

Her father touched her arm, his eyes warm with concern, and it almost broke her. "What?" he asked.

"I…When I was in there, I was given two choices. This staff and the power of the moon."

"And?"

Her parents both watched her, waiting.

"And I chose…" She glanced towards where the others had disappeared but didn't see anyone. She dropped her voice anyway. "I chose them both. *And* I kept the necklace."

Her mother nodded. "Good. You'll need every weapon you can find."

"No, it's not good. There's…Vedhe can explain it better…There's a balance that has to be maintained. And by taking both weapons, as well as keeping the necklace, I upset that balance. It may mean that Aran's gods can now give him enough power to defeat us."

Her father patted her arm. "I wouldn't worry about it. Like you said. There has to be balance. So he won't be given any more power than you have."

"But I can only use one of the objects at a time. And his gods may give him one weapon that can match all of ours."

He shrugged. "So give Badru one of the weapons."

"Even if I do that, we're still short one person. And…" She grimaced. "Vedhe doesn't know I took the moon power. And I don't want her to."

"Why not?" Her mother asked.

"Because I may need to use it against her if she turns on the tribes."

"Why would she do that? She's your friend."

"I know. But you haven't seen the way she looks when she holds that sun orb. Or some of the things she's said. Mom…she's…not right."

Her mother shook her head, dismissing K'lrsa's concerns. "I'll admit, I didn't like the girl at first, but I never saw anything like that in her. And I spent as much time around her as you have. You need to learn to trust people, K'lrsa. You're too used to doing things by yourself, that's all."

K'lrsa looked to her father, hoping he'd give different advice, but he nodded. "Your mother's right. You need to trust others. Or you're going to lose."

"You don't know that..."

M'lara burst out of the trees behind them. "Come on. It's time for dinner. You should see all the food. This place is the best." She turned and ran back towards the campfire.

K'lrsa looked back and forth between her parents. "You can't tell anyone what I told you, okay? Not yet."

They both frowned at her, but at least they didn't argue as they walked back to join the others.

There was more food than K'lrsa had ever seen—even in Toreem—spread out for them to eat. Every single dish she'd ever tasted and then some. It smelled delicious, especially since K'lrsa hadn't eaten all day.

As she took a seat next to Vedhe and started to eat, she felt a small stab of guilt that she was keeping something so important from her friend. But as they ate and talked and laughed, Vedhe's hand kept drifting towards the pouch where she'd stashed the sun orb, like she couldn't stand to be parted from it.

And her eyes had a distant look, like she was once more staring into a world no one else could see.

Watching her, K'lrsa knew she'd made the right choice. Both in taking the moon power and in keeping it a secret from Vedhe.

The only question that remained was, should she tell Badru?

CHAPTER 50

After the meal, K'lrsa went to rest. No point in leaving until the moon had risen and the horses could fly. (Even though it seemed to always be daytime in the city, she knew that it was still midday in the real world.)

She intended to close her eyes for a moment and relax, but as soon as she lay down she fell into a deep, dreamless sleep. It was one of the best sleeps she'd had in a long, long while and she woke up completely refreshed.

A new set of riding leathers was waiting for her, folded next to her sleeping pallet. She stripped out of her old clothes, throwing them in a pile in the corner, and carefully removed the necklace, setting it next to her belt pouch before she went to take a bath.

She'd acquired a taste for baths in Toreem and as she sank into the perfectly hot water, she luxuriated at the feel of it against her skin, soothing away the last bits of tension as she sank in up to her chin, inhaling the scents of lavender and eucalyptus.

She closed her eyes and leaned her head against the edge of the tall bathing tub, trying not to think of anything. Soon enough she'd have to make choices she didn't want to make. For now she just wanted to relax and enjoy the moment.

A scuffling noise from the direction of her tent interrupted her reverie and she sat up, scared that maybe

Vedhe was trying to steal the staff.

"Who's there?" she demanded.

"It's just me." M'lara came to stand outside the bathing tent so K'lrsa could see her. She had her hands clasped behind her back and wouldn't quite look at K'lrsa.

"Were you in my tent?"

"I wanted to see if you were up yet."

K'lrsa watched her with narrowed eyes. Something was off, but she didn't know what.

Sighing, she climbed out of the tub and grabbed a cloth to dry herself—pausing for a brief moment to appreciate how soft and supple it was, just like the ones she remembered from the Daliphana.

As K'lrsa dried herself off, M'lara came to lean against the side of the tub. "I want to go with you."

"You can't. You're too young."

M'lara thrust her lower lip out in a pout. "But you need another person. I can use the necklace and you can give Badru the moon power."

She whirled around, staring at M'lara. "What did you just say? How did you know about the moon power?"

"I heard you talking to Mom and Dad." M'lara glanced at her and away again, her jaw was set.

"You know better than to eavesdrop like that!"

"But nobody tells me anything. They think I'm just a child."

"You are."

"Am not. I can take care of myself." Her brow furrowed and she looked ready to cry.

"M'lara. You're not even nine summers old yet. You are not ready to face a man like Aran. *I'm* not ready to. None of us are. He's horrible."

M'lara lifted her chin with a sniffle. "You said you need someone else. Who else is there?"

K'lrsa opened her mouth and then shut it again. She sighed. "The necklace won't make a difference. And I refuse to put you in danger like that."

"Vedhe thinks it could. She was explaining to me about the balance. She actually thinks the necklace may be the key. That's why she's glad you're going to meet up with Badru before you go after Aran."

"Did you tell her about the moon power?" K'lrsa glared at her sister.

If she had…

"No. I can keep a secret."

"Good." K'lrsa finished drying herself off and set the towel aside. "M'lara…"

"Don't. It's not fair. I *can* help you."

"You're too young."

M'lara backed away, tears in her eyes. "No, I'm not. And I'm going. Whether you want me there or not."

She held out her fist, the necklace chain dangling from between her fingers.

"M'lara! That isn't yours. Give it back." K'lrsa lunged for her, but M'lara was gone.

She'd used the necklace.

Didn't she realize how dangerous it was? Even now she could be a tangled mess of bones and muscle, already dead. Or coughing blood. Or unable to breathe, alone in the desert somewhere…

What had she done?

K'lrsa collapsed to her knees, unable to breathe.

CHAPTER 51

K'lrsa threw on her new hunting leathers as she shouted for her parents.

Her father came running, her mother close on his heels. "What? What is it?"

"M'lara. She took the necklace. She wanted me to take her with us and when I refused, she used it. I don't know where she is."

"We'll find her. She can't have gone far."

K'lrsa nodded, but she wasn't so sure of that.

As her parents pushed through the trees, shouting out M'lara's name, K'lrsa made her way to the campfire and told the others what had happened. They fanned out, looking for her and calling her name, but eventually everyone returned to the fire.

Her father wrapped an arm around her mother's shoulders as they leaned into one another for support. "She's gone."

K'lrsa nodded, trembling with fear as she imagined where M'lara might be now. "Lady Moon!" she shouted, unable to contain her fury and desperation. "Where are you? We need you. Now!"

The Lady glided into the room, gorgeous as always, her face slowly shifting between the young maiden, the matron, and the crone as it did when she appeared in the moon dream.

"You called?" Her voice was like silk and steel entwined, soft but lethal.

K'lrsa didn't flinch. "My sister is gone. She used the necklace. Where is she?"

The Lady looked into the distance for a long moment. "Hm. Clever girl."

"Where is she?"

"Moving across the desert. She's already left the city."

"Is she hurt?" K'lrsa's voice shook.

"No. She's moving in small little hops. Seems she paid more attention to how the necklace works than you did." The Lady's smile was sharp with cruelty

K'lrsa didn't care. All that mattered was getting M'lara back safely. "Where is she headed?"

The Lady shrugged one shoulder. "Shelter, if I had to guess. Right now she's just hopping from sand dune to sand dune. I assume eventually she'll either stop to wait for you. Or…" She nodded to herself as she looked into the distance again. "Find Badru."

"Bring her back." K'lrsa balled her hands into fists. "Now."

The Lady half-laughed. "No."

"She's just a child."

"Seems fine to me."

K'lrsa glanced in the direction of the tent where she'd left the staff. Could she use it to force the Lady to help? She knew the Lady was scared of the power it contained, but she didn't know *why* she was scared of it.

Perhaps…

The Lady stepped so close they were almost touching.

There was a vastness to her that K'lrsa had never sensed before—like the Lady contained the entire night sky in her person. "Don't you ever again think of using one of those objects on me, child. I will not only banish you to the nothingness between worlds, I will send every single person you love with you." Her voice was beautiful in its controlled fury.

K'lrsa licked her lips, tempted to stand up to the Lady despite the warning, but one glance into those star-filled eyes and she knew she'd never survive long enough to try.

She stepped back, forcing a smile. "I wouldn't dream of it."

The Lady wasn't fooled. She gave K'lrsa a long, dark look before stalking out of the room.

CHAPTER 52

As soon as the Lady was gone, K'lrsa's mother stepped forward. "What do we do now?"

"It's okay. She'll go to Badru. We'll find her there and then I'll get the necklace back and take her to D'lan. She would've been safer here with you, but I won't have time to bring her back. That's the best I can do."

K'lrsa's mother nodded once. "You should get going then."

Herin stepped between them. "Pzah. The moon isn't even up yet. They'll move faster if they fly the horses. You should eat."

K'lrsa's mother glared at Herin for a long moment but then nodded and moved to the far side of the fire, away from K'lrsa. Her father followed, pulling K'lrsa's mother close and talking softly to her. She nodded at whatever he was saying and leaned into him, resting her head on his shoulder.

K'lrsa forced herself to look away, shaking her head. After all these years she shouldn't be surprised that they'd turn to one another for comfort and not even realize that maybe she needed a bit of reassurance as well.

She glanced at the others. Lodie and Vedhe sitting together, talking quietly. F'lia nestled next to L'ral; she hadn't said much since they'd arrived, but every once in a while she smiled at him and it was like she was her old self, all sunlight and happiness.

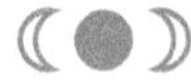

It hurt to see how changed her friend was, but K'lrsa was glad she'd found some small measure of joy in her pain.

Last, she turned to where Herin stood, Garzel a silent presence at her side. "Can we talk? While we eat?"

Herin nodded and they sat down together away from the others.

"What will you do after we leave?" K'lrsa bit into a fresh orange slice, savoring its tangy freshness while she could.

"Probably move on to the Promised Plains. Or beyond."

"You won't wait here, to see if we succeed?"

"Pzah. Why would I wait around to find out you finally did what I couldn't?"

K'lrsa picked up a small packet of green leaves, inhaling the complicated scents of meat and vegetables tucked inside before taking a bite, enjoying the different textures and tastes before finally swallowing. She was going to miss this.

She leaned closer to Herin. "I don't think we're going to succeed. I made a mistake."

"Of course you did." Herin sighed. "Well. Out with it. What did you do?"

She made sure none of the others were listening before she told Herin about keeping all three objects and what that might mean.

"You fool," Herin hissed. "Aran is the last man who needed more power."

"I know...I...If I'd realized..." K'lrsa stared at the ground, ashamed all over again at how foolish she'd been to think she could keep all three objects without consequence. She should've known. Vedhe had. "I ruined it all."

"Oh, enough of that. You don't have time to feel sorry for yourself. And this is on the gods as much as you. The Lady let you do it, didn't she? And even if you'd just taken the staff and Vedhe had the orb, the two of you would still be leaving here with two of the most powerful objects ever made."

"Why do you think they let it happen?"

Herin snorted. "Why do gods do anything?"

K'lrsa set aside her food, no longer hungry. Herin was right. Who really knew what the gods were thinking. "Should I tell Vedhe about the moon power?"

"No."

"Why not?"

Herin scoffed. "You don't want to tell her, so you ask me if I agree. I do, and now you need me to explain it to you?"

"I…Yes?"

Herin watched Lodie and Vedhe for a long moment with her hooded grel-like gaze. "Think about it. Who is Aran to Vedhe? She's never met him. He's never done anything to her. She's never even been to Toreem to see what he did to others. Why should she care if Aran dies?"

"I don't know. But she does. More than I do, I think."

Herin shook her head. "She just wants someone else to suffer the way she has. She'll kill Aran if it gets her closer to her goal, but what she really wants is to return to that northern home of hers and kill the man who killed her family. I expect she'll take anyone in her path out along the way."

"I saw what he did. I understand why she'd want that."

"Do you? How nice." Herin turned her dark gaze on K'lrsa. "Will you still be so understanding when the tribes stand between her and her vengeance?"

"I won't let her hurt them."

"No. You won't. That's why you have the moon power and why you won't tell her about it until you need to. Those objects, each and every one of them, twist their users. Each time you touch them, each time you use them, they twist you a little more."

Like the staff she'd wrapped in three blankets and left in her tent because the power of its call had been so strong.

"That sun orb?" Herin continued, "It'll latch onto the hatred in Vedhe's soul and twist her beyond recognition. And when it does and it looks like nothing can stop her…You will. But not if she knows what you're going to do."

K'lrsa looked across the fire at Vedhe, who was smiling slightly as she spoke to Lodie, the scars on her face twisting her mouth. She was so young and what had been done to her wasn't her fault, but…there was a darkness there.

"I don't want to hurt her. She's my friend."

Herin didn't answer. She didn't have to.

"What about Badru? Should I tell him?"

"Pzah. Of course."

K'lrsa held Herin's gaze. "Can I really trust him, Herin? Could I give him the staff and trust him to use it properly?"

"The staff? Why would you do that?"

"I don't know. I just wanted to know if I could."

Herin stared into the fire, her brow furrowed, the wrinkles in her face deepening as she spoke. "Badru loves you more than anything. The choices he made as Daliph and in entering the Hidden City prove that."

She met K'lrsa's gaze. "And he'll do anything to defeat Aran. But…" She shook her head. "He won't help you destroy the Toreem Daliphate. You have to know that. Even though he knows the truth of his parentage now, he'll still want to protect it. Give him the staff and he'll be able to stand against you. You won't be able to free your parents."

K'lrsa bit her lip. "Are you sure?"

"Pzah. Of course I am."

K'lrsa sat back with a sigh.

Herin was right. Badru would never want to destroy Toreem. He loved her, but not enough to stand aside while thousands died.

She stared into the fire, wondering what she was going to do. Defeating Aran was going to be hard enough, but when she couldn't even trust her allies…

CHAPTER 53

When at last it came time to leave, K'lrsa hurried through her goodbyes. Even though she was sure that M'lara was headed for Badru, she still wanted to get there as soon as possible. M'lara was too young to be on her own—even if she had been raised in the tribes where children were trained to hunt and gather food for themselves from the time they could toddle. That wasn't the same as traveling across the desert, alone, using a strange necklace that could easily kill her.

What was M'lara thinking? That she could stand with Vedhe, Badru, and K'lrsa when they confronted Aran?

No. Never.

She wouldn't allow it.

Fallion and Kriger were waiting for them when they exited the labyrinth. K'lrsa ran to Fallion and threw her arms around his neck, burying her face in his mane. "I missed you, *micora*."

As he whuffed at her hair, she wished he could speak. He'd been the only steady presence in her life through all of this, the one she could depend on no matter what. But, as remarkable as he was, he was still just a horse.

A beautiful, flying horse sent by the gods, but a horse nonetheless. Unfortunately, she had to make her own decisions.

She scratched his ears for a moment and then touched his forehead, willing him to transform.

With a shudder, he did, the light of a thousand suns shining under his coat, his eyes glowing, his beautiful wings stretched out behind him. Breathtaking as always. She kissed his nose and then mounted, looking down at the others who had come to see them off.

F'lia was tucked under L'ral's arm, a small smile on her face. K'lrsa hoped more than anything that the time her friend spent in the city would heal her from the loss of her child. She wanted her best friend back. But she suspected that when she returned, F'lia would have already left with L'ral. Or would refuse to return to the tribes. It's why K'lrsa hadn't told her about him initially.

She hadn't wanted to lose anyone else.

But bringing F'lia to the city had been the right thing to do.

No matter what it cost K'lrsa personally…

Her parents were standing together off to the side but not touching. They didn't need to. It was like the space around them was their own little world.

She bit her lip to keep from crying. "You'll be here? When I come back? Even if Father Sun frees you before that?"

Her father shook his head slightly. "Not if he frees us. I'm not about to miss my chance to leave this time. Sorry."

As she swallowed back her tears, he stepped forward and squeezed her foot. "I love you. We love you. Always know that." He glanced to her mother who nodded.

"I love you, too." She couldn't stop the one tear that escaped and ran down her cheek.

Her father stared up at her, his gaze intense. "And I have faith that you'll make the right decision when the time comes."

She wanted to beg him to tell her what that was. Did he want her to save people he'd never even met because they didn't deserve to die just for him? Or did he want her to honor the promise she'd made so he could be free?

But he wouldn't tell her, even if she asked, so she just nodded, holding the rest of her tears back as best she could.

As her father stepped back, K'lrsa looked to where Herin, Garzel, and Lodie stood. "And you?" she asked.

Lodie lifted her chin. "I'm leaving. Going straight through the Promised Plains and on to what comes after. My child and my husband are somewhere out there, and they need me."

Herin turned to her sister. "We'll go with you. If you'll have us."

"You don't want to stay in the Promised Plains for a while? Rest and recover after this horrible life?"

Herin snorted. "Pzah. What would I do with pretty rolling hills and abundant food?"

Lodie grinned fiercely and hugged Herin tight. The emotions passing across her face were so powerful K'lrsa's knuckles turned white where she gripped Fallion's reins.

"Good luck." K'lrsa's voice cracked and she shook her head slightly, surprised by how sad she felt at the thought of losing them for good.

She didn't even like Herin. Not really. Although…

"I'll miss you," she said, meaning it.

"Pzah." Herin gave her a beady-eyed look, but she couldn't hide the smile that twitched at her lips. "Tell Badru I love him."

"I will."

Herin turned away, Garzel following after, before either of them could embarrass themselves further.

Lodie stepped closer, looking back and forth between K'lrsa and Vedhe. "Don't forget your purpose. Aran must be destroyed. Nothing else matters more than that."

Lodie's gaze lingered on Vedhe, and K'lrsa looked just in time to see Vedhe smooth the annoyance from her face.

She shivered.

How much could she actually trust Vedhe? She'd assumed all this time that Vedhe would help her defeat Aran before anything else, but…Would she? Or did she have plans of her own? What was keeping her from flying Kriger north, towards her home and the man who'd killed her family?

K'lrsa looked back to Lodie, but she'd already turned away.

"I guess it's time." K'lrsa studied her parents and F'lia, trying to memorize every line of their faces. Just in case.

Her father met her eyes. "I have faith in you, K'lrsa."

She nodded, still unsure what that meant. "Thank you. I love you." She looked at each of them in turn, biting her lip to keep from crying more than she already had. "Goodbye. I'll miss you."

They waved as she turned Fallion away.

With three graceful beats of his wings, Fallion launched into the sky, Kriger and Vedhe right behind them as they left the Hidden City and its eternal sunshine.

On the fourth beat of Fallion's wings, they entered the land of the moon dream, the moon shining half-full in the sky above. K'lrsa watched Vedhe, waiting to see if she'd turn Kriger north, towards her own home, but she didn't. Her attention was focused ahead, on the distant mountains where Toreem lay.

As they flew onward, in that world that wasn't a part of the real world, K'lrsa wondered what would happen now.

How powerful would Aran be? Could she trust Vedhe to fight by her side? And what about Badru? Would he turn on her when she tried to destroy the Daliphate? Which was stronger, his love for her or his love for his former home?

And where was M'lara? Was she okay? Or had she pushed too hard with the necklace and injured herself, perhaps fatally?

CHAPTER 54

They stopped at a small cave as the moon set. As always, it had just enough food and water for the horses and humans, but no more. Vedhe prepared a small breakfast for them while K'lrsa tended to the horses, both working in silence.

K'lrsa took the bowl of grains and greens that Vedhe offered and sat down across from her in front of the small fire. Vedhe was silent, her gaze focused on the dancing flames.

"Vedhe? Are you okay?" K'lrsa wanted desperately to ask her about why she hadn't turned north, but she didn't want to put the idea into Vedhe's mind if she hadn't already thought of it.

Vedhe looked at her. Was it her imagination or did Vedhe's eyes have a hint of fire in them?

Vedhe touched the pouch at her waist where the sun orb was, her hand shaking. "It calls to me. It begs to be used. To burn everything."

K'lrsa glanced at the fire. "Did you use it? To start the fire?"

Vedhe nodded.

"And?"

She shuddered. "I didn't want to stop there." She nodded towards the fodder for the horses and the dry grasses that covered the ground where they drowsed. "It would be so easy. To burn it all."

"But you resisted?"

She nodded, but her fingers twitched towards the pouch once more.

K'lrsa licked her lips, nervous. "Maybe…Maybe I should carry it for a while?"

"No!" Vedhe clutched at the pouch. "It's mine."

This time K'lrsa was sure there were flames in Vedhe's eyes. She held her hands out in a calming gesture. "Okay. Sorry I suggested it. I just…I know how powerful that call can be. It's why I have the staff wrapped in all those blankets."

K'lrsa touched the pouch where the moon power was stored, surprised it didn't call to her in the same way. It was different somehow. Powerful, but more…passive.

She needed to understand the weapons they were going to use, but she didn't dare use either one. Not yet. "Vedhe? Do you know anything about the sun orb or the staff? About what they can do? How they were used in the past?"

Vedhe shook her head, her eyes focused once more on the fire. Its flames made the scars on her face twist and change as if alive.

"Vedhe? Look at me."

But Vedhe was lost in the dance of the flames, her hand clutching the pouch at her waist.

K'lrsa watched Vedhe through the rest of the meal, but she never took her eyes from the fire. She didn't even eat, her small bowl sitting forgotten at her side.

Finally, K'lrsa had had enough. She doused the fire with water.

Vedhe glared at her, the fire in her eyes flaring once more, but K'lrsa didn't flinch. She pointed to the bowl of untouched food. "Eat. Rest. We'll move again once the Trickster's time has passed, and keep going until it's too hot to continue. I'm sure the gods will provide another shelter when we need it and we need to catch M'lara before she harms herself."

Vedhe picked up her now-cold food and shoveled it into her mouth in sullen silence. When she was done, she moved to the far side of the cave and lay down. She turned her back on K'lrsa and was soon snoring softly.

K'lrsa placed her sleeping roll as far from the horse fodder and firewood as she could—just in case—and then she too lay down. She fell asleep immediately.

CHAPTER 55

I t was much harder for the horses to walk through the
desert than to fly, so they quickly gave up on the idea of
traveling during the day. K'lrsa used her moon stone to find
another shelter—this one was smaller than the other one,
but cooler, too—and they settled in to wait for moonrise.

K'lrsa tried to sleep again, but she couldn't. It was too
hot and she was too restless. Finally, when she realized that
Vedhe wasn't sleeping either, she sat up and leaned against
the wall, staring across the small space to where Vedhe sat,
the sun orb cradled in her hands.

"Vedhe…"

Vedhe looked at her, flames dancing in her eyes.

"Please put that away. We need to talk."

Vedhe hesitated, but finally she tucked the sun orb back
into its pouch. The flames in her eyes didn't disappear, but
they at least dimmed a bit.

"It's affecting you, you know. I can see it in your eyes."

Vedhe shrugged one shoulder. "It's the side effect of
the sun orb. You take the sun into yourself to use it."

"Can it kill you?"

Vedhe ran her finger along the curved path of a scar
that ran up her arm, refusing to look at K'lrsa or answer.

"Vedhe? Can using the sun orb kill you?"

"Of course it can. Just like using the staff can kill you."

K'lrsa glanced across the cave to where she'd left the

staff, still wrapped in its three layers of blankets. Even this far away and wrapped up, it called to her, longing to be held and used, whispering to her how easily she could turn this dry desert into an oasis. All she had to do was try.

She licked her lips, forcing her attention back to Vedhe. "Is there a way to use them safely?"

"No." Vedhe leaned against the wall, resting her arms on her knees. "It's never safe for a mortal to use that kind of power. Didn't you realize that the first time we were in that room? Every item in there was barbed, designed to eventually punish the mortal who dared to wield the power of a god. They're our lesson when all else fails."

"And yet you keep playing with the orb, even knowing that it can hurt you."

Vedhe touched the pouch where she'd stashed the orb, a small smile on her lips. "I'd rather burn out from the power I wield then ever again be at the mercy of a man like Ivan or Harley or G'van."

"But you're safe right now."

Vedhe didn't answer for a long moment. K'lrsa touched the pouch at her waist, wondering if she was going to need the moon power. And, if so, how to use it.

"Am I?" Vedhe leaned forward, the flames in her eyes flaring just the slightest bit. "What aren't you telling me? What else happened in that room?"

"What are you talking about?" K'lrsa crossed her arms across her chest and leaned back, trying not to look guilty, but from the slight smile on Vedhe's face as she too leaned back, Vedhe wasn't fooled.

"I'm not a fool. Something happened. It's why M'lara took the necklace. And it's what you discussed with your parents and Herin."

"I just wanted their counsel."

"Hm."

K'lrsa bit her lip, thinking. Should she tell Vedhe? It might help. Vedhe knew the dangers of the sun orb. Maybe she knew about the moon power and the staff, too. But…

She sighed. Surprise might be the only advantage she had. She couldn't risk letting Vedhe know. Not yet.

She leaned forward. "What do you think they'll give Aran? Do you think it'll be like the moon power? Something that can defeat us like the moon power can defeat the sun orb? Or do you think it'll be a stronger weapon?"

"Who told you that?"

"What?"

"About the moon power. Who told you it could defeat the sun orb?"

"The Lady. The first time we were there. When I thought you'd choose it, I asked her what I could choose to counteract you and she told me the moon power. It appeared because I asked that question."

Vedhe shook her head. "It won't defeat it."

"It won't? But I thought…" K'lrsa tried to hide her panic as Vedhe shook her head.

"It protects against it. That's different." She narrowed her eyes and studied K'lrsa. "Why did you choose the staff? You had to have other choices. Better choices. What good is the ability to call water in a fight like this one?"

"I don't know. I…I almost chose it the first time. It just seemed to call to me. But the Lady didn't want me to choose it. She kept standing between me and the staff. And so I thought maybe it scared her because it was so powerful, but I don't know why."

"What were your other choices?"

"Just the staff and the moon power." She met Vedhe's eyes. "I almost chose the moon power."

"Why? What good did you think that would do?"

She bit her lip, scared to confront her friend, but she needed to if they were going to succeed. "To stop you. When you go too far. When you turn on the tribes."

Vedhe laughed softly and touched the pouch at her waist once more. "Oh, I don't think it'll come to that."

"No?"

"No. The orb will destroy me long before then."

"*Destroy* you?"

"I told you. They each have their price. And the amount of power I'll need to wield to defeat Aran and destroy all the men with him will kill me."

"And you're okay with that? Why?"

Vedhe shrugged one shoulder. "The Trickster tells me I have to do this if I ever want to go home. It's the only way he'll give me Kriger."

"But you think you're going to die. So why do it?"

She pulled her knees close to her chest, looking as young as she actually was. "I don't want to continue like this. At least if I kill Aran before I die, I'll have done something good with all this pain and rage."

K'lrsa moved closer, staring into Vedhe's eyes. "Is it really that bad for you?"

"Yes." Tears flowed silently down her cheeks. "Every night when I sleep, if the Trickster doesn't come for me, I relive what was done to my family. Or what it felt like to burn as I walked across that desert. Or what G'van did in that tent. It's like being in the labyrinth and facing my deepest fears every single night."

She stared at something K'lrsa couldn't see, shaking. "It comes during the day, too. It's not constant, but… There'll be a moment when I'm not even expecting it, and suddenly I'm back there, watching my home burn or with those men's hands on my body." She shook her head, curling up on herself even more. "I never know when it'll happen. I can't guard against it. It just comes when it wants and then leaves again. I can go days, thinking I'm fine, and then, BAM." She slapped the ground. "It strikes."

K'lrsa reached out a tentative hand to touch her knee. "I'm sorry, Vedhe. I…I didn't realize."

Vedhe shrugged and moved away, breaking the contact. "It's not your fault. It's theirs."

"It'll get better. In time."

Vedhe shook her head. "Maybe for you, but not for me." She turned away from K'lrsa, curled up on her side and pretended to sleep.

K'lrsa slunk back to her own bedroll, wishing she knew what to do to help her friend, but feeling powerless.

She watched Vedhe sleeping. It was her fault Vedhe had been in that tent. That part of her friend's misery was a direct result of K'lrsa's actions and no matter how much time passed or how much she did, she'd never make up for that.

And worse. Now she was taking Vedhe with her to kill Aran—a man she'd never met and didn't care about—and Vedhe fully expected to die because of it.

That, too, was K'lrsa's fault.

But how could she save her? How could she make it all right?

CHAPTER 56

Two days later—after traveling in silence, each lost in their own thoughts—they found Badru in the camp at the edge of the barren lands. The women and children from the Daliphate were gone, moved to safety somewhere else, replaced with Riders from the other tribes mixed in with the former soldiers from the Daliphate.

There wasn't a man or woman in the camp that wasn't bandaged or bruised in some way.

K'lrsa slid from Fallion's back and raced to Badru's side. He had a strip of cloth tied around his upper thigh and a nasty gash on his forehead, but when he smiled her heart skipped a beat like it had the first time they met. "Are you okay?"

He nodded. "We've managed to keep them at bay so far. It hasn't been easy, but we've done it. I'm not sure how much longer we can hold, though."

Vedhe joined them, the sun orb cupped in the palm of her hand. "I can take care of them next time they come."

K'lrsa swallowed, imagining hundreds of soldiers burned to nothing in the space of a breath. Not to mention what it might do to Vedhe to use that kind of power. "Do you think that's wise? I'd hate for you to use it now and not be able to use it against Aran later."

Vedhe looked at K'lrsa for a long moment, her eyes full of fire and darkness—enough to consume the world.

225

K'lrsa shivered as Vedhe tucked the orb back into the pouch at her waist and walked away.

"What was that?" Badru asked.

"Vedhe has the sun orb now. And I have the staff of power. The Lady let us choose new weapons." She glanced around the camp. "Didn't M'lara already tell you? Isn't she here?"

"M'lara? I thought she was with you."

"She was. Until she stole my necklace and escaped. The Lady said she was headed towards you."

"She never made it. Why'd she steal the necklace?"

K'lrsa fought the urge to grab Fallion and keep riding until she found M'lara. The only thing that stopped her was not knowing where to go. Had M'lara made a mistake with the necklace and injured herself? Was she even now trapped in a cave somewhere in the desert, coughing up blood? Or had she continued on? Not wanting to risk Badru or anyone else stopping her.

She wasn't that foolish, was she? Then again, she was K'lrsa's sister and K'lrsa had been that foolish not so long ago…

K'lrsa shoved thoughts of M'lara to the side. She couldn't do anything about her right now and thinking about her little sister would destroy her if she let it.

She needed to rest and plan. They'd only have one chance to defeat Aran.

She looked to Badru. "Do you know where Aran is? Is he with his troops or in Toreem?"

"No. I don't know."

"We need to. Can you send scouts? We have to act before Aran has a chance to master his new powers."

"New powers? What are you talking about?"

She stared into his beautiful blue eyes. So much had happened since she last saw him in the cave. He needed to know, but she didn't have it in her to tell him. Not just yet.

She squeezed his arm. "Can I tell you everything after I've eaten a hot meal and had a chance to sleep for a bit?"

He frowned but pointed her towards a tent on the far side of the camp. "Sure. You can sleep in my tent. I'll have one of the men bring you some food."

"Thank you."

She kissed him on the cheek. It probably wasn't fair to leave him in the dark like that, but she still hadn't decided how much she was going to tell him. She wanted to trust him, but… could she?

Her gut was screaming at her that she needed to trust both Vedhe and Badru if they were going to have any hope of defeating Aran. But at the same time the only way to stay in control was to keep the existence of the moon power to herself. And as much as she'd been through with both of them, she wasn't sure she could let go enough to tell them everything.

She sighed.

She was so tired…

She just hoped the gods left her alone while she slept. She needed rest, not more of their interference.

CHAPTER 57

Of course, as soon as K'lrsa fell asleep she found herself in the moon dream.

She wasn't in the desert this time. She was in the midst of the barren lands, the earth blackened and dead all around her, pools of stagnant water that reeked of decay dotting the landscape. The whole place was gray and oppressive. Fog drifted along the ground, wrapping itself around her legs like a living, breathing nightmare.

Cursing the gods, she kicked at the skull of an animal unfortunate, stupid, or desperate enough to drink the tainted water.

A shrill giggle filled the air around her.

"Show yourself, you little brat," she yelled, looking in all directions for the Trickster.

Because of course that's who had summoned her here. Who else would spend any more time in this horrid place than they had to?

He stepped out of the grayness, this time in the shape of an old man, twisted and bent. But he still had the same fat belly as his child form.

It occurred to her that the Lady hid behind her beauty, Father Sun behind his fierce warrior nature, and the Trickster behind his vicious cruelty. Masks, all of them. That hid a rotten core.

She glared at him. "What do *you* want, little man?"

"Oh-oh. Forgotten that you should respect the gods, have you?" He capered closer, his maze-like eyes studying her face. "Think you can do it all yourself now? Protect your people? Keep them healthy and safe? Feed them even in the worst of times?"

She shook her head. "I never said that. I just want a decent night's sleep without one of you traipsing through and telling me what I have to do."

"Oh. I see." He raised one eyebrow in amusement. "Have my parents been bothering you again? My apologies. They get bored so easily. When you've been here as long as we have, it gets harder and harder to find anything entertaining in the day-to-day lives of you short-lived little creatures."

"Then move on."

"And lose? No."

"Lose what?"

He tilted his head to the side, studying her. "The battle, of course."

"What battle?"

He shook his head as if disappointed. "Surely you know by now we aren't the only gods."

"Yes. I've figured that out. Aran has his death walker gods and Vedhe has something, I'm not quite sure what."

"Oh there are many others besides them. Hundreds."

"And you're all at war with one another?"

"War? No, no, no. That would be too much effort." He grinned, showing blackened teeth. "It's more…a battle of the minds. Like one of your little games you like to play around the fire. Except you, my dear girl, and others like you, are our pieces. And there are no rules. Other than the balance." He eyed her shrewdly. "Unless you're my clever mother, of course."

"Why? What did she do?"

He laughed, rubbing his hands together in glee. "*She* took the playing board and threw it in the air. All the pieces are scattered now. Every carefully made plan, every stratagem and trick—some that have been in the making for hundreds of years—gone in a flash."

"Just because I took an extra object?"

"*Two* extra objects. And, no. Not because of that. That was more like you stomping on the board after it had been overturned already." He rubbed his hands together, grinning. "No. Your re-entering the room at all upset the balance. And when you chose the weapons you did?"

He chortled. "Between you and my chosen one, you brought back the three most powerful objects that have ever existed. In one day. On one side of the battle!" He wiggled with glee. "The others are beside themselves. They don't know what to do."

"Vedhe thinks they'll give Aran the power to stand against us. So that the balance can be maintained."

"Oh, Aran's gods will give him power alright. That's a certainty. Already have. The question is…What will all the other gods do?"

She stared at him. Hundreds of gods, he'd said. How many sides were there to this battle?

His eyes lit up with excitement. "They're scrambling right now. Gods that haven't spoken in a thousand thousand years are reaching out to one another, trying to form alliances and debate strategies. All the lines are being redrawn. Every single one!"

"And you're happy about this?"

"Things haven't been this exciting since we first arrived here."

K'lrsa glared at him, hating him and the Lady and Father Sun.

She wished they'd just go away. Better to stumble through alone than be subject to the whim of the gods.

As if reading her thoughts, he leaned closer. "You do need us, you know. The tribes rely on their gods more than most. You can't survive the desert without us."

She didn't want to admit he was right, so instead she asked, "What are they going to do? These other gods?"

"Ahhh. That *is* the question. Do they give more power to their own people so they can stand against you or Aran, whoever wins? But if they do, then how does it ever stop? It'd take millennia to achieve balance again. And what if someone grows bold enough to challenge them? To take on the gods themselves?"

"Is that possible?"

The Trickster looked at her closely, first with his left eye, then with his right, like a strange, broken bird. "Why do you ask? Do you want to challenge the gods?"

"Just curious." But she watched his face with an intensity she couldn't hide.

He stepped closer, narrowing his eyes. "Hmmm. Do you really dislike me that much, little one?"

She snorted. "No. I don't care about you. I care about my parents who are trapped right now in the Hidden City because Father Sun is holding them captive to a vow I didn't mean."

"Ohhh…." He peered at her again. "So you'd challenge my father, would you?"

He laughed merrily and danced away. "That would be worth seeing!"

K'lrsa turned away, disgusted. "Why am I even here? Why isn't Vedhe here? She's your chosen one, isn't she?"

"True…And she needs me to keep the nightmares away. But you're the one it all hinges on."

"What do you mean by that?"

He stepped closer, lowering his voice. "What kind of world do you want to live in, K'lrsa dan V'na of the White Horse Tribe?"

"What kind of world? What are you talking about?"

"Do you want to live in a world where people like you and Vedhe and Aran have the power to kill thousands with a mere flick of the wrist?" He wiggled his eyebrows. "Or do you want to live in the world you grew up in, one where food is always scarce and death a close companion, but people are too powerless and concerned with their own survival to bother much with threatening yours?"

"Isn't there some other choice? Maybe one where food is plentiful and death comes at old age and I don't have to worry about someone taking what I have away?"

He tilted his head to the side. "No…Not really. That stage never lasts. A couple hundred years at most. No more."

K'lrsa backed away. "Why are you even asking me this? I thought it was out of my control now. We already took the objects and we can't put them back."

"Mmm…You might be surprised." He leaned closer. "We gods are a conservative bunch for the most part. We don't like change. Not like this. Most of the gods are sitting back, waiting to see what you do. You and Vedhe and Badru."

He stepped back. "See, the question is this: Will you use the objects to defeat Aran—who really was becoming a bit too much with his overuse of that death walker magic— and then give them up after? Or will you cling to them, desperate to protect yourselves at any cost?"

"If we give them up?"

"Then the world goes back to what it was before."

"And if we keep them?"

He held his arms out, shrugging. "Then I sit back and watch as the gods scramble to create the most powerful object they can imagine, each one creating an object more powerful than the last until…" He shrugged again. "I don't know. Death? Destruction? Perhaps a new balance with everyone that much more powerful than before. The world stable once more but on a smaller pivot point, waiting for another Aran to come along and wreck it all?"

K'lrsa shivered. "I have no interest in keeping the power after Aran's defeated. I just want to be left alone. And for my parents to be able to move on to the Promised Plains."

He pursed his lips, studying her. "Can you say the same for your companions? Will a man like Badru, who knows the preventative value of superior strength, be willing to let go? And what about Vedhe? Can she give up the only power she has after being made to feel so powerless for so long? Especially when her enemies still walk the earth?"

K'lrsa shivered, wondering if either of her friends would give up their weapons, even knowing the destruction it might cause if they kept them.

She was afraid she knew the answer already.

The Trickster shrugged and turned away. "So there you have it. The world is watching you K'lrsa dan V'na of the White Horse Tribe. Don't let us down."

As the fog swirled closer, hiding his form, he added. "Oh! Almost forgot—Aran is in Toreem. But not sure that matters, because his army will be attacking your camp before the sun sets. And they have ten times more men than you do. Should be fun!" He disappeared with one final cackling laugh.

CHAPTER 58

K'lrsa jolted awake, the Trickster's laughter still echoing in her head. It was past midday already. The Daliph's troops would be attacking soon. She had to warn Badru.

But first she called to Vedhe, who was curled up asleep on the other side of the tent. "Vedhe. Get up."

Vedhe sat up, already reaching for her clothes. "The Trickster just told me. Aran's men are coming."

"Did he tell you they have ten times as many men as we do?"

"It doesn't matter. Between the orb and the staff they won't be able to stand against us."

In the murky light of the tent, Vedhe's eyes danced with flames.

"I'm not sure we should use them, though." K'lrsa finished dressing and reluctantly grabbed the staff before leading the way out of the tent.

"Why not? Why would you let even one Rider risk injury if we can defeat them with our weapons?"

"I think this is a test." She pushed her way through camp, looking for Badru. "Or a challenge. Herin said every time we use the objects they'll change us. So what if Aran is trying to force us to use them before we fight him so we're too weak to defeat him when the time comes?"

There was no sign of the approaching soldiers, but it was only a matter of time before they arrived. K'lrsa spotted

Badru at the edge of camp and turned towards him.

Vedhe trotted at her side. "If we can defeat Aran's soldiers, we should."

They reached Badru. He was directing a group digging a ditch between the barren lands and the camp. "Rested?" he asked, smiling.

"Hardly."

He looked back and forth between them. "What? What is it?"

"The Trickster came to us in our dreams. He said Aran's soldiers are going to be here before sunset and that they have ten times more men than we do." K'lrsa glanced at the ditch. "What's that for?"

"Not much at the moment. I was hoping we'd have another day or two to finish it. Once it was deep enough we were going to put sharpened sticks in it and then cover it over with cloth and some dirt. I was hoping the soldiers wouldn't see it and they'd fall in."

"Killing their horses?"

He nodded.

K'lrsa grimaced.

"Better than my men."

"I know. I just don't like it. What did those horses ever do to anyone?"

Badru started to laugh, but stopped when he realized how serious she was.

Vedhe pulled out the sun orb. "We don't need that. Or anyone else. We can defeat them with this. And with the staff." She glared at K'lrsa. "If you ever bother to unwrap it."

K'lrsa glanced at the bundle in her hands. "I don't trust it. It calls to me."

"As the sun orb calls to me. They were made to be used." Flames danced in Vedhe's eyes, and K'lrsa shivered as she pictured Vedhe using the orb on living, breathing men. Men with families and children and homes to return to.

"Maybe we can scare them away. Do you think you can set a path of flame before them? Or maybe I can cause the river to overflow and block their path?"

"Scare them? They'll just come back later. We have to

stop them. Now."

"Vedhe…"

Vedhe shook her head in disgust. "If you don't want to use the power you chose, then don't. I can do this myself."

Badru looked back and forth between them and K'lrsa realized she hadn't told him about the nature of the objects. Or what Vedhe had been like on their trip from the Hidden City. Or the balance. Or her dream. Or any of it.

"No. I'll do it. Save the sun orb for Aran."

Worst case scenario, K'lrsa could still use the moon power against Aran, whatever good it would do.

She unwrapped the staff, peeling back each layer slowly, reluctantly. It throbbed with power, begging to be used, to call the stream and turn it into a mighty river that would rage so fierce none could cross it.

She sighed as she removed the last layer and gripped the smooth wooden surface. "Like you pointed out, I'm not sure how I'd use the staff in Toreem anyway."

"Toreem?" Badru asked. "What makes you think we need to go all the way there?"

"The Trickster told me that's where Aran is." She stepped past him and stood in front of Vedhe, trying to get her attention. "Vedhe? Did you hear me? I'll use the staff. You can put the sun orb away now."

Vedhe stared into the barren lands, her fingers white where they clutched the orb, her eyes full of fire.

"Vedhe?" She poked Vedhe's arm.

Vedhe raised her fist, the orb in her hand alight with red fire.

"Vedhe! What are you doing?" She stepped back, hands raised, wondering how to defend herself against fire. "I'm not your enemy."

Vedhe's arm shook as she struggled to lower the orb. She stared at K'lrsa, eyes wide with fear as fire spat from her hand.

Slowly—too slowly—she brought her hand back down and shoved the orb into the pouch at her waist.

"Vedhe?" K'lrsa stepped closer, trying to meet her friend's eyes. "Are you okay?"

Vedhe nodded, but wouldn't look at her. "It wants to be used…" she muttered.

"I know. But not until we confront Aran, okay?"

Vedhe didn't answer. Her fingers were still twitching towards the pouch. K'lrsa gripped her hand to stop her from taking it up again.

Badru came closer. "Maybe we should hide it away until we get there."

"No!" Vedhe turned on him. "It's mine. I won't give it up."

"Okay. Sorry." Badru backed away, hands up. "It was just a suggestion."

"Vedhe? Are you okay now?" K'lrsa asked.

Vedhe nodded. "I have it under control."

But her hands still twitched towards the pouch at her belt and flames still danced in her eyes. K'lrsa flicked a glance at Badru and he stepped closer, taking Vedhe's elbow and pulling her to the side. "Here. Come with me. We don't want to get caught by whatever K'lrsa's about to do."

Vedhe resisted at first, but then she let him lead her away.

One of the Riders digging the ditch shouted and pointed towards the barren lands.

There, just on the horizon, was the first sign of Aran's soldiers. Ten men across, they appeared, marching forward in precise lines. Row after row after row of them.

K'lrsa shivered as she gripped the staff tighter. She didn't want to do this. But she had to. Vedhe was right. Why risk the Riders when they had the power to defeat the soldiers without risking a single life?

She moved towards the stream.

If this failed…

She shivered, picturing what it would be like for Vedhe to release the fire that burned inside her with so many men so close. In the throes of the sun orb's power, she wouldn't know friend from foe.

K'lrsa had to succeed. For everyone's sake.

CHAPTER 59

K'lrsa walked towards the stream, her hands so sweaty she could barely hold the staff, her legs jittery with fear. She tried to find the Rider's version of the Core, but it was elusive, just out of reach.

The closer they got to the water, the more the power of the staff beat against her mind, demanding to be used. The stream was about four paces across and knee-deep at its deepest. It provided a nice source of water to drink and maybe wash off, but it certainly wasn't enough to keep an army at bay.

How was she going to turn something so small and peaceful into the raging torrent she'd need to defeat Aran's men?

Was it even possible?

She had to try.

Or else Vedhe would send fire into their ranks. And maybe the Riders' as well.

She shuddered as she imagined men burning, their flesh blackened and twisted, while Vedhe smiled, wielding death and destruction upon them.

K'lrsa stopped at the stream bank, her feet sinking into the mud at the water's edge. She glanced to where Badru and Vedhe stood, watching her, waiting to see what she could do.

She planted the staff in the water and closed her eyes, letting her awareness settle on the spot where her palms

met the wood of the staff, following the well of power she sensed down the staff's length to the ground.

She traced the stream in her mind's eye, following its meandering path northward towards where a great body of water lay. She could draw that water to her, bring it crashing down the length of the stream, building it ever higher until it was powerful enough to destroy her enemies.

But it was too far away to call in the time she had.

She moved her awareness away from the stream, seeking in all directions for any other source of water she could use.

The barren lands were like dark sludge and she shied away from their seeping poison, looking elsewhere.

Down. Deep, deep, down in the earth, she found a vast pool of water that had gathered over the ages one slow drip at a time. Still and silent, it called to her.

And she called to it.

She pulled the water from its hidden home, straining as she brought it through layer after layer of earth, carving a path to the surface.

She braced herself with the staff as the ground erupted at her feet, thousands of years' worth of dirt and rocks shoved aside to make room for the geyser of water she'd called from the depths of the earth.

It shot upward into the sky, answering her call, responding to the power of the staff. Water that had trickled and flowed through cracks and fissures over thousands of years came to the surface in just a few heartbeats, unstoppable and overwhelming in its force.

Distantly, she heard screams. Aran's men or her own, she didn't know, she was too lost in the power of the staff, in the communion with the water that rushed through the rent she'd made in the earth.

The water shot high into the air and then plummeted back down at her command. She directed it towards the approaching soldiers and it crashed through their ranks like a giant fist, sending men flying in all directions like pebbles strewn by a careless hand.

None could stand against it.

The power of the staff filled her, vibrating through every part of her body, demanding more. It wanted her to reach for that distant water to the north, to call it to her and drown this dark and barren place in life-giving water.

Aran's soldiers—those who could still move—fled back the way they'd come.

But she didn't let go of the staff.

She couldn't.

A small part of her desperately wanted to stop, but the call of the staff was too powerful.

She reached for that vast, endless stretch of water to the north…

Someone wrenched the staff out of her hands and flung it to the ground. She cried out, dropping to her knees, crawling after it through the mud and what little remained of the stream.

Distantly she could hear Badru screaming her name as he pulled her back, trying to keep her from reaching the staff again.

She fought him, desperate to renew that connection, to feel that power once more, but he wrapped her in his arms and pinned her to the ground.

She sobbed.

She was hollow, empty inside. Dead.

She needed the staff. It made her whole.

She fought Badru once again, kicking and biting and elbowing him. Screaming for him to let her go. But he held on, refusing to release her.

"I hate you."

"Stop, K'lrsa. You did it. It's enough. Let it go now."

Vedhe stepped around them and wrapped the staff back up in its three layers of blankets. She took it away, walking back towards camp.

With each step the call of the staff faded.

K'lrsa lay there, gasping, still wanting the staff, but no longer overwhelmed by her need for it. Slowly, she calmed herself.

"It's okay, Badru. You can let me go."

"Can I?"

"Vedhe has the staff. And the sun orb. I'm sure she can keep me from taking it back."

He let her up, wiping the worst of the mud from his arms. She was covered in it. It clung to her face and her hair and her clothes. She moved towards the stream to wash the worst of it off, but the stream was gone.

She clutched her arms across her stomach as she studied the carnage she'd wrought.

The ground was buckled and broken, like a giant had crumpled it in his fist. Aran's soldiers were scatted everywhere. Or at least their bodies were. Bent and broken. Some buried in mud. A hand stuck out of the earth a few paces away, but no other sign of the soldier remained.

A few paces beyond that a man lay, his body twisted at an angle that shouldn't be possible, his eyes frozen open in horror.

K'lrsa shook uncontrollably. "How many did I kill?"

"A lot."

"Enough?"

Badru nodded.

K'lrsa turned towards the Riders' camp. The destruction there was less, but her own hadn't been spared. The trench Badru's men had been building was full of water, a man in Rider's garb floating facedown in the center.

K'lrsa buried her face in Badru's soldier. "What have I done?"

She'd never wanted to kill. She'd just wanted to hunt and ride Fallion and spend time with her family.

But in this one moment, this one day, she'd killed more men than anyone she knew had ever killed.

And worse.

Even now, even seeing what she'd done, she longed to hold the staff and call that distant water from the north down upon them. To drown the world and cleanse it.

She couldn't be trusted to use the staff again.

She'd kill them all.

CHAPTER 60

K'lrsa stumbled through the wreckage of the camp, Badru by her side. Even though Vedhe had the staff and it was wrapped in three layers of blankets and on the other side of camp, it called to her, telling her where even the smallest drop of water was and how easy it would be to gather that water to herself and use it.

A Rider ran up to them, her head bleeding from a nasty gash. "Badru."

"Report."

"Five dead. They were in the trench when the…" She glanced sidelong at K'lrsa. "When whatever it was struck. We rescued two, but were too late to save the others."

K'lrsa shuddered. She'd thought using the staff would save lives, but it hadn't. She'd killed those Riders. Her. It was her fault they were dead. They might've survived a battle, but how were they supposed to stand against a raging torrent of water?

Badru squeezed her hand, but kept his attention focused on the Rider. "Any others dead?"

The Rider shook her head. "No. But we have a lot of injuries. A few broken legs or arms, some cuts. If the soldiers come back we won't be in any position to stand against them."

Vedhe, who'd just joined them, answered, "They won't come back. And if they do, I'll handle them."

The Rider looked back and forth between K'lrsa and Vedhe her eyes wide with fear.

"Thank you." Badru rested a hand on her shoulder as he spoke, and she visibly relaxed. "I appreciate the report. Now, go. Take care of that cut."

The Rider ran away after one last frightened look at them.

K'lrsa winced, but it was to be expected, wasn't it? She was a monster. Look what she'd done. Without even trying.

Badru squeezed her hand one last time before moving away from her to issue orders. He walked through the camp with ease, like he belonged there, and everywhere he went people listened and acted, newcomer and Rider alike. Calm spread from him like ripples in a pool, and soon the camp fell into order once more, the panic that had tinged the air fading away.

"How does he do that?" K'lrsa asked Vedhe.

"Do what?"

"Command them like that. He's new to the tribes. Why do they listen to him?"

"It's only natural to listen to someone who speaks with certainty in a moment of panic. Most are good at following orders, but few can lead, especially at a time like this."

K'lrsa nodded. It made sense. But still she was amazed by how easily Badru asserted control, and how calm he remained as he walked among the broken remnants of the camp.

"What did you do with the staff?" K'lrsa asked.

"I put it in the tent. But you should keep it with you. What if someone takes it?"

"Let them. I never want to touch it again."

"But it's yours. It was given to *you* by the gods. They expect you to use it."

"You don't understand, Vedhe. It calls to me. It wants me to drown the entire world. To cleanse it. Do you know how close I was to calling water from the north and killing us all?"

Vedhe touched the pouch at her waist, her eyes burning with fire.

"Does the sun orb call to you like that?"

"All the time."

"How do you resist it?"

"I don't." The flames danced in her eyes. "I promise it that soon I'll do as it wishes and rain fire on the world."

K'lrsa shuddered. "You can't do that, Vedhe."

"Why not?"

"Because…Because it isn't right. We need to defeat Aran. But then…These things need to go back where they came from. We aren't strong enough to keep them. And what if they fall into the wrong hands? What would a man like Aran do with something like the orb?"

Vedhe laughed. "You're worried about Aran?" She looked around at the destruction in the camp and then back to K'lrsa. "You should be worried about us."

Vedhe stalked away before K'lrsa could respond, but she was right. Look what one of those weapons had done when it was used one time by someone who wasn't evil, who'd just been trying to protect her people.

K'lrsa shivered imagining what it would be like when Vedhe used the orb.

Or worse, if they didn't return the objects to the Hidden City and the world descended into a chaos of ever-more-powerful weapons handled by more and more humans who weren't strong enough to control them. Forget how precarious the balance would be with so many weapons loose on the world; each weapon, every single one, would create an opportunity for something like this to happen.

For a single person to kill hundreds—or thousands—with no more than a thought.

She couldn't let that happen. The weapons had to go back.

After they'd defeated Aran.

She just hoped they could last that long without destroying the world.

CHAPTER 61

That night, Badru, Vedhe, and K'lrsa sat around a campfire far removed from the rest of the camp. It wasn't intentional, at least not on their part. But as the others had cleaned up the camp and replaced their tents, each had made the choice to move away from Badru's tent.

Not because of him, obviously—they all adored him—but because of K'lrsa. And Vedhe.

Throughout the last bit of the day as K'lrsa and Vedhe had tried to help, the others had avoided them, shying away, finding excuses to be elsewhere or doing something else until finally K'lrsa had turned away in disgust and defeat.

As they ate dinner that night—a tasteless meal of grain past its prime and a few straggly bitter greens that were almost too bitter to be edible—they were silent, each lost in their own thoughts. K'lrsa had already filled Badru in on everything that had happened in the Hidden City, so they were all thinking of what needed to happen next.

Finally, Badru broke the silence. "We need to find M'lara first. Where do you think she is?"

"If she's alive…" K'lrsa grimaced and set the remainder of her food on the ground. She wasn't hungry enough to force it down. "I assume she's on her way to Aran. Although, how she knows where to go…"

"The Trickster." Vedhe added another stick to the fire, smiling as the flames danced higher.

K'lrsa shivered, wondering how much worse she'd be after she'd used the sun orb on Aran and his men. "You think he visited her in her dreams, too?"

"Why not?"

K'lrsa licked her lips, not wanting to state the petty thought that crossed her mind, but it had to be said. "She's not a chosen of the gods like we are."

"You think there can only be three? One for each god?"

"Yes. Don't the horses prove that?"

Vedhe shrugged a shoulder and her lips twisted into a half-smile. "Perhaps M'lara is the chosen of the Moon Maiden, the Lady's daughter."

"But she already passed on. The others gods forced her to leave."

Badru leaned forward, interrupting their conversation. "So we think she's headed to Toreem? Okay. Then we go there and find her before we confront Aran."

"Why? I mean, I want to find my sister as much as anyone, but shouldn't defeating Aran be our priority? Especially now that he's going to be even more powerful than before?"

"No. We need that necklace."

K'lrsa shook her head. "It won't make a difference, Badru. I'm telling you, compared to the power of the staff, or the sun orb, that necklace is nothing."

"It may be nothing, but I need a weapon if I'm going to stand with you. Even one as weak as the necklace."

"You can have the staff. I'm not touching it again."

"But then you'll need the necklace."

K'lrsa touched the pouch at her waist. Should she tell them about the moon power?

"K'lrsa, you can't face Aran without a weapon. We need the necklace."

She ignored him. "Vedhe? You said the moon power can't actually defeat the sun orb. What *does* it do?"

"What does that matter now? Aran's gods won't give him a power like that."

K'lrsa bit her lip as she looked back and forth between them.

She was probably about to make a mistake, but she couldn't trust herself to wield the staff a second time, so she needed to learn about the power she could wield. And her gut told her she had to trust them. If she didn't, they'd fail.

She reached into the pouch and held out the small container of moon power.

"What is that?" Vedhe leaned closer, peering at it.

"The moon power."

Vedhe sat back, staring at K'lrsa in alarm. "Where did you get it?"

"From the room at the center of the labyrinth. The Lady let me take both."

Vedhe lurched to her feet and then slowly sat back down. "Why would you do that? Didn't you...?" She shook her head in disbelief.

"The Lady told me I could do it. I only had the two choices—the staff and the moon power—and I couldn't decide between them, so I asked if I could have them both, and she said yes."

Vedhe stared at the small container, her mouth slightly open, her eyes wide with horror.

"What? What is it?"

"The balance..." Vedhe reached towards the container and then pulled her hand back as if burned. "I thought it was bad before, but this...Do you know what you've done?"

"I think so. After what you said when I kept the necklace, I have a pretty good idea."

Vedhe shook her head. "No. This is so much worse."

"Well, that's why, when we're done with Aran, we *have* to take all of the objects back to the Hidden City."

"And do what with them?"

"Return them. That's what the Trickster told me. He said the other gods are waiting to see what we do. If we keep them, the other gods will create weapons to match them. But if we return them, they won't. They're waiting on us right now."

Vedhe continued to stare at the container, shaking her head slightly.

K'lrsa put it away. "So? What can it do? Because I can't

touch the staff again without drowning the world. Which means Badru will have to use it."

Vedhe turned her attention to Badru, studying him. "Is that wise?"

He snorted. "Is letting you handle the sun orb wise?"

"Stop. Both of you. We need to stand together against Aran. Unless there's someone else you'd trust more to handle the orb and the staff? Because I can't think of anyone."

They both shook their heads, but they were eyeing one another warily.

"So? What does the moon power do if it doesn't defeat the sun orb?"

"It neutralizes it."

"Isn't that defeating it?"

"No. It just protects you against its power. It doesn't stop it from working. Or protect anyone else from its use."

K'lrsa winced. "That doesn't seem like much."

"It is. If I tried to use the sun orb on you, I'd fail."

"What if you used the sun orb to set the building I was in on fire?"

"It can't protect you against something like that. But any power Aran has, if he tries to direct it at you, will fail."

"Unless it's like the staff, right? Because that calls water and it can't protect me against water." She sighed. "Hardly seems worth it."

Badru shook his head. "No. Think about it. What kind of weapon is Aran likely to choose? Something offensive, something he can attack you with. He won't want to call water or shake the earth. He'll want to attack you directly. Which means it is valuable for this fight. More valuable than the staff."

He narrowed his eyes.

"No, Badru."

"What?"

"You can't have it."

"Why not?"

"Because there's no way I'm touching that staff again, which means that you need to be the one to use it, and that leaves me with the moon power."

"And what about the necklace?"

"I told you. It won't matter." She sat back. "I'd love to find my sister, but, wherever she is, she's on her own. We don't have time to find her and we couldn't use the necklace even if we did."

Vedhe threw another stick in the fire. "It doesn't matter. None of it does."

"What are you talking about?"

"It's too late. When you took the moon power and the staff, you destroyed the balance. Nothing we do can save it now."

K'lrsa shook her head. "That's not true. The Lady said nothing can destroy the balance. It always restores itself."

Vedhe laughed softly. "Maybe it does eventually. But not every creature survives the process. The gods will, but we won't."

"But we're only going to use them once and then return them."

Vedhe stroked the pouch at her waist.

"Vedhe? You agree with me, right? We use them once to defeat Aran and destroy the Toreem Daliphate, and then we're done. We take them back to the Hidden City."

"Right. Why keep the only weapon we have to stand against evil? What was I thinking?" She stalked away into the darkness, her shoulders stiff with anger.

"Vedhe…" K'lrsa called after her, but she didn't turn back to them and K'lrsa let her go.

Badru was studying the fire, his brow furrowed. What did he think? Did he agree with Vedhe? Would he be able to use the staff once and then let it go? Could he give up that kind of power once he had it?

She tried to imagine the upcoming battle—with Vedhe burning everything and Badru flooding everything and her there in the middle trying to stop them—and shuddered.

She wanted to take the objects back to the Hidden City now, before it was too late.

But she couldn't.

Aran had to be defeated. No matter the cost.

CHAPTER 62

They left camp the next morning. No need to slink and scurry like they had when they'd fled Toreem. They had the power of the staff and sun orb and even if they didn't use them, word of what they could do would spread before them like wildfire.

That was obvious when they rode out of the barren lands and into the camp of Aran's soldiers just as the sun set. Men eyed them warily, some bandaged and still dirty from the mud that had washed them down when K'lrsa unleashed the staff's power.

Badru rode Midnight into their midst as K'lrsa and Vedhe hung back. He spun Midnight in a circle so that he could make eye contact with every man willing to do so. They were sullen and angry, but none spoke out against him.

"Listen to me, soldiers of the Toreem Daliphate. My name is Badru Palero. I was Daliph of the Toreem Daliphate until Aran Palero, my grandfather, took my throne from me. He is a death walker who was brought back to life by infernal means after he was poisoned by the slave known as Lodie. I'm riding to Toreem to defeat him."

K'lrsa bit her lip as she watched him, sitting tall and proud on Midnight as he addressed the soldiers. How had she allowed herself to believe that he'd walk away from this?

That he'd agree to live in a tent, with barely enough food to eat, and give up his power for her? He may have given his life to help her and her people, but to live out his days in the tribes? Why would he do that when he could be a Daliph instead?

The men mumbled to one another, but none spoke.

Badru circled Midnight once more, staring them down. His voice swelled with power and he sat up straighter. "Hear this. Any who strike at the tribes from this day forth, I will destroy. They are your allies. You need them to cross the desert. They give you access to the trade that has raised you above what you were."

He met the eyes of the men once more. "Do you really want to go back to the way it was before? To squabbling amongst one another for scraps? To being the main source of slaves for the other Daliphana? No? Then leave the tribes alone."

A man stepped forward. He had a multi-colored sash tied at his waist, marking him as one in favor with the Daliph and likely an officer. "If we don't follow the Daliph's orders, he'll have us killed."

Men nodded to one another.

"And if you do, *I'll* have you killed." Badru touched the staff where it was bundled to his saddle.

Vedhe nudged her horse forward and pulled the sun orb from the pouch at her waist. "You saw the power of the staff yesterday." She held the orb above her head, her hand shaking as it pulsed with an angry red light. "But it's not our only weapon. You might survive a flood, but will you survive fire?"

A man scoffed from the back of the crowd and Vedhe turned on him, eyes burning with flames. The orb spat fire as Vedhe struggled to control it.

"Enough. Vedhe, put that away." K'lrsa rode Fallion between Vedhe and the man, not sure what she was actually going to do if Vedhe didn't back down. She turned to the crowd. "We will defeat Aran. Be sure of it."

Slowly, struggling to do so, Vedhe put the sun orb back in its pouch.

K'lrsa looked at the leader. Did he believe them?

He needed to. Because the tribes couldn't stand against these men if they attacked again. And if they did attack, it wouldn't matter that she'd defeated Aran if the tribes were decimated.

Before they'd left the Rider camp, Badru had issued the order to leave the entrance to the barren lands unprotected. There wasn't enough food, the stream was dry, and they couldn't stand against so many soldiers.

But by the time they'd left, no one had moved on. And they didn't look like they would.

These soldiers needed to believe them. It was the only way to protect her people.

The moon appeared on the horizon and K'lrsa leaned forward, stroking Fallion's neck. She whispered in his ear. "Transform for me, *micora*. Please. Show them your beautiful wings."

Nothing happened for a long moment and then Fallion shivered, and the light of a thousand suns rippled under his coat as his beautiful wings stretched out from his back in glorious challenge.

He reared onto his back legs as K'lrsa let out the ki-ki-ki of the Rider's call, drawing the attention of any who hadn't noticed them yet.

As Fallion returned to all fours, Kriger and Midnight transformed as well—Kriger's coat the misty silver of the Trickster's fog and Midnight's coat seeming to encompass the entire night sky.

The soldiers backed away, whispering and pointing, some in awe, some in fear.

All except the one who'd spoken before.

He stepped closer, reaching for Midnight. "May I?" he asked.

Badru nodded and the man reverently touched one of Midnight's ebony wings. "I'd heard the rumors, but I didn't believe them."

"Well now you know the truth of it. And when I tell you that we'll defeat Aran, I mean it. I'm not asking you to follow me. All I ask is that you don't fight me."

The man nodded once and stood back. "Very well. I'll give you five days. If we haven't heard of your victory by then, we'll have to attack the tribes again."

"Thank you." Badru nodded once. He looked at the men in the camp, quietly judging them before he turned to K'lrsa and Vedhe. "Ready?"

"Ready," they answered in unison.

Midnight launched into the air, Kriger and Fallion right behind him.

K'lrsa watched the soldiers' camp until they were so far away the men looked like ants. She hoped they'd keep their word and wait, but there was nothing to be done about it now.

Either they would or they wouldn't. Either she'd have a tribe to return to or they'd be gone.

She turned her attention forward, towards Toreem and Aran, hoping Badru was right and they really could defeat him.

Because if they couldn't…

And he now had more power than before…

No one would be able to stop him.

CHAPTER 63

They flew through the night and found a rundown barn to sleep in as the moon set. Badru wanted them to travel during the day as well, but K'lrsa refused. She wasn't willing to expose Vedhe to any more of the Daliphana than she had to, not with the way her eyes constantly danced with flame.

Plus, she didn't want to face Aran on what little sleep she could find during the Trickster's time. This was going to be hard enough as is. No need to add exhausted and confused to their list of challenges.

Badru tried to tempt her with finding M'lara, but K'lrsa refused to consider it. Her little sister was probably lost somewhere, hopefully safe, but she couldn't let herself hope that they'd find her in Toreem. Because if they didn't find her there, K'lrsa would be devastated, and she needed to have all of her focus if she hoped to stand against Aran.

As they settled down to sleep—Badru snuggled up against her back, his arm thrown around her waist—K'lrsa had to ask about the speech he'd made. "Badru…You told those men you were going to Toreem to defeat the Daliph."

"Mmhm." He nuzzled her neck, but she swatted him away. This was not the time or place for that.

"You…You talked to them like you were their leader."

He rolled away, sighing.

"What?" She turned to look at him.

"Did you listen to my words, K'lrsa? Did you actually listen to them?"

"Yes."

"Then you should know that I never claimed to be their leader." His brilliant blue eyes pierced her like a knife.

"But you said you were going to defeat Aran."

"And I am. We are."

"And…"

"That's all I said, K'lrsa. I could've told them I was their rightful Daliph. That they should follow my orders because when I defeated Aran I was going to be their ruler. I didn't." He held her gaze. "Because I won't be. I know how you feel about the Daliphana. And I know how I feel about you."

He tucked a strand of hair behind her ear. "I want to be with you, K'lrsa. I love you. More than the Daliphate, more than my life. Haven't I already proven that to you?"

She bit her lip. "Yes, but…I don't know. I figured…If you had the chance."

"I don't want that life back, K'lrsa. I want you."

"You're really okay living in a tent, never having a home, and eating bad food for the rest of your life?"

He laughed. "The food's not that bad. Wild-caught hare is actually quite good. And who knows what will happen when this is over. Maybe we'll settle down in the tribes. Or maybe…" He quirked one eyebrow at her. "Maybe we'll travel across the desert and see if we can't start a trading empire on behalf of the tribes. I do speak five languages, you know."

"You do?" It was all she could think to say, her heart was bursting with such happiness. He wanted to be with her, no matter the cost.

"I do. Now let's get some sleep. We have to defeat Aran before we can do anything else."

She stretched out alongside him, resting her head on his chest, listening to the steady beat of his heart, smiling.

As his breathing slowed and steadied, she closed her eyes, savoring the moment. No matter what happened when they confronted Aran, she'd found a man she loved and who loved her—something she'd thought was impossible.

Maybe someday, when this was all over, she really could live that vision the Lady Moon had shown her. The one of the little dark-haired girl—hers and Badru's—dancing and laughing happily as F'lia played the flute and Badru sat by her side.

She closed her eyes and dreamed about a wonderful, bright future with Badru by her side.

CHAPTER 64

As they flew through the night, K'lrsa studied what she could of the Daliphate—the rolling hills; the fields of grains and fruit trees; the baru grazing in their pens, ready for the slaughter; the small homes and towns scattered across the countryside.

A land of abundance built through hard work over hundreds of years.

And she was supposed to destroy it.

Father Sun had said it was up to her what that meant, but she knew that to truly destroy the Toreem Daliphate she'd have to destroy it all. Every last paving stone, every home, every orchard, every fence and farm.

It made her sad. To take something so amazing and seemingly impossible to create and to raze it to the ground.

True, it had all been built on the backs of slave labor. But she couldn't deny the value of it. She couldn't bring herself to contemplate erasing everything just because evil was at the heart of its construction.

Maybe…

Maybe destroying the Toreem Daliphate could mean destroying its culture instead. Tearing down the blackness at its core. The slavery. The way women were treated.

Badru had tried. A bit. He'd said slaves could be freed if their owners so chose. But it hadn't worked. She'd heard those men say that as long as anyone else kept slaves that they'd have to as well, to be able to compete and survive.

To end slavery, it would have to be eliminated entirely. All of it. Immediately.

And then what? Take from those at the top to give to the slaves? Split each farm into pieces so small that none could survive? Give a little patch of dirt to each worker where they could starve in freedom?

Or let the owners keep what they had but share the wealth amongst the workers? Pay them for their efforts. But at what rate? And how? How to enforce that? How to make it fair so that what came after wasn't equally as horrid?

And what about those who wanted to go home, back to the families they'd left behind? How could she make that happen?

It was overwhelming.

And, if she was honest with herself, not a task she cared to take on.

Easier to burn everything to the ground.

To wipe the entire nation from the earth with fire. To purge everything and everyone. To burn away the old so something new could grow in its place, enriched by the ashes of what had come before.

She smiled, imagining the leaping flames as they consumed everything in their path, burning ever hotter, ever higher...

White-hot. So bright you couldn't even look at them.

She imagined that man who'd beat his daughter, with flames licking his skin as he screamed, and smiled. A fitting end for one such as him.

K'lrsa shook herself and shoved the horrible thoughts out of her mind.

What was she thinking? She wasn't like that.

K'lrsa whipped her head around to stare at Vedhe who was flying Kriger to her left. She had the sun orb out and was holding it high, its malevolent red light shining on her face, twisting her scars into a mask of death.

"Vedhe! Put that away. Now."

Vedhe glared at her, eyes red with fire.

"I can feel it, Vedhe. It just had me imagining what it would be like to burn a man to death. Put. It. Away."

Reluctantly, Vedhe tucked the sun orb back into its pouch at her waist.

It helped, but K'lrsa could still feel the orb pulsing with evil, calling out to be used, to burn the world to the ground. Flames, soaring high, everywhere the eye looked…

"We need to land." She nudged Fallion towards the ground.

Badru, who was flying on her other side, hadn't been affected. He called after her. "K'lrsa, wait. We can't land yet. The moon is weaker each night. We need to fly for as long as we can."

He was right. The moon was already half her normal self and with each night she grew thinner, meaning the horses had less time they could fly. But…

Something had to be done about the sun orb. Immediately. Even if she had to fight Vedhe to make it happen. That thing was too dangerous to be unguarded for another moment.

"No. We land now." She nudged Fallion to land in a large field. A herd of baru huddled together at the far end of the space, eyeing them warily but unable to flee like their instincts told them to.

Badru and Vedhe landed next to her, but neither one looked happy about it.

She didn't care. If that infernal orb was invading her thoughts, who knew what else it could do.

She slid from Fallion's back and made her way to Kriger's side. Vedhe stared down at her, expression closed and distant. At least she didn't have flames dancing in her eyes.

"Vedhe. I need you to get down."

"No." Kriger danced sideways as Vedhe glared at her.

"Vedhe…"

"I'm not giving it to you. It's mine." Her eyes flashed with fire as she reached for the pouch at her belt.

"Don't touch it!" K'lrsa grabbed her arm and wrestled her hand away. "Don't you understand that every time you

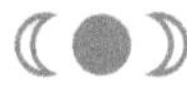

touch it it worms its way deeper into you? If we had a mirror I'd show you the flames that dance in your eyes when you hold it. And just now, while we were flying, that thing had me thinking how I was going to burn the Toreem Daliphate to the ground and enjoy it."

"You would."

"Vedhe!"

Vedhe looked away, her lips pressed tight together.

Badru came to join them. "Is there anything in your memories about shielding the objects? The staff has started calling to me, too, even through all those blankets."

K'lrsa nodded. She could feel it also, but not as strongly as the sun orb.

Vedhe answered. "There's a metal that shields them."

"Good. We'll stop in a town tomorrow and have containers made."

"No. We don't have time. It takes at least a week to make and isn't something anyone will just have lying around."

K'lrsa studied Vedhe for a long moment. Was she telling the truth? Or did she just want to keep the sun orb close and unshielded? "Is there another way to dampen the effect of the objects?"

Vedhe twitched her hand towards the sun orb and then away again with a grimace. "Distance."

"Okay. We can do that. Badru can carry the sun orb tomorrow and you can carry the staff…"

"No! The orb is mine." She grasped the pouch and her eyes flared red. A small patch of grass at K'lrsa's feet started to smolder, wisps of smoke drifting into the air.

K'lrsa stomped on it. "Control yourself."

Badru looked towards Midnight and Fallion. "What if we put the staff and the orb on one of the horses and then ride the other two? The horse carrying the objects can fly far enough away from us to dampen the effects. That would work, right? And Vedhe, you wouldn't have to worry that one of us was going to steal the orb. What do you think?"

Vedhe nodded, but she didn't look happy. "That might work. But no one else touches the sun orb. I put it on the horse's saddle every night and remove it every morning."

"Done," K'lrsa said. At least this way she wouldn't have to touch either of the vile things.

"Okay," Badru said. "Which horse should we use to carry the objects?"

Vedhe nodded towards Midnight. "One of yours. And you two fly together."

She was still twitchy, so K'lrsa just nodded. "Fine. We'll have Fallion fly with the objects and I'll ride with Badru on Midnight."

"Works for me." Badru winked at her and she smiled back.

It was only for a little bit, but she liked the idea of getting that much more time to spend with him, especially when they didn't know what might happen once they reached Toreem.

CHAPTER 65

With the objects farther away, K'lrsa found her mind was much more clear than it had been in days.

But all that did was lead her to obsess about M'lara. They hadn't seen any sign of her the whole trip. She couldn't possibly know where she was going—unless, of course, the gods had directed her to Toreem—in which case they were going to answer to K'lrsa when this was all over for putting a young girl at risk.

They'd probably claim that she'd wanted to go, like K'lrsa had when she set off to avenge her father.

Didn't they see that she was still a child?

She didn't know what she was getting herself into. She couldn't make those kinds of decisions. And using the necklace could kill her.

And what if it fell into Aran's hands? What if he captured her sister?

K'lrsa shuddered to think about it.

She also worried what they'd find when they reached Toreem. Would Aran be there, waiting for them? Or would they have to somehow sneak their way into the palace to find him?

And what power would he have to balance theirs? Would they be able to control the power they had long enough to defeat him? What good would the moon power be?

262

Could Vedhe wield the sun orb even once without losing control? The more time passed, the stronger its hold on her, and the more concerned K'lrsa became.

Twice K'lrsa had had to stomp out the beginnings of a fire while Vedhe slept with the sun orb cradled to her chest. She and Badru had started taking shifts sleeping just so someone could be awake to watch for signs of fire.

If Vedhe couldn't control it now, how was she going to control it when she allowed its full power to flow through her?

They reached the plains outside of Toreem in the middle of the night, but there was nowhere to land without being seen. The city was built for defense, with a large open plain in front, a tall mountain behind, and a large wall that surrounded the city to protect it from any attackers foolish enough to approach.

"What do we do now?" K'lrsa asked as they flew towards the palace that stretched the entire length of the city, dominating the skyline. It was at least six stories high and, although not visible at night, decorated in bright colors—greens, reds, blues, yellows, oranges, black, white—interwoven to form mesmerizing patterns on every surface. A stark contrast to the drab brown buildings that clustered the mountainside below it.

"We find Aran and end this." Badru's sat stiff-backed, his jaw clenched as he stared towards the palace that had once been his.

But where were they were supposed to land? They were invisible as long as they were flying, but they couldn't fly forever, and the roofs of the palace and the surrounding buildings were too steeply sloped for the horses.

Seeing Badru's intensity, she stayed silent. Even though he'd said he was done with the Daliphana, it had to be hard to come back here and be reminded of how he'd been forced to flee when his own men turned on him.

Badru had Midnight fly over the city and farther up the mountainside past the palace to a small courtyard nestled amongst tall trees and next to a long-abandoned stone building, its thatched roof sagging and rotted in places.

As soon as they landed, K'lrsa found herself drawn to the building. She left the others behind, unpacking the horses.

There was a doorway on the side facing the courtyard. Carved into the stone above it was the moon in all of her phases. It was clear from the bits of paint that still clung to the stone, that at one point the images had been painted in bright colors sometime long ago.

She walked around the side of the building and found a second doorway with a second carving. This one had a mazelike pattern that reminded her of the Trickster. She studied the pattern for a long moment, trying to see if there was a way out of the maze, but each path she followed dead-ended or twisted back on itself.

The third side also had a doorway and a carving, this one of a giant sun.

She continued around to the fourth and final side of the building. Whatever had been carved above that doorway had long since been hacked to pieces, chipped away until there was nothing left but the scars of its destruction.

M'lara slept in the shadow of the doorway, a blanket draped over her shoulders, her thumb in her mouth, whimpering softly in her sleep. A small pack of provisions sat next to her—looking better stocked than what they'd brought.

The necklace was wrapped tight in her fist, twined around her fingers so that it couldn't be removed without waking her.

K'lrsa tried not to cry as waves of relief and fear rushed through her.

M'lara looked exhausted. There were dark circles under her eyes, her skin was dull, her hair limp. And she slept the sleep of a child—heedless to all around her.

K'lrsa fought the wave of pure rage that threatened to overwhelm her. How dare the gods send her sister here? She had no part in what was to come. She was too young for this.

Before the others could call out and wake M'lara, K'lrsa returned to them. "I say we find Aran and end this now."

Badru frowned at her. "Don't you want to rest a bit, maybe? Wait until morning? Or…"

"No. We go now. Every moment we spend here is a moment we risk discovery."

He frowned, knowing she was keeping something from him, but he didn't argue.

Vedhe had, of course, already reclaimed the sun orb and was eager to begin, flames dancing in her eyes.

Badru carefully unwrapped the staff and held it in his bare hands for the first time, trembling slightly with the power of it.

He met her eyes and she could see his fear, but it didn't show in his words as he said, "Okay. Follow me. Watch your step. The path is steep."

CHAPTER 66

They made their way down a narrow, rocky path towards the rear of the palace. The whole time, K'lrsa expected to hear the shouts of soldiers and their running feet as they came to confront the intruders in their midst. But it never happened.

They reached the palace without incident and crouched against a wall next to a small door to regroup.

"Why aren't there any soldiers?" K'lrsa looked around, still tensed for an ambush.

"No one has ever attacked from this direction. The mountain on the other side is so steep it's impassable. And there's a garrison of soldiers at the base to shoot down anyone who tries. The only way to reach the temple is through the palace."

"It's a temple to my gods."

He nodded. "They were once worshipped here before the unnamed gods became more powerful."

K'lrsa shifted where she crouched against the wall, uncomfortable with the realization that her gods had once been more powerful than they now were. Maybe that explained why the Lady had done what she'd done…

Badru nodded to the pouch at her waist. "Get out your moon power."

"What for?"

"I don't know what we'll face once we go inside. We

need to be ready. For whatever happens."

Sighing, K'lrsa drew the container with the moon power out of its pouch. Unlike the sun orb and the staff, it didn't pull at her to be used. It felt like nothing at all. Or, more particularly, the absence of everything.

But it was better than touching the staff again. Even though Badru carried it now, it still called to her.

Vedhe stood up. "We should go now. I can't hold this forever." Her eyes were full of dancing flames.

Badru opened the door, leading the way along a deserted hallway that ended in a kitchen where women talked and laughed as they made the first bread of the day. K'lrsa tensed. If they walked into that kitchen, with its fires and people who might sound the alarm, Vedhe would strike.

They couldn't have her lose control this close to the end.

Fortunately, Badru ducked into a small storage room instead of continuing forward. He shoved a stack of boxes aside and pushed on a trio of rocks embedded in the wall. The wall slid open to reveal a hidden passage like the one she and Sayel had escaped through when they'd fled the throne room with Badru's dead body.

"Here. Hold this." Badru handed K'lrsa a lamp from inside the passageway and then reached back inside to grab a fire rock to light it with. But before he could, Vedhe passed the sun orb over the lamp and it sprang to life, the flames dancing almost high enough to burn K'lrsa's fingers.

"Gee, thanks." K'lrsa handed the lamp back to Badru and sucked on her hand where the flames had come a little too close.

Vedhe's eyes were twin flames. "I had to channel the fire somewhere. Get me away from that kitchen. Now."

Badru led them down the passageway at a fast jog, Vedhe on his heels and K'lrsa behind her. Soon, they'd left the heat and comfort of the kitchens behind as they followed the cold, dark, abandoned passages.

K'lrsa wanted to ask where they were going and how long it would take and how Vedhe was doing controlling the sun orb and how often the passages were used—it didn't look like often—and who else knew about them and any number of other things, but she kept silent.

She didn't want anyone to hear them, assuming that was possible through the thick stone walls.

She also didn't want to distract Vedhe who was sweating now, sparks flying from the sun orb with each step. Or Badru, whose knuckles were white where he gripped the staff.

They climbed upward at every chance they had until they reached the topmost level of the palace. Only then did Badru slow. He blew out the lamp and set it on the ground. K'lrsa wiped her palms on her pants as they waited for their eyes to adjust.

Finally, Badru crept forward, one agonizingly slow step at a time.

K'lrsa didn't know how he could see where he was going. All she could see was the vague outline of him and Vedhe as they slowly moved farther along the passage. But he continued, slow step by slow step, as silent as could be, the only light at all coming from the sun orb as it spit sparks of flame.

After what seemed like forever, Badru stopped and turned back, gathering them close together so they were huddled around the sun orb. Whispering so quietly she could barely hear him, he said, "Okay. We're here. At the Daliph's quarters. Now…"

The wall next to Badru burst inward, spraying rocks and dust in all directions. K'lrsa ducked, but not in time to avoid a large rock that sliced her forehead. She peered through the haze of dust and blood; a large man grabbed Badru and threw him into the ornately-tiled room beyond.

"Glad you could join us," someone else said. "Thank you so much for the lovely gift, grandson. It'll make a nice addition to my collection."

Aran. K'lrsa would've recognized his voice anywhere.

CHAPTER 67

K'lrsa had dropped the moon power when the wall burst. She didn't know where it was and didn't have time to find it.

Vedhe wasn't moving, and there was no sign of the sun orb either.

Aran's man had already grabbed the staff.

K'lrsa scuttled backward, desperate to flee, knowing what Aran had done to Herin and Lodie and how powerful he must be with whatever weapon the gods had given him to balance theirs.

She'd go back to M'lara. Get the necklace. Find a way to use it against him.

But she had to get away first.

Before she could sneak away, Aran stepped into the passage, his toad-like face twisted into an evil grin. "Don't leave now, my dear. The fun is just getting started."

K'lrsa turned to run, but she only made it two steps before she ran into a man so large he took up the entire passageway. She stumbled backward, caught between Aran and the giant.

She dropped into a fighting stance. She wasn't about to give up that easy. The space was too narrow for most of the hundred and five attacks, but she tried anyway. It was like fighting a wall. The man didn't even grunt when she hit him.

Aran laughed, his voice filling the small space where she was trapped.

Someone dragged Vedhe out of the passage as K'lrsa attacked the giant again, lunging for his eyes this time, desperate to get away.

He grabbed her wrist and squeezed.

The agony as he crushed her bones was excruciating. He twisted her arm in a direction it wasn't meant to go, and she collapsed to her knees, sobbing.

"Enough, Manen. Bring her out."

The man grabbed K'lrsa by her hair and dragged her out of the passage, the jagged edges of the broken wall scraping her arms and back. The room on the other side of the wall had likely once been a large bedroom and sitting room combined, but most of the furniture had been emptied from the space. There was a bathing area in the far corner like she remembered from her own rooms in the palace, but where her bed would have stood was a single long table.

The center of the room was bare—except for Badru and Vedhe who'd both been dumped on the multi-colored tiles. Neither one was moving. Badru was bleeding from a nasty slash across his forehead. Vedhe was covered all over with tiny cuts. K'lrsa longed to help them, but she there was nothing she could do, so she continued to scan the room, looking for weapons or ways to escape.

On the side of the room opposite the table, a small group of soldiers and courtiers stood, stationed against the wall, awaiting orders. There were two pallets nearby with a small table between them. The table was covered with black candles and metal bowls that seemed to absorb the light—death walker tools.

K'lrsa shivered as Manen dumped her next to Vedhe, wondering who Aran planned to kill or torture and then heal with his evil magic.

She fought to find the Rider's version of the Core, to set the agony in her wrist aside so she could think. And act. She had to get away. To find M'lara and the necklace. To save Vedhe and Badru.

But each time she reached for the Core, her thoughts shattered and scattered away from her, the fear too strong for her to set aside.

She crawled to Vedhe's side.

Was she dead?

No.

Her chest was still moving—barely—but she had hundreds of tiny cuts all over her face and body. She'd taken the brunt of the wall's collapse.

"Larek. Heal this one first." Aran pointed to Vedhe and a man dressed in brown except for a black sash around his waist, came forward to grab her.

"No. Don't touch her." K'lrsa stumbled to her feet, placing herself between the man and Vedhe.

"Don't be a fool, girl." Aran stepped closer, looking down at Vedhe like she was a bug he wanted to squash. "She'll die if Larek doesn't heal her. Not that it looks like that would be much of a loss. Ugly, isn't she? So pale. And scarred." He turned away in disgust.

"Why do you want to heal her?" K'lrsa glared at Larek as he once more tried to take Vedhe away.

"Why? It's no fun to just kill someone. That's so easy. Especially now." He flexed his right hand. He was wearing some sort of glove woven of a dark metal that seemed to suck up the light. "Like my gauntlet? You'd be amazed what it can do. *That* was nothing." He nodded towards the wall.

"Why'd you do that?"

"Why, why, why. Can't you say anything other than why?" He shook his head. "I will never understand what Badru sees in you. I mean, you're pretty enough, I guess. But..." He kicked Badru who moaned and rolled away from him. "Not worth a Daliphate, that's for sure. And not nearly as interesting as Herin was. I bet you kill yourself the first chance you get. Whereas Herin..." He grinned. "She was a fighter. Worth the effort it took to break her."

K'lrsa spat at him. "I wish you'd stayed dead when Lodie killed you. I can't believe someone cared enough to bring you back."

He stared at the spit on the ground for a long moment and K'lrsa shivered with fear, wondering what he was going to do to her as he stepped closer. "Some people know how to choose the winning side. You, my dear, are not one of them. First Badru, then the tribes, now trying to oppose me. As for the wall…I did it because I could. And because it surprised you. Seems to have worked pretty well if you ask me."

One of his men brought the sun orb from the passage and he gestured towards the table at the end of the room where the staff already was. No moon power. Yet.

K'lrsa glanced towards the gaping hole in the wall. If she ran for it…

Aran would strike her down before she even reached the passageway.

The giant picked up Vedhe and carried her to the corner, Larek following behind. K'lrsa watched, her fists clenched in anger as they brought out a young child to heal Vedhe's wounds. Why did men like this always use the innocent?

It disgusted her.

She watched as Larek went through the death walker ritual—lighting the candles, taking blood from Vedhe and the child, saying his words. It didn't take long. It was a simple ceremony. No wonder Herin had learned it after all the times Aran had hurt her and healed her again.

Vedhe sat up, her wounds gone, completely healed.

All of them.

Even the scars from crossing the desert. Where her skin had once been patchy and red, there were now fine white lines that blended into her fair skin.

She held her arms out in front of her and cried, tracing the lines of the scars with a fingertip.

She was beautiful. Almost as beautiful as that idealized image of her they'd seen in the mirror at the heart of the labyrinth. She was still too pale, her nose too narrow, her cheeks too thin, but there was a symmetry about her face that was strangely compelling.

Aran laughed in delight. "Ah, much better! Now that's a girl I could spend some time with." He licked his lips as he

stepped closer to Vedhe. "Tell me, child, what would you do if I took this beauty from you again?"

Vedhe touched her cheek. She glanced towards a full-length mirror standing in the corner and away again, crying even more. "I don't want it. Take it." She glared at him. "Carve me up," she growled. "And then leave me be."

"You don't want it? You're rather be ugly? Scarred?"

"Yes," she screamed. "Why do you think those slavers killed my family and took me? Because of this."

She tried to claw at her face, but one of the soldiers stopped her before she could do more than cut one small groove into her cheek.

Aran turned away. "Restrain her. If anyone's going to cause her harm, it'll be me."

The soldier bound Vedhe's wrists behind her back and returned her to the center of the room, dumping her at K'lrsa's side.

"Are you okay?" K'lrsa asked.

"I'm fine."

But she wasn't. Her eyes were wild with panic.

K'lrsa leaned closer, whispering. "Can you use the orb from here?"

"No. I need to touch it."

"Okay. Forget Aran for now, Vedhe. He isn't going to harm you. We'll kill him before he can. Do you understand? No one will hurt you again. We'll get you to the orb and then you can use it on him and every other person in this room."

Vedhe focused on K'lrsa's face, a calm coming over her. She nodded. Once.

Aran came closer and bowed gracefully as he waved towards Larek. "Your turn, my dorana. Unless you want to lose the hand?"

K'lrsa cradled her shattered wrist to her chest. She'd been healed by death walker magic twice before. She didn't want it again, especially if a child was harmed to do it.

"I'm fine."

Aran crossed his arms and glared at her. "You understand I can't let you keep your hand the way it is? So you have a choice. I call a surgeon in, he chops your hand off just above the injury, puts the stump in a fire to stop any further bleeding, and we hope for the best. But if the wound festers you will still need to be healed, you just won't have a hand. Or…" He gestured to Larek again. "We heal you now. So…What'll it be, *Rider?* Can you shoot a bow one-handed? Or ride a horse one-handed?"

K'lrsa flinched. She didn't want to lose the hand, but she wasn't going to let some child lose their hand because of her either.

Aran narrowed his eyes and stepped closer. "Hm. Maybe I'll just have him take the hand now and heal you anyway. Not like I need your cooperation for the ritual, as you already learned with Herin."

As K'lrsa opened her mouth to argue further, she noticed movement in the passageway behind him, at the edge of the broken wall. She moved so Aran was directly between her and the passage, pretending to look at him while she tried to figure out who it was.

M'lara. She peered around the edge of the wall, eyes wide with fear.

What was she thinking? If Aran saw her…

He started to turn.

She stood. "Fine. Heal me. Here. Look. I'm going. Right now." She backed away from him, making sure he stayed focused on her as M'lara ducked back behind the broken wall.

CHAPTER 68

Two men dragged out a young servant girl, her head down, and pinned her to the pallet next to K'lrsa. She struggled against them, but she was too small to resist as they tied her hands and feet into place. Her body—what was visible as they bound her—was crisscrossed with scars the way Herin's had been.

She had to be no older than M'lara. K'lrsa shuddered. *This* was the fate that awaited her sister if Aran noticed her.

As the girl thrashed on the table, she met K'lrsa's eyes and K'lrsa choked. It was the girl from the stables. The one without a tongue that K'lrsa had spared the night she fled.

Spared but left behind to the cruelties of Aran and his men.

This girl's fate was K'lrsa's fault.

She cradled her shattered wrist to her chest. The hand was useless. Injured beyond repair. Aran was right, if she wasn't healed, she would lose it. She could probably still ride Fallion—he was such an amazing horse he'd adjust—but she'd never shoot a bow again. She wouldn't be a Rider anymore.

And wouldn't be welcome in the tribes either.

But this girl...

What she'd suffered already...

And to lose her hand on top of it?

No. She didn't deserve that.

K'lrsa stepped away from the pallet. "I changed my mind. I don't want to be healed."

Aran turned from where he'd been taunting Vedhe. "Why? Are you feeling sorry for the girl?" He came closer.

The girl trembled uncontrollably, scrabbling to free herself, her eyes white with fear.

K'lrsa stepped between them, afraid Aran might kill her just because. "Why are you like this? Why do this to people?"

He studied her, a slight smile twisting his fat lips. "Your hand is shattered. The man you love is on the floor, in desperate need of attention. If we leave him much longer, he'll probably die, and then Larek will have to kill this girl to bring him back. And you want to know why I do what I do?"

She looked past him to where Badru lay, unmoving, blood pooled by his head.

"Yes."

Aran smiled and the menace in it chilled her to the bone. "Perhaps I *can* see a little bit of what my grandson finds so intriguing about you. But now is not the time." He nodded to Larek. "Finish it. Force her if you must."

K'lrsa moved back to the pallet and lay down as two guards moved towards her. She turned her head so she could meet the girl's eyes. "I'm sorry," she mouthed as silent tears trickled down the girl's cheeks.

The ritual was quick. Larek efficiently collected a small bit of K'lrsa's blood in a bowl and then did the same with the girl. He placed the bowls within a circle of black candles that smelled of death and decay, and muttered words she couldn't quite understand over them. When that was done, he marked both K'lrsa's and the girl's foreheads with the blood and muttered another series of words before clapping his hands together.

And, just like that, K'lrsa was healed. She flexed her hand and bent her wrist. As good as new. Just like when Herin had used death walker magic to heal her after the fight with Balor.

They dragged the sobbing girl out of the room, her wrist now shattered like K'lrsa's had been, and rage burned through K'lrsa like fire. She glared at Aran, wanting him dead more than anything she'd ever wanted before.

But how?

Badru was bleeding to death, Vedhe was huddled in a ball weeping, and K'lrsa had no weapons to attack him with. He'd taken both the staff and the sun orb and who knew where the moon power was—not that it would do her any good in defeating him.

And, of course, M'lara was lurking in that passageway just waiting to be discovered and used against them…

How had they failed so miserably?

CHAPTER 69

As K'lrsa moved back towards the center of the room, trying to see if M'lara was still hiding in the passage, two soldiers dragged Badru's limp body past her. He moaned softly as they moved him, and K'lrsa breathed a sigh of relief. He was still alive.

Aran would've brought him back one way or the other, but at least this way no one had to die for him. Again.

Although, looking at the young boy they'd brought in, she wondered if living another day was actually a mercy. His feet were so deformed he couldn't walk and there were fresh burn marks on his face and hands. He didn't even try to struggle as they strapped him into place, every line of his body resigned to his short, miserable existence.

Once more, rage pulsed through her body.

She moved towards where the staff rested, positioning herself so she could see into the passage at the same time. No sign of M'lara. Maybe she'd fled when she saw what had happened to them.

Not likely, though. She was K'lrsa's sister after all, and just as stubborn and foolish.

Aran watched her through his bulging, hooded reptile eyes as she eased her way closer to the staff.

It called to her, begging to be used.

She could sense every drop of water in the entire palace. *And* the vast reserve of water below the city—an amount of water so vast and deep that it could swallow not just the palace but the entire city of Toreem.

All she had to do was call on it and it would come to her. Even now. Even without the staff in her hand.

But she didn't want to do that. She'd destroy every man, woman, and child in the city, including Badru, Vedhe, M'lara, and the innocent children Aran was using for his dark magic. And every slave forced to be here against their will.

Everyone would die. Both the evil and the innocent.

She would die.

She didn't want that. Not yet.

But…

If that's what she had to do to defeat Aran? To purge his evil from the world…

She'd do it.

Not yet, though.

There were still other options. If she could just get Vedhe close enough to the sun power…

Or the sun power close enough to her…

She glanced towards the passage. She needed the necklace. She needed M'lara.

Behind her, Badru gasped as they completed the ritual. K'lrsa didn't look at him, even though she was glad he was back. She was too busy trying to figure out how to get the necklace from M'lara without Aran noticing.

Unfortunately, his attention was completely focused on her. He clenched his gauntleted fist. "One more step and I'll blast you into that wall."

She turned away from the table. "I don't get it. Why do this? You're a powerful man. Why hurt people like you do?"

Aran stepped closer. "What's the point in being the favored one of the gods if you never do anything with the power they've given you?"

"So you hurt people so you can use the power of the gods?"

He nodded.

"That makes no sense."

In the darkened passageway behind Aran, a shadow shifted, and K'lrsa tensed.

What was M'lara doing? She was going to get caught.

She wrenched her attention away from M'lara, hoping Aran hadn't seen her reaction. Instead she turned to smile at Badru as he made his way back to the center of the room.

"Badru!" She forced herself to step past Aran and ignore M'lara as she moved to Badru's side. It was the hardest thing she'd ever done, ignoring her sister, but she had to do it. Aran couldn't know M'lara was there.

She threw her arms around Badru. "I thought I'd lost you," she cried, loud enough for Aran to hear.

As Badru pulled her close, she pressed her lips to his ear and whispered, "M'lara's here. In the passageway."

He tensed for just a moment as he pulled her closer.

Aran interrupted them. "Enough. Sit down. Now that everyone's healed, it's time to see what you brought me. And then the fun can really begin."

CHAPTER 70

K'lrsa sat down next to Vedhe, making sure she could see the passageway without Aran noticing. "Are you okay?" she asked, searching Vedhe's face for signs of her earlier panic.

Vedhe shrugged, pulling her knees tight to her chest. She flinched each time one of Aran's soldiers moved, but otherwise she seemed fine.

"Silence!" Aran shouted. He picked up the staff and ran his hands down its length, studying each whorl and notch in the wood. "Ah, the Staff of Life. A good tool to have in the desert, but not much of a weapon, is it?"

K'lrsa glared at him. The power of the staff called to her, begging her to use it, to show this arrogant little man what a fool he was. To drown his corruption and debauchery and wash away his filth.

It would be so easy…

She shoved the thought aside.

Not yet.

Not if she could get the sun orb for Vedhe.

He set down the staff and picked up the orb. "Now this is more interesting. The Sun Orb. The power of Father Sun himself." It burned red in his hands and he raised it high as he looked at each of them in turn. "Hm. Which to test it on? The one already burned by the sun once? The fool who lost his throne to a pretty face? Or that pretty face?" He focused on K'lrsa. "Do you want to know what it feels like to burn, my little desert Rider?"

K'lrsa flinched, but Vedhe nudged her knee and spoke loud enough for Aran to hear her. "He can't use it unless he takes off the glove."

Aran nodded and set it back down. "True. But how did *you* know that?"

"I learned it in the labyrinth."

"Ah, yes. You've all three been to the center of the labyrinth. Except…" He studied the objects on the table and then looked towards the passage. "There are only two objects here. Where is the third? Is it still in the wall?"

"Badru didn't get to choose." K'lrsa said, desperately needing him to look at her and away from where M'lara was hidden. She wanted to dash across the room and block the broken hole with her body, but she resisted.

"What?" He turned his attention back to her.

"Badru didn't get to choose the first time because he came to the Hidden City as a death walker. He was dead as soon as he crossed the threshold."

"And yet here he sits. How?"

K'lrsa bit her lip. Why had she told him that? He hadn't known until she said it that Badru had been healed with death walker magic. And now he knew a death walker could leave the Hidden City. He'd use that knowledge. He'd follow it like a string unraveling from a rug until he figured out how to do it himself.

"How?" he thundered.

K'lrsa cowered as he raised his gauntleted fist.

"Father Sun." Badru stood, confronting his grandfather. How anyone could've thought that Badru in all his beauty was in any way related to Aran, she'd never know. "He's the one that freed me."

"And how did he free you?"

"You think a god would tell a mere mortal his secrets? I don't know. He said he could and he did."

Aran flexed his fist. "Hm. I'll have to talk to him someday. See what he cares to tell me."

"You'd challenge a god?" K'lrsa asked.

"What are the gods, really? Powerful, yes. But all-powerful? No. And with this?" He clenched his fist and held it high. "And these." He gestured towards the staff and the sun orb. "I, too, am powerful."

K'lrsa shook her head. "They'll destroy you."

"Perhaps. But I'll take that risk. You said Badru didn't get to choose the first time. What happened the second time?"

"He was already gone. Father Sun freed him before we returned to the Hidden City."

"And what of the necklace you used to send the twisted and bent remains of my men back to me. A nice gesture by the way. Well done. Against a weaker opponent that might've had some meaning."

"The balance." Vedhe lurched to her feet, her hands still bound behind her.

K'lrsa risked looking towards the passage. Was that a shadow with a small vial clutched in its tiny fist? Had M'lara found the moon power?

"What about it?" Aran asked, sneering at her.

Vedhe took a step towards him. "I gave up my viewing tube. I couldn't keep it and maintain the balance."

K'lrsa bit her lip, waiting for Aran to stop her. Instead, he laughed.

"Like the balance would be affected by that little viewing tube you took." He shook his head. "You foolish women. You were given access to any weapon you could possibly want, and you chose a viewing tube and a necklace. I hear they were pretty, at least."

K'lrsa held her breath as Vedhe took another step closer. "Not all of us want to destroy the world."

"Destroy it?" He leered at her. "I don't want to destroy it, little girl. I want to rule it. And what do you want? Pretty dresses? Fancy jewels? Men to adore you?"

Vedhe took another step.

She was within arm reach of the table now, but her hands were still tied behind her back. Was she close enough to use the orb yet? Did she need to touch it?

"What do *I* want?" Vedhe asked, her voice as sweet as

honey, sounding every bit like the little girl he'd called her. *"I* want the world to *burn."*

The sun orb flared to life, shooting flames in all directions.

CHAPTER 71

A ran screamed as his clothes caught fire, flames racing up and down his body, licking at his flesh. He wasn't the only one the flames struck. Manen, who'd been standing off to the side, burned like a torch, screaming until he collapsed to the ground in moaning agony.

The curtains on the windows were consumed in an instant and the table smoldered.

K'lrsa could hear men screaming behind her as well—the only thing that had saved her and Badru was the fact they were seated on the floor—but she didn't turn, her attention focused completely on Aran and Vedhe.

Vedhe had done it. She'd defeated Aran.

But even as K'lrsa thought it, Aran held his gauntleted fist out and clenched it closed. Vedhe screamed in agony. The flames disappeared as her chest collapsed. It was as if a giant hand were squeezing her body to a pulp.

K'lrsa shouted at him to stop, but he continued to squeeze, his face twisted with rage. At last he stopped, throwing what remained of Vedhe against the wall where she hit with a sickening splat.

"I'll make you burn, bitch." He screamed.

K'lrsa ran to Vedhe's side even though it was too late. No one could survive that kind of damage.

But her body had landed next to the passage where M'lara hid. She had to save her. She had to...

K'lrsa glanced over her shoulder. Aran was taking off the gauntlet, his hands trembling with rage as he pulled at each finger.

"Give me the necklace," K'lrsa hissed into the darkness of the passageway, hoping her sister was there and would listen. Now was not the time for her to decide to be a hero.

K'lrsa glanced over her shoulder again, just in time to see Aran tuck the gauntlet into his belt and grab the sun orb.

His eyes filled with fire as the orb latched onto the darkness inside his soul and fanned it to a frenzy of destruction.

CHAPTER 72

"K'lrsa, here. Take it." M'lara pressed the necklace into her hand.

Aran's smile widened. "Another one? Good. We'll have fun together. Do you like fire, child?"

K'lrsa gripped the necklace, feeling the metal curves press into her flesh, wanting nothing more than to use it to flee this horrible room that smelled like burned flesh and death. But it was too late for that. Too late to pretend there was anywhere in the world or the Promised Plains that would be safe from Aran.

He took another step towards them, clearly fighting to control the power of the sun orb. A blast of fire shot out from the orb and struck one of the guards on the other side of the room. He screamed in agony as the others fled, leaving him to burn.

There was no point trying to find the Core. She was too scared for that. Instead she just gritted her teeth and focused on what she needed to do. M'lara was safe—she had the moon power. Which meant K'lrsa needed to attack.

Now.

She focused on the gauntlet, and with a flick of her mind, flung it at Badru, who'd been trying to sneak up on Aran from behind, a slim dagger clutched in his fist. Badru caught the gauntlet and dodged to the side as Aran turned and blasted fire at him.

K'lrsa ran to the back of the room, looking around for any sort of weapon she could find as Badru continued to run from Aran, struggling to put the gauntlet on as he ducked and rolled and dashed left and right.

A blast of fire almost caught K'lrsa, but she managed to hide behind the burnt body of one of the soldiers, gagging on the stench of him, trying not to see his burned flesh and empty eyes. He had a half-melted sword buckled at his waist, but it was useless.

She reached for his calf, hoping he'd stashed another weapon there, as Aran turned back to Badru. He threw another blast of flame and Badru cried out. He was on the ground now, crawling away from Aran, the flesh of his left leg burnt and smoking. Aran laughed, raising his hand to strike the killing blow.

M'lara ran from the shelter of the passageway, the moon power clutched in her tiny little fist. "Don't," she screamed, placing herself between Aran and Badru.

Aran laughed and threw another bolt of fire, this one headed straight for M'lara's chest.

"No," K'lrsa screamed.

CHAPTER 73

K'lrsa lurched forward, desperate to put herself between Aran's fire and M'lara. But she was too late. The fire reached M'lara in less time than it took to blink.

But then…

Nothing.

The fire just disappeared.

It wasn't there anymore.

For a count of five they all froze, trying to figure out what had just happened. Then M'lara started crying and Aran screamed in rage and threw another bolt of fire at her but it too disappeared into nothing. K'lrsa veered away from them at the last moment as she finally realized what had happened.

The moon power was protecting her.

But it wouldn't protect K'lrsa. She dove for the bathing area, hiding behind the half-wall that seemed to have survived the fire so far, batting at her hair where it had been singed by a random spit of fire as she passed Aran.

She peeked over the top of the wall. Aran was advancing on M'lara, still throwing fire balls at her. She was stumbling away from him, safe for now. But not for long. The moon power couldn't protect an eight-year-old child against the physical harm a grown man could do if he managed to catch her.

Badru staggered to his feet, the gauntlet on his left

hand. "Grandfather," he shouted. "Your time has come." He reached out and squeezed, lifting his hand into the air as he did so.

Aran rose off the ground, screaming in agony as his body crumpled in on itself and his bones ground together. The sight and sound of it was too much for K'lrsa. She retched until there was nothing left in her stomach and then retched some more.

When she finally stumbled to her feet, it was over.

Aran lay on the multi-colored tile floor, his bright red blood covering a checkered section of black and white tiles, his eyes staring at nothing. He'd been crushed in half, his entire chest area no wider than her thigh.

She stumbled across the floor, fighting the urge to run away and never look back.

The sun orb lay by his side, still spitting fire as if alive, soaked in his blood.

She swallowed her bile and picked it up, fighting the urge to burn the world down. To turn it on everyone and everything and cleanse them in the holy fire of Father Sun.

Only one man in this room needed cleansed.

Aran. She focused on him, directing the flames of the sun orb at his broken body, watching him burn until there was nothing left. Not a tooth, not a fingertip.

Nothing.

Aran was dead. Gone.

Forever this time.

No one could bring him back.

She dropped the orb and turned to the others.

CHAPTER 74

B adru stood in the center of the room, the gauntlet at his feet, leaning heavily to one side, hurt but alive.

M'lara stood off to the side, shaking, her eyes wide with horror as she sobbed.

K'lrsa wanted to go to her, but she didn't. Instead she went to Vedhe. Just in case. Just in case she'd somehow survived what Aran had done to her.

Even though Vedhe had come to the Hidden City expecting to die, it still hurt to see her friend lying there on the floor, her eyes open and unseeing, dead. K'lrsa closed her eyes and brushed her pale hair back from her forehead.

She hadn't deserved this. Hadn't deserved any of it.

K'lrsa sobbed, letting all the fear of the last few moments finally overwhelm her.

Badru knelt beside her, pulling her into his arms. "I'm sorry, K'lrsa."

"It isn't fair. Everything she went through and…For it to end like this…" She shook her head, wiping at the tears that continued to flow.

It wasn't fair. Vedhe deserved her revenge. Her chance to track down Ivan and make him pay for what he'd done to her family. And she deserved a chance to heal, to find happiness, to know that her life wasn't just about the moments of suffering, but that there could be joy, too.

And love. Love like K'lrsa had found with Badru.

She deserved better than to be crushed to death as part of a fight that meant nothing to her.

A man moaned nearby and K'lrsa flinched. She'd left the sun orb in the center of the room for anyone to take. Fortunately, the soldier was burnt too badly to move.

He was no threat; he'd be dead soon.

She lurched to her feet.

Badru joined her. "What? What is it?"

"We can save her."

"What?"

"We can save Vedhe. That man's going to die anyway. We can use death walker magic to save her."

He gripped her shoulders. "K'lrsa…Maybe she doesn't want that."

"Of course she does." She tore free from him. "She deserves better than this, Badru. She gave her life to kill a man who'd never done her any harm. She came here instead of going home to avenge her family. She deserves to live."

"K'lrsa…"

"No. It's not like I'm not killing someone to save her. That man's dead no matter what. She can't argue against this."

Badru looked like he wanted to, but he didn't.

"Go get Larek. We don't have much time."

Badru hesitated and K'lrsa shoved him towards the door. "Go. Now."

As he left the room, she turned to M'lara. "Come on, little one. Help me move Vedhe to the table."

M'lara stared at her and then at Vedhe's broken body. She burst into tears and turned away.

"M'lara…" K'lrsa stood between them, torn between comforting her sister and saving her friend.

Larek and Badru returned, Larek staring around the room in horror. "Where's the Daliph?"

"Gone. You can't bring him back this time."

"So why am I here?" He glared at her.

She pointed to Vedhe. "Save her. You can use him." She pointed to the man moaning in the corner, the flesh that was visible blackened and cracked.

Larek hesitated.

"Now!" K'lrsa screamed, her hand twitching to grab the sun orb and use it on him. It sparked where it lay on the floor and Larek jumped backward. He moved towards his bloody tools.

"Badru, help me move her."

Larek turned back to them. "No. They can stay where they are. They're close enough for it to work. And…" He grimaced. "Right now she's still in one piece. You move her she might not stay that way."

K'lrsa's stomach flipped, threatening to purge itself once more, but she fought against it. "Fine. Just…Hurry."

CHAPTER 75

As Larek prepared the bodies, a few of Aran's soldiers crept back into the room. K'lrsa turned on them, her hand twitching towards the sun orb where it still lay in the middle of the room. These men were her enemies. They'd kill her given the chance.

One of the men stepped away from the others. "My Daliph?" He wrung his hands as he looked at the carnage. Burned and broken bodies scattered around the room, the stench of it almost overwhelming.

"Your Daliph is dead," K'lrsa spat, glaring at him.

"No." He nodded towards Badru. "He's our Daliph."

K'lrsa tensed, turning to Badru. He'd said he wanted to be with her. To live in the desert or wherever else they wanted to go. That he didn't want to be Daliph anymore.

But these men. They were all looking to him, expectant.

Could he walk away from that? From the power and comfort? From the riches and security?

He limped to her side, dragging his injured leg along the tiles. He held out his hand, holding her eyes with his impossibly blue ones.

She hesitated, worried what came next, but she took his hand, tensed to hear him utter the words she didn't want to hear.

He turned his attention to the soldiers. "I am not your Daliph. Aran Palero was not my grandfather. My grandfather

was G'zen of the Summer Spring Tribe and my father was L'ren of the Black Horse Tribe. I am a member of the tribes and I intend to return to them. Call the Council, tell them what I've said, and have them choose a new Daliph from one of the founding families. When he's ready to trade with the tribes he can find me there and we'll negotiate terms."

The man stared at him. "But…"

"I am not one of you. I never was." He leaned close and kissed her cheek, whispering "Is that what you hope to hear?"

K'lrsa bit her lip, fighting not to cry in front of so many strangers. "Yes."

"Good. Because I meant it, K'lrsa. I'd rather be by your side than anywhere else in the world."

CHAPTER 76

K'lrsa flung herself into Badru's arms and hugged him until he winced and pushed her back. "Careful. I'm still injured."

"Right." She stepped back. "We need Larek to heal you."

"No. I won't let another child be hurt on my behalf."

K'lrsa clenched her jaw, thinking. There had to be someone they could use to heal him…

But before she could think who that might be, Vedhe sat up, gasping, and K'lrsa ran to her side. "You're back."

Vedhe glared at her. "Why?"

"What?"

"Why did you bring me back?"

K'lrsa blinked, surprised by her anger. "Because you deserved a better life than that. You deserved the chance to avenge yourself on Ivan and to move on and find some measure of happiness. A husband. A child. A…"

"Don't you understand? I didn't want to survive this!"

"But…"

Vedhe shoved to her feet and moved away from K'lrsa, shaking with anger.

"Vedhe…"

Vedhe ignored her, scanning the room, her eyes resting on the sun orb with lust. "We need to contain these objects. Now." She turned on Larek. "Do you have any boxes made of lanelium?"

He nodded.

"Good. Get them"

He licked his lips. "How many do you need?"

"One for that orb. One for that staff. One for that gauntlet." She shrugged. "And if you have a few smaller ones left, two more, although those aren't as necessary. Go! Now. Unless you want me to burn this whole place down."

He nodded once and took off at a dead run. Clearly whatever he'd seen in her eyes had convinced him she meant it.

CHAPTER 77

Vedhe turned on M'lara next, her expression softening slightly. "M'lara?"

"Yeah." M'lara hiccupped. Her face was wet, but at least she'd stopped crying.

"I need you to take each of those objects and move them to the far corner of the room. Can you do that for me?"

K'lrsa stepped between them. "No. I don't want her to touch them. I'll do it."

"You can't. You've used them. If you touch the objects, they'll consume you. Can't you sense how the orb has grown in power?"

Vedhe was right. K'lrsa had only used the orb once and yet it called to her, demanding to be used again.

"If it's more powerful, then how can you expect a child to handle it?"

"Because she's innocent. There's no anger in her soul for it to feed off of."

"Who says?" K'lrsa crossed her arms. "She lost both of her parents just like I did."

"I'm sure she's sad. But that desire you have for revenge? To destroy what destroyed your world? She doesn't have it." Vedhe clenched and unclenched her fists and said through gritted teeth, "Please ask her to take the orb to the far corner of the room. Now."

K'lrsa hesitated a moment longer, but then turned to M'lara and nodded. "Do it."

Vedhe relaxed slightly as M'lara picked the orb and gauntlet up and ran to the far corner of the room with them. "Better. Not perfect, but better."

They didn't have long to wait until Larek returned, a servant boy trailing along behind him, both of them with an assortment of metal boxes piled high in their arms. Vedhe stopped Larek at the door and sent the boy to M'lara. The two children worked together, finding containers for the orb, the staff, and the gauntlet while the adults watched from the other side of the room.

Only when they were all safely stowed in their containers did K'lrsa realize how much she'd been fighting the call of both the staff and the orb. It was like someone had removed an incredibly heavy weight from her shoulders.

She sagged to the ground, suddenly exhausted. When was the last time she'd eaten?

"So?" she asked. "What now?"

Vedhe shrugged. "Depends on you, I guess."

"How so?"

"Well…Are you going to destroy the Toreem Daliphate like you promised Father Sun you would?"

K'lrsa rubbed at her face. She'd forgotten all about that.

She stared around the burnt and scorched room, at the crumpled and dead bodies and the boxes in the corner filled with the weapons that had caused all this.

She was done.

Done with killing.

Her father would understand.

She hoped.

She shook her head. "No. I'm not going to do it."

Her hand started to burn like she'd plunged it into a fire and she screamed.

CHAPTER 78

K'lrsa clutched her hand to her chest, the pain so intense she wanted to chop her hand off rather than suffer through it for a moment more. She'd forgotten about the binding.

She grimaced as she opened her hand to reveal the red fire burning her palm.

Larek stepped closer. "That's a binding."

"Yes." She spoke through gritted teeth, wanting to hurt everything and everyone around her.

"A god did that."

K'lrsa gasped as the pain intensified, tears streaming down her cheeks. "Yes."

He gripped her face between his hands. "Focus on what you're supposed to do. Pretend it's something you want to do."

She focused on how to destroy the Toreem Daliphate. She could use the sun orb to call fire and burn the city to the ground. Or use the staff to bring that vast reserve of water to the surface, drowning everyone and everything for as far as the eye could see. Or take the gauntlet and bust through every wall, tearing the city to its foundations.

Slowly, with each thought, the pain lessened.

But it didn't go away.

She gasped, nodding to him. "That helped. But it still hurts."

"It's tied to your will. You know deep down you aren't going to complete your task. If you move from here or stop thinking of ways to complete it, the pain will come back."

"Can you remove it?"

He stepped back, looking between her, Vedhe, and Badru. "Yes. But I want something in return."

Badru glared at him. "You're a death walker. You don't deserve anything except to die."

"Badru." K'lrsa glared at him as her thoughts slipped and the pain came back.

"It's true. Death walker magic is evil."

Larek shook his head. "No, it's not. Our magic is a healing magic. It's men like Aran who've polluted its true purpose."

"And yet you brought him back after Lodie killed him."

Larek bowed his head. "It wasn't me. And it wasn't the men who trained me. There are some who've learned our ways who don't understand our true purpose. Who use our magic to torture. Men who see it as a source of power. Those are the ones who brought Aran back."

"And you want me to believe you aren't one of them?"

"I'm not. I'll swear it on any god or any object you want."

K'lrsa winced as her thoughts slipped and the pain came back, twice as bad as before. "Badru."

Badru lifted his chin. "Fine. What do you want in return for removing the binding?"

"To live. And to use my magic the way it was meant to be used. To heal the sick and bring back those whose lives have been cut short before their appointed time."

K'lrsa glared at him. "You used children in your magic."

He bowed his head. "I'm not proud of what I've done. But I want a chance to make it right. To take my religion back to what it once was."

Vedhe stepped forward, her eyes dark and cold. "And what about the men who brought Aran back? The ones who know your magic and would use it to torture others? Or to bring power to themselves. What about them?"

Larek met her glare, unflinching. "*They* must die. But they won't die in vain. We'll use them to heal the children that were harmed. And you." He nodded to Badru.

Vedhe nodded. "Yes. Heal the children."

"And the binding?" Badru asked.

"I can transfer it. To myself."

"But then you'll just be in pain like I am."

"No. I can transform it. Change its purpose. Bind myself to the right path."

K'lrsa clutched her hand to her chest. It burned like she was slowly roasting it over a fire. She couldn't take this much longer. "Fine. You live. You take the binding. You heal the children and kill those who'd pollute your magic. And then? What happens when another man like Aran tries to turn you from your path?"

"Aran had an oath rod. We'll use it to bind all who remain. We'll each swear to only use our magic to heal others and to never do so in the service of those who seek to torture or harm."

K'lrsa looked at Badru and Vedhe. They both nodded. "Okay, then. That works."

Larek nodded once. "Give me until sunset. I need to prepare and then we can transfer the binding and handle the others." He glanced around the room. "I'll send a servant to lead you to new quarters. I'm sure you could use some food and rest."

K'lrsa winced. It wasn't even midday yet and her hand was throbbing with pain. But at least an end was in sight.

CHAPTER 79

L arek was as good as his word. A servant appeared almost immediately and led them down a series of hallways until they reached a large room with four windows, open to the early spring day, the mountain visible in the background.

A bed big enough to sleep at least four people dominated the corner of the room, gauzy curtains tied to each post. In the center of the space were bright cushions arranged in a circle to form a seating area. In the corner near the bed was a large bathing area and in the corner opposite that there was a table and a chair, the table covered with various jars.

"Is this my old room?" K'lrsa asked, moving to the nearest window to confirm her suspicion.

"Yes," Badru answered, turning to instruct the servant on what food to bring.

K'lrsa shivered, looking around the space where she'd spent so many days struggling to be something she wasn't, all for a chance to kill a man who hadn't even been responsible for her father's death.

It felt like a lifetime ago.

The smells of food drove every thought from her mind except how hungry she was and she moved to sit with the others, admiring the fresh fruits and nuts, the warm discs of bread, the soft cheeses, and the meats floating in heavily-seasoned sauces.

They ate in silence, too exhausted to talk about what had happened with Aran.

And about what happened next. Because this wasn't over.

Not yet.

CHAPTER 80

That night, they watched in silence as Larek transferred the binding from K'lrsa's hand to his own and then had each of ten death walkers swear an oath to only use their magic to heal.

Just like on the gathering grounds, there was one man who tried to swear a false oath and was burned to nothing for his lie. But for the others it was a simple process.

When that was done, Larek brought in five men who were completely healthy, the black sashes at their waists marking them as death walkers, and a large group of children, each with wounds visible on their arms and legs and faces.

The girl from the stables was one of them—her shattered wrist clutched tight to her body as she tried to disappear behind the others.

The men fought when they realized what was about to happen, but Larek and his death walkers bound them into place with a cool efficiency.

K'lrsa watched as the men were used to heal the children, nodding in satisfaction as each broken bone, burn, and bruise disappeared from soft young flesh. She didn't feel the least bit sorry for the men. They deserved this—to taste the same suffering they'd inflicted on so many.

The girl from the stables was the last one to be healed.

Even seeing what had happened with all of the others, she held back. K'lrsa had to lead her forward and hold her good hand as Larek performed the ritual. And even then her eyes were wide with fear as he marked her forehead and said the words that had brought so much harm before.

Only when he clapped his hands and the half-healed wounds on her body disappeared, did the little girl finally believe. She smiled—a smile more beautiful than any K'lrsa had ever seen before.

K'lrsa turned to Larek, still holding the girl's hand. "What happens to them now?" She'd abandoned this child once, she wouldn't do it again. Not without knowing she'd be taken care of.

"These children know the death walker magic. So we'll take them into our order. Teach them the true ways of our religion. That we have a sacred duty to heal those who've been harmed. That in sacrifice, we find a higher meaning."

The little girl flinched.

"You won't use them to heal others, will you?"

He shook his head. "No. Not the children. In the old days it was the elderly or those too far gone to save who willingly took on the suffering of others. In extreme situations we offer ourselves. But only as adults, fully sworn into the order. And only if we're willing to do so. None will be forced to heal. You have my word on it."

K'lrsa nodded. She looked to the little girl. "Is that okay? Do you want to stay here? With them?"

The girl nodded. She pulled her hand free from K'lrsa's and ran across the room to hug a boy slightly older than her with the same brown hair and dark eyes. Clearly a brother or cousin.

K'lrsa hesitated a moment longer, but then shrugged. She'd done what she could. She walked back to where Badru and Vedhe stood, waiting for her. M'lara was curled up asleep at their feet, her thumb in her mouth, whimpering as tears rolled down her cheeks.

She wished she had time to comfort her, to sit in these rooms and rest and eat good food and recover. But there wasn't time. The Daliph's troops were still camped on the border of the barren lands. They needed to return the objects to the Hidden City before the other gods decided to act.

And she needed to free her parents. Even if it meant challenging the gods.

CHAPTER 81

They left Toreem at moonrise. The horses transformed without being asked, as if eager to leave. K'lrsa turned to look down at the city one last time. It was beautiful in its way, but she hoped to never see it again.

She'd be happy to spend the rest of her life riding Fallion across the plains, hunting baru by day, and sleeping in Badru's arms by night.

A part of her worried that she'd made the wrong choice by not doing more. She could've demanded they free all slaves. Or treat all women as equals. Forced them to change with the threat of the sun orb or the gauntlet. Dragged them kicking and screaming to a better place.

But it wouldn't have lasted. If they didn't believe in their own hearts that all were equal, that people didn't earn their fates, that women could do what men could, it wouldn't last. They had to change on their own. They had to grow to learn what she already knew.

Maybe she could've stayed and forced them to pretend until they truly believed, but...

She didn't want that life.

She helped M'lara into Fallion's saddle and then mounted up behind her. The gauntlet was tucked away in her saddlebags, the sun orb in Badru's, the staff with Vedhe. Even shielded they'd decided it was best to keep them as far away from those who'd used them as possible.

"Ready?" she asked the others.

They both nodded.

"Fly, *micora*," she whispered. With three great beats of his wings, Fallion launched into the air, Midnight and Kriger close behind.

CHAPTER 82

They flew until morning. The horses were tiring as the moon waned, but they made it to the abandoned barn they'd stopped in the first time they fled Toreem.

All K'lrsa wanted to do was sleep, but the minute they'd led the horses inside and handed out some of the food they'd brought from the palace, both Badru and Vedhe started to speak.

"One at a time." K'lrsa held up her hand. She already knew what they were going to say. And she didn't care. "Vedhe, you first."

Vedhe squared her shoulders. "Okay. I'm keeping the sun orb. The Trickster said if I survived the Hidden City, I could take it back home with me."

"Vedhe…"

"Ivan deserves to pay. Aren't you the one who said I deserved a chance at revenge?"

"What about the balance?"

"I don't care about the balance. I will not live in a world that has a man like that in it." She dashed a tear from her cheek as she glared at K'lrsa.

"Vedhe, you can't control it. You almost burned down the last barn we stayed in."

"It's contained now. It'll be safe until I need it."

"And what happens when you use it? How many innocents will you kill just because you want to kill Ivan?

You saw what happened in the palace. You saw how many died just because they were standing nearby when it was used."

Vedhe glared at her, jaw set. She wasn't going to be convinced otherwise.

K'lrsa closed her eyes, took a deep breath, and turned to Badru. "And you?"

"I think we should keep one of the weapons. Either the gauntlet or the sun orb or the staff."

"Why?"

"The Daliphana respect strength. If they know we have one of the weapons, they won't attack us."

"Now that Aran's gone and they have no means of crossing the desert other than our help, why would they attack at all?"

He shrugged. "That's now. But what happens if another man like Aran comes to power? Or if one of the other Daliphana hear about the Hidden City and decide to go after what's stored there? What if another Daliph marches an army across your lands in search of it?"

"So we keep the weapons out of fear? We upset the balance because of what-ifs? We let the world become even more dangerous than it already is, because someday someone might threaten us?"

Badru nodded.

"That's ridiculous."

"That's the way the world works, K'lrsa. If you're strong, none dare challenge you. Only the weak have to actually fight."

"And what happens when someone comes along and they want to use those weapons we kept? They want to attack the Daliphana? Or just use the weapons to get what they want? What then?"

"It won't happen. We'll...We'll come up with rules about when they can be used. We'll make sure no one person can use them."

"It seems to me that's what the Hidden City does. Only those most desperately in need would go there and choose a weapon."

"It's too far away."

She looked back and forth between them. "So neither one of you want to return the weapons?"

"No."

She bit her lip. "So I'm outvoted?"

"We want you to agree, K'lrsa." Badru squeezed her hand, staring into her eyes with his impossibly blue ones.

"Right. Of course. I think…" She stood. "I think I'll go outside and think about it a bit. I understand what you're both saying. It's just…The balance. I don't want to live in a world where there are hundreds of objects like these that could fall into the wrong hands. It's not just about us and how we use them. It's about the other weapons the gods will create and how their chosen ones will use them."

They both nodded, but it was clear they'd made up their minds.

CHAPTER 83

K'lrsa paced outside the barn, back and forth, back and forth. The right thing to do was return the objects to the Hidden City.

Yes, it might make them vulnerable, but they'd be no more vulnerable than they'd been before.

And, yes, it might make it harder for Vedhe to get her revenge. But K'lrsa had gone to Toreem with nothing and managed. Ivan wasn't a god. He was just an evil, horrible man. He could die from an arrow through the eye just as easily as anyone else.

They didn't *need* the weapons.

But she felt it, too. She understood. That desire to hold on to what you had. To not give up power. It was one thing to never have it, another to have it taken from you, and another to willingly give it back.

She understood. But that didn't make it right.

They couldn't keep the weapons. They had to return them.

She kicked the dirt wishing she were more like Badru— a leader, someone that others turned to and trusted. Someone who could weave her words in such a way that she could convince them of what she knew in her gut.

But she wasn't.

She was a person of action. She could fight, she could do what needed to be done no matter how hard or painful

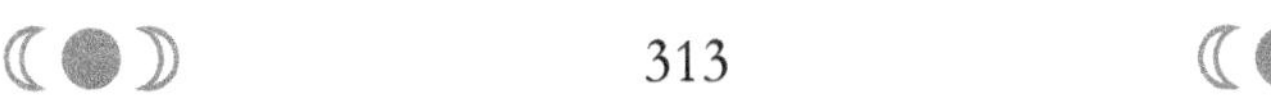

it might be. But she couldn't convince others. She couldn't persuade and cajole.

All she could do was act.

She turned back towards the entrance to the barn.

M'lara was standing there, watching her.

"Hey, little one. It's been a rough couple of days, hasn't it?"

M'lara nodded, scuffing the ground with her foot.

K'lrsa sat on the ground and let M'lara crawl into her lap. "You okay?"

M'lara shook her head. "That was horrible. All the fire and the dead people and…what Badru did to that bad man."

"I know. I'm sorry you had to see that."

M'lara cuddled against her. "I don't want to see that ever again."

"Neither do I, little one. Neither do I."

"Then take them back. Take them back to the Hidden City so no one can ever use them again."

She kissed M'lara's forehead. "That's what I'm trying to do."

"They won't let you. They want to keep them."

"I know. But we'll convince them. Somehow."

M'lara shook her head. "No."

"What do you mean, no?"

She pushed herself off of K'lrsa's lap and ran inside. K'lrsa followed, confused.

Badru and Vedhe were already laying down, eyes closed, breathing steady, each on an opposite side of the barn. Vedhe had the box with the sun orb tucked against her chest; Badru had the box with the gauntlet under the wadded up blanket he was using as a pillow.

K'lrsa grimaced. Of course they did.

M'lara met her at the entrance to the barn, holding another small box. The one with the necklace in it.

"M'lara, what are you doing?" She knelt down and spoke quietly so the others wouldn't wake.

"They have to go back," she whispered. "Now. You can do it."

K'lrsa looked at the box. Should she? Should she ignore the wishes of her friends and send the objects back to the

Hidden City? And what if she did and then it turned out Father Sun wouldn't release her parents? Didn't she need the sun orb or the gauntlet to confront him? To force him to do her will?

But that made her as bad as Badru and Vedhe, didn't it? Holding on to something she shouldn't, just in case she needed it? Especially knowing what harm that might cause if she did.

The others hadn't realized she could use the necklace to send the objects back. But when they did…

The opportunity would be lost.

She took the box from M'lara. She had always been better at action than words, after all…

CHAPTER 84

It was done in a moment. She sent the staff and the moon power back first since no one would notice their absence. And then the sun orb, quickly followed by the gauntlet.

That woke Badru up, since his head thunked backward as soon as it disappeared. He sat up, confused, looking around until he saw her, standing in the doorway, the necklace still in her hand.

"K'lrsa. What did you do?" he demanded.

"What I had to do to restore the balance."

Vedhe turned to glare at her. "Why did you bring me back if you weren't going to let me avenge myself on Ivan?"

"You can. You don't need the sun orb for that."

"You're wrong." She stood, shaking all over. K'lrsa couldn't tell if it was from anger or fear or some other emotion. "You should've never brought me back. It wasn't your right."

"Vedhe…"

Vedhe shoved past her.

K'lrsa turned to Badru. "Do you hate me too now?"

He shook his head and sighed. "No. I understand why you did it. I don't think it was the right thing to do. I think we'll pay for it eventually. But I understand." He stepped closer. "You could've at least talked to me about it."

"No." She looked away. "I'm not good at words. And was there honestly anything I could've said to convince you?"

He hesitated. "Maybe."

She stared him down.

"Okay, no. Probably not. I was raised to believe that superior strength is always better."

She glanced towards where Vedhe had disappeared outside. "Will she be okay?"

"I hope so. Eventually. It's hard. You have to know that. Knowing that someone is out there who has hurt you and hurt those you love and you can't do anything to stop them from hurting others. You had your revenge. I've had mine. But she hasn't had hers yet."

K'lrsa nodded. He was right. But someday Vedhe would have her revenge. She was sure of it.

CHAPTER 85

The rest of the trip back to the Hidden City was uneventful. They stopped on the edge of the border lands to make sure the soldiers hadn't attacked the tribes—not that they could've done much about it if they had—and found that the soldiers had received a notice from Toreem to disperse and return to their garrisons. That let them notify the newcomers and Riders camped on the other side of the barren lands that they could move on as well.

K'lrsa had expected most of the newcomers to return to Toreem, but after a long discussion with Badru most decided to stay and help him establish a trading route to the north. Some planned to relocate to those foreign cities and act as representatives of the tribes, while some looked forward to transporting the goods back and forth between the Daliphana and the north.

Even with Aran gone, most had no desire to return and face punishment for desertion.

K'lrsa had intended to leave M'lara behind when she continued on to the Hidden City—she didn't know what she might find there or how dangerous it might be to confront the gods—but M'lara begged and pleaded to go with her and she finally relented.

Vedhe insisted on accompanying them, too. K'lrsa suspected she wanted another chance to choose a weapon, she just hoped the Lady wasn't that foolish.

318

And Badru went as far as he could with them, stopping in the caves just outside the city to wait for their return. "You didn't have to come this far, you know," she told him as they said their goodbyes.

"I couldn't wait back in camp, wondering if you'd survived. If you aren't back in three days, I'm coming in. So don't make me die again. Unless, you know…"

They kissed and she drew away, reluctant to be separated from him once more, but she had to do this. It was her fault her parents were trapped there. She had to make this right.

They flew to the Hidden City as soon as the moon rose—just a sliver of her normal self—and rode along the crowded street to the labyrinth in silence. Vedhe led the way as they walked down the never-ending white hallway, M'lara and K'lrsa trailing behind.

With each step, K'lrsa's dread grew. She didn't want to confront the gods—look what Father Sun had done to her parents. One touch and he'd made them forget all their anger. Made them happy to be trapped here. What if he did that to her?

And what was Vedhe going to do? If the Lady let her choose another weapon, what destruction might she cause? Not just with the weapon itself, but for everyone. If she upset the balance, it would affect K'lrsa and Badru and M'lara and everyone they knew.

Finally, they reached the center of the labyrinth. The Lady wasn't there like she had been the times before. Father Sun was. He watched them approach, arms crossed, eyes like banked coals.

"You returned. Why?" His voice was like a lash, stopping them where they stood.

Trembling, K'lrsa pushed her way forward. "I came to free my parents. They don't deserve to be trapped here forever because of what I promised. If you have to keep someone…" She swallowed. "Keep me."

She didn't want to be trapped here forever. She wanted to go back to Badru and live a life with him and then pass on to the Promised Plains. But if anyone deserved to be stuck here, it was her. Not them.

"Oh, right. Your parents. They left. Days ago."

"What?" She stared at him. "What are you talking about?"

"As soon as Aran died, I released them."

"But…The binding. And…My vow…" She stared at him. "I don't understand."

"I never wanted the Toreem Daliphate destroyed. You did. I wanted Aran dead. You did that. So I released them."

"I almost destroyed an entire culture because of you. Thousands of people. Everything they'd built over hundreds of years. I almost destroyed it."

"But you didn't."

She stared at him, mouth hanging open in surprise. "I don't understand you."

"Of course you don't. You're not a god." He stepped closer, his eyes dancing with flames. "Don't forget that, K'lrsa dan V'na of the White Horse Tribe. I don't know what you thought you could do against me, against us, but you are a mere mortal. You cannot challenge the gods and don't you ever dare think you can. Now go. Be gone from this place before I decide to punish you for your hubris."

She stumbled backward. "Wait."

"Wait?"

"I…" She reached into her packs and held out the box with the necklace in it. "I wanted to return this. You already received the other objects, didn't you?"

He nodded and took the box, his hand so warm it almost burned. "Thank you."

"And…"

"And?" He glared at her, but she didn't back down.

"F'lia. Is she still here?"

"No."

K'lrsa's heart sank. "She left with L'ral?"

Father Sun smiled slightly and shook his head. "No. She asked to go home, back to her tribe. You'll find her there when you return."

K'lrsa laughed, clapping her hands in delight. "Truly? She's okay now?"

"She lost the man she loved and her child. She'll never

be okay again. But she lives and she continues onward. As you all do."

"Thank you." K'lrsa backed away and took M'lara's hand. Vedhe didn't.

Father Sun turned to her. "I know you wanted to find my wife here and be given another weapon, one that could defeat the man who killed your family. But you won't find her here. And after this, after you leave this place, you won't find this city again. Go. Live your life, child."

"He deserves to pay for what he did."

"And he will. But you don't need my power or hers or any other power to defeat him. You have friends who will stand by your side no matter what. And you are strong, strong enough to stand against him. To make him pay for what he did. You don't need us to make that happen."

Vedhe trembled and a tear rolled down her cheek. "But…I'm not."

"Yes. You are. Have faith in yourself, child. Have faith in your friends. Now, go. Unless you want to be trapped here forever."

The walls shuddered and dust filled the air.

Vedhe didn't move.

"Vedhe, come on. You heard him. We have to go. Now."

K'lrsa grabbed her hand and dragged her back down the long, white hallway as the walls continued to shake, large cracks forming, M'lara running ahead of them.

At first, Vedhe resisted, but when a chunk of ceiling narrowly missed crushing them, she finally gave in. They ran as fast as they could, bursting out onto the street outside the labyrinth just in time. It collapsed in on itself, dust clogging the air.

All around them, the other buildings of the Hidden City were shaking and breaking apart and collapsing in on themselves. The long avenue they'd followed from the gate buckled like it was a living and breathing snake.

Fallion and Kriger were there, waiting for them, and launched into the sky as soon as they were in the saddle. As they flew away from the city, it broke apart, sinking into the desert, the sand swallowing it until nothing was left.

CHAPTER 86

Father Sun had told the truth.

F'lia was back with the White Horse Tribe and she confirmed that K'lrsa's parents had passed on to the Promised Plains as soon as Aran was killed. She looked better, but she wasn't yet her old self. And talking to her, K'lrsa realized she might never be again. The girl who'd shone like the sun was still kind, still soft where K'lrsa was hard, but her light had been dimmed. And no wonder.

Tragedy did that to you. It took a little bit away. Left behind a reminder that at any time the perfect day could turn dark. The love could go away, the storm could come.

K'lrsa knew that feeling, too. She'd lost her father and her mother and that belief she'd had that she could do anything, be anything, conquer anything. She'd won her battles, but it hadn't been easy. And she'd been changed by it all. Hardened in some places, softened in others.

She hoped, at least for a bit, that the world would leave her alone now. Give her time to enjoy what she had left. To raise her sister, to spend time with the man she loved, and with her two friends who'd been through so much and were still hurting.

EPILOGUE

K'lrsa stood in the center of the tent, nervously adjusting the thin strips of fabric that covered her body. She waved her hand through the air, watching as the strips of cloth danced and flowed through the air.

She'd never felt this nervous in her life. Everything she'd been through. Everything she'd done…

This one moment scared her more than all the rest of it combined.

She touched her hair—long and flowing down her back—and stared into the small hand mirror that had once been her mother's, wishing for some of Sayel's makeup to brighten her cheeks or define her eyes a little more.

But she didn't have that. She just had herself to offer.

She bit her lip and stared at the tent flap, too nervous to move.

"K'lrsa? Are you ever going to come out?" Badru called. "It's a gorgeous night…"

She took a deep, shuddering breath.

No point in waiting any longer.

The moon was full and ripe, and it was a beautiful night, not too hot, not too cool. They were all alone, in the midst of the desert where none could see them.

At last, after so many moons of waiting and wanting, she could dance the Moon Dance with the man she loved.

She took one last deep breath and stepped outside.

323

GLOSSARY OF TERMS

Amalanee: An extremely rare type of horse known by the teardrop mark in the center of its forehead.

Daliph: Leader of a Daliphate. Usually a hereditary position. The current Daliph can designate any of his sons or grandsons as his successor using any criteria he chooses.

Daliphate: One of seven territories ruled by a Daliph. (plural: Daliphana) Male-dominated society that engages in slavery and is heavily reliant on trade.

Death walkers: A secret religious sect that can heal someone's wounds or bring someone back from the dead if done within a short time after their death. Must trade one life for another when they bring someone back to life.

Dorana: One of a Daliph's chosen consorts. Considered the highest honor a woman can receive. The more dorana a Daliph has, the more powerful he is. A dorana can be released from her service. She is given a golden ear cuff for each year she serves as dorana.

Grel: Type of desert vulture with gray, greasy wings and red, beady eyes. Move slowly and are known to start eating before their prey is fully dead.

Hidden City: A city in the middle of the desert, put there by the gods to make it harder to find. Where the dead and the living can meet and also where dangerous artifacts are kept.

Moon Dance: A dance done under the full moon either to honor the gods or with one's lover as a sign of love and commitment.

INDEX OF PRIMARY CHARACTERS

Aran: Current and former Daliph of the Toreem Daliphate. Badru's grandfather. A death walker capable of coming back from the dead. Kidnapped Herin. Cut out Garzel's tongue.

Badru: Former Daliph of the Toreem Daliphate. Rider of the *Amalanee* horse, Midnight.

B'nin: K'lrsa's father. Former Rider of the White Horse Tribe.

D'lan: K'lrsa's brother. Rider for the White Horse Tribe.

Fallion: K'lrsa's *Amalanee* horse.

F'lia: K'lrsa's best friend. Member of the White Horse Tribe. Had intended to wed L'ral before his death. Pregnant.

Garzel: Husband of Herin. Formerly of the tribes. Has been in the Toreem Daliphate serving as Herin's poradom. Has no tongue.

Herin: Grandmother of Badru, wife of Garzel, former captive of Aran's. Formerly of the tribes. Missing the top joint on each finger as a result of each attempt she made to kill Aran.

K'lrsa: Member of the White Horse Tribe. Sister to D'lan and M'lara. Daughter of V'na and B'nin. Rider of the *Amalanee* horse, Fallion.

Kriger: Vedhe's *Amalanee* horse.

Lodie: Herin's sister. Formerly of the tribes. Former slave.

Luden: Former solider in the Daliph's army. New member of the tribes and of the Council.

Midnight: Badru's *Amalanee* horse.

M'lara: K'lrsa's sister. Eight years old. Both parents dead.

Vedhe: Pale-haired and —skinned slave girl brought from the North by a slave caravan. Fled to the White Horse Tribe with the assistance of K'lrsa and Lodie. Rider of the *Amalanee* horse, Kriger.

V'na: K'lrsa's mother. Former Rider of the White Horse Tribe.

SUMMARY OF RIDER'S REVENGE
(BOOK 1)

K'lrsa loves her life as a Rider for the White Horse Tribe. She spends her days riding her *Amalanee* horse Fallion and her nights avoiding her mother's attempts to settle her down. But there's unrest in the tribes. Trade has brought change and her father is concerned by the way the other tribes have succumbed to the temptations brought from the outside.

When her father finds out that one of the tribes, the Black Horse Tribe, is also helping bring slaves across the desert, he campaigns amongst the tribes to have them expelled.

But before that can happen, the White Horse Tribe is raided by men from the neighboring Toreem Daliphate. Her father rides out to confront them along with his other Riders, but leaves K'lrsa behind.

When her father doesn't return, K'lrsa goes looking for him and finds him dying in the desert, staked to the sand with his eyes gouged out and belly slit open. She swears to avenge him by going to the Toreem Daliphate and killing the Daliph.

Her father doesn't want her to go.

She promises him she won't to appease him, but then secretly vows to do so.

Her father begs her to kill him and put him out of his misery. She does even though it devastates her to do so.

That night she dreams of Father Sun who shows her a trading caravan that will lead her to the Toreem Daliphate.

She lets the caravan capture her, almost killing herself and Fallion in the process.

The healer traveling with the caravan, Lodie, is a slave and former member of the tribes who recognizes that K'lrsa's wounds are self-inflicted. Instead of turning K'lrsa in to the caravan master, Harley, Lodie counsels K'lrsa against going to the Daliphate.

One of the slaves in the caravan is a pale-blond woman

who they were going to present as a Northern Princess but has been ruined by exposure to the sun. Harley gives K'lrsa the choice to take the woman's place and be sold as a "Desert Princess" or to just be one of the rest of the slaves made to walk across the desert and sold at the earliest opportunity.

K'lrsa chooses to take the woman's place.

After watching how the woman is abused as a result, K'lrsa feels guilty and helps the woman and Lodie escape. In order to do so, K'lrsa makes Lodie a sister of her blood and gives Lodie her moon stone. They steal a horse belonging to G'van of the Black Horse Tribe and flee.

When G'van discovers his horse missing, he attacks K'lrsa. She fights back.

Harley breaks up the fight, but when G'van then threatens Harley, Harley kills him.

Most of the slaves are sold off in Crossroads, but Harley takes K'lrsa and a handful of slaves deeper into the Daliphate.

The Toreem Daliphate is completely foreign to K'lrsa who is used to a nomadic life where all are equal. She struggles to adapt to its different ways.

She befriends one of her captors, Barkley, and eventually confesses to him that her plan is to go to Toreem and kill the Daliph. Barkley arranges for a friend of his in the city to write to Harley offering to purchase K'lrsa if Harley will bring her to Toreem.

On the plains outside of Toreem, their small party—now just Harley, Barkley, Reginald, and K'lrsa—run into a man on a black *Amalanee* horse, Badru. He's the same man K'lrsa has been dreaming about the entire journey.

He's accompanied by an old woman, Herin, who knowns Harley and tells him to leave. She's also Lodie's sister. As they're turning away, K'lrsa calls on their blood connection and demands that Herin help her.

Herin has the party arrested and orders the soldiers to kill anyone who speaks.

They're taken to the dungeons of Toreem where all the others are killed except K'lrsa.

She wakes up in a luxurious room in the palace to find that she's been chosen as a dorana—an honored concubine—to the Daliph of the Toreem Daliphate. Herin is furious, K'lrsa confused. But it's the best chance K'lrsa has to avenge her father.

K'lrsa finds training to be a dorana incredibly hard. She's not allowed to look at anyone, not supposed to speak. They dress her in ornate costumes that keep her from moving freely. Her fingers are bound with the *meza* so that she can't even feed herself. And, even if she could, she's not supposed to.

Everything she needs is done by her poradoma—Sayel, Tarum, and Morel. Sayel is her head poradom and very fond of her although exasperated by her inability to be a proper dorana. Tarum hates her and takes liberties when he dresses or feeds her. Herin is there to supervise with her constant companion, Garzel.

Weeks later, Badru finally comes to see K'lrsa. She's still been dreaming of him every night and is so grateful to see a friendly face that she confesses to him her plan to kill the Daliph.

He tells her she can't do that and leaves. She waits in her room, certain he'll betray her, but instead Herin and Sayel come the next day and tell her it's time to present her to the Daliph.

She's dressed in even more ornate clothing than normal, including the *tiral*—a full-length coat crocheted of gold that binds her movements to the point she knows she won't be able to attack the Daliph.

Finally, she's brought to the throne room. Just outside they run into Badru who she learns is actually the Daliph. He's furious she's there and demands that Herin take her back to her rooms. K'lrsa is devastated to realize that the man she loves and the man she wants to kill are the same.

She refuses to continue training as a dorana and is punished by being left alone, unattended with no food or clothing, her fingers still bound by the *meza*.

Eventually, she continues her training and is once more brought to see Badru. This time she enters the throne room, still conflicted about whether to kill Badru or not, but before she can reach him, she overhears a man insult her and turns to confront him, something a dorana is not supposed to do.

Badru sees what happens and declares that an insult to his dorana is an insult to him and has the two men responsible whipped even though they are both senior advisors of his.

After, Herin tries to convince K'lrsa to escape, but K'lrsa refuses, not trusting her.

Badru comes to her rooms and she attacks him, but fails to kill him. He swears to her it wasn't his men who killed her father but she still doubts him.

She asks Badru to free her because she can't possibly be with him if she isn't free to choose to be with him.

The next day he takes her out riding and frees her from slavery and gives her Fallion back. He also declares that any slave owner who chooses to can free their slaves and that any freed slaves can have their property back. His court is in an uproar over the decision.

A courtier insults K'lrsa while on their ride and Badru banishes him even though the man is the son of an important advisor.

When they return, Badru has to leave to attend to an urgent matter and K'lrsa is left alone in the stables where she overhears the arrival of K'var of the Black Horse Tribe who demands more weapons and soldiers to destroy the tribes that oppose him.

She confronts Badru about K'var's demands and he says he'll have no choice but to back the Black Horse Tribe unless K'lrsa can find his people another way across the desert.

K'lrsa throws him out of her room.

In the middle of the night, Tarum comes to kill K'lrsa. She manages to kill him first, but he uses a poisoned blade in his attack and she collapses shortly after.

She awakes to find Herin at her bedside. Her wounds are fully healed and Herin tells K'lrsa she has been accused by Balor, another poradom, of having an affair with

Tarum. Balor claims he's the one who killed Tarum when he found them together.

The penalty for a dorana cheating on the Daliph is death by beheading performed by the Daliph himself. Herin leaves and informs Badru and the others that K'lrsa confessed to the affair.

K'lrsa is able to convince Sayel that she's innocent by showing him the healed scars from the attack. He tells her she was healed by death walkers, those who can also bring back the dead and are feared above all others, and agrees to stand by her side.

At the trial, Badru clearly believes K'lrsa even though the crowd is against her. Since Balor claims he subdued her by force, Badru proposes that they battle to the death to see who is actually telling the truth.

Before the fight, Balor takes a poison that makes him incredibly powerful. K'lrsa shatters her foot and Balor crushes her arm during the fight, but the poison eventually kills Balor and she's declared the winner.

Herin and her husband, Garzel, spirit K'lrsa away immediately after. Sayel follows.

K'lrsa and Sayel learn that Herin was the death walker who healed her wounds the night before in an effort to protect Badru. Herin says she learned the death walker magic from the former Daliph, Aran, who would use it to kill Garzel and bring him back to life again and again in order to torture Herin. She heals K'lrsa again.

Sayel tells Badru that Herin and Garzel are death walkers. Rather than turn them in to the temple where they'd be killed, he banishes them to their quarters.

K'lrsa begs Badru to let her go home and warn the tribes about the threat from the Black Horse Tribe, but Badru asks her to give him three more days. He has her attend court where she learns that K'var was the one who killed her father and that L'ral, who was going to marry her best friend, F'lia, was the one who lured her father to his death.

One of Badru's senior advisors demands K'lrsa's death because he claims she cheated in the trial by combat. Badru replies that there are no rules to such a trial and that if she did poison Balor that was allowed.

Badru frees K'lrsa from being his dorana and brings her to court dressed as a Rider and places her at his side, something no one approves of. He calls K'var of the Black Horse Tribe forward and accuses him of conspiring against Toreem and sentences him to death.

Before the sentence can be carried out, the former Daliph, Aran, shows himself and demands his throne back. In the chaos of the ensuing fight, Badru is killed by one of his own guards.

Sayel and K'lrsa fight their way to Badru's side and flee with his body through a hidden passage behind the throne. They take Badru to Herin and Garzel to be revived.

All four are trapped in a room and running out of time. Sayel gives his life so Badru can be brought back.

Badru wants to stay and fight to regain his throne, but they convince him they have to flee.

They wait until night and then make their way towards the stables.

K'var is waiting for them. K'lrsa fights and kills him, avenging her father at last.

Herin, Garzel, Badru, and K'lrsa flee Toreem on the two *Amalanee* horses.

They stop outside the city and Garzel uses his sun stone to "awaken" the horses who can now fly. They leave before the guards can reach them, racing to warn the tribes that Aran is sending troops to destroy them.

SUMMARY OF RIDER'S RESCUE
(BOOK 2)

K'lrsa, Badru, Herin, and Garzel flee Toreem on Fallion and Midnight in an attempt to warn the tribes that Aran has sent troops to attack them. The only hope for the tribes is to reach the gathering grounds where they'll be safe until K'lrsa and the others can go to the Hidden City and bring back a powerful enough weapon to defeat Aran's soldiers.

However, when they reach the White Horse Tribe, K'lrsa is taken into custody and accused of murdering her father. While she did technically kill him, no one will listen to her and let her explain what happened. She eventually is able to tell her story to her sister, M'lara, who then tells the story to K'lrsa's brother, D'lan, who sides with K'lrsa.

She's released, but people still distrust her. She also learns that her best friend, F'lia, gave herself to the sands after K'lrsa and L'ral went missing.

No one believes K'lrsa about the threat represented by Aran's soldiers. And even those who do, think the better option is to flee to one of the other tribes instead of to the gathering grounds. They do at least send out scouts to confirm her story.

In the meantime, K'lrsa and the others are reunited with Lodie and Vedhe (the unnamed pale-skinned slave girl from *Rider's Revenge*), and learn that Vedhe now has an *Amalanee* horse, Kriger.

While they're waiting, K'lrsa, Badru, and Vedhe learn how to make their horses fly and that they can only fly at night and when the moon is shining. They fly to the gathering grounds and find that the Black Horse Tribe has the grounds surrounded already and that there's no way through without fighting.

When they return, they learn that the Daliph's troops have circled behind the tribes and are going to drive them towards the gathering grounds so that they're trapped between the two forces.

K'lrsa leaves to warn the other tribes while the White Horse Tribe makes its way to the gathering grounds.

When she returns, they follow Badru's plan and use the horses to fly the children and non-Riders to safety in the gathering grounds. But the next day four members of the White Horse Tribe betray them and escape to the Black Horse Tribe.

The Black Horse Tribe attacks. The White Horse Tribe manages to fend them off, but K'lrsa is devastated by having killed someone she knew.

The next night they manage to get most of the rest of the tribe to safety, but K'lrsa's mother refuses to go. In the morning she confronts the Black Horse Tribe and kills many of their leaders before she herself is killed.

The other tribes arrive, but there's no way to get them to safety because as the moon wanes so does the horses' ability to fly.

The Daliph's troops appear on the horizon and everyone knows that the next day they'll attack and the tribes will be slaughtered.

Vedhe says she can lead everyone to safety and does so by taking them along the Trickster's pathways which are not part of the real world. But the Trickster taunts K'lrsa while she's traveling them and, on the last trip, K'lrsa and her group are lost in the fog.

K'lrsa manages to have Fallion light their way and lead them to safety in the real world. They appear in the center of the platform where all of the tribes have gathered.

K'lrsa sees F'lia with the other members of the Black Horse Tribe. She's pregnant and initially angry with K'lrsa.

At the invocation for the gathering, the Lady Moon appears and gives the tribes a choice. Renew their vow to the gods or go their own way. After a day and a half of speeches and discussion, the tribes vote.

It's a tie.

But then Herin steps forward and asserts her right to vote as a member of the Summer Spring Tribe. When Herin, Lodie, and Garzel's votes are included, the final vote is to continue to follow the gods. All members of the tribes are required to take a new oath or leave. Many of the members of the Black Horse Tribe choose to leave and they join the Daliph's troops which have surrounded the gathering grounds.

When it comes time to leave for the Hidden City, Herin tries to keep Lodie and Badru from joining them, but they both insist on coming along even after the Trickster appears and says some of them will die.

K'lrsa, Badru, Vedhe, Herin, Garzel, and Lodie go to the Hidden City. At the center of the city is a labyrinth that will test their body, mind, and spirit before they can choose a weapon which will let them save the tribes.

The first challenge is a dragon. Almost immediately, it kills Herin and Garzel but the knowledge Herin gives them before she dies allows Badru to slice the dragon's belly open and defeat it.

K'lrsa can't stand watching the magnificent creature suffer, so she and Vedhe kill it by driving arrows through its eyes. She blames the gods for Herin and Garzel's deaths as well as the dragon's.

In the next challenge they have to solve a puzzle that involves pictographs.

Next, they step through an archway and are each met by someone they love. Lodie is led away by a giggling little girl. Vedhe is led away by a man who looks like her brother.

And K'lrsa sees her father. He tells her she's reached the center of the labyrinth and she now has a chance to rest and spend time with him before she chooses her weapon.

K'lrsa lets herself believe it. Her father is everything she remembered and they spend days talking and playing games until Badru finally finds her and tells her that this is the third challenge and that the man isn't her father, but just an illusion.

K'lrsa is devastated and a part of her wants to stay even though she now knows the truth, but she forces the man to lead them to Vedhe and Lodie.

Vedhe is willing to leave. Lodie refuses. She says she's already dead and that she knows she has no hope of finding her daughter in the Promised Plains because it's been too long since she died and children move on quickly.

When K'lrsa demands an explanation, she learns that anyone who has been revived by death walker magic—which includes Herin, Garzel, Lodie, and Badru—can never return to the real world after they enter the city. This is why Herin tried to keep Lodie and Badru from coming with them.

K'lrsa is furious with Badru, but he says it was his choice to make and he wanted to help her succeed and save her people no matter what it cost him.

K'lrsa, Vedhe, and Badru step through the final arch and are assaulted with all of the knowledge of the place. Vedhe manages to last longer than K'lrsa, but they both learn a lot before they collapse.

Vedhe can now speak fluently in K'lrsa's language and K'lrsa can understand hers.

L'ral is there and apologizes for betraying K'lrsa father. He asks her to tell F'lia that he's waiting for her. K'lrsa doesn't care.

K'lrsa's dad is also there. The real one. And they talk. She gets to see her mother again as well. Herin and Garzel are also there, waiting for them.

The Lady Moon takes Vedhe and K'lrsa to a room to choose one object to take back into the world with them. Vedhe almost chooses a sun orb that could destroy not only the Daliph's troops but the tribes, because she was mistreated by both. K'lrsa convinces her to choose a viewing tube instead that lets her see a person's true nature.

K'lrsa can't bring herself to choose one of the weapons she's offered and instead chooses a necklace that allows her to move people any distance she wants.

When she returns to the others, Herin and Badru criticize their choice of weapons, but K'lrsa's father is proud of her.

K'lrsa uses the necklace to return her and Vedhe to the gathering grounds. It makes her cough blood and she realizes it can't be used safely since the more people she moves at once and the greater the distance, the more harm it does to those moved.

Instead, she uses the nacklace against the leader of the Daliph's troops and demands that the men leave or she'll use it on all of them. She gives them a day.

Some of the Daliph's soldiers come to ask for sanctuary and K'lrsa grants it after Vedhe judges them with her viewing tube. The only requirement is that they marry into the tribes.

K'lrsa doesn't want to return to her old tribe and most of the Black Horse Tribe has left, so she decides to form a new tribe to replace them. Many of the newcomers join her and Vedhe as well as some young Riders from the other tribes. K'lrsa also takes on responsibility for her sister, M'lara, and convinces F'lia to join them and leave the Black Horse Tribe.

Most of the Daliph's troops leave on their own, but the leaders refuse and K'lrsa has to use the necklace to banish them.

They have a celebratory feast that the threat is ended and K'lrsa looks forward to her new life with her new tribe and her friends, both old and new.

ABOUT THE AUTHOR

Alessandra Clarke has been losing herself in the worlds of fantasy novels since she was old enough to borrow her first book from the library.

She loves the worlds of Darkover, Valdemar, and Pern, and wishes she could live a hundred lives just so she could read all the books on her to-be-read shelves while still having timeto write, take her pup to the dog park, and see her friends and family.

You can reach her at aclarkewriter@gmail.com or on her website at alessandraclarke.com.

www.ingramcontent.com/pod-product-compliance
Lightning Source LLC
Chambersburg PA
CBHW070426170726
48291CB00002B/373